I0760331

SERPENT'S TOUCH

DUET

MARINA SIMCOE

THE RIVER OF MISTS

Serpent's Touch
World of the River of Mists

Marina Simcoe
Marina.Simcoe@Yahoo.com
Facebook/Marina Simcoe Author

Spelling: English (American)
Editing by Cissell Ink
Proofreading by Nic Page

Cover design by Hannah Sternjacob, from www.hannah-sternjakob-design.com

Illustrations by Chuck Monty,
Twitter @ProductiGhoul and @SeductiGhoul

This book contains graphic descriptions of intimacy and discussions on adult themes. Intended for mature readers.

Serpent's Touch

COMPLETE DUET

MARINA SIMCOE

MARINA SIMCOE

PART 1

THE RIVER OF MISTS

Chapter One

AMIRA

"Enjoy the show." I handed two tickets to the elderly couple in line.

They headed towards the striped tents on the outskirts of the fairgrounds, the man supporting his female companion by her elbow.

Despite it being January, it was a warm, sunny day in the southern US. The multi-colored lights around the painted sign "Madame Tan's Menagerie" over the entrance to the tents had been turned on, but their light paled in the sunshine.

I couldn't remember the name of the town where the fair was taking place this week. Not that it mattered, anyway. The next week, there'd be another town, another name I'd quickly forget.

Radax, one of Madame Tan's men, let the elderly couple inside the tents, then pulled down the flap of striped canvas after them, closing the entrance. Madame was about to start the tour of her menagerie.

A young couple rushed to my booth.

"Oh, no!"

"Did we miss it?"

The man tightly gripped the arm of the woman who held a wad of cotton candy on a stick in her other hand.

I stretched my lips into a smile that Madame demanded from all her staff when customers were around. "The next show is in forty-five minutes. You can wait here or come back later."

The young man, who was really still a boy, probably a high school student, ran a hand over his neat, dark cornrows.

"What do you want to do?" he asked his companion. "Wait?"

The girl shrugged, biting off a piece of her cotton candy. "I don't really care. We can hang around."

"Okay. Two tickets, please." The boy slipped a fifty-dollar bill through the cut-out in the plexiglass that separated me from the rest of the world. He glanced proudly at the girl, as if to make sure she noticed the money. Or maybe he was just happy he could afford to treat her.

She smiled, flipping her thin, black braids over her shoulder.

I counted out the change and handed him the two tickets. He shoved the tickets in his back pocket and stepped aside, dragging the girl with him.

She tore a piece of her cotton candy and offered it to him. "Want some?"

He held her wrist while eating the candy from her hand, then licked her finger. She giggled, jerking her hand away. He caught her around the middle.

"It's sweet. Just like you." He kissed her full, smiling lips.

It looked like a private moment, even if they did it in the middle of the crowded fairgrounds. I shouldn't be watching them, but I couldn't tear my gaze away.

The couple were a few years younger than me. Though no one knew how old I really was. Radax, who found me almost twenty years ago, thought I might be about twenty-four or twenty-five now. Yet, unlike these kids, I'd never been kissed. Other than a rare, friendly peck on a cheek or a quick hug from Radax, who had always been like an older brother to me, I'd never been touched by a man at all.

The boy squeezed the girl's backside, then slid his hand under the hem of her shirt. I imagined his palm pressed to her dark, smooth skin under her top. What did his touch feel like?

The girl hooked her arm around his neck, pressing herself to him. What did it feel like being kissed this deeply?

"How much is a ticket, beautiful?" A male voice yanked me out of my musings.

Startled, I jumped on my wooden stool. Ogling people instead of doing my job—that was a sure way to get in trouble with Madame.

A group of men stared at me from behind the plexiglass.

I cleared my throat, pointing at the painted sign to my right. "The price is here."

The man in the front, with wind-swept overgrown blond curls and deeply tanned face, studied me closely. Did he catch me watching the teenagers kissing?

Heat warmed my cheeks. I drew my chin into the wide scarf I wore around my neck despite the heat inside my booth.

"Is the show any good?" the blond man asked, not even glancing at the sign with the price.

"It's the only one of its kind," I repeated mechanically the words I knew by heart. "Never before seen by people of Earth."

"How about those people?" He pointed at the group of visitors that started filing out of the exit from the tent.

The latest tour of the menagerie was over. A line of new customers was already forming behind the blond guy and his friends, waiting to buy tickets for the next one. Madame gave several tours a day, in addition to her VIP shows.

"Those guys have just seen it, so you can't claim it hasn't been seen by anyone." The blond guy snickered, poking the nearest of his friends with his elbow, inviting him to join in the fun.

I looked straight into his baby-blue eyes. "*They* have seen it, but not you. Would you like to buy a ticket?"

He jerked his head to his friends. "She's kinda snappy, isn't she?" He squinted back at me. "And cute, too, in a goth kinda way."

Goth?

I'd heard the word before, but I didn't know its exact meaning. Despite being born and raised in this world, I knew little about life outside of the menagerie.

One of his friends scoffed, giving me a side eye. "She's cute alright.

Like Wednesday Addams. I bet all her dolls were missing heads when she was a kid."

What was that supposed to mean?

I had no dolls growing up, or any toys for that matter. I'd had no time to play. For as long as I remembered, I'd always worked at the menagerie, and my chores grew in number the older I got. Like school, friends, or family, dolls were an abstract concept to me. I knew what they were, but I'd never had any.

Also...if I'd had dolls, why would they be headless?

The men made no sense. Or at least they made no sense *to me.* Unease itched my skin. I wished the group would just go away, whether or not they bought the tickets.

Unfortunately, they appeared to be having too much fun to move on.

Another one gave me a measuring stare. "She looks like a ghost, Brad."

I withdrew deeper into my scarf, wishing I could disappear in it completely.

"Would you like to buy tickets?" I repeated, avoiding eye contact.

The blond guy, Brad, placed a plastic card on the counter. "Impatient, aren't you?" He smirked.

I didn't touch his card. "Um, cash only, please."

Madame refused to bother with the machines necessary to process any other forms of payment. "If people don't have cash, I don't want them here," she would say. "It's bad enough that I'm reduced to accepting their pathetic paper money. I'm not going to deal with plastic credit promises of humans who break their promises all the time. Respectable folks trade in gold and jewels."

I'd never been offered any gold or jewels for a ticket to the show. So, I guessed, none of the people in this world were "respectable folks" in Madame's eyes.

Brad glared at me, obviously irritated. "What? Why cash only? What's wrong with my card?"

He grabbed the card then slapped it against the plexiglass, leaning so hard on it, I feared he might break the flimsy partition.

"Huh? What's wrong with it?" he practically screamed.

I flinched, shifting as far back on my stool as was possible without falling off it.

"Hey, you're scaring her." One member of the group reached from behind Brad and placed a hundred-dollar bill on the counter.

I slipped my hand through the small window to snatch it, but Brad caught my wrist.

"Nope." He smirked. "I want you to get out of that booth, beautiful, and take it from me here." One hand wrapped around my wrist, he yanked the bill out of my fingers with the other. "Come out and take a stroll with me."

"I have to work..." I tried to wrench my wrist away from him, but he held tight.

"Work can wait."

A man in line behind the group protested on my behalf. "Let her go!"

"Hey! What's going on?" someone else yelled. "Get your tickets and move on. We're waiting here."

"Fuck off!" Brad snarled over his shoulder.

"Is there a problem?" Radax's deep voice boomed nearby as he approached the agitated line of people, his large figure towering over everyone.

"And who the hell are you?" Brad snapped at Radax, squaring his shoulders.

His bravado melted away quickly, however. Most trouble-makers reconsidered their behavior the moment they saw Radax.

At least a head taller than any person in line, Radax was much broader, too. He crossed his arms over his wide chest. His thick biceps bulged out, stretching the short sleeves of his black t-shirt.

"What's going on?" he demanded from Brad, who gave him a long once-over. The blond man had to tilt his head far back to meet Radax's dark eyes high above him.

Radax was a *brack*, one of Madame's people. And all her *bracks* looked very much the same—tall, broad, with bald heads and huge muscles. All had a tattoo that circled their necks and covered their entire right arm. Unlike the rest of them, Radax also sported a full beard, which didn't make him look any more approachable.

The *bracks'* appearances were not deceiving. They were dangerous. I'd witnessed their non-human strength on more than one occasion. Any of them could easily lift this booth, with me and the stool in it.

Radax stretched his thick neck. The lines of his tattoo moved as the muscles flexed under his skin.

"I asked if there was a problem here?" he repeated as Brad appeared to be lost for words.

The blond guy swallowed hard, then straightened his back, coming out of his stupor. "Yeah? And what if there was?"

He cocked his head, taking a wider stance. Despite the challenge in his tone, he let go of my hand. I snatched it back and hid it in my hoodie.

Met with Radax's glare, Brad stepped back. He must've thought he was moving out of reach of Radax's fist. Little did he know that *bracks* moved fast, much faster than their size and weight should allow. If Radax got angry enough, no place was safe from him and his rage. Luckily for Brad and the likes of him, Radax had impeccable self-control.

"If there's a problem, I have a solution," he said evenly. "You either buy a ticket or take your money elsewhere." He leaned in ever so slightly and added with a growl of warning, "Either way, you'll leave the girl alone."

Brad froze under Radax's stare.

His friend quickly grabbed the hundred-dollar bill from him and nudged him with an elbow. "Let's go, man."

"Fuck this stupid show," another one of their group drawled. "Let's go find some beer."

The rowdy posse finally departed, dragging their feet along the packed dirt of the fairgrounds.

I slid a grateful glance at Radax. *"Go,"* I mouthed to him and flicked my gaze to the tents.

The next tour would start soon. Madame needed him there. If she found him missing, she'd be displeased. If she found out his absence was because of me, she would likely get angry and punish him. Again.

Because Radax was the one who had brought me to the menagerie,

Madame often held him responsible for my mistakes. Radax had been whipped more times than I wanted to remember.

"Go," I mouthed again, tipping my head toward the entrance where a new group of customers had gathered already, including the high school sweethearts I'd sold the tickets to earlier.

I turned back to the line of people behind my window.

"How many?" I asked the next customer.

From the corner of my eye, I saw Radax going back to the tent and released a breath of relief. Hopefully, there'd be no punishments shelled out today.

Chapter Two

AMIRA

I had almost finished sweeping the empty room inside a tent when Krin, one of Madame's *bracks*, carried in a huge wooden crate. A truck had delivered it earlier that morning and unloaded it in the yard while *bracks* were having breakfast.

"Get out of the way," Krin hissed at me.

I scurried closer to the striped canvas wall as he maneuvered a massive metal frame out of the crate.

A large creature was chained to the frame. It was upright, its arms and legs spread like a sea star, ankles and wrists locked into metal manacles.

Over the years, I'd seen many peculiar animals join Madame's menagerie. The *bracks* hunted and trapped them in Nerifir, the world where Madame and the *bracks* had come from to Earth. Madame could not return to Nerifir, Radax had told me. But her *bracks* traveled between dimensions, bringing marvelous things and magnificent beasts from the magical kingdom.

This one appeared disturbingly human-like, however. His distorted proportions made it look like the most grotesque version of a man.

It was most certainly a *he*—a huge penis dangled between his muscled thighs. The creature was partially covered in black fur. There was not enough of it to conceal his entire body, though. Patches of fur sprouted on his wide shoulders and narrow hips, some of his crotch area and thighs, leaving his gray skin bare in other places.

"Where does Madame want him?" Krin asked another *brack*, Dez, who followed him in.

I hadn't seen Dez for the past few months. He'd been away from the menagerie, but not in Nerifir. Madame had mentioned once that Dez was taking care of a beast in another location in the country for her. I wondered if this creature was the beast Dez had been guarding.

Dez shrugged. "Put him right here for now."

The beast snarled, snapping his needle-sharp teeth. Saliva dripped from his fangs. It sizzled and steamed when it hit the packed dirt of the tent floor.

"Easy, *voukalak*." Dez shoved a fist into the ribs of the animal. The beast snarled and clacked its teeth, narrowly missing Dez's arm. "Easy!" The *brack* jumped back, then noticed me as I tried to hide in the shadows by the wall. "Hey! What are you doing here?"

Madame had ordered me to sweep this room for the crate's arrival. She'd mentioned the creature would be her new VIP exhibit. I'd finished and was on my way out when Krin had blocked my escape route.

I lifted the broom in my hand, explaining my presence in the room to Dez without words.

Dez made a face as if he'd stepped into gum on a sidewalk, harmless but annoying. Except for Radax, the *bracks* didn't care much about me. For them, I was mostly a nuisance they had to share the space with. No matter how much I tried to keep out of their way, it wasn't always possible to avoid them in the small world of the menagerie.

"Get out of here," Dez dismissed me, jerking his head toward the exit.

Clutching the broom and dustpan in both hands, I hurried to the exit when Krin yelped in pain. Leaping away from the frame with the beast, Krin slammed into me. Blood dripped from the deep scratch on the pad of his thumb.

I staggered backwards, trying to regain my balance.

"What the fuck are you still doing here?" Krin shoved at my shoulder, knocking me to the ground.

The broom and dustpan tumbled out of my hands. I painfully slammed my tailbone against the hard ground but swallowed the groan of pain. There'd be no sympathy from the *bracks*. My cries would just irritate them further.

"Fucking *voukalak!*" Krin punched the chained creature in the head. The beast howled and thrashed in his restraints.

"What did he do?" Dex moved toward the animal, his fists at the ready.

"Scratched me with his claw." Krin sucked on the wound on his thumb.

Dez huffed a laugh and landed a blow in the animal's ribs, then turned to Krin. "Lucky for you, it was his claw. If it'd been his fangs, you'd be dead."

Gripping the broom handle, I collected the dustpan, then scurried behind the fabric partition into the narrow passage behind it. Only once I was out of the *bracks'* sight could I draw a full breath.

The morning was steadily running away from me. Many chores remained to be done, but I hurried to one of the storage rooms located in the bowels of the interconnected tents.

Despite being with the menagerie most of my life, I had no room of my own. Madame used a travel trailer or stayed at a hotel if she found one to her satisfaction. The *bracks* shared a few trailers between themselves. I usually remained in the tents.

I didn't need much space, and there was always a bundle of rags or a pile of bags for me to sleep on. Neither did I have enough clothes to require a closet. I wore what the *bracks* wore—black t-shirts and hooded sweatshirts. Their clothes were several sizes too big for me, but I didn't mind. They were warm and easy to hide in.

Besides that, I picked up lost things on the fairgrounds sometimes. That was how I'd gotten the gray scarf I now wore day and night. It was made from thin but soft material, wide and long. I loved how warm it felt coiled in thick folds around my neck and how I could bury my face in it by drawing my head into my shoulders. It made me feel safer somehow.

After putting the broom and the dustpan away, I found a dark place behind another large crate in one of the stuffy little storage rooms in the maze of the canvas walls. I wedged myself between the wooden side of the crate and the dusty canvas partition.

Cleaning Madame's trailer was next on my list of chores. But maybe she wouldn't notice if I took a moment?

Leaning with my back against the crate, I drew my head into my shoulders, buried my chin into my scarf, and hugged my knees, taking as little space as possible. Here, in this hiding place, I could pretend I was invisible.

The man at the ticket booth, one of Brad's friends, had called me a ghost. And sometimes I wished I were one—invisible, untouchable, ethereal. Impossible to hurt.

My tailbone ached, and I shifted into a slightly more comfortable position. I released a long breath. It came out shaky, but without tears. There was no point in crying. I learned long ago, tears never changed a thing.

A scratching noise came from the crate behind me. I jerked away, startled, then settled back down. Animals scared me far less than people.

This crate had been traveling with us for quite some time now. For whatever reason, Madame had been holding back from displaying the creature inside it to the public. Judging by the size of the crate, the beast must be big, maybe the size of a lion. But it was just another animal from Nerifir. Contained in the crate, it wouldn't harm me. I leaned back against the wood.

Of all the otherworldly beings in Madame's menagerie, I preferred the company of her animals. *Bracks* were heartless and often acted cruel.

Except for Radax. Had Radax been around when Krin pushed me to the ground, he would've certainly confronted Krin—punched him in retaliation, most likely. Then Madame might've ordered him whipped again.

All my life, Radax had been watching over me, but it came at a price. Madame detested the attachment between him and me. I believed that by punishing him, she tried to pry us apart. And in a way, it worked. I kept away from Radax whenever possible. I thanked the stars he had been busy elsewhere that morning. But there were so many other times...

"Where is it?" Madame's sharp voice sounded just outside of the room with the crate.

Panic rushed me, chased by icy fear.

Was she looking for me? How long had I been sitting here? Too long?

"Where did you put him this time?" Her voice sounded closer.

I stilled, halting my breath. Fear froze my insides, paralyzing my limbs—my usual reaction to Madame's presence.

"He's here, Madame," Krin's voice replied.

"He" not *"she."* Madame wasn't looking for me, for once. I allowed some tension to drain, relaxing my stiff shoulders.

"Put the mirror here," Madame ordered sharply, the sound of her footsteps stopping in front of the crate I hid behind.

Other footsteps joined hers—heavy stomping of *bracks'* boots. There were more *bracks* who came with her, not just Krin. I tried to make myself even smaller, hoping they wouldn't look behind the crate.

"Get me a chair, too," Madame demanded.

Too scared to be discovered, I didn't dare look out from behind the crate, keeping as quiet as possible.

"Open the crate," Madame commanded. "He's chained, isn't he?"

"Yes, Madame," Krin replied. The *bracks* complied with her orders, judging by the screeching sound of nails being wrenched out of the wood. "He has his hood on, too."

She huffed. "I don't trust their hoods. I'm not looking at a gorgonian directly. Neither should you if you treasure your life. Place the mirror so I can see him in it."

More shuffling and rustling sounded as the *bracks* complied. Then came the slamming of one side of the crate falling open.

"What a pathetic state to be in for a future High Lord," Madame murmured with a mocking note in her voice.

A rattling of chains came from inside the crate, as if the creature kept in there moved.

Madame chuckled. "Surely, working for me couldn't be any more demeaning than spending your days chained in a crate like an animal."

"I'd rather die as an animal than live as your slave." It was said in a low, cracked voice, barely audible. Yet the sound of it slammed over me like a hammer.

It wasn't an animal but a person in that crate! A person who could speak, think, feel...

How long had he been in there?

I'd never received the order to feed the occupant of this crate. Did someone else feed him?

"My slave?" Madame scoffed. "Like my *bracks?* No, honey. I'm not offering you the honor of becoming one of them. All I'm asking from you is a partnership, a business arrangement, if you will. You'll become my next VIP act. I want you to use your magic to wow my human audience, but without harming them. Dead can't pay, can they?" She chuckled. "Then I'll think about releasing you back to Nerifir one day. All I need is your promise to cooperate."

"You won't get it," the reply came. "I don't make deals with disgraced goddesses."

Quiet as the voice was, it carried the force of defiance and contempt. Madame's prisoner appeared to mock her. I marveled at how brave he was—stupid, but brave.

Stunned by his insolence, I almost missed the fact that he'd called her a goddess. Was *that* what Madame really was?

Madame's chair suddenly crashed to the ground with a slamming noise. She must've leaped to her feet.

Way too familiar with her temper, I drew my head into my shoulders, even though I knew she couldn't see me.

"Look at you!" she screamed. "You're pathetic! Shriveling and drying out from thirst. You haven't had a drop of water in months, and you're sure not getting any until you agree to work for me. Resist, and you'll die most pitifully. No one in Nerifir will ever know about your fate. You'll perish here, in this sad human world. Nameless!"

A soft, dry chuckle came from the crate. The person must be insane, laughing in her face. "I dare you to look at me directly, Goddess Ghata. Instead of hiding behind that old mirror like the coward you are—"

"Enough!" Madame's voice thundered, sending a bolt of terror through my chest. "Close the crate. Let him rot inside."

The *bracks* moved to obey her orders.

"His hood!" Madame suddenly yelled in warning. "Krin. No!" Genuine fear—an emotion I'd never encountered in Madame before—vibrated in her voice. "Zuso, Nerkan, close your eyes!"

The sound of a punch came.

Grunts of pain.

Then something hard and heavy crashed to the floor.

I covered my ears with my hands, trying to block the noises of whatever horrors were happening in front of that crate—things so terrifying, they scared *a goddess.*

The slamming of the crate being shut came, then the sound of the nails being hammered in.

"All done, Madame," Zuso, another *brack*, said.

"Clean this up," she ordered in a somewhat shaken voice. "And no water for the gorgonian. He made his choice. Let him die."

Afraid to breathe, I stayed behind the crate long after all sounds in the room ceased—the shuffling of the *bracks*, the sweeping of the broom, the footsteps of everyone leaving.

In the quiet that followed, I ventured to press my ear to the crate. The faint sound of the shallow, labored breathing came from inside.

A man?

A monster?

Fear surged through me with a shudder.

Trying to make as little noise as possible, I crawled from behind the crate on all fours. My hand landed on a piece of something hard on the floor. I picked it up.

Strings of white light hung high under the ceiling of the tent, aiding the sunlight filtering through the canvas in illuminating the space.

I examined the item in my hand. It was about an inch long, gray, and hard like a rock. It was shaped like the tip of a finger—a thumb—complete with the smooth, short nail on one end. When I turned it over, a long gash on the thumb's pad came into view, the scratch from the beast's claw.

Struck by horror, I tossed it away and ran from the room as fast as I could and as far from the crate as possible.

I had no idea what exactly happened in that room that morning. But I was fairly certain I'd never see Krin again.

Chapter Three

AMIRA

Somewhere between the nightmares of the night and the horrors of the day lay a few fuzzy moments of early morning. Wrapping my arms around me, I kept my eyes closed, trying to stretch these moments just a little bit longer.

Few sounds filtered through the fabric walls of the tent—chirping of the birds, distant hum of traffic, rustling of wind between the strings of lights outside. There was no noise of people moving around yet. I was usually the first one to rise.

Without a permanent accommodation at the menagerie, I slept in whatever hidden corner I would find. Last night, it happened to be a storage room with the spare rolls of oiled canvas. Piled together, they made a decent bed for someone like me, who never had a bed to compare it with.

I slept fully dressed, but the chill of the morning snuck through the tent walls and under my clothes. I hugged myself tighter, huddling into my hoodie.

Like a new dream, dressed in the golden haze of the morning, the memory of the young couple kissing in front of my ticket booth entered my mind. The girl was giggling as the boy cradled her head with one hand, his other hand splayed on her back under her shirt.

A tingling sensation spread down my body—pleasurable and warm. I slid a finger along my bottom lip, trying to imagine what a kiss on the lips would feel like. Soft and tender and barely there?

Then I thought about the girl's back arching as the boy leaned over her. Wouldn't the passion like that be more punishing, claiming, invigorating?

I had no idea.

Living at the menagerie, I was surrounded by Madame's *bracks*—all young, strong, and conventionally handsome men. But *bracks* weren't human. They felt no need for a woman other than Madame.

Radax treated me like his little sister, to be looked after and protected. The rest of the *bracks* paid me little attention. They put up with me, begrudgingly, sometimes with annoyance, oftentimes with clear disdain. And, I preferred it that way. The thought of a *brack* touching me in any intimate way brought fear with a dash of repulsion.

Madame chose one or two *bracks* to take to her trailer nightly. If I happened to pass by, I heard their growls, grunts, and groans coming from inside the trailer. The sounds filled me with dread rather than excitement.

I knew what was happening between Madame and her *bracks* at night. I knew of sex, even as I'd never had it myself. I'd seen animals' couplings in the menagerie. I also read. I regularly found abandoned paperbacks on the fairgrounds all over the continent. Most of them were heart-racing thrillers or blood-curdling horror mysteries. But some were romance novels that sent my heart racing for different reasons.

Occasionally, the fair set up next to a drive-in movie theater. Then I'd stay up every night, hiding behind the chain-link fence that separated the drive-in from the fairgrounds and watching every single movie that played. I heard no sound, of course, and the screen would often be positioned at a wrong angle for me to see it properly. But movies were like a window into the ordinary lives of people of my world. The life I'd never experienced—family, school, friends... Love.

Longing warmed my body. Some of it was physical, pressing between my thighs and tingling in the peaks of my breasts. But a huge part of it lived much deeper inside my chest. Loneliness crushed my heart. Sometimes, it felt like there wasn't enough room inside me to contain the desperate need for something or...*someone* in my life.

Silence had kept me safe at the menagerie. But sometimes, the need to hear a kind word from someone, to have a simple conversation with another person seemed even more important than life.

I tried to imagine kissing a man openly, in front of the tents, for Madame to see...and I couldn't. Terror gripped me, like it always did at a mere thought of Madame.

I drew in a long breath, then released it slowly.

In a few seconds, I'd have to get up and start the string of endless chores. The worries of the day already threatened to rush in. I chased most of them away, but the memories of Madame's confrontation with the person in the crate came crashing in.

I didn't fully understand what had happened yesterday. Krin was nowhere to be seen today, which didn't surprise me. Madame sulked, but made no announcements about him or her prisoner whom she'd called "gorgonian."

If I asked Radax about that, he might not reply or he might get in trouble if he did. Most likely he'd just brush me off as he usually did when I asked questions about the many puzzling things that took place at the menagerie.

"Some things are best for you not to know, Amira. It's safer that way," he'd say.

With a long sigh, I opened my eyes and climbed off the pile of the canvas rolls. I left the tent and padded across the parking lot to one of the *bracks'* trailers. There, I used the bathroom, then started to prepare breakfast for Madame. My chin buried in my scarf, I quickly fried some eggs, the way Madame liked them, toasted a slice of her favorite bread, then arranged berries and yogurt in a bowl.

The thunder of the *bracks'* snoring shook the trailer while I worked. Only a thin partition separated the tiny kitchenette from their sleeping area with rows of bunk beds.

I hurried, wishing to be out of the *bracks'* quarters as soon as possible. Once awake, they would take up the entire space, huge as each of them was. I would surely get in the way and make someone angry.

After quickly arranging the food and a pot of tea on a tray, I sneaked out of the trailer and headed to Madame's trailer parked nearby.

Hers was far more lavishly decorated than the *bracks'*. A red runner lined the stairs, with a colorful tapestry hanging over the door. Mystical beasts and plants I'd never seen were woven into the tapestry, but I never had the time to stop and study the beautiful picture, always rushing from one chore to another.

"Breakfast." I knocked on the door quietly.

"Well, bring it in!" Madame ordered.

If she ever slept, I didn't know. For over a decade now, I'd unfailingly served her breakfast daily, unless she stayed at a hotel. And whenever I showed up with my tray, Madame was always up, no matter how many *bracks* she'd had in her trailer the night before.

Madame sat in front of her dresser, brushing her long, red hair.

"Set it on the nightstand over there." She waved her hand. Candlelight from the candelabrum on the dresser broke into a million tiny sparks in the precious stones of the rings on her fingers. "Did Vuk bring Lorsan Lily honey from Nerifir?"

"No, Madame." I put the tray down on the night table. "He said the honey was very hard to find where he landed in Nerifir."

Bracks didn't report to me about their trips to Nerifir, of course. But they often spoke to each other in my presence. I'd overheard Vuk complain to Leslo about not finding the honey Madame liked having in her tea.

"*Hard*, doesn't mean *impossible*," Madame hissed through her teeth, shoving her golden hairbrush into my hands. "He obviously didn't make enough effort. Lazy, useless slave."

Her displeasure sent a shiver of dread down my spine, as if it was *my* fault that Vuk didn't find the honey. Chances were Vuk would be punished now, and I flinched, as if already hearing the sound of the whip splitting open the skin on his back.

"Braid my hair," Madame ordered curtly. "Then give me my tea, with that disgusting local honey, and get out of here."

I did as I was told, trying not to tangle her luscious fire-red locks with my trembling fingers. She preferred elaborate hairdos that had taken me a lot of practice to get just right. Tiny little braids interweaved with each other into flower-like designs on the back of her head, then merged into one wide plait running down her back.

I ran the brush down a strand as gently as I could. Yet it tugged at a tiny invisible knot.

"Ugh!" Madame inhaled sharply, snatching the brush from me.

"I'm sorry..." I mumbled, fear solidifying my insides.

"Useless!" She struck me across the knuckles with the heavy metal brush. "You just never learn."

Sharp pain lanced through my hand. I sucked in a breath, holding in a whimper. Any sound of crying or complaining would make it worse—so, so much worse. Madame had an explosive temper, and her cruelty knew no bounds.

"Finish it!" She tossed the brush on the dresser. It landed among the framed pictures of her dressed up in elaborate silk gowns.

Holding my breath to the point of nearly passing out, I adorned her braid with a few bejeweled clips. My fingers shook so badly, it was a miracle I didn't pull on her hair again.

"Done." I exhaled the word, not meeting Madame's coal-black eyes.

She eyed her hairdo in the mirror critically, turning her head this way and that. A frown of displeasure firmly settled on her beautiful face, the way it always did in my company.

My heart raced with worry as her silence stretched. My hands grew clammy with sweat as I waited for her assessment of my work.

Madame kept studying her reflection in the mirror. She was undoubtedly the most beautiful woman I'd ever seen. Tall and stately, she had intense black eyes that set off her flaming red hair in a most stunning way. Her unblemished skin appeared to glow, her naked body barely covered by an open silk kimono that morning.

"Goddess," the prisoner in the crate had called her. She very well could be that. If gods were real, it'd be easy to imagine Madame among them. And who was to say for sure that gods didn't exist?

I'd spent my life surrounded by things and creatures that didn't belong in this world. I knew other worlds existed, all connected by the mysterious river the *bracks* called the River of Mists. I'd hardly seen anything outside of the canvas walls of the menagerie, but those walls held plenty of evidence for me to believe in things others would deem extraordinary.

It didn't make much difference to my life who or what Madame was, though. My role remained the same—do whatever she says and do it well to avoid her displeasure.

"Fine." Madame pressed her full, red lips together, turning away from the mirror. "Now, give me my tea and get out."

Once out of her trailer, I dared take a deep breath again. The dust of the grounds and the exhaust fumes of the parking lot nearby felt more refreshing than Madame's perfume. The fragrant air inside her trailer had been suffocating.

I grabbed onto the railing, walking down the trailer's few steps, and winced in pain. Redness spread across my knuckles where Madame's brush had hit it. My skin puffed up, bruises already forming underneath.

It was my right hand, and I still had a day-worth of chores lying ahead of me. Cradling my hand to my chest, I allowed a whimper to escape. Everything would take that much longer if I only had one fully functioning hand, my *left* hand.

Maybe if I took no breaks today, I could still get everything done? But I had to hurry. My hand started to throb, and I shoved it into the pocket of my hoodie on my way to the tents.

When feeding the animals, I had to use extra caution to not let them escape while keeping the doors to their enclosures open and getting their food with the one healthy hand I had. When cleaning Madame's trailer afterwards, I could barely hold back tears. It hurt too much even to hold the broom.

By the time I got to dusting the display area of the menagerie, my right hand had swollen twice its size and was throbbing hot.

I yelped in pain, trying to lift a metal box, one of Madame's unanimated exhibits. It wasn't very large, the size of a medium music box, but the aged, golden-green metal it was made of was heavy. Intricate gears were visible through the various cut-outs of the outer layer, indicating this was a device, but I didn't know how it worked. Madame told her customers it was a communication box from the Wetlands of Lorsan in Nerifir.

The heavy object slipped from my fingers, hitting the shelf with a thud. Tears sprung to my eyes. I could no longer ignore the pain.

Sneaking into the *bracks'* trailer when no one was looking, I got some ice from the freezer, put it in a plastic bag, then wrapped it in the end of my scarf. The cool pack eased some of the burning pain the moment I placed it on my injured hand.

Cradling my hand with the cold pack to my chest, I kept my head down on my way back to the tents.

The fairgrounds were about to open. The first tours of the menagerie would start shortly after. I'd have to go back to the ticket booth soon. There was no time for a meltdown, but I couldn't stop the tears flooding my vision.

Rushing into the nearest dark room inside the first tent, I squeezed into a corner out of sight and let the tears fall. The pain got the best of me. I sobbed, lifting the ice pack to inspect my hand. Thick bumps rose over the bones just below my knuckles. Dark bruises formed. And it hurt. Dammit, it hurt so much.

I sobbed, tears dripping into my scarf.

"Are you having a bad day, little one?" came a raspy voice, like a whisper of the breeze in a pile of dry leaves.

I choked on a sob in shock. Wiping the tears with my sleeve, I realized I was sitting next to the wooden crate with the gorgonian.

"Tell me who hurt you," the voice rustled from the crate. "Sometimes just telling someone helps."

It sounded eerie, horrifying, and...kind.

And it was the kindness that broke me. I was starved for it so much, I would've given whatever was left of my miserable life for just one warm hug.

A loud sob tore from my throat. I scrambled to my feet and ran. I fled the room with the crate and the creature in it.

Whoever he was, however, he couldn't be a bigger monster than the one I'd been working for most of my life.

The morning shows started, and I took my place in the ticket booth. Radax manned the front entrance to the menagerie, as usual. I sent a quick smile and a wave of a hand—my left hand—his way. He inclined his head to me in greeting.

At noon, I made lunch for Madame and a quick egg salad sandwich for myself. As I walked through one of the passages inside the tents, looking for a hiding place to eat my sandwich, the *brack* Nerkan stopped me.

"Madame wants you to get these for her." He shoved a piece of paper into my hand.

It was a shopping list with different powders and spices, all of which I could probably get at the local grocery store.

"I'll need to be back in the ticket booth soon," I reminded him softly.

He wrinkled his nose, obviously annoyed. "Fine, I'll sell tickets until you come back. Take the van. And make it quick. The booth is too hot. I hate it there."

I snuggled into my hoodie on the way to the van in the parking lot. High noon temperatures had chased away the freshness of the early morning, but I didn't take off either the hoodie or the scarf. They were more than just clothes, they were my security blanket, my one safe place, even as they weren't a place at all.

Radax had taught me how to drive, both manual and automatic transmissions. Madame had allowed it, likely foreseeing the usefulness of my having the skill. She often preferred sending *me* to run errands rather than one of the *bracks*. I attracted much less attention as compared to them with their tall, muscular bodies, bald heads, and tattooed arms and necks.

I pulled over into the parking lot of the local store and parked the white, windowless van of the menagerie.

Madame's list wasn't long, but it was specific. It took me some time to locate all the items. Once I'd collected them all, I got in line to the cash register and occupied my time by watching people.

They were my one true window into the world outside of the menagerie. I rarely spoke to anyone, but I always watched carefully, trying to guess the life they all led, the life I would never be allowed to have.

A young woman was holding the hand of a man. Was he her boyfriend? Just a friend? Or a relative?

A man had a toddler strapped into the baby seat of his shopping cart. The boy was happily munching on a cookie from an open box. Was this a single dad? Or did mom stay at home?

An older woman bent over to tie the shoelaces of a little girl. Were they a grandma and a granddaughter, spending time together?

All those mundane things people did every day while interacting with each other were a mystery to me. What was it like to have a grandmother, a child, a family?

A teenage boy in line in front of me opened a bottle of water and took a drink. His friend squeezed the bottle while he was drinking, spilling its contents on the boy's chest.

"Hey!" The boy in the soaking wet shirt shoved his friend away, both laughing loudly.

Water...

As I watched it run down the boy's shirt and uselessly drip on the floor, my mind veered to the creature left to die from thirst in the crate inside one of Madame's tents.

He was dangerous—the image of the piece of rock shaped like Krin's thumb rose in my mind. The prisoner might be a true monster.

But he was suffering.

"Are you having a bad day, little one?" His voice had sounded listless but kind—raspy because his throat was dry.

His suffering came from something so easily fixed as lack of water. Even I—the "weak, pathetic human" as Madame often referred to me—had the power to help him.

If I gave him water, though, I'd violate Madame's direct order—an offence punishable by death. In the dark world of the menagerie, I was but a shadow. As a shadow, I could survive, but I needed to remain invisible—do nothing, say nothing, see nothing...

The cashier scanned my purchases. "Anything else?"

In my sweaty hand, I crinkled the twenty-dollar bill Nerkan had given me.

The cashier glanced at me expectantly. "That'd be seventeen dollars and fifteen cents."

A sticker on the shelf inside the glass door of the refrigerated display stated the price of a bottle of water as ninety-nine cents. That was all it'd cost to stop someone from suffering a horrible death from thirst—ninety-nine cents for a bottle of water and...quite possibly, my life if Madame ever found out. She might also hurt Radax for my offense, as she often did.

"I'd rather die as an animal than live as your slave," the gorgonian had said to Madame. His quiet voice had carried so much strength when he'd said that—the strength I did not possess but couldn't help to admire. He dared defy the goddess, choosing to pay with his life for his freedom.

I stepped away from the cash register and grabbed two long cucumbers from the vegetable stand nearby.

"These, too," I croaked, slamming the cucumbers onto the belt.

A cucumber consisted mostly of water. Yet it was *not* water. Would that make a difference if Madame discovered my feeding it to her prisoner? Probably not. But defiance came easier to me when it wasn't about breaking her direct order.

I wasn't strong enough to defy a goddess. But maybe I was smart enough to find a way *around* her orders? And maybe I could be stealthy enough to avoid getting caught?

"Hey! You're from the freakshow, aren't you?" The girlish voice startled me.

I froze on my way across the parking lot to the van.

A slim girl in frayed denim shorts and a worn leather jacket was leaning against a parked pickup truck.

“I saw you in the ticket booth this morning.” She blew a pink bubble from the chewing gum in her mouth.

Keeping my head down, I circled the girl, giving her a wide berth, then laid course back to the van again.

She peeled her back off the pickup and jogged after me. “Hey, what’s the matter? I’m not going to hurt you. I just want to ask you something.”

Whatever it was, I already knew I wouldn’t be able to answer. Madame didn’t allow speaking about the menagerie with strangers. It was always a wise choice to remain quiet.

The girl blew another gum bubble, then popped it with a loud sound. I drew my head further into my shoulders until both my mouth and my nose were buried in the scarf around my neck.

“So, what’s the deal with all those things you guys have in there?” the girl asked, blocking my way.

I had no choice but to stop, finally taking a good look at her.

Her copper-red hair was shaved off on one side, reaching down to her shoulder on the other. Shiny metal piercings decorated her lip, one nostril, and an eyebrow. Several rings and hoops glistened on each ear.

She was a colorful character, almost as colorful as Madame. Unlike Madame, though, she didn’t look evil. I liked staring at her.

The girl smirked, shoving the gum behind her cheek with her tongue.

“I’m Amber.” She offered me her thin, bony hand. “What’s your name?”

Clutching the paper bag from the store with one arm, I kept my injured hand in my pocket.

She shrugged, shoving her unshaken hand into the pocket of her shorts, but didn’t move out of my way.

“I need to go,” I mumbled, avoiding the girl’s hazel eyes.

“But are all those things in your tents real?” Her face split with a wide grin. “The animals, too?”

I nodded.

The animals of the menagerie were very real to me. Yenric, the two-headed piglet that, according to Madame, should’ve had three heads but was born with a defect and ended up with only two; the red snake-birds that looked like feather boas with claws and wings; the glow-in-the dark bog turtles that burst with colors brighter than any fireworks I'd seen—all of them were more real to me than this world's cows or horses that I'd never seen up close.

"Cool!" Amber kept gazing at me with curiosity.

A sudden roar of an engine made me flinch and stagger back a few paces. A man on a motorbike pulled over behind Amber, his face concealed by a black helmet.

"Shoot, I've got to go. Well, bye, ticket girl." She hopped on the seat behind the man and gave me a wave before circling his waist with both arms.

Wind caught her bright hair as the motorbike sped up along the dirt road, raising clouds of dust in its wake.

I stared after them, watching the dust settle. I'd never ridden a motorbike. Now I wondered what it felt like. Wind rushing by. Road ahead, endless as it could be.

Freedom.

Amber swept away on a motorbike was the epitome of being free when I was tied by invisible chains to the place I could never escape.

I squeezed the key to the van in my hand. I had a vehicle with enough gas in the tank to take me hundreds of miles away from Madame and her menagerie.

Except, where would I go?

Madame often said that money was everything in this world. I had none to my name, not a penny. I knew people earned money by working, but I had no idea how one would even get a job.

So much about the world outside of the menagerie confused and terrified me. Every now and then, I heard fragments of people's conversations in the fairgrounds. Taxes, IDs, bank accounts, social security, college, rent, loans were the words often used by people. They sounded like a foreign language to me.

Radax was my one source of information, but he couldn't help me with any of that either. He belonged to the menagerie, to Madame. Like me, he'd never really *lived* in this world, either.

Getting in the van and driving as far as it would take me was tempting. Except that this plan had no final destination and therefore ended nowhere.

Climbing into the driver's seat, I started the engine. Then, I headed back to the fairgrounds and to Madame's tents—to the tried and familiar, to the only place in the world where at least one person cared about me.

Chapter Four

KYLLEN

His throat constricted with a swallow. Only there was nothing to swallow—there was hardly any moisture left in his body. His throat felt like dry sand in a desert. Any movement hurt.

"You'll die here. Nameless," Ghata had said. And it looked like he was well on his way to fulfill her prophecy.

The mortal drought had set in, shriveling his insides and drying his skin that by now resembled tree bark. Soon, his brain would shut down, and his body would slowly turn to dust.

Great Serpent, this was not how he'd thought he'd die. As a child, like every gorgonian boy, he'd wished to wrap his name in glory through an honorable death on a battlefield.

Of course, his parents always hoped he'd live long enough to take his father's place one day and die of an old age as the High Lord of Ellohi in the Kingdom of Lorsan in Nerifir.

And here he was, drying to death in the remote, unknown world of humans.

The alternative was even worse than death—centuries of servitude to the disgraced goddess of werewolves. Her own people had chased Goddess Ghata out of Nerifir. She had no decency, and her lack of honor made any chance of a fair deal impossible. She was a goddess, not a fae. Promises didn't bind her. Making a deal with Ghata would be like placing lifelong shackles on himself, without any guarantee of her ever holding up her end of the bargain. His life and his honor would be forever in her hands.

He preferred death.

His back started to cramp from sitting in the same position for too long. He lay on the wooden floor carefully, trying to avoid cracking his dry skin any more than it already was. It hurt when that happened. The cracks no longer healed.

The iron chains rattled and clanked as he shifted his legs. The space wasn't long enough for him to stretch them out completely. Neither was the crate tall enough for him to stand up. The construction of it must be a part of the devious plan to torture, no doubt.

In this position, the small opening in the top part of the crate came into view. Crossed with thick, rusty bars, it was his only window into the world. Except that the world had been reduced to the strapped fabric overhead, with a string of yellow lights.

During the day, the sunlight filtered through the fabric like it was now. At night, it was dark, save for the lights.

He had no idea how much time had passed since the *bracks* had trapped him like a wild animal and brought him here. The thirst had blurred his mind a lot lately. He passed out often. This could've been going on for months, years, or maybe even centuries.

Not that it mattered anymore. At this rate, he wouldn't last much longer.

Noises reached him more frequently than the sights. Feet shuffling. Ghata's voice—sometimes sugary sweet, but often brutal and harsh. Her *bracks'* voices, either confirming her orders or reporting on their execution. Sounds of packing. Then vibrations of being driven somewhere. Then, the same noises all over again, spinning in an endless, maddening cycle.

Sound of footsteps reached his hearing, then a shuffling noise brushed along the wall of the crate. Someone was sneaking around his prison. The footfalls were light, so light he wondered if it was one of the many hallucinations the brutal thirst had forced on him.

"Um..." someone cleared their throat softly.

Were they trying to get his attention?

Shoving back his hood to expose his ears, he strained his hearing.

"I brought you something," the voice said, hesitantly.

The speaker was clearly a woman, and judging by her voice, a young one. He wondered if it was the same human whose soft sobbing he'd heard earlier. Was she also a prisoner? Or did Ghata send her here, to try and succeed where the goddess herself had failed?

It could be a trap.

"Um..." the woman hesitated. "Can you hear me?"

He'd spoken to her when she'd cried, hadn't he? He couldn't remember the exact words he'd said to her, but he'd meant for them to be comforting.

His dehydrated brain functioned slowly, but an idea was forming in his mind while the woman waited for his reply. She'd cried. Something or someone had made her unhappy. And if so, maybe he could use her misery to his advantage? Gods knew he could use an ally, even an unwitting one.

Maybe, just maybe, she could become his key to freedom?

It might be the thirst or desperation or both, but for the first time in what felt like forever, hope fluttered in his drying heart.

He was still pondering the best words for his reply when something long and slim obstructed his view in the opening above. The woman slid the object between the bars and...let go of it.

His reflexes being much slower than they used to, he didn't roll away in time. The long object hit him straight in the eye.

"Hey!" He jerked back into a sitting position. His eye ached, and he rubbed it. "What, by Great Serpent, was that for?"

The woman squeaked.

"I'm so...so sorry," she half-whispered. Then, the sound of her scurrying away came.

"Wait!"

But she was gone.

What, by all the gods of Nerifir, had just happened?

He'd expected new kinds of torture from Ghata and her people. But this... Well, this was just ridiculous.

He rubbed his eye a little more. The soreness dissipated quickly. Whatever she'd tossed at him wasn't nearly hard or heavy enough to be lethal. She hadn't appeared trying to kill him.

What did she do this for? And what was that thing she threw at him?

He searched the floor by touch, his hands closing around a smooth, long object.

A cucumber?

The woman had just tossed a cucumber into his crate, whacking him in the eye.

He chuckled, staring at the vegetable in disbelief. It looked very much like cucumbers in Nerifir—green, long, and probably juicy.

He brought it to his nose and inhaled the fresh, crisp scent. It always reminded him of the cool water running between the roots of his father's palace.

Water...

Closing his eyes, he sank his teeth into the dark green skin. The clear, watery juice ran from under his fangs, dripping on his bottom lip and trickling down his chin.

So much like water.

He inhaled the fresh scent again, biting a huge chunk off from the side. The tender flesh of the vegetable slid down his parched throat, soothing it with moisture. He took another bite, then another.

Before long, the entire cucumber was gone. And he wanted more.

His insides, which had hardly seen any food or water since the day he was taken, appeared to instantly absorb every bit of moisture and nutrition from the vegetable. His stomach still felt empty. His skin remained dry like paper, but some clarity returned to his brain. He felt better than he had in a very long time.

Exhaling slowly, he leaned against a side of the crate.

Maybe he should've been more cautious when ingesting anything that came from Ghata and her people. Chances were the woman worked for her. It could all be a trick after all—a trap.

He couldn't bring himself to care, though. For the first time in a long time, there was food in his belly. The scorching dryness receded.

He closed his eyes, not in a fog of delirium for once, but in a deep, restful sleep.

Chapter Five

AMIRA

I hit him with a cucumber.

I wanted to do something brave for once, help in some way, and instead ended up hitting him with the cucumber...

Shame and mortification wracked me. Madame was right. I never could do anything properly.

A day later, the fair ended. The *bracks* tore down the tents and packed up the trucks. The menagerie was moving farther south in Georgia. After that, I overheard, we were leaving the United States for England at the end of January.

All those locations were mostly just sounds to me. When traveling with the menagerie, the differences between places and countries were subtle. Instead of a tent, there might be an exhibition hall. Instead of a truck, we'd take a plane. Other than that, my life didn't change much, no matter where Madame chose for us to travel.

Instead of being tossed and shaken in the cabin of a truck, Madame took a plane to the nearest airport to the next fair. She'd be waiting for us in a hotel when we got there in a couple of days.

With her departure, breathing got a lot easier. The *bracks* were still bossing me around, and I ended up working just as much as if she were here. But not hearing her voice, not expecting it to rise to the shrill of displeasure at any moment, felt like a weight had been temporarily lifted off my shoulders.

I moved quickly, helping to break down the menagerie and our camp while also trying to stay out of the *bracks'* way as much as possible.

My hand had been healing. The bruise bloomed in every shade of blue, yellow, and red, but the swelling and the pain had gone down. By keeping my hand tucked inside my sleeve, I managed to hide it from Radax and avoid his questions.

When we were almost done, I took one of the few things that still needed to be loaded—a bucket with tubes and other pool paraphernalia, left from when Madame had a giant water tank. She had displayed a siren man in it, Zeph. But Zeph escaped in November, and she'd sold the tank. The bucket with spare tubes and cords remained because Madame probably forgot to give the order to get rid of it, and the *bracks* didn't do much without her orders.

Walking along the open tractor trailers, I found the one with the crate where Madame kept her prisoner, the gorgonian. I shoved the bucket in, then loitered around, pretending to be busy with arranging the things inside the trailer.

Ever since my fiasco with the cucumber, I'd been keeping away from the gorgonian's crate. He must be angry with me for hitting him, and I didn't need to have one more person yelling at me.

I did wonder, however, what happened to the cucumber. Did the gorgonian eat it? If he did, it wouldn't have lasted long. By now, he must be hungry and thirsty again.

Placed deep inside the trailer, the crate must've been one of the first things loaded today. It'd been sitting in the hot truck for a while now. I couldn't help thinking how hot and stuffy it must be inside that wooden box, and how thirsty the person in it must feel.

Then another thought entered my mind. What if he *didn't* eat the cucumber? I had no idea what kind of creature the gorgonian was. What if cucumbers weren't what they ate?

Then, the stupid vegetable would be lying on the floor of his crate, rotting. Not only would it make the conditions inside the crate even more uncomfortable, but if a *brack* or Madame ever discovered the rotting cucumber, they would demand to know how it got there.

If he didn't eat the cucumber, I absolutely had to get it back.

Once all was done and packed, I found Radax.

"Ready?" he asked, standing next to a truck.

I nodded. "I'll go in the back, with the animals."

"Are you sure you don't want to drive in the front with me?" he asked.

Dez climbed into the driver's seat of the truck Radax was pointing at. If I went with them, I'd have to listen to Dez bragging about his time with Madame, what he'd brought for her from Nerifir the last time he went there, and how much she praised him for it.

"Maybe later?" I said tentatively, reluctant to say no to Radax.

He didn't look happy about my decision but didn't argue. "We'll stop for dinner later in the evening. You'll let me know if you changed your mind. Do you have anything to eat until then?"

"I do." I produced a wrapped sandwich and a plastic water bottle from the deep pockets of my hoodie.

"Well, climb in, then." He held the back door to his truck open for me.

"Um... I need to get something first. You go ahead. I'll get Vuk to lock the doors in a minute."

Dez stuck his bald head out of the driver's side window.

"Come on, Radax!" He slapped the outside of the door with his hand to attract our attention, as if his booming voice wasn't loud enough. "Time to get going!"

Radax touched my arm. "Well, take care. I'll check on you at the next stop."

That wasn't good. He'd be checking on me in his truck while I'd be in the one with the crate. I'd have to think of something to explain it to him later.

I waited until Radax jumped into the cabin of his truck. Then I locked his back doors before climbing inside the truck with the crate and crouching behind a pile of stacked boxes. The truck's doors were closed and locked shortly after. Then, our entire caravan was on the move. I found a comfy enough spot between the rolls of tent fabric. Then I sat and silently stared at the crate.

The truck shook and jumped on the dirt road before we came to a paved one. It couldn't be comfortable riding in the crate with nothing but chains holding one in place. Yet not a sound came from inside the crate.

I was never the one to start a conversation, but I feared I had no choice in this case. Trying to get my nerves under control, I cleared my throat.

A shuffling noise finally came from the crate, accompanied by the rattling of chains.

"I'm ready," the gorgonian said.

"For what?" I blinked in confusion.

"If you're going to toss another vegetable at me, do it now, while my head is out of the way." His voice sounded smoother and stronger this time, somewhat grumpy, but with a soft teasing note, too.

"Oh, no. Did I hit you in the head?" A wave of mortification flooded me anew.

"My eye, to be precise."

"I'm so sorry," I half-whispered, hiding my mouth behind my hand. "Did I hurt you?"

"Horribly."

How awful.

Though he didn't sound angry. In fact, a smile prominently sounded in his voice when he spoke again. "No apology would ever fix the injury I sustained. The only way to remedy the situation would be to throw another cucumber my way."

He laughed—the soft, merry chuckle filtered through the wooden partition between us.

I blinked again, confused whether he was mocking me. It was difficult to say for sure without seeing him. However, if we were speaking face to face, I'd probably just stay silent, like I often did. Not seeing the person I was talking to made the speaking part easier.

"You want another cucumber?"

"Please," he said. "That'd be amazing."

"So, did you eat the one I gave you last time?"

"Absolutely. It was delicious."

I released a breath in relief—he'd eaten the evidence of my disobedience. Of course, just by talking to him, I was already breaking another one of Madame's orders—she didn't even like me speaking to *bracks*, not to mention anyone else.

"So?" her prisoner urged. "Please tell me you brought another cucumber?"

"No... I don't have another one."

The second cucumber I'd bought at the store that day I'd sliced into a salad for Madame's dinner the very same night to justify my purchasing them. She often went through my store receipts to verify expenses.

"No?" His voice dropped with disappointment.

"You like cucumbers?"

"My dear human friend," he said with a soft huff. "I hadn't drunk or eaten anything for a very long time before you so generously dropped it in my eye. I can honestly say it was the best thing I've ever had in this world."

"I..." I rummaged through my pockets. "I have a sandwich and a bottle of water."

I'd made the sandwich from the leftovers of Madame's breakfast after she'd left for the airport that morning. She never forbade giving her prisoner food. There'd be no harm in sharing my sandwich with him. I took it out and held it up as if he could see it through the wood.

"It's an egg sandwich. We can share. Or you can have the whole thing if you want." I would get dinner when we stopped, as Radax had said.

"Did you say you had water?" he asked hurriedly, greedily. If it was possible to sense someone else's thirst through their voice, I just did. My own throat grew dry, and I had to swallow to even continue breathing.

I wrapped my fingers around the plastic bottle. It felt cool from the liquid inside. Refreshing. Just what he needed, I imagined.

Giving him water would be breaking Madame's order. I'd done some things before I knew she would disapprove of. Or I'd skirted around her instructions and even slightly bent the rules sometimes. But I had never disobeyed a direct order.

"Would you share your water with me?" the prisoner asked sweetly. "Please? Just a sip."

There was so much hope in his voice. I just couldn't crush it. Madame wasn't here, anyway. No one would tell her. Right? No one would know if I just gave her prisoner one tiny drink of water.

I blew out a breath. "Okay. I'll share. But you can't tell anyone."

"I won't," he said quickly. "You can trust me fully and completely."

I didn't know him enough to trust him, but he had nothing to gain from telling on me to Madame.

"Let me just figure out how to get it to you." I got up, holding on to the edge of the crate. Its height reached just above my chest. Leaning over, I could reach the small, barred window in the crate's roof. "The bottle wouldn't fit through the bars of the window. Should I just open it and tip it over so you could drink?"

"No." He sounded anxious. "Don't. You'll risk spilling and wasting it." To him, every drop of water was obviously precious.

"Okay. Just give me a minute." I searched around for something I could use as a straw or a funnel, then remembered the bucket I had loaded earlier. Finding it, I pulled out a bundle of plastic tubes and untangled one from it.

"This should work." The tube was almost as long as I was tall. I threaded one end of it through the opening between the bars. "Do you think you could use this as a straw?" I dipped the other end of the tube into the open water bottle in my hands.

Instead of an answer, the gorgonian sucked the air out of the tube, filling in with water. Within seconds, my bottle was empty. He practically "inhaled" the water in a few long, deep gulps.

"Wow. That was quick." I turned the empty bottle in my hands, dumbfounded. How could anyone drink that fast? "You were really thirsty..."

"You have no idea," the reply came in a slow, satisfied voice.

"Feeling better?" I sat back on the pile of canvas rolls.

He hummed contently, then asked, "Why are you doing this, little human? Don't you know Ghata forbade giving me water? You work for her, don't you? You're one of her people."

That was too many questions to answer at once. Especially since I wasn't clear on the answers myself.

Did I work for Madame? I wasn't formally employed, but I did things for her and followed her orders. I got no compensation other than room and board, which were a pile of rags to sleep on and whatever food I scavenged from the kitchen.

Was I one of her people? I didn't belong to her the way the *bracks* did. Yet I wasn't free from her, either.

The hardest question to answer was why I went against Madame's direct order. I couldn't even use the excuse that it was just a cucumber this time. I had given him an entire bottle of water.

"I... I heard you speak to her," I started, searching for words. "I didn't know she imprisoned people."

No, that was a lie. I knew. Or I should have known.

Madame had imprisoned and displayed Zeph, the siren-man, for money before. But I had chosen to believe her lies that the siren wasn't a sentient being, that he was simply a magical fish or a marine mammal from Nerifir and only visually resembled a human. It was easier for my conscience to accept his being locked in a water tank if he had no thoughts, no awareness, and no life to give up when she'd captured him.

Just like now, it would've been easier to pretend the gorgonian was some wild beast, too.

Except that beasts didn't talk.

"It's not right to keep people in a crate," I said.

"No, it's not," he agreed. "Would you help me get out, then?"

I choked on my next breath at that demand.

Freeing him would be a much greater act of defiance than getting him some water to drink. Even if I had the ability to release him—which was questionable, considering he was locked in chains and I had no key—it'd have severe consequences. Death, most likely. For both Radax and myself.

"What scares you?" the gorgonian asked when I hadn't replied.

Fear was an undividable part of me. I lived with that chilling, sinking feeling inside for so long, it had become my second nature. I could not imagine a life without it.

"Are you afraid of Ghata?" he insisted. "The one who the *bracks* call Madame?"

Madame was the source of many horrors. I'd witnessed her do things that would haunt me in my nightmares forever. I'd heard her brag about even worse things still.

She raised her hand to me often, almost daily. A shove, a push, a slap across my face were the norm. Lashings were frequent, too, with whatever she could grab when she was in a sour mood and I was close enough for her to take it out on me.

But what frightened me even more than what she did was what she *could* do. Madame had the power to hurt people far more than physically, and she could make the pain last for an eternity.

I cleared my throat again, finding just the right word to describe her. "She's evil."

A long sigh rose from the crate.

"That she is, my little human friend, that she is." He didn't pressure me to release him. And for that, I was grateful.

Chapter Six

AMIRA

The drive was long. The truck rolled with only a minimal disturbance along the highway. I welcomed the chance to have a companion for once. I couldn't remember the last time I'd had a real conversation with anyone.

I sat with my back against the side of the crate. I had no idea what position the gorgonian was in, but I imagined him sitting with his back pressed to the same spot from the inside. If the crate wasn't there, we'd be back to back. Like friends.

He'd called me that, didn't he? He'd called me his friend.

I'd never had a friend, other than Radax. But caring for me brought nothing but abuse to him. In the menagerie, it was best not to have any friends. It was best not to care for anyone, either.

The gorgonian interrupted my gloomy thoughts. "Tell me about yourself."

I exhaled a short, nervous laugh. "There isn't much to tell."

"What's your name?"

I'd never introduced myself to him, had I? It felt safer somehow to be a nameless, faceless person who could slink back into the shadows at any moment and disappear without a trace. Names were records—footprints left in memory. A name made a person real when I preferred to remain a shadow.

I hesitated, the silence between us growing longer. Once again, the gorgonian was the one to break it.

"My name is Kyllen," he said. "Son of the High Lord of Ellohi Court in the Wetlands of Lorsan in the Kingdom of Nerifir."

That was the longest name I'd ever heard. Mine seemed practically non-existent in comparison.

"I'll never remember it whole," I muttered under my breath.

He laughed—a genuine, hearty sound that pleasantly resonated through my chest. "Please, just call me Kyllen. That's what my friends and family call me. The rest are just titles and lands."

"Kyllen." I tested the sounds of his name. I liked how smoothly it slipped off my tongue. It sounded both sleek and strong.

"Will you tell me your name now?" he coaxed sweetly. And I couldn't deny him any longer. He'd given me his name. It was only fair I gave him mine.

"I'm Amira."

"Amira," he drawled. "It's a beautiful name. It makes me think of a flower."

Flower?

I smiled.

The meaning of my name was "princess" in Arabic or "treetop" in Hebrew, as I had learned from a wooden plaque sold in a merchant stall at a fair years ago. The woman selling the name plaques complete with their meanings had also told me that the direct translation of my name was "one who speaks," which was ironic because I spoke little.

Come to think of it, I'd probably said more words to Kyllen today than I would normally say to anyone in an entire month.

"Where are you from, Amira?" he asked.

I rubbed my forehead. That was a question I really had no answer for.

Radax said he took me from a street ruined by bombings while the menagerie traveled in the Middle East. I'd seen a map of the Middle East and learned that the region included many countries. He didn't remember which one it was where he found me.

Bracks lived for many centuries. Their memory mostly retained information relevant to Madame and their service to her. My past wasn't relevant for Radax to remember the details. I didn't blame him. I hardly remembered all the places we'd been to here in North America myself.

For years, I'd tried to figure out where I came from. I watched people at every fair we'd been to. I listened to their conversations for the mentions of the countries they came from or had visited. I compared the color of their eyes, hair, and skin to those of my own, searching for my countrymen, my tribe, my home.

I wondered if I might be from Syria or Israel. Could I be from a Jewish family that came from Europe or Russia? Had I been a visitor to the region because my skin was so pale—"like a ghost?" Though my name suggested the region might've been my home.

Deep inside, I realized I might never get the answer. There was no way to confirm anything. I would never learn what street I'd been standing on the day Radax found me. I'd never know who were the dead people around me. I'd never know where my home was.

"I don't know," I exhaled softly. "I don't know where I'm from."

"You don't?" he sounded confused. "But where is your family? Your parents?"

My parents belonged to the world that only came to me in nightmares now. It was full of darkness, ruined buildings, deafening explosions, and bodies half-buried by rubble. It came from what Radax had told me about the place he'd found me. I had no clear memories of that part of my life. Which was probably a blessing.

"My parents are dead," I said.

"I'm sorry to hear that," he replied somberly.

I decided to pre-empt any further questions in that area. "They died when I was little. I don't remember them or anyone from my family."

My family, my neighbors, the life I was meant to have were all gone. Maybe I should've been gone, too. And often it felt like I actually had. Only a shadow of me remained in this world, always hiding and always silent.

"How old are you, Amira?" Kyllen asked again.

It was impossible to remain silent when he asked me questions. Though this was another one I couldn't really answer.

"I'm not sure," I said.

"How so?"

"Radax thinks I was between three to five years old when he found me. That was twenty years ago."

Bracks rarely paid attention to human children, even at the fair. Radax admitted he might be inaccurate in his estimation of my age.

"So young," Kyllen exhaled.

"How old are you?"

"Seventy-eight. Well, I *was* seventy-eight when I was taken. I'm not entirely sure how long I've been in this cursed box," he grumbled, shifting inside the crate. The chains clunked as he adjusted his position.

"Seventy-eight?" I knew *bracks* were immortal. Many of them had lived for centuries. But seventy-eight sounded so human. "Are gorgonians immortal?"

"No. The fae life span is about five hundred years."

"So, you're a fae, then?"

"Yes, just like everyone who lives in Nerifir."

"I've never met anyone from Nerifir before, except for *bracks*, of course."

But *bracks* normally didn't remember their life before Madame. Radax had told me about the sister he'd lost. Her death was the only thing he remembered from before Madame had made him the *brack*. He said I reminded him of his little sister when he first saw me. I believed that was the reason he'd saved my life and had been looking after me ever since.

Most of what I knew about Nerifir came from Madame's speech she made to the visitors of her menagerie. She spoke about each exhibit she had. The curious objects, she claimed, came from either Lorsan Wetlands, Mountains of Dakath, or Sarnala Plains. She'd said that the siren came from the Olathana Ocean. According to her, all these places were in Nerifir.

"I know Nerifir is home to sirens," I offered tentatively.

He hummed in affirmation. "And to gargoyles who live high up the snowy mountains. And to werewolves who take a ghastly appearance every full moon. To sky fae who live high above the clouds. And to many more magical beings that the human world doesn't have. We're all fae, Amira."

That world sounded like a fairy tale.

"Is it true that fae have magic?"

"Yes, every kind of fae has their own type of magic. " He sounded rather smug about it.

"What magic do *you* have?" I asked.

Silence followed my question.

"Bring me something mechanical," he finally replied. "A broken watch, a music box, bolts, gears, springs—anything. And I'll show you my magic."

My mouth dropped open at that odd request. Then excitement of anticipation buzzed through me. Would I really get to see something magical?

"Oh, I'll get you—"

A loud slamming against the trailer door made me jump.

"Amira!" Radax's voice roared from outside.

I hadn't realized the truck had stopped.

"I'm here!" I yelled back, then added quietly to Kyllen, "No one can know we've spoken."

"Why not?"

"Shhh! Be quiet." I yanked the tube off the crate and tossed it back into the bucket on my way to the doors.

So absorbed I'd been by the conversation with Kyllen, I'd never thought of what to tell Radax about my switching trucks.

Radax wrenched the back doors open with a crashing noise.

"What are you doing here?" he demanded. "You were supposed to be in my truck."

I froze, faced with his fury. Radax had never hurt me, but his deep frown along with his thundering voice were intimidating. "I'm sorry..."

"How did you end up in this truck?" He wouldn't give up.

I shifted my gaze aside. "I... This one seemed comfier." I pointed at the tent fabric rolls.

It hurt me to lie to Radax, but the less he knew, the less he could tell Madame, even if she made him. The safer he would be.

He rested his penetrative stare on me.

"I'm fine. It's all good. Where are we? Is there a bathroom here?" I asked, eager to escape any questioning.

"Over there." He gestured in the direction of the building of the truck stop, with our caravan parked nearby.

The sun was setting already. The parking lot was lit by the few streetlights nearby.

"Thanks." I climbed out of the trailer. "I'll be right back."

When I returned from the bathroom, Dez came by with two paper bags in his hands and a bottle of water under each arm.

Radax snatched one of the bags from him and shoved it in my hands. "Here. Take this."

Dez gave me a look like he'd just noticed me.

"And this, too." Radax grabbed a bottle from under Dez's arm.

"Hey!" Dez protested. "That's *my* dinner!"

Radax tipped his head back to the truck stop building. "Go get more."

I shifted the bottle under my elbow, then reached for the other one that Dez held under his other arm. "Can I have this one too, please?"

"What? No!" Dez stared at me in shock. I never asked for anything. Especially this blatantly.

Radax frowned, giving me a concerned look. "You want two bottles?"

"Yes..." I tried to keep my voice normal. It wasn't easy because *normally* I didn't speak at all. "It's just... It's hot in the truck."

Radax casually grabbed the second bottle from Dez and silently gestured for him to go to the truck stop building.

Dez opened his mouth to argue, then just shook his head. He pressed the remaining bag of food into Radax's hands, then begrudgingly headed back to the building.

"You really should be traveling in the front, Amira," Radax said.

"I'm fine in the back," I protested.

The conversation with Kyllen proved addictive. I didn't want to end it. Especially if that meant listening to Dez droning on for hours instead.

Radax shot a glare at the crate shrouded in the shadows inside the truck.

"How has your trip been so far?" he asked cautiously.

"Fine. Quiet." I faked a yawn. "I slept most of the way. I'll go back to sleep right after dinner, too."

Radax flexed his jaw, moving his beard. "It'd be more comfortable in the front."

I shifted from one foot to the other, clutching the bag of food in my hands and pressing the two bottles to my chest with my arms. "Not if Dez doesn't shut up, which you know he won't."

It was so unlike me to argue. My insistence would normally raise suspicions. Thankfully, Radax's mind must be so preoccupied with the move, he let it slide.

"Fine," he finally conceded. "If you travel in this one, so will I. Hey, Leslo!" he yelled at the *brack* who was about to climb into the driver's seat of my truck, a bag with the takeout in his hand.

"Get out. I'm driving this one."

"Why?" Leslo made a face.

Radax shoved him aside and got into the driver's seat himself. He pointed his stare at the bottles in my arms. "Make some noise if you want me to stop for a bathroom break on the way."

Leslo glanced at me with clear resentment on his face. Avoiding his glare, I climbed in the back again. Eventually, someone shut and locked the doors, and I made myself comfortable by the crate.

"You can speak now," I said to Kyllen as the truck moved again.

For the first time in my life, I was actually excited about the long, dusty ride in a pile of old tent fabric.

"Where are we going?" Kyllen asked.

"To another location for the show, further south. I didn't ask the name of the town."

He scoffed softly. "The town name makes no difference to me."

That was very much my sentiment as well. Maybe Kyllen and I weren't that different at all. In many ways, I was Madame's prisoner, too.

Chapter Seven

KYLLEN

He took another sip through the tube Amira had found for him to use as a straw. Cool, clean water filled his mouth and slid down his throat with a swallow. It was his third bottle today, and he could finally drink slowly, savoring every drop.

His skin remained uncomfortably dry, tugging when he moved. But inside, he felt almost normal again. His lungs drew in air easier. His heart pumped the gradually increasing amount of blood. His brain functioned well. And his words left his well-hydrated throat so much more smoothly.

The iron manacles around his wrists chafed and burned his skin, but there was nothing he could do about them. They were made from Nerifirian iron, a metal hazardous to all fae. To remove them, he needed tools. To obtain items he could convert into tools, he needed Amira.

The human girl had been timid and shy, but she'd returned to his crate after the stop, which gave him more time to work on gaining her trust. He made himself as comfortable as was possible in this abhorrent box. His back to the wall of the crate, he stretched his legs in front of him.

"Tell me more about yourself," he asked Amira, leisurely sipping the life-bringing water.

He no longer believed she was acting on Ghata's orders to ruin him. The girl couldn't lie to save her life. Even without seeing her face, he could hear it in her voice whenever she was unsure about something, and she seemed to be unsure a lot.

"There really isn't much more to tell," she said softly. She always spoke and moved *softly*, as if afraid to disturb the balance in her world by making any kind of noise.

He heard her shift against the wood of the crate. She must be sitting in a similar position to his, leaning against the same wall of the crate, right behind him.

"There must be more to your story," he insisted, for several reasons.

One, he was bored, having sat in this crate for gods knew how long. The conversation entertained him.

Two, he needed to get to know her in order to figure out the best way to use her to his advantage. Maybe he could even manipulate her into setting him free?

And three, he was curious about this human woman who'd spent her life in the household of a disgraced werewolf goddess and her pack of monks.

"And don't tell me humans are boring," he warned.

"But we are," she replied. "We have no magic."

He scoffed. "Magic may make a person more powerful, but not necessarily more interesting."

She paused, possibly pondering his words.

"Listen," she said. "How did you know I was a human? I never told you. You never asked."

"Oh, that was easy." He chuckled. "Only a clueless human would come anywhere near a gorgonian. Everyone else would know to stay away."

Contrary to his intentions to lure her in, his words had the strong potential to frighten her away. But he felt the need to warn her. She had to know he was dangerous, lest she do something stupid and unwittingly get herself killed.

Silence hung between them, long enough for him to worry he might've ruined his one chance at freedom, as slim as it had been.

"What did you do to Krin?" she finally asked, her voice barely audible.

"Who's Krin?" The name told him nothing.

"The *brack* who was in the room when Madame spoke to you last."

That jolted his memory.

"That's right. You were there, too, weren't you? The sneaky little thing that you are."

She gasped. "How do you..."

"I have good hearing." He smirked. "And you have a distinct way of moving around. No one steals and scurries in this place but you."

"Please don't tell Madame," she begged. "I wasn't supposed to be there. It was an accident."

He filed that piece of information away, adding a weapon to his arsenal against her. However, the thought of blackmailing Amira didn't sit well with him. This weak, frightened woman didn't represent a formidable adversary. Harming her in any way would feel like kicking a kitten, he imagined—not something to be proud of.

"Don't worry," he assured her. "I'm not exactly on friendly terms with Ghata. There's no risk of me spilling your secrets to her in a friendly chat during an afternoon tea."

"Madame doesn't take tea in the afternoon." Amira's voice lightened. The idea of him having a friendly chat over a cup of tea with her "Madame" must have amused her.

He smiled, pleased with himself for lightening the mood of this somber, quiet girl.

Not for long, though. Her voice came solemn again. "I found Krin's thumb. He cut it that day. The wound was still there—a scratch on the pad. The thumb was a rock."

He let go of the tube with water, blocking its opening with his thumb, and released a long breath.

Would the truth terrify her? Would she run, taking away his only hope?

"What are you, Kyllen? What does *gorgonian* mean?" Her voice was wary.

He wondered if he'd jumped to conclusions about her way too quickly. She might be inexperienced and hungry for company—even if the company was someone like him—but she wasn't stupid. Her sense of self-preservation must be high for her to survive in Ghata's household for that long.

She'd also lived through Ghata's interrogation of him when the goddess had foolishly ordered to open his crate. Amira survived when that Krin guy didn't.

"Gorgonian is just another type of fae, Amira." He kept his voice soft and pleasant so as not to spook her any more than she already was.

Her fear didn't stop her from asking more questions. "How do you turn a man into a stone? That was what happened to Krin, wasn't it?"

He had to put her mind at ease and make her trust him completely, even if that meant lying to her. But he just couldn't lie. If she senses the insincerity, whatever understanding had formed between them so far would be irrevocably broken.

"Yes. I was the one who turned Krin into stone," he replied honestly, hoping she was strong enough to handle the truth.

She sucked in air sharply. "How did you do it?"

"Through eye contact, Amira. If you want to live, never look me straight in the eye, or in the eyes of my *senties.*"

"Senties?" she echoed. "What are those?"

"The feelers I have on my head instead of hair. Twenty-four of them. And each has eyes. Twenty-four extra pairs of eyes I use to watch for danger around me. And twenty-four extra pairs of eyes you have to avoid looking into."

"How can one avoid that?"

"Exactly. It's impossible. That's why you should never look at me directly if you don't want to end up like that poor fellow Krin."

Krin was a *brack*. He might've been one of those who tricked and captured him back in the forest of Ellohi. Kyllen found no sympathy for Krin in his heart. He doubted Amira was heartbroken over his death, either. She appeared to be more shocked by it than saddened.

"Did you kill him on purpose?" she asked.

He cleared his throat to win some time before replying, "Krin had the misfortune of stepping in my line of sight."

She didn't need to know that he'd managed to get Krin's attention just before the *brack* was about to close the crate. Krin had been facing his way when Kyllen shoved his hood back and moved, clanking his chains. Sometimes a glance was inevitable, even if one knew it was deadly. At the sound of the chains, the *brack* couldn't help but look up. Now, there was one *brack* less in the world—not a huge loss.

Sadly, it'd been just Krin who had glanced at him. Ghata had observed the scene through a large mirror, cleverly avoiding looking at him directly.

"Can you stop it? Your power?" Amira asked.

"Can you avoid looking at someone?" he retorted.

"Easily. I just close my eyes."

"How long can you stay with your eyes closed? A minute? An hour? A day? Can you live your life like that?"

He heard her blow out a breath.

"It wouldn't be easy, would it?" he said. "People often think it's simple. Close your eyes. Turn away. Don't look. Could you have a conversation with someone without ever looking them in the eye, not even once? It's hard to do, even if you only have two eyes. And I have fifty."

"But can you...like, turn it off?"

"Turn off the magic?" He chuckled.

Gods, she *was* naïve. Or maybe just ignorant. Humans didn't possess any magic. How would she know anything about it? Obviously, no one here in Madame's establishment had taught her about these things, either. No one had thought she'd ever need this knowledge.

"No, Amira. Magic cannot be *turned off.* A fae is born with it. One can strengthen it. Sometimes magic can be lost. But no one controls it enough to turn it on and off at will."

"So, the only way for you not to kill people would be..." She paused, probably thinking about his little speech about avoiding eye contact.

He didn't lie to her. It often was impossible not to look. One glance, no matter how brief, was all it took for a gorgonian to turn any living creature to stone outside of the Lorsan Wetlands.

"If we need to, we wear hoods that conceal the *senties* and cover our eyes," he explained. "A gorgonian can't turn another gorgonian to stone.

Neither can our power harm the animals that live in Lorsan lands. We don't travel outside of our kingdom that often. Our craft is valuable everywhere in Nerifir. However, gorgonians are not welcome outside of Lorsan. For obvious reasons." He exhaled a humorless laugh.

"Others are scared of you, aren't they? I'm sorry, Kyllen, but I can't blame them. Your...um, gift is terrifying."

She got that right. The *gift* often felt like a curse outside of Lorsan's borders.

"It's a good thing you can't harm each other." Her voice lifted.

"That is a good thing." He smiled at her attempt to find something positive for him. "Procreation would be very difficult otherwise. No one likes stone-cold sex."

She took another pause, then said with some uncertainty, "You're teasing me."

He grinned wider. "Just a little."

It felt good to smile again. To jest, to flirt. All those things he had enjoyed before and had been deprived of for so long.

"Do you have a big family?" Amira switched the subject. Or maybe his mentioning of sex brought her to the topic? He was still figuring out how her mind worked.

"Not very big. Just my parents, myself, and my brother."

"Tell me about them." A rustling against the wood on the other side told him she must have shifted her position a little, and for a moment he wished he could see her sitting out there.

He made himself a little more comfortable, too, by rearranging his chains. The truck had been traveling along a relatively smooth road, with minimal jolting.

"My family? Well, my father is the High Lord of the Court of Ellohi. He's honorable, brave, and beloved by his subjects, of course. My mother is a true lady—fair, kind, and elegant. A noble family. Boring in its perfection."

It was true. His parents were perfect. The hardest part of his life so far had been to fit in and to prove himself worthy of their flawless legacy.

"And your brother?"

"Udren? He's younger than me by over six decades. He was sixteen when I was taken."

"How did you get taken?" she asked.

He winced at the shameful memory of his defeat. "They trapped me."

"How? You said you have fifty eyes to look out for danger."

She was sharp, throwing his own words back at him.

"In that particular instance, the eyes didn't help," he replied. "The *bracks* set up their trap underwater. My brother and I were at the Teal Stream, away from the palace. I was helping him select a water serpent to ride. He decided to test one."

"Serpent is a snake, isn't it?" she interrupted. "How do you ride a snake?"

"Water serpents are much bigger than regular snakes. They live in the wide, shallow rivers of the Wetlands."

"How big are they?" She seemed to be drawn into his story, with eagerness in her voice and thirst to know more.

"Wider than you and me together and as long as the trees are tall. We ride them by sliding a harness over their heads and standing on their necks, right where their heads merge with their bodies. If you pull the harness up, the serpent will hold its head above water. But if you do it wrong, it will do everything it can to shake you off."

She made a noise of astonishment. "Why on earth would anyone want to ride a monster like that?"

He smiled, thinking back to his training. "For fun. For sport. My father holds a tournament every year when the best of the warriors from his lands come to compete. I've won them all for the past decade," he added smugly.

"But your brother is only sixteen. Isn't there an age limit for when to start taming the giant snakes?"

"My brother has long started his training." Kyllen himself had first tried to climb on a serpent when he was eight. Of course, that hadn't gone so well. "I wasn't angry with Udren for trying to ride a serpent. But I was upset when he fell off. I saw him splash into the water, and when I got to that spot, he was trapped in the net below. I dove in to free him, but my knife couldn't cut the net. I managed to untangle it from around him. The moment the net released him, it coiled around me. Then, a thick, black fabric shrouded me. The *bracks* hooded me, chained me in iron, and locked me in this crate." He couldn't help a heavy sigh. "The rest you know."

"That's horrible. You sacrificed yourself for your brother."

"How is that horrible?" he scoffed. The human obviously didn't get it. "My family and the people of Ellohi will view it as an honorable act on my part." That had been the hope he nursed when faced with certain death from thirst and dehydration, that at least back home his people would think him a hero.

"Is that why you sacrificed yourself for him?" she asked. "To make your parents proud?"

She did get it, after all. She was way too sharp for her own good, he thought with some irritation. He kicked himself for letting his protective instincts and his love for his brother take over and land him in this crate. Yet if faced with the same situation again, he'd act the same.

"What would you do, Amira, had you been in my place? Would you let the *bracks* take your little brother? Or would you try to save him, even if it cost you your freedom?"

Silence stretched a little longer this time. He wondered if she was trying to imagine what having a brother would be like.

"No," she finally said. "You did the right thing, the *only* thing to do in that situation. It's just that... You're trapped here, now."

"And you don't like that?" he asked quickly, too quickly, he feared.

"No," she admitted.

"Then find a way to get me back home." The words were on the tip of his tongue, begging to be said. But it was too soon. She was like a fish on his hook. If he yanked too hard, too soon, too carelessly, she'd run, leaving him to rot in this loathsome crate forever.

Amira was his one faint hope for freedom, and he had to tread carefully. He bit his tongue and kept silent.

"Tell me about your home." Amira seemed insatiable in her desire for knowledge.

He didn't mind feeding it. "My father's palace is the greatest in Ellohi. It's the most magnificent of all the High Lords' in Lorsan—fit for a king." It wasn't empty boasting. The Court of Ellohi was one of the oldest and most affluent in the Kingdom.

"What does it look like?"

"Three great royal marsh trees comprise its core, with the waters of Layahi Bay flowing between their roots."

"You live in a tree?"

He huffed a laugh. Did she think gorgonians were like cat monkeys? Building nests in the tree branches?

"I said I lived in *a palace*," he replied indignantly. "It's built inside and around the trees."

"The trees are a part of the palace?" She sounded amazed and mesmerized.

"Yes. A hundred rooms are nestled between their branches. Stairs and bridges connect the sections. The grand hall is on the lower level, with the tree trunks forming its walls."

"Do the trees have leaves?"

"Millions of them. Green and soft on one side, gold and glossy on the other. When the breeze blows, which it often does, the leaves turn and flip. It makes it look like the entire castle is showered with gold coins."

"Wow... It sounds... Beautiful."

"It is spectacular," he agreed. "My room is one of the highest in the castle. As a child, I had a habit..." His lips twitched in a smile at the memories of his childhood. "Well, I tended to sneak out with my friends to ride rapids on my water board or to watch the blue serpents in the bay down the stream. My mother nearly collapsed with worry after finding my room empty one morning. So, my father ordered me moved as high as possible."

"Did that stop you from escaping again?" There wasn't much faith in her tone.

"No!" He laughed. "But I learned to return earlier, before the servants would come into my room to wake me in the morning."

She kept silent for a minute, maybe going through the images he'd created in her mind. He enjoyed being plunged back into his past—the life he longed to return to one day.

"Do you have a lot of friends?" she asked.

"I do. So many, I lost count."

"Must be nice," she said wistfully.

He sensed loneliness in her. Loneliness so ancient and enduring, it made her sound much older than her twenty-somewhat years. The weight of it seemed to spread, seeping through the wood of the crate and pressing on his heart.

He rubbed his chest through his tunic. "When you're the heir to a High Lord's throne, making friends is easy. The challenge is figuring out which ones are genuine. Not all friends are real."

"I guess..." she said hesitantly, then added, "Seventy-eight is not old for a fae, is it?"

"No, it's not." He stretched his shoulders. With water rejuvenating his body, he felt as young as ever. His muscles filled with strength, urging him to move. "I've heard fae and humans age the same at the beginning. Both grow and mature physically until their twenties or early thirties. After that, our aging slows down for centuries. We don't start growing old until the very end of our lives."

"So, in fae years...you'd be about my age, then? Right?"

That was a ridiculous notion. He'd lived three times as long as she had. He would be that much wiser and more mature, too, wouldn't he?

Yet, there was something in her voice that stopped him from dismissing her question outright—hope, vulnerability, longing. It felt as if she searched for a connection between them. As if she really needed a friend.

He couldn't be her friend, of course, but maybe he could pretend for a while?

"Right," he conceded. "In fae years, I'm about your age."

"Do you...have a girlfriend?"

He nearly choked on his next sip of water, spattering precious drops on his chin and chest. The question came unexpectedly.

She sounded innocent—curious, nothing more. Her life probably didn't leave much room for a romantic relationship, though she was of age. Her interest shouldn't be a surprise. It was his fault he'd been thinking of her more as a child than a woman.

He avoided answering her question directly. "In Lorsan, one doesn't concern themselves with finding a mate until they're about a hundred years of age or older. And if one is an heir to anything of significance, their marriage is a matter of state importance, unless a mating bond happens, of course."

"A mating bond? What's that?"

"It's when one finds his other half. The legend says that gods rip a soul in half before giving each part a body and life. If two parts manage to find each other, theirs is the strongest, most powerful union of all."

"And do they always find each other?" She sounded captivated.

"It doesn't happen often for gorgonians. But if it does, it's truly remarkable. My parents are a bonded couple. Their strengths and weaknesses complement each other, making them stronger. Their love is unconditional, and their loyalty is unshakable. Their rule over our land is absolute. Nothing and no one can stand in their way."

"Wow. That's... It's nice to know there's someone for you out there. Someone to complete you, so you'd never be alone."

For him, a mating bond meant added power—useful for a ruler but not necessary to assume a throne. He'd hardly ever contemplated it as anything else before. Surrounded by courtiers and servants eager to fulfill his every wish and competing for his attention, he had never really been alone until Ghata locked him in this crate.

For Amira, the bond meant something far more personal, it seemed.

"Is that why you don't have a girlfriend?" she asked. "Are you waiting for your other half?"

He didn't say he hadn't had women in his life. He'd had many. Flirting was fun. And there were plenty of females at his father's court who enjoyed his attentions and gladly allowed him to go way past flirting, too.

But he realized Amira was talking about someone more serious than the fun conquests he'd had.

"I don't have what you'd call a 'girlfriend,'" he replied. "But my parents do have someone in mind for me to marry. Lady Eiphed, the daughter of another Lorsan High Lord."

"Do you love her?"

Love? Did she have any idea what she was talking about?

"I met her once, about six years ago." Ever since, he'd been working hard to postpone the marriage to Lady Eiphed for as long as possible. "She's nice. I've nothing against her."

"But something isn't right, is it? You don't sound happy. You're not in love." It appeared, he wasn't the only one who could read emotions in a voice.

"No. I'm not opposed to the idea..." He wasn't waiting for his true mate—though finding one would be nice—but he was waiting for *something*. Something great, exciting, different had to happen in his life before he settled down into his father's throne with a wife, a family of his own, and all the boring responsibilities of a High Lord. "It's just too soon for me."

Of course, the only "special" thing that had happened so far was his abduction and imprisonment by Ghata. He sighed. Even marriage didn't seem as restrictive in comparison.

A sudden noise snapped him out of his gloomy thoughts. It came from outside. A battery of tiny thuds pummeled the roof of the vehicle they transported him in.

The stuffy air inside the crate quickly saturated with moisture. He sensed it first with his *senties,* then with the whole expanse of his skin.

"What is it?" he asked. "It sounds like rain."

"It is rain," Amira confirmed. "It starts suddenly like that sometimes. Good thing the truck is fully covered."

He wished it wasn't. Then he could've possibly caught a few drops through the barred opening in the top of the crate.

"Tell me, Amira, what does rain look like in this world?"

"Rain? The same as everywhere, I think. A bunch of water falling from the sky."

Water.

He shoved back his hood, fanning out his *senties* around his head. Lifting his face up to the barred opening in the crate, he closed his eyes. Listening.

He felt the vibration of each droplet acutely, imagining it hitting his skin. He pretended he was there, outside, in the rain. Water would be running down his face and along his *senties*. It'd soak his clothes, pool in his boots, make his skin supple and soft again, allowing it to breathe.

Never before had he wished to be free of this crate so much.

"What is rain like in Ellohi?" Amira's soft voice broke through the pattering of the droplets.

The rain back home was a true blessing.

"In Ellohi, a rainy day is a cause for celebration." He kept his eyes closed, allowing his mind to transport him back to the Wetlands of Lorsan. "The creeks and rivers swell. New ones form. The fountains in the palace run higher. The many waterfalls we have streaming between the rooms down the branches of the giant trees grow wider. The air impregnates with moisture, nourishing every cell of one's body. Joy reigns over the Kingdom, mightier than the King himself."

"Tell me more," she begged. "Please, tell me about the fountains and the waterfalls."

Wonder floated in her voice. Amira was obviously hungry for something different from what life had dealt her so far. She was soaking up his every word.

She wanted more?

He would give her more. He would tell her about Lorsan until his mouth went dry again, if only that would keep bringing her to his crate again and again. He needed time to gain her trust and pull her to his side.

Then maybe one day, the tales about his home world and Amira's voracious appetite for them would lead him to freedom.

Chapter Eight

AMIRA

After years of traveling, tearing down, and setting back up, the *bracks* had gotten the routine perfect. It took them a day to set up, and the menagerie was ready for its first visitors the very next morning.

At this location, just like at any other before, there was no difference in the schedule for me, except that now I had Kyllen.

I made my "bed" out of sandbags and spare fabric rolls in the storage room behind his crate. After the menagerie would settle down for the night, the *bracks* would leave, and Madame would get busy with one of them in her trailer. I'd snuggle into my hoodie behind the crate, and Kyllen would tell me about Nerifir and his childhood in the Kingdom of Lorsan.

He was a great storyteller. From his vivid descriptions, I could almost see the grand palace of the High Lord of Ellohi, the richly dressed courtiers, and the lavish balls they held. I could smell the scents of his childhood home, filled with plants and water features. I envisioned the tournaments that Kyllen loved so much and the school lessons he loathed as a child.

Over just a couple of days, I'd assembled quite a collection of things for him. I never found the watch or music box he'd asked for. But with my eyes always to the ground, I picked up anything that didn't belong in the dirt.

I brought him every screw and spring I found, pieces of electric wire, hair elastics, a broken necklace with blue and green beads, a hoop earring, and several other lost or discarded things. Whether all of them were useful, I didn't know, but he gratefully accepted everything, and it made me happy.

"Do you know what all these things are?" I asked him once, sliding my newest loot—a bent metal fork and a mechanical pen with no ink—through the bars of his crate.

"It's not hard to figure out," he replied, staying out of sight while I was near the crate. "The more I learn about your world, my friend, the more I see how similar it is to mine."

"Similar? From your stories, all I see are differences."

"There are both," he agreed. "But the basic, fundamental things are very much the same. The ancient legends say all worlds of the River of Mists were one, long ago. We share more than may appear at first glance."

More than for the objects, Kyllen was especially grateful for the water I brought to him every chance I got. He drank so much that eventually it got me worried. What went in had to come out, hadn't it? He was locked in the crate twenty-four seven, with no access to a bathroom.

After a couple of days, I mustered enough courage to bring up the bathroom issue with him. He laughed when I finally managed to ask my question after some stammering and tripping over words.

"My dear Amira," he said. "I've been denied water for so long, every drop is fully absorbed by my body and used for energy. This world is too dry. I need a lot of water to function. Trust me, there won't be anything left in me for a bathroom visit for a long time yet."

I wondered how much water he really needed to no longer be thirsty at all. Since his physical needs were so different from mine, I also wondered how much different he would look. I was curious, though I made no attempt to sneak a glimpse, knowing that seeing him might kill me.

A few days after the move, I flew through my chores as quickly as I could, looking forward to hearing another one of his stories. Before the first shows were to start, I brought Kyllen another bottle of water I'd smuggled from the kitchen.

"So, what is it going to be today?" I asked in eager anticipation. "What will you tell me about, today?" Carefully threading the tube through the bars for him, I inserted the other end into the bottle I'd brought.

Kyllen took a long drink of water before speaking. "Did I tell you about my first time eel fishing?"

"No. What happened? Did you fall in the river?"

He chuckled. "Nothing quite so trivial."

"Tell me please." I made myself comfortable behind the crate and got the egg salad sandwich from my pocket—my late breakfast.

The sounds of *bracks* getting ready for the first shows filtered through the canvas. But they were far enough for us to continue our quiet conversation.

"On the other hand," Kyllen said. "That story is too long for the quick break you get in the morning. I'll save it for tonight when we hopefully get more time."

Before Kyllen, if I had a moment for breakfast, I ate it near the enclosures with the animals. With the birds chirping and other animals moving around, it didn't feel so lonely.

Now, I spent every spare second here, with him. His stories were addictive. When I listened to him, a whole new world rose in my mind and splashed all around me. Reality disappeared, and I didn't miss it.

"Is there a king of the entire Nerifir?" I unwrapped my sandwich. Egg salad was quick to make, and we always had eggs at the menagerie because Madame liked having them for breakfast.

Kyllen took another drink, the water level in the bottle dropping to almost half at once. "No. There are many kingdoms in Nerifir, and each has its own king. Lorsan has one, too."

"Have you met the King of Lorsan?"

"A few times. I even played with one of the princes at the King's Palace, Prince Zeldren, ones or twice. He's a couple of years older than me. He loved sword fights, probably still does." He chuckled softly at the memories.

"Are there any safe hobbies in Nerifir? Or are they all just riding giant snakes and trying to kill each other with swords?"

"Safer?" He sounded puzzled.

"Yes. You know, like painting, reading, needlepoint? Anything with a lower risk of injury or death than what you enjoy?"

He laughed—a deep, rich sound that never failed to make me smile in return. A smile no longer felt foreign to my lips. Kyllen had made me practice it daily, without even knowing or trying.

"Of course, we have all those things, too," he said. "But painting or reading would require one to stay put for a long time, something I could never do as a child. I could barely wait for the end of my classes every day, so I could run out to play."

I shook my head, even if he couldn't see it, and muttered, "It's a miracle you even made it to the ripe age of seventy-eight with that behavior."

"Life is too boring without taking risks, Amira. One just needs to be smart about what risks are worth taking. Would you really rather have absolute safety at the price of never having any fun?"

Would I? All my life, I'd had neither. I never felt absolutely safe. Every moment of every day, I lived in fearful anticipation of punishment. And sooner or later, it always came, no matter how hard I tried to do everything right.

Sleep was often filled with nightmares. The past I didn't remember haunted me in my dreams. Shadows of danger and deafening echoes of explosions kept me awake. I slept in my clothes, ready to run for my life at a moment's notice, even though there was nowhere to run.

"I… I don't know, Kyllen. I don't know what exactly 'fun' means," I said, then added, "Or 'absolute safety.'"

He went quiet, and I finished my sandwich in silence.

"Amira," he said slowly. His somber voice got my attention. I stared at the crate, trying to envision him behind its walls. "Why do you put up with this life?"

I balled the plastic sandwich wrap in my hands.

Why?

Because I had nowhere else to go. Because if I protested, I'd be killed, and Radax would get hurt. Because this was the only life I knew, and I had no idea how to break away from it.

"This is all I have," I exhaled.

"But what if I offered you something better? Much, much better." His soft voice filtered through the wooden walls like a warm breeze from another world, coaxing and tempting.

There was danger in its seduction.

I shouldn't listen.

Nor should I reply.

I should turn around and run, but I asked, "How?"

"I can take you to my father's palace. At my side, you'll always have peace and respect. No one will hurt you ever again. I'll take care of you for as long as you live. You'll want for nothing. In Ellohi, you'll have both fun and security. I can give you a new life, Amira."

I listened to his voice, luring and mesmerizing. But his promises sounded like little more than a rustle of leaves in the wind—soothing, but fleeting. For Kyllen to take me to Lorsan, he needed to be free himself.

"All of it is impossible, Kyllen."

He shifted inside the crate, and I realized one sound had been missing throughout this conversation—the sound of rattling chains.

Had Kyllen freed himself from his restraints? But how?

"Oh, it's very possible, Amira, my dear human friend." The voice continued to tempt, sweet and tender like a lover's. "You need some courage to change your life, but you are strong and courageous."

Strong and courageous? Me? That was a lie.

"I..." I tried to protest.

But he wouldn't let me say a word. "Look at how far you've come already, how brave you have been by taking care of me."

I had defied Madame's orders, hadn't I? I'd broken the rules and continued breaking them daily. I wished to be brave...

The footfalls of a *brack* passing by stole my voice and made me shrink further into the shadows behind the crate.

So much for being brave. Every sound scared me. I wished to be strong, but my actions had consequences. If I were discovered...

Chills ran down my back. All it would take was a *brack* or Madame catching me speaking to Kyllen. I dreaded to think what she would do to me then, what she'd do to Radax...

"I have to go." I scrambled to my feet.

It was time for me to leave, anyway. Madame had several shows for her VIP clients scheduled every day. She served them food and a special drink that I had to prepare from the ingredients she gave me.

This was my reality.

Kyllen's beautiful tree palace was literally in another world. And to me, it would never be anything more than a dream.

"Wait," Kyllen stopped me. "I have a present for you."

"For me?" I paused with a rush of surprise. Other than a cupcake for my birthday from Radax each year, I never got any presents.

"Step back from the crate," Kyllen warned. "Make sure you're not looking inside."

I took a step backward as instructed, but kept my eyes on the opening in the roof of the crate.

A hand slid through the bars, holding something. The hand had four fingers and a thumb, just like mine. His skin was lighter on the palm, deep tan with a faint tint of green. The color darkened over his knuckles and on top of his fingers, with a mesh pattern of tiny, elongated diamonds—similar to the designs on a snake's skin. It looked almost black in the muted light inside the tent.

His hand fit easily through the bars, with no metal cuff around his wrist to stop it. He released his fingers that looked both strong and elegant, leaving a small object on top of the crate.

"I made this for you." The hand disappeared back into the crate.

The object shimmered. It appeared to move, illuminated by the strings of lights above.

I didn't get presents. If someone saw me with this one, there'd be questions. I shouldn't touch it. I should just leave.

But curiosity got the best of me. I stepped closer and quickly snatched Kyllen's offering, as if it would disappear if I lingered.

It was a dragonfly. Beautiful and fantastical, it appeared real at the same time. Its iridescent blue-and-green wings moved, trembling delicately, as if the magical creature was about to take off and fly away. Its shimmering glow spread over my palm where I held it.

"It's for your hair," Kyllen explained. "Do you like it?"

I realized it was a barrette, with the clip on the bottom. It was the most beautiful thing I'd ever seen. Even the most elaborate hair accessories from Madame's collection lacked the lifelike tenderness of this one.

I stared at it, speechless.

"You do have hair?" Kyllen asked, concern in his voice. "Most humans do, I believe. But maybe I should've asked you first."

I smiled. "Yes. I have hair, Kyllen." I fingered my long, dark braid, most of its length tucked inside my scarf and hoodie. "Lots of it, actually."

"Good." He sighed in relief.

"You made this. It's amazing." The dragonfly looked more beautiful than any I'd seen in nature, yet it seemed alive.

"I promised to show you what my magic can do. Here it is." He sounded pleased with my delight.

The barrette was a true miracle, and Kyllen made it from all those loose bolts, beads, and wire strings people had discarded and I'd collected for him. I vaguely recognized the colors of the beads of the broken necklace, the copper of the wires, possibly the spring from the pen, but the rest of it was unrecognizable, new, and...undeniably magical.

A shimmering feeling of wonder enveloped me when I stared at Kyllen's gift. Magic seemed to swirl all around me, almost tangible and very real.

"Amira!" Madame's voice shot though my bubble of wonder like a bullet, shattering it to pieces.

I froze in horror.

"Oh, no... I really have to go." I shoved the dragonfly into my pocket, dashing out of the room.

I found Madame in the VIP room next to the large, round cage that was empty. Radax was there, too. Madame held his arm, digging her long, sharp nails into his bicep.

"I'm here!" I nearly screamed, my eyes drawn to the thin trickle of blood running down his tattooed skin from under her nails.

"The *camyte* drinks are not made," she stated tersely.

It was still early. The VIP clients hadn't shown up. There was still time. But of course, I was at fault. I always was.

"I'm sorry." I dropped my gaze.

"Hurry, you useless human," she snapped. "And you..." She shoved Radax my way, finally releasing his arm. "You make sure she doesn't slack this time."

She stormed out of the room.

"Are you alright?" Radax headed to the dark mahogany bar in front of the cage and started taking out the tall glasses we used to serve the *camyte* drink to the VIPs.

Blood crawled down his arm in a thin trickle. He didn't bother whipping it off.

"Are *you* alright?" I asked in turn, finding his eyes with mine.

"Me? Sure." He gave me a smile, which nearly broke my heart. Once again, he'd gotten hurt because I hadn't been where I was supposed to be. I had given in to the temptation of having a friend in Kyllen when I should've known better.

Spending time with the gorgonian had given me comfort I rarely felt. It reminded me of the times when Radax had taught me how to read when I was a kid. He would place me in his lap, his tattooed arm wrapped around my shoulders, while he pointed at the letters in a children's book he'd sourced from a Lost and Found at the fair where the menagerie had stopped last.

Back then, I used to believe that nothing bad would ever happen to me as long as Radax was with me. He'd been my protector for as long as I remembered.

As I got older, I realized Radax needed protection, too. As a *brack*, he belonged to Madame, body and soul. His life and death were under her absolute control.

Madame had dozens of *bracks* in this world, but she'd singled out Radax for her punishments. No one had been abused as much as he had, and it had everything to do with me. I hid my face in my scarf and started helping him with the glasses.

I had to be better. I could do better. Instead of hanging around Kyllen's crate, I had to stay closer to Madame, invisible but available on a whim. I had to anticipate being needed to keep her from taking out her frustration with me on Radax.

As I passed by the garbage can behind the bar, I yanked the dragonfly barrette out of my pocket and tossed it away.

No more breakfast breaks with Kyllen. No more daydreaming.

I had to protect the one man who had been the closest to a family I'd ever had. I had to protect Radax.

Chapter Nine

AMIRA

Living without dreams was hard. Giving up the only magical, beautiful, wonderful thing in my life proved excruciatingly painful. But staying true to my resolution of perfect obedience, I kept away from Kyllen, focusing on my work.

Unfortunately, my chores required little thinking. Even the lingering ache in my injured hand didn't distract me enough. As I worked, my mind wandered, and it inevitably ended up in the room with the crate and Madame's prisoner inside it. I imagined him sitting there—alone and thirsty—and my heart twisted in compassion so strong it hurt.

Kyllen had no one to bring him water, no one but me. Every minute I stayed away, he suffered.

Without him, I suffered, too. Over the short period of time I'd known him, he'd become an important part of my life—the most exciting part, too. Without him and his stories, the world felt dull and cold, monotonous and...unbearable.

When the shows were done for the day, I saw Vuk taking out the garbage from the VIP room.

"Wait!" I screamed, rushing after him. "I left something in there. I need it back."

He stared at me as if I'd lost my mind while I ripped the bag open and rummaged through the dust and litter inside.

"Hey!" he yelled in disgust. "I'm not cleaning this shit up now. Clean it yourself, you weirdo."

I went through the entire bag to find the barrette I'd tossed away. Clutching it with both hands, I sat back on my heels and closed my eyes. It wasn't a birthday cupcake that would get eaten. This was the only present I'd ever gotten that I could keep. And I'd thrown it away. Because I was afraid. Fear had cost me so much already. I couldn't sacrifice Kyllen's present to it, too.

Shoving the barrette into my pocket, I felt the bottle of water I'd been carrying with me since lunch and the orange I'd taken from the kitchen but hadn't eaten. I was determined to be good, to avoid aggravating Madame, and to keep Radax safe from her. Yet I kept squirreling away things for Kyllen, even as I knew I couldn't see him.

Flexing my jaw in determination, I hurried out of the tents. I found a small cargo trailer in our camp, climbed inside, and spent the night there, away from the tents and from him.

I managed to stay away most of the following day, too.

Once the day was over, however, I'd finished cleaning up for the night but lingered inside the tents.

This late hour had become my favorite. I would look forward to it the entire day, waiting for Madame and the *bracks* to finally leave, so I could spend the night next to Kyllen. I loved hearing his voice, deep and soft, with just a bit of rasp left. His stories transported me far away from the menagerie, to the magical place he came from.

Kyllen was a gifted storyteller. His tales were witty and engaging, with vivid descriptions and entertaining characters. It was like watching a movie, and I couldn't wait to "see" more.

I put away the cleaning supplies and stood in the corridor near the exit from the tent, torn between the need to leave and the desire to stay. If I left, Kyllen would suffer from thirst. If I went to him, I risked the little I had in this world, including Radax.

"I'll have to leave the *voukalak* behind, then?" Dez's booming voice reached me through the flimsy fabric partition.

By the sound of it, the *brack* was heading my way from the center of the tent.

"Yes." The reply came in the melodious voice of Madame that had the effect of a thundering explosion on me.

Panic spiked through me. My chest squeezed painfully, making it hard to breathe. I spun around, frantically searching for a place to hide before they spotted me. At this hour, Madame didn't need me, which meant nothing good would come from this encounter.

"All live exhibits would have to travel with me, including your *voukalak*," she continued in that enchanting voice of hers. "It's too risky to ship them ahead. I need to deal with customs and inspections personally to avoid complications."

I dropped to my hands and knees and crawled under the canvas partition. Then I lay low, afraid to breathe as their voices came closer.

"Right. How about the gorgonian?" Dez asked.

"Is he still alive?" Madame enquired casually.

"Not sure. I'll check tomorrow. But does it make any sense to bring him along, even if he's still alive? He's been denying you all this time."

She clenched her jaw so tight, I heard her teeth grind. Madame was not used to rejection. Kyllen's resistance must infuriate her.

"It'd be easier to just ditch him here," Dez suggested.

"No," she snapped. "I want to watch him break or see him dead." She sighed deeply, speaking more calmly. "If he's alive, I hope he comes to his senses. I have a really good act for him. It includes turning rare animals into stone for the VIP patrons to watch. I would then sell the figurines to them at an extra charge. He could make me money still."

"Enough to warrant taking him all the way across the ocean?" Dez sounded skeptical.

"I'll take him to Europe, but no further. Either way, he doesn't have much time left."

"As you wish," Dez conceded. His voice dropped a notch, a sultry note slipping in. "Since I'll be leaving for England before you, I'll have less time here than the others. Can I come to your trailer tonight?"

Madame released a melodious peal of laughter. "It's not your turn, my pet. I believe Leslo needs me the most tonight. Go find him."

By the shuffling of Dez's feet, he wasn't in a hurry to leave her. It appeared he just moved closer to her.

"I always need you the most—"

His words, filled with desperation, were cut short by a ringing sound of a slap—her hand against his skin.

"What you need is patience and restraint." Madame's voice turned sharp like a knife, no longer enchantingly musical. "Go get Leslo, slave."

She stormed out. Dez stomped to deliver on her order. And I sucked in a breath.

Dez said he'd check on Kyllen tomorrow. Obviously, he wouldn't do it by opening the crate. Maybe he'd try talking to him or moving the crate around to hear if Kyllen would make any noise.

No one knew I'd been giving Kyllen water. Dez would expect him to be near death. He had to confirm Kyllen was still alive, so Madame would take him with us to England. If she left him here, he'd surely die.

I couldn't let that happen.

Chapter Ten

KYLLEN

Amira didn't show up all day. She didn't sleep next to his crate that night, either. He stayed up for hours, straining his hearing for the sound of her light footfalls but heard nothing.

He fisted his hands, as if he could hold on to that one chance of returning home that was slipping away between his fingers.

He'd pushed Amira. He'd told her what he needed from her, and he'd scared her. Impatience had urged him to nudge, but now he feared he might've been too forward. Patience had never been one of his virtues.

As the hours of the following day ticked by with no sign of Amira, he began to worry for other reasons.

Amira served a corrupt goddess who had no honor and no morals. What if the poor girl had been discovered helping him and had paid for her kindness? What if she was hurt? Or...dead?

He shouldn't have given her that hair clip. He'd made it for her, wishing to place a smile on her face, even if he couldn't *see* her smile. But he might've put her in danger by that.

Anyone from Nerifir who saw the dragonfly barrette would know it was made by a gorgonian. They'd know Amira would've gotten it from him. They'd know she broke their stupid rules.

What would they do to her then?

Rage against Ghata flared higher, burning his insides with a thirst for revenge. Guilt wrecked him. He'd get out of this cursed box and sweep through this entire place, turning them all to stone. The whole rotten lot of them—the *bracks*, Ghata...

But what if Amira was still alive? He'd risk accidentally harming her, too. The idea of hurting her in any way made his stomach churn.

As the night approached, the light above the opening in the top of the crate dimmed. Lost in the storm of his worries and rage, he didn't hear anyone approaching until the familiar sound of a person clearing their throat reached him through the walls of the crate.

Amira!

Relief rushed over him like a blissful deluge of rain in the forest.

"I missed you." He blurted out the first thing that leaped into his mind.

It was childish, spontaneous, and...absolutely true. He'd missed her —the sound of her voice, the light scurrying of her footfalls. He missed that soft, hesitant noise she made before speaking, like she made right now, clearing her throat again.

"You...what?" she asked, sounding utterly confused. His sentiment obviously came as unexpectedly to her as it did to him.

It was his turn to clear his throat as he scrambled for a reply. "I...um, was worried. Is everything all right? You've been away." And now he sounded desperate. It was simply pathetic how much her absence had wrecked him.

"I've come to warn you," she said somberly. "After the fair is over, in just over a week, Madame is moving us to England—"

"Where?"

"To another continent," she explained. "Dez, one of her *bracks,* will be coming by sometime tomorrow to check if you're still alive."

He smirked. "How so very thoughtful of him."

She didn't smile at his sarcasm, her voice remained serious. "You can't speak to him. If you do, he'll know you've been getting water all this time."

"Right." If it wasn't for Amira, he'd be lying here, unable to move, not to mention speak in any coherent way.

"But you'll need to make some sound to confirm you're alive," she continued. "Otherwise, they may leave you behind."

That couldn't happen. He had to be with Amira until they were ready to leave this cursed world for good.

"I'll make sure to grunt or groan," he conceded begrudgingly, not looking forward to an interaction with one of Ghata's monks, no matter how short that might be. "Don't worry, I'm good at performing. The *brack* will be satisfied."

"Good," she said. He heard her shuffle her feet, but she wouldn't come any closer.

"Amira—"

"You must be thirsty," she blurted out quickly, as if afraid of what he might say. "I brought some water. Just give me a minute." The noise of her moving around the crate came, then a clear tube descended from between the bars.

He *was* thirsty—he always was in this wretched world. Incredibly, the thirst had not been his main concern while she was gone.

"What happened, Amira? Why didn't you come last night?"

A long pause followed his question. Her silence was nerve-racking.

"Did someone hurt you?" he growled, really *growled* in a most barbaric fashion. The mere thought of Amira getting hurt made him see red.

"No," she said, then hurriedly switched the subject. "I...I brought you an orange."

"An orange?" he repeated, dumbfounded. Her change of topic came quick as a whiplash.

"Yes. I know you don't eat much, but you liked the cucumber. So, I thought you might like an orange, too."

Was it a peace offering on her part? For leaving him alone for a night and a day? He might not be the only one feeling guilty during their time apart.

"Sure. I'll take the orange." When water was scarce, he preferred drinking to eating. Even the juiciest fruits and vegetables had fiber that required precious water to digest. But he'd take anything she'd give him if that would keep her by his crate a little longer.

"Do you have oranges in Lorsan?" she asked. His heart fluttered excitedly at the tendril of the usual curiosity in her voice. "You have cucumbers, don't you?"

"Yes, we do. We have oranges, too, blue-bell oranges. They'd be way too big to fit through these bars, though."

"Blue-bell?" She hummed in wonder. "Well, mine is a mandarin orange. It'll fit. I'll peel it first."

A strong citrusy smell drifted through the bars as she peeled the fruit. It smelled very much like the blue-bell oranges from Lorsan. They grew inside giant flowers so big, they could be used as umbrellas if their petals weren't so delicate and fragile.

"What color is your orange?" he asked.

"Color? Well..." Was there a smile in her voice? What wouldn't he give to *see* that smile. He hoped so much to hear her laugh one day, too. "It's...orange color."

He chuckled. How uninventive. In this language, the word for both the fruit and the color was the same.

Amira must be thinking about the language, too. "Kyllen, does everyone in Nerifir speak English?"

English.

Was that the name of the language they spoke?

"If not, then where did you learn it?" she asked.

"I didn't have to learn it. It was the language *bracks* spoke when they trapped me." He rummaged through his memories of the almost-forgotten lessons. "I've heard that when traveling between worlds, the first language you hear becomes your own."

She shifted, coming closer by the sound of it. Worry spiked inside his chest.

"Careful," he warned. He'd grown too comfortable with Amira, risking to forget she wasn't his kind and he could easily kill her. "Just put the orange on the bars, then step back, will you? Please."

"Okay." She leaned against the crate, stretching her arm over it to the opening in the top.

He hid in the shadows inside the crate. Shoving his hood lower over his eyes, he twisted his *senties* into a tight knot under it, not allowing any to escape.

Peeking carefully from under the edge of his hood, he saw her hand holding a small, round fruit. Slim, pale fingers with trimmed nails in the same color looked almost translucent against the light above. On impulse, he reached for them, wishing to feel her skin.

She gasped in surprise and dropped the orange as he seized her hand.

"Kyllen..." she exhaled a shuddering breath, but didn't take her hand away.

He closed his eyes, holding her hand. It felt cool and fragile, like the delicate paw of a pond gecko, and almost as small. Her skin was soft and smooth, in contrast to his rough and dry. He ran his fingers over the hard patches of calluses on her palm—she clearly was no stranger to physical work.

"Tell me, Amira, please," he said gently, using the most tender voice he could. "Tell me, my friend, why did you stay away? Are you afraid of me?"

"What? No. Of course not." Her fingers tightened over his, holding his hand back.

He didn't think she feared him. She might've been wary of him at the beginning, but her natural curiosity helped draw her out of her shell. Until yesterday, she'd appeared to seek his company any chance she got.

"Are you scared of getting caught here with me? Are you afraid of Ghata? Madame?"

She inhaled deeply. "I'm always afraid of her."

He used to think he needed to win her trust, but that had proven easy enough to do. Amira was a trusting person. Life hadn't treated her fairly, but it hadn't killed her faith in people. She longed for a connection, drawn to him and his silly stories. He knew she enjoyed their time together. Without even noticing when or how, he started to enjoy spending time with her, too.

It wasn't about earning her trust that he had to worry but about conquering her fear.

"Let me take you far away from here, to a place where Ghata would never find you."

"To Nerifir?"

"Yes. Ghata won't return to Nerifir. She fled, escaping a prosecution, and she risks being captured, tried, and most likely executed if she ever sets her foot back in that world."

"Is she really a goddess?"

"A disgraced one," he scoffed. Fallen gods were pathetic, even if they remained dangerous.

Unlike werewolves, gorgonians stopped creating physical embodiments or living effigies of their gods long ago. The ethereal spirit of Great Serpent and its court of disembodied deities remained in their divine realm where they belonged, communicating solely through their priests and priestesses if needed.

"Ghata committed too many crimes back in Sarnala, the land of werewolves," he continued. "People stopped believing in her, which caused her to lose most of her power. The werewolves wish to get their paws on her and hold her accountable. She'll never go back. You'll be safe with me. Help me, Amira, and I will help you. Or...you can go and forget I exist." He released her hand. It was a gamble, but gambling was something he was good at—the right timing was everything for success.

She didn't leave. On the contrary, she clung to his fingers as if her life depended on it.

"How do you want me to help you, Kyllen?" she whispered.

Oh, this was great progress. They'd moved from a firm "no" to "how."

"Leaving the menagerie won't be difficult," he assured her. "I got rid of my shackles with the tool I made from the things you've found for me. Nothing binds me. Soon, I'll be strong enough to open this box. But I'll need to know how to get from this world back to mine."

"I don't know anything about traveling between the dimensions, Kyllen."

Sadly, neither did he. Now, he wished he'd paid more attention to his tutors when he was a child. Somehow, he'd thought there'd be time to catch up on the lessons when he was older. That time never came, and now he needed the knowledge he'd missed.

He tried to remember the little he'd learned. "There must be a way to open the portal between the worlds. The *bracks* do it all the time. I need you to find out how. Can you do that for me, my friend?"

"I'll try," she said.

He couldn't believe his ears. Did she finally relent? Did he convince her, after all? Thrill rushed through him in effervescent tingles. Hope grew stronger.

It was good. But not enough.

He proceeded carefully. "I don't know this world. I don't want to roam through it, turning its inhabitants to stone everywhere I go."

Oh, he would, if he had to.

Now that his hands and feet were free of the iron and his strength was slowly returning, he'd make it out of this crate.

But then what?

Turning *bracks*, Ghata, and every unsuspecting human in his path to stone wouldn't bring him any closer to getting back to Nerifir. Rocks didn't talk. He needed someone to tell him how to open the portal that would take him home.

"I need a guide," he said. "Someone who will help me find my way back home. I need you to come with me. And in exchange, I'll do anything you ask once we're in Nerifir."

She released a long sigh. "I can't come with you, Kyllen. I can't leave Radax."

"The *brack?*"

"You said it as an insult," she reprimanded.

He shook his head, even if she couldn't see it. "Not insulting, just stating the fact, Amira. Radax is a *brack*, Ghata's monk. He's given his life, his mind, and his conscience to her in exchange for immortality. A *brack* is just a mindless slave, a husk of a man. There's really nothing left to save there."

Her fingers tightened on his.

"Don't say that about him. Radax... He's not like the rest of them. He raised me. He taught me everything I know. He's my family, the only one I have. He can no longer cross dimensions. Madame stopped sending him to Nerifir long ago. I can't bring him with me. And I just can't... I can't leave him behind."

That was a serious obstacle. As weak and fragile as this woman appeared, she possessed some strong, enduring qualities. Loyalty, apparently, was one of them.

"You deserve so much better than this life, Amira." This was a line meant to flatter and entice her, but he genuinely believed what he said. Unlike *bracks*, she wasn't a slave. She deserved better than slaving away her short human life for an ungrateful creature like Ghata. "Radax can't leave. He's connected to Ghata for an eternity. But it doesn't mean that you have to stay and suffer here with him. He can't leave, but you can."

"No." She tugged at her hand in an attempt to free it, but he held tight. He was no longer willing to release her. What if she ran away, and he would never see her again? He couldn't allow that.

"I care about you, my friend." He employed the sweet, coaxing voice again. "I want you to be free, to see the world—whichever world it may be—to enjoy the short life you were given."

"I really can't, Kyllen. If I leave, Madame will kill him."

He was right about the challenge of combating her fear. But it wasn't the fear for herself that was the problem. It was her fear for another—an undeserving *brack* of all people.

"If I leave, Madame would think Radax helped me," she said.

"Then make it so that she knows he has nothing to do with your escape."

"I—"

He couldn't allow any arguments or any doubts to stand in her way. "Think about it, my little friend. If Ghata punishes him for the things *you* do, wouldn't it be best for both of you if you were no longer here?"

She went still. He appeared to have stumbled on the right thing to say.

He had to keep pushing. "She'd have no more reasons to punish him, would she? And if she tortures him to teach you a lesson, then there'd be no more audience for her to perform the torture for."

She remained silent, her breathing fast and shallow. Her fingers in his hand grew colder.

"I'll see what I can find out about the portal," she finally said. "But I won't be coming with you, Kyllen."

It shouldn't matter whether or not she came with him to Nerifir, as long as she helped him get back home. Yet the thought of leaving Amira behind tinted his excitement with a bitter streak of disappointment. He wished to take her along.

Maybe he could still make it happen? He just needed to work harder at convincing her to join him. He wasn't good at waiting, but he'd muster patience.

Her fingers slipped from his hand. She stepped away from the crate.

"Don't go," he pleaded. "No one is around. Stay with me tonight. I still haven't told you the story about my ill-fated eel fishing, remember?" He didn't even try to keep the desperation out of his voice. Now that he had tasted the pleasure of her company once again, going back to thirst and loneliness felt unbearable.

"Is it the story when you *didn't* fall in the water?" she teased.

He loved to hear humor and curiosity in her voice again. The teasing was new for her, and it thrilled him.

"Oh, I did fall. Later." He chuckled. "But it was just one part of my misadventures that day. The eels snuck into my pants—"

She gasped. "Oh no! What happened then? Do eels bite?"

"Take a seat, Amira, make yourself comfortable. I better start from the very beginning."

She obeyed, and he released a breath in relief. He heard her snuggle in her usual spot against the crate. He leaned with his shoulder against the same side from the inside. If the crate weren't there, they'd be cuddling, he realized. The thought made him snort. Normally, he had so many better things to do with a woman than cuddle. But the shortage of water had made arousal difficult for him. He felt no lust and for now, he didn't even miss it.

His current pleasures didn't come from sexual desire. Having Amira near eased the tension in his chest. It almost made the world right again, even though he was still in this abhorrent crate.

He yanked his hood off, spreading his *senties* over his shoulders, and drew in a cleansing breath. The clear tube dangled from the roof of the crate. He caught it and took a long drink of water, soothing his throat. He'd have to find the orange she'd brought. It must be on the floor of the crate somewhere.

But first, he owed her a story.

"I was not supposed to go eel fishing on my own," he started. "But as you know, I was a rather unruly child."

"I've learned *that* by now," she retorted lightly.

This promised to be a good night. One of the best ones he'd had in this world.

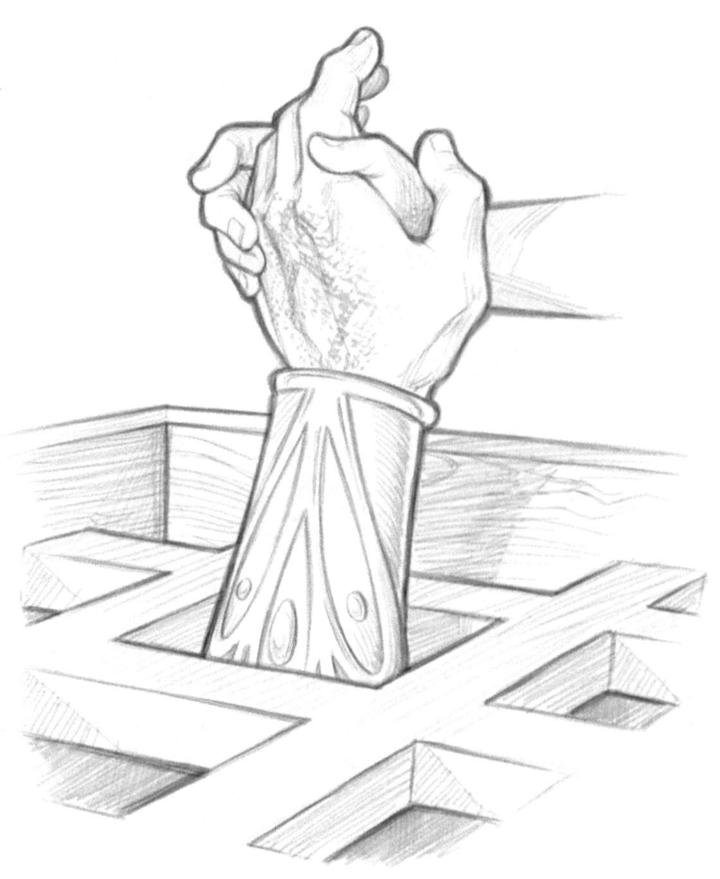

Chapter Eleven

AMIRA

I stayed with him, and Kyllen told me another one of his stories. He'd been choosing funny ones lately. Maybe he was trying to make me laugh? I never laughed openly. It felt like making too much noise. But he succeeded in making me smile when he told me about his eel fishing.

"The nasty creatures invaded my pants!" His outrage was genuine, which made the story even funnier. "One bit me right in the bollocks!"

"Where?"

"My sack," he explained pointedly. "Come on, Amira, I know we're not the same kind, but the male gorgonian equipment down there couldn't be that different from humans'. Legends say we can mate and even reproduce."

"Oh." Heat of blush spread up my face when I finally realized what area of the body he was referring to. I had only a vague idea about the appearance even of the human male "equipment," having never seen one myself.

"They say the scar is still there if you look closely," Kyllen revealed.

"Not that I'm flexible enough to search for it myself. But if you're curious—"

"Um, no thank you," I blurted out. "I'm good. I'll take your word for it."

"Suit yourself." His voice changed, the rasp in it turning more prominent. "But I assure you, you're missing out on a glorious sight. And I'm not talking just about the scar."

Was he flirting with me? Was that why my blush flared even hotter, spreading downwards? The sensation was so sudden, and the more aware of it I became, the more intense it grew.

"You're quiet, Amira," he stated in that changed voice of his. "What are you thinking about?"

Thinking?

I couldn't think about anything but him at the moment. My crazy mind was trying hard to conjure a naked image of a man I'd never seen, either in or out of clothes. Warmth tingled in my chest, gathering in the tips of my breast and making me wish for something I couldn't name.

"Let me guess—"

"No!" I cut him off, afraid he'd actually guess what was happening inside me. "Don't...I-I was just thinking I could never enjoy the...um, the *glorious sight* you're talking about because looking at you would kill me, remember?"

"Right." He heaved a long breath. "How do I keep forgetting about that? Somehow, you don't feel like 'other,' you know?"

I believed I knew. I didn't think of Kyllen as a stranger anymore, either. He became closer to me than anyone in the world.

Closer than Radax, I realized.

The thought was alarming, but not that surprising. In the past few days, I'd spent more time with Kyllen than I'd spent with Radax in years. He'd been much more open with me than Radax had ever been. Never in my entire life did Radax's voice cause the same reaction in me as Kyllen's did just now.

Radax was family. Kyllen was...something else entirely.

I rested my chin in my hand, giving up on sorting out my feelings for now.

"What happened to the eels?" I asked, going back to a topic that felt much safer to discuss.

"The eels? They ended up in a soup, of course. One of the best soups I've ever had because it was seasoned with revenge," he added with a dramatic flair that made me smile again.

"Did *you* make the soup?"

"Of course not. My father's chef did. He's one of the best in Lorsan."

That got me thinking. "What other things do people eat in Lorsan? Other than soup?"

He made a clicking sound with his tongue. "Oh no, let us linger on the soup a little longer, shall we? My father's chef can prepare hundreds of different kinds."

"Hundreds of kinds of soup? Really?" It made sense, though, as gorgonian bodies required a lot of liquids.

"Yes. There are at least a dozen ways to prepare the cattail root soup alone."

"Sounds like gorgonians take their soup seriously," I teased.

"That we do." He matched my light tone of voice.

"But do you have eggs?" They were my favorite food, maybe because I ate them most often.

"Every possible kind," he assured me. "Duck eggs, goose eggs, fish eggs, frog eggs—"

"Frog eggs?" I exclaimed in shock. Surely, he was joking. "Do you really eat them?"

"Mmm," he stretched the humming sound of pleasure. "If pickled just right, they are delicious."

"So, no chicken eggs then?"

"Well, we can certainly find you some chicken eggs. I am the heir to a High Lord, after all. But trust me, duck eggs are not much different. You wouldn't even notice."

I knew what he was doing. He spoke as if I'd already agreed to come with him, planting things in my brain that would make it easier for me to imagine myself in his world. But I drank in his every word like sweet poison.

Deep inside, I wished to go to that magical land. I caught myself fantasizing about finding a home in that far-away place called Lorsan and had to remind myself those were just fantasies, things I couldn't have and shouldn't wish for.

I spent that night by Kyllen's crate, and returned again the following night.

Then, two days later, after cleaning Madame's trailer, I snuck back to the storage room to say a quick hello to Kyllen between my chores, and found his crate gone.

The sight of the bare ground where it used to stand was like a punch to my stomach. I gaped at it, refusing to believe my eyes.

He was gone...

But where?

And how? How did I miss this? I had slept right there, by that wall that used to be hidden behind his crate. I'd gotten up early to make Madame's breakfast, like always. Then, I fed the animals and cleaned her trailer. In that time, the crate had disappeared.

Did Madame decide to get rid of him after all?

The thought made me sick. A sinking feeling hollowed my stomach.

"Where is it?" I didn't realize I asked out loud until the reply came.

"What?" Leslo stopped behind me, an eyebrow raised. He was carrying a toolbox and appeared to be on his way out of the tents.

"The crate that was just here this morning." I frantically gestured at the wall that had been a part of my sleeping place.

He gave me a curious look. I must be exposing my connection to Kyllen right now. But panic rose in me, and I couldn't hide it.

"Do you know where it went?"

He tilted his head. "When in the morning did you see it?"

I couldn't possibly tell him I slept here last night. Swallowing the lump of panic choking me, I collected my thoughts the best I could, choosing words carefully.

"Before breakfast. I swept the floor in here. Now, I need to clean it again." I pointed at the dusty square patch of the ground that had been covered by the crate before, pretending it was the extra work that made me so upset. "See?"

Leslo shrugged. "So. Clean it again. As if you have anything better to do."

He turned to go on his way, but I hurried after him. "Do you know where that crate is now?"

"On its way to the airport, I take it."

"Airport?"

"Yeah, we're going to England next. Don't you know?"

Of course, I knew about the move and that some of the menagerie cargo was being shipped earlier. Dez and a few others went ahead to arrange things with the new venue in London. Dez spoke to me earlier, leaving instructions on how to feed the *voukalak* beast in his absence.

"Yes, but not until next week, right?" I clarified. "Aren't all live exhibits supposed to stay here until then?" That was what Madame had said.

But maybe she didn't consider Kyllen fully "live?" Without my giving him water, he would've been in a near dying state, after all.

"Right. But we sent some stuff ahead early. Some bulky equipment and inactive exhibits, like the dragon statue and the gorgonian." Leslo tipped his head back toward the storage room where Kyllen had been held.

We exited the tent, and Leslo turned toward the *bracks'* trailer.

I had to jog alongside to keep up with his long strides. "What is all that *stuff* going to do in England?" This was more than I'd ever spoken to Leslo. Thankfully, he appeared more annoyed than suspicious.

"The same thing they were doing here—absolutely nothing." He scoffed. "They'll be sitting in a warehouse somewhere until we pick them up next week. Fucking freeloaders." He spat through his teeth.

I pressed my hand to my chest, waiting for my heart rate to return to normal as my panic subsided. They didn't get rid of Kyllen. He'd just been moved. I didn't lose him for good, just for a few days.

Leslo stopped in his tracks to stare at me. Did I make him suspicious after all?

"Well..." I sank my chin into my scarf, backing toward the tents. "Thanks. I'll go sweep that room again, then."

He shook his head, probably calling me a weirdo or a lazy freeloader in his head, then went on his way.

I dragged my feet, walking back to the tents. Kyllen was no longer there, and without him, the place had lost its soul. Everything magical, beautiful, and fun he'd brought with him disappeared.

I stopped in front of the tents and took a good look at them.

Dark and scary, the menagerie had been the only home I'd ever known. I used to see it as a place full of mystery, the gateway to another world. But for the first time in my life, I saw it for what it was—a bunch of dusty tents and beaten up trailers, ran by a heartless, egotistical deity. The place of constant fear and little comfort.

It could never be a true home to anyone.

Chapter Twelve

AMIRA

"Amira!" Vuk's deep voice boomed from inside the tents after dinner. "Where the fuck is she?"

Somehow, I was always expected to be right there the moment someone needed me.

I closed the gate of the enclosure with the fog turtles and shook the dusty remnants of their feed off my hands. The creatures didn't like loud noises, especially while eating their dinner. So, I rushed out of the room before raising my voice. "I'm here!"

Vuk stormed out from one of the passages nearby, a gun in his hand. "Have you fed the fucking *voukalak* yet? We need to pack him in the shipping crate."

Panic speared through me. I completely forgot about the beast.

"Oh no." I gasped. "I... I was just about to feed him."

Unlike the rest of the animals in the menagerie, the beast that *bracks* called *voukalak* wasn't my usual responsibility. Dez had been taking care of him. But Dez left for England, and he'd ordered me to take over his duties for the next few days.

He'd chosen me over a *brack* because he'd reasoned if I made a mistake, Madame would kill me. In his opinion, it was a strong enough motivation for me to follow his instructions precisely.

He wasn't wrong, except that with the sudden disappearance of Kyllen's cage that morning, I forgot all about my added duties.

The poor beast had missed the morning feeding. Night was approaching. He must be starving. That upset me even more than any potential punishment.

Vuk rolled his eyes, like he wouldn't have expected anything better from me, anyway.

"Great." He tucked the gun into his belt. "Now we won't be able to pack him until after the tents are down."

Dez had mentioned that it'd be easier to shoot the beast in the head before packing him in the crate. Apparently, like *bracks*, the beast couldn't be killed with human weapons, but it would incapacitate him for a while, making him easier to handle.

Vuk glared at me. "What are you standing there for? Go, feed him, you idiot!"

I rushed to the kitchen for the meat that Dez had prepped for the beast by sprinkling some yellow substance from Nerifir over it. In addition to feeding the beast, I was also to smear some smelly stuff from a jar on his neck.

As simple as these tasks sounded, they seemed nearly impossible when I faced the creature.

The animal was huge, chained to a thick metal frame in the upright position. Covered in thick black fur in some places, he had patches of skin visible in the others. His front paws looked almost like hands, his fingers tipped with long, black claws.

Madame had displayed him in a round metal cage to her VIP clients. But the cage was now gone. Nothing would protect me if the beast were to attack but the restraints attached to the frame. Even chained, he was dangerous. If just a drop of the poison from his teeth touched my skin, I'd die.

Another reason Dez assigned the care of the *voukalak* to me must be because he didn't want to risk a *brack's* life. If the beast bit and killed someone, Dez would obviously prefer it'd be me.

In one hand, I squeezed the key to the beast's collar that Dez had given me. In the other, I held a leather noose that he'd told me to put over the animal's maw to keep him from biting me.

The creature looked fairly docile at that moment. His head leaning toward one shoulder, he appeared to be asleep.

I carefully slid the leather strap over his elongated nose and jaw, then removed his collar. The metal band Dez had put around the beast's neck had long spikes, pointed inwards. They had pierced the animal's neck, causing rivulets of blood to trickle out when I removed it.

The design of the collar could only have one purpose—to torture. Except that I couldn't understand why. As depraved as *bracks* often acted, they didn't torture without a reason.

The beast opened his crimson-red eyes and watched me as I gently washed the wounds on his neck. It wasn't just mindless following the movement on his part. There was something human in his gaze, despite the inhuman color of his irises.

And it wasn't just in his eyes, either.

I stepped back, taking him in. He looked very much like the beast he was, but the humanlike part of him appeared more prominent tonight than it was the last time I saw him. His front paws looked even more like hands. Even his snout didn't seem as long as it had been, like the bones in his nose and jaw had shrunk somehow.

Holding his collar in one hand, I took the plastic-wrapped meat out of my pocket.

The beast roared through the noose around his snout, lunging for the meat. The restraints threw him back. But I jumped in shock, dropping the meat into the bucket of water I'd used to wash his neck.

"Amira!" Madame's sharp voice terrified me even more than the beast ever could. Startled, I accidentally dropped his collar into the bucket, too.

"Where is that girl when I need her?" Madame barged in. "Oh, there you are."

I snatched the beast's collar from the bucket, and she thrust Yenric, her two-headed pet pig, into my hands.

"Take him," she ordered. "He needs a bath."

With my hands occupied, I couldn't grab the piglet fast enough. The little rascal twisted out of her arms, making her drop him.

Pour Yenric landed on his side with a piercing squeal. Scurrying to its hooves, he dashed to me to hide behind my legs.

"Get him, you useless human!" Madame screeched. She yanked the heavily beaded leather belt off her waist, then lashed with it at me.

The blow landed on my shoulder as I bent over to pick up the piglet. The next one came right after. It hurt, but my hoodie absorbed some of the sting. Hiding the piglet in my arms, I took another lash.

I clenched my teeth, bracing for more. Madame's temper often cooled off as quickly as it flared up. I just had to wait it out.

The next lashing whipped around my elbow. The end of the belt nipped at my chin with a sharp sting of pain.

I bit my lip. I could take it. Sooner or later, she'd calm down, and it'd be over.

The fabric flap over the entrance flew open, and Radax stormed in. "What's going on here?" His thick brows furrowed into a frown, his teeth bared in a scowl, he looked furious.

Oh no. Nothing good would come out of Radax getting angry with Madame.

I groaned inside when she whipped around to face him. Raising her free hand, she slapped him across his cheek.

"This stray runt you've found will not live long enough to die of old age!" she raged. Tossing her belt at me, she spun on her heel and stormed out of the room.

I crouched on the floor, my arms around Yenric, my chin buried in my scarf. I was shaking from head to toe. I hated it, hated how half-paralyzed with horror Madame's rage always left me.

"Amira." Radax went down on his knees at my side. "Let me see." He gently lifted my face out of the scarf.

The scratch on my chin burned, but the pain in my chest was much more agonizing. There was no reason for Madame to lash out at me tonight. No reason at all.

Unable to hold back a sob, I closed my eyes.

"It'll be okay," he said soothingly.

And normally, Radax's voice soothed me. But not this time. Because it wasn't just pain that burned inside my chest. It was the all-consuming anger at the injustice.

"No." I shook my head. "It won't be okay, Radax. Not if I stay here."

The truth became blindingly clear.

I had tried so hard to be perfect, but Madame didn't want perfect obedience from me. If she did, she could've *made* me obey. She had the means to bend the will of humans to her wishes. Government officials, custom authorities, animal welfare inspectors, her VIP clients—all ended up doing her bidding after accepting a drink or a snack from her laced with magic from Nerifir.

No, she had a different purpose for me. Radax was not like other *bracks*. Madame's control over him had been waning. I could sense it. Surely, she felt it, too, and she used me to manipulate him.

Kyllen was right. Without me, Madame would lose a piece in her game, and Radax's life might actually improve.

"I need to leave," I whispered, shocked by my own words.

Radax caught me by my shoulders, turning me to face him. "What are you saying, Amira?"

His dark-brown eyes had thin red streaks radiating from the center around the pupils, like spokes on a bike. People usually found it unsettling when a *brack* looked at them directly. But not me. In Radax's bizarre eyes, I saw affection, something I never found anywhere else.

I cupped his chin, my fingers nearly disappearing into his thick beard. A red spot was blooming on the side of his face where Madame had hit him, just under his eye.

"Tell me how to get to Nerifir," I said.

He shrank back as if I'd slapped him. "What?"

"How do I open the portal?"

Yenric squeaked in my arms, and I settled him more comfortably in my lap.

Radax looked shocked and worried. "Why?"

"You've been like a family to me," I tried to explain. "I love you like a brother. Madame knows it, and she can't stand it. She is hurting you..." My voice broke, as did my heart. "I need to get away."

He slowly moved his head from side to side. "I can't go to Nerifir, Amira. Even if I could, she'd pull me right back to her. I'm a *brack*. I'm tied to her for eternity."

"I know." Leaving him behind gutted me but staying would only hurt him more. I could see it now. "I know you can't leave her, but I can." I lowered my voice. "Without me, you'll be safer, too. You can finally stop risking your life to protect mine. Can't you see? She's been using us against each other, punishing you for me. Neither of us will ever be safe unless I leave."

Radax dropped his shoulders.

"I can't watch over you in Nerifir. If you leave, I'll never see you again." He stared at me intensely. "I love you, Amira, like the daughter I never had or the sister I've lost. Please, let me take care of this. Let me find a safer place for you here, in this world."

Shifting Yenric under my arm, I took Radax's hand in mine.

"I can't stay in the same world as her. You know she will search for me, if just out of spite. And sooner or later, she'll find me."

Radax gripped my hand tighter, as if anchoring me to him.

"You don't know life outside of these tents, girl, not in this world, not in any other. Nerifir can be a dangerous place. You won't be safe there on your own."

I couldn't hold his stare and glanced down at Yenric snuggling peacefully in my lap.

"I won't be alone," I admitted.

"What do you mean?" Radax frowned. "Who will be with you?"

"The gorgonian. His name is Kyllen. He promised to come with me."

"The gorgonian? Amira!" he raised his voice, and I hushed him by waving both hands at him. "Have you been talking to him? You know it's strictly forbidden."

I knew it was, and yet I broke that rule. I'd broken way too many rules to even think I'd be safe if I stayed.

"He'll die here, Radax. Madame will kill him sooner or later."

Radax huffed impatiently. "The gorgonian is a fae. He's much more resilient than you realize. But more importantly, Amira, gorgonians are extremely deadly. You can't go with him."

A sound of chains rattling came from the frame with the animal.

Radax jerked his chin at the beast. "Are you done with him for tonight?"

I glanced at the bucket with the meat on the bottom concealed by the murky water. The meat was now ruined, but it'd been laced with the powder I knew nothing about. Just as I had no idea what the gel I was supposed to put on the beast's neck wounds would do to him.

Madame had several magical substances at her disposal. No one had explained their purpose to me. But I'd noticed that the *camyte* drink we served to our VIP clients made them happy and forgetful. It altered their perception of reality and made them enjoy Madame's shows without questioning what was behind them.

I peeked at the beast again. Nothing that came from Madame could be benign. What if there was a sinister purpose to the yellow powder or the gel? I decided not to use either, at least not until I knew more about both.

"Yes. I'm done here." Setting Yenric down, I grabbed the spiked metal circle off the floor, then approached the beast. "Are you going to bite me?"

He closed his eyes. A threatening rumble vibrated in his chest, but he held still.

I raised the collar to his neck, then locked it in place as gently as I could.

"Come." Radax tugged me away by my arm after I'd picked up Yenric again. "I'll think of something, but we shouldn't discuss anything here, in his presence."

The way he said it made me take a closer look at the beast's eyes again. He watched me carefully, with awareness clearly above the animal level.

"He is just an animal, isn't he?" I asked, squinting at the beast.

"Amira." Radax shook his head. "You of all people should know, in Madame's establishment, nothing is what it seems."

Chapter Thirteen

AMIRA

Radax studied my face as we exited the room, leaving the beast alone.

"Is Madame hurting you more than I know?" he asked grimly. "Is that why you want to leave?"

I buried my chin in the folds of my scarf, hiding the cut from Madame's belt. He didn't need the visual reminder of her lashing out. I adjusted the scarf, using my right hand as Yenric was tucked under my left arm.

"What's this?" Radax's frown deepened. He spotted the bruise blooming over my knuckles and grabbed my wrist. "Did she do this, too?"

It'd been over a week since Madame had hit me with the brush. My hand didn't hurt nearly as bad anymore, but the bruise looked more colorful than ever, with yellow shades added to the blue.

"I'm fine." I tried to take my hand away from him.

We came to the room with the animal enclosures, and Radax let go of my hand long enough for me to place Yenric back in his little space with a comfy pile of felt to snuggle in.

Radax's expression remained stormy as we exited the room.

I touched his arm. "It's okay. Honestly—"

"Radax." Madame sauntered down the hallway between the canvas walls. "You're coming with me tonight."

Bracks viewed the night spent with Madame as the highest reward possible. Any one of them would jump with joy at her invitation. But Radax's frown didn't ease. It grew deeper as she approached.

I drew my head into my shoulders and searched for the best way to disappear, but Radax grabbed my wrist again.

He faced Madame. "You hurt her."

Dread rushed through me, making my head spin. A *brack* could never stand up to Madame. Yet this was exactly what Radax was doing. The resentment in his voice was unmistakable.

Madame tilted her head, resting her hands on her voluptuous hips. "What was that, my pet?"

He held her stare. "You can do anything you wish to me. But stop hurting Amira."

"Radax..." I whispered, hoping he'd come to his senses before she destroyed us both.

"Huh!" She stared at him in genuine disbelief. "You dare tell me what to do, slave?"

Her eyes narrowed. Cold, cruel sparks flashed in them, sending a chill down my spine.

"I took her in as an act of *charity*." She curled her lips, as if the word disgusted her. "And I can do whatever I want with her. Her life belongs to me, just like yours does."

She grabbed the back of my neck, long fingernails digging into my skin through the fabric of my scarf.

I whimpered in horror.

"No!" Radax moved on her, murder in his eyes.

She raised her hand, and the tattoo around his neck and the right arm burst to life. Red sparks ran along the black lines. She'd done this before. The tattoo was burning his skin and squeezing his neck under her command.

"Please... Please don't hurt him," I sobbed, but she paid no attention to me.

Madame glared at Radax.

"You are my slave," she seethed, pronouncing every word slowly, as if laying a curse on him.

He raised his chin.

"I am, but Amira isn't." The words sounded strangled leaving his throat, compressed by the magical tattoo tightening like a noose around his neck.

Other *bracks* started gathering around us, never ones to miss free entertainment. They had no compassion, not even for one of their own. No one really cared about the others in this cursed place.

"Both of you!" Madame bellowed, tightening her grip on my neck. "Both of you belong to me!" She flicked her wrist, and Radax lurched closer, manipulated by his tattoo like a marionette on a string. "One day, this entire world will be mine, too," she hissed in his face. "All humans will be my servants, Radax. And no one can stop me."

He could no longer reply. The tattoo around his neck choked him. Veins bulged in his forehead as he gasped for air. My heart tore to pieces at the sight of him, yet I couldn't look away.

"I'll have to teach you a lesson. You both need one." Madame shoved me toward the *bracks*. "I want them both whipped," she ordered.

Bracks grabbed my arms. I didn't struggle against their hold. I knew better. Any of them could snap my neck between their fingers. I couldn't fight them.

I could only plead.

"Please..." I begged. "Let Radax go. He did nothing. It was me..."

Madame scoffed. "He found you and brought you here, didn't he? That was a big mistake on his part."

"I'll leave!" I screamed as tears ran down my face. "I'll go away. You'll never see me again. Just please don't punish him."

"Oh no, you're not going anywhere, you little runt. Your life is mine. Tie them both." She gestured at the nearest support pole inside the tent.

Directing with her hand, she forced Radax next to the pole. The *bracks* dragged me to the other side of it.

"Take those dreadful clothes off her," Madame smirked. "I want her to feel every lash."

They stripped me naked. They ripped off my scarf, my hoodie, the long baggy t-shirt I had underneath. Layer by layer, they peeled away the little dignity I had left, baring me for the scourging.

I screamed. I cried. And now, I fought them, even though I knew it was useless. I clawed at their hands as they ripped off my bra and underwear. I drew blood, which earned me a punch in the face.

They yanked my hands above my head and tied them to the pole, positioning me to face Radax with the pole between us. I felt the heat of his body. He was so tall, the top of my head barely reached his chest.

The whip hissed through the air. Radax jerked, taking the first lash. The pole shook. I sobbed.

"I'm so sorry." The film of tears obscured the view of him in front of me. "I'm so sorry..."

I didn't want to exist. I wished to vanish into the shadows, dissolve into the night... Disappear. Then none of this would be happening. And Radax wouldn't suffer because of me.

With a hiss, the whip landed on my bare back. I screamed in searing pain.

Radax yelled, too, "Stop it! Let her go!"

Another lash of the whip burned my back like a lick of fire.

"Make sure you don't break her skin," Madame murmured. Watching us being hurt had calmed her temper. She sounded cheerful now. Pleased. "Humans are so weak. I need her to work in the morning. But do your worst with him. I'll let him heal soon enough."

Radax gritted his teeth as the whip lashed across his back, but he made no other sound.

I prayed to the gods of both worlds for this to be over. But the whip came down again and again. The pole shook from our bodies convulsing. The pain burned my skin like fire. But an even bigger agony racked my soul. Sorrow burned through my heart like acid.

Radax slumped in his restraints. I hoped for his sake he'd passed out and felt no more pain.

"Cut him down," Madame ordered. "Take him to the trailer. Let him heal. And get back to packing. We're leaving tomorrow."

They cut the ropes. My knees buckled, and I sank to the ground.

The *bracks* hauled Radax away, blood from his wounds dripping onto the packed dirt.

I hugged my knees and curled into myself, lying on my side.

"You." Madame wasn't done with me yet. She stepped closer until her shoes decorated with silk flowers came into my view.

I didn't move, no longer caring what she did to me.

"I'll wipe this from his memory," she said tersely. "Don't even think you can use his rage against me. He's mine."

She stepped back and was gone, leaving me in the dust on the dirt floor of the tent.

I wanted to crawl over to the trailer where they had put Radax. I'd sneak under it and spend the night there, listening to every sound inside, guessing how he was doing and whether he was healing well.

But the longer I lay naked on the dirt ground, the further the sorrow receded and anger took over.

"Don't ever think you can use his rage against me," Madame had said. Maybe she was right. Radax's rage belonged to her and her alone, just like everything else he had.

But the rage that bubbled and burned inside me right now was all my own. It belonged to no one but me.

For years, I'd fought my anger. When I was hurt, I blamed myself.

"Why do you put up with this?" Kyllen had asked me once. And suddenly I couldn't remember the reasons why.

I didn't have to continue enduring this. Kyllen had given me a way out, and I was going to take it. But I had to do it on my own, without Radax. He couldn't know anything about my escape. Madame could never blame him for what I was about to do.

Wiping the tears and dust off my face, I found my clothes and got dressed. Holding on to the pole, I got up to my feet. My legs shook, and my back felt as if it'd been doused in burning gasoline. But the skin wasn't broken. I had no open wounds, no blood. The *bracks* hadn't gone against Madame's orders.

Instead of going to the trailer, I went into the room with Madame's exhibits. I took the key I used when dusting inside the displays and unlocked a glass cabinet with the collection of jewelry. Each piece was fiercely beautiful, made from black and white spikes set in metal. Madame claimed the spikes were werewolves' teeth and claws.

I took out a tall diadem and turned it in my hands. The black spikes on it looked exactly like the claws of the beast Madame kept chained. And the white ones had the same appearance as his teeth.

"Nothing is what it seems," Radax had said. He'd also added that I, of all people, should know that.

I would, had I looked closely at what had been happening around me. But I'd chosen not to see, not to listen, and not to analyze. Because not knowing felt safer.

I'd chosen to go through life like a shadow, unseen and uncaring. Because caring hurt. There was so much pain in the world I grew up in, it would've crushed me had I absorbed it all. So, I blocked it off.

Now, I had to be strong enough to face it all. It was time to see things for what they truly were.

Chapter Fourteen

AMIRA

The beast was hanging in his chains. I knew better than to believe he was simply sleeping. I now doubted he was simply a beast, too.

Roaming my gaze over his body, I picked out the visual signs of a man within the animal. And the more I looked, the more of them I found. The features of a man smoothly merged with those of an animal. It looked natural, as if both were a part of one person—a werewolf.

Keeping a safe distance, I poked him in the arm with the diadem.

"The black thorns in this crown are werewolves' claws," I said. "The white ones are their teeth. Both are just like yours." I paused, trying to gauge whether he understood me or even heard me. His eyes remained closed. "You're a werewolf, aren't you? From Nerifir?"

His eyelids, trimmed with thick black eyelashes, fluttered open. Red flashed within. His top lip curled, bearing long, needle-sharp teeth. A growl resonated through his chest.

I shrank back, dropping the crown. He was bone-chillingly terrifying. Everything inside me urged me to flee. But he was my one and only chance. I forced my feet to stay where they were. Pressing my hands to my chest, I tried to calm my racing heart.

"Can you speak?" I ventured a question.

His chest rose and fell with heavy breathing. He made no sound in reply.

I took in the uneven patches of fur, the front paws that looked so much like hands, his feet that were more like clawed wolf paws, the face with features of both a human and a beast. Whatever had been done to him wasn't natural, even for the magical being that he was. He seemed stuck between two forms.

Dez had been giving him two substances—the yellow powder he'd sprinkled on his food and the gel he'd put on his wounds. He obviously did it for a reason. I needed to find out exactly what each substance did to this creature.

He might be suffering more than I realized.

Compassion squeezed my heart like a steel band. It helped me conquer the fear. I took from my pockets another portion of tainted meat I'd sourced from the kitchen and the jar with the fragrant gel.

"Dez said to give you both daily. I've given you neither because I don't know what they'll do to you. Which one will help you speak?"

He licked his lips with the long dark tongue, the lethal saliva dripping from his fangs as he stared at the meat.

"This?" I glanced at the meat suspiciously. Maybe he was just too hungry to think rationally? "Dez laced it with something, a yellow powder. Are you sure that's what you want?"

He appeared to struggle, hesitating, then shifted his crimson stare to the jar.

"This? Will this help you speak?"

He released a roar. It sounded soft, not aggressive. He was trying to communicate with me, not scare me.

I shoved the package with meat back in my pocket, then came closer, holding the jar.

He drew in some air, sniffing me, then yanked on the chains, snapping his teeth. Saliva dripped to the floor, scorching the ground.

Fear jolted me. I leaped back, evading his teeth. Sentient or not, he could hurt me.

He could kill me.

I kept my distance, figuring out what to do. Dez had said to smear the gel on the spikes of the collar. It would then get into the beast's bloodstream. The werewolf's wrists caught my attention. Rubbed raw under the manacles, they were but open wounds.

"This should work," I muttered under my breath.

Staying away from his teeth, I opened the jar and smeared the gel on his wounds under the iron, both wrists and ankles.

He groaned and gritted his teeth at the gel's contact with his exposed flesh.

"Sorry it hurts." I tried to be as gentle as possible.

He leaned his head back against the frame and groaned again. This time, the sound held more contentment than pain.

"Better?" I asked with hope.

He breathed deeply, and I watched him...change.

His maw shortened, the fangs shrinking to hide behind his lips. His skin turned from gray to pale. It shimmered as the black fur slipped under it, disappearing completely from most of his body.

The fur turned to a tousled mop of dark hair on his head, a generous sprinkle of it on his chest, and a nest of dark curls in his groin area. There wasn't nearly enough of it left between his thighs to fully conceal his...um, sizable "male equipment."

I averted my eyes. "You've changed."

He turned to me. Red leached from his irises, replaced by serene gray.

"Thank you, Amira." The words came in a dry croak.

He spoke!

Of course he spoke. He looked like a person now. There was nothing left of the beast. Only the color of his hair was the same as his fur used to be.

And he knew my name. Which meant he must've been listening to the conversations around him all along.

"The yellow powder brings out the beast in me," he explained. "The *womora* gel impedes it. Dez uses both, to keep me in between."

That must be torturous.

Something clanked deep in the tent somewhere, and I froze. The *bracks* were tearing down the tents on Madame's orders.

"They're packing up to move," I said in a low whisper. "They'll be here soon. We need to hurry. Quick, tell me how to open a portal to Nerifir."

He gazed at me, his eyes still slightly unfocused.

"You don't open a portal." His voice was raspy, with a soft purr of a French accent. "You find one."

He knew! I released a contented breath. I'd guessed correctly. He was from Nerifir, and he knew how to get there.

"You weren't abducted straight from Nerifir, were you?"

He shook his head. "No. I came to this world on my own, long ago. The portal I used is near Paris, France."

That explained his accent. As Kyllen had told me, the first language the fae heard when coming to this world became their mother tongue. The werewolf's first language must have been French.

Oh, this was real. I could bring Kyllen home. Tingles of anticipation scattered along my arms.

"Listen." The man eagerly shifted in his restraints. "I'll tell you everything I know, but you need to answer some of my questions, too. Deal?"

Deals could be dangerous when made with fae. But I felt ready to make one with Kyllen. For that, I needed the werewolf to tell me all about the portal. I just had to negotiate carefully and state my terms clearly.

"If you take me to the portal, I'll set you free." A rush of adrenaline coursed hot through my veins. I could do this. I would set him free. Dez had given me the key to his collar and chains. It'd be like stealing the prisoner from under Madame's nose.

Thrill shot through me at the thought. Fear would no longer stop me.

"How would you free me?" the werewolf asked suspiciously.

"The key for your collar is the same that opens the locks on your restraints. But I'll only have the key until we move."

He winced, either in discomfort or concentration. "Move where?"

"To Europe. England first, then France."

It occurred to me that since the portal was near Paris, it'd be convenient to stay with the menagerie until we got to France. I knew so little about traveling on my own.

However, if the werewolf took my offer and I released him, I'd have to get out of here as soon as possible, too. I harbored no illusions. Madame wouldn't let me live if I released her VIP act. Radax wouldn't be safe from her wrath, either.

The prisoner yanked at the chains, looking alarmed. "I can't go to Europe. I have...someone I need to protect in this country. Let me go, and I'll tell you exactly how to find the portal. I'll also tell you the rules of traveling through one."

"There are rules?" A wave of concern washed over me.

He nodded. "Rule number one. Once you cross the River of Mists that connects the worlds, you will never be able to come back to this time or place. If you cross back to Earth, you may end up a month in the past from now or a thousand years into the future. There is just no way to predict with any certainty."

I drew in a shuddering breath. Now I vaguely remembered overhearing *bracks* talk about something like that once. Back then, I didn't understand what that meant. Now, worry spiked in me anew. Kyllen wanted to return to his world, his family, and the throne that waited for him. What would he think about going too far back into the past or too much forward into the future?

"Who's going with you?" the werewolf asked.

I threw him a cautious glance, unsure if I should tell him about Kyllen. If this failed, I wanted neither Radax nor Kyllen to deal with the consequences. "Does it matter?"

"It does. Your travel companion has everything to do with rule number two that I haven't mentioned yet."

"What is rule number two?" I frowned.

"I need you to answer my questions first."

Faint sounds of shuffling and packing came through the canvas walls again. The *bracks* were nearby. We needed to hurry, but a deal was a deal.

"Fine, what do you need to know?"

It turned out he had many questions.

First, he wanted to know about the siren man Zeph, whom

Madame had in her possession last year. Zeph must be his friend, and the werewolf appeared to be really worried about him. But Zeph had escaped about two months earlier. I truthfully answered every question the werewolf asked about him.

"What do you know about Madame's trade to supply her menagerie?" the werewolf asked me next.

I didn't have much to tell him about that. Madame had her *bracks* bring her many things from Nerifir. But I didn't know how she paid for them. She didn't involve me in that part of her business.

He asked me about the dragon-man statue Madame had. It was a life-size depiction of a winged man sitting on a piece of rock carved from obsidian stone. I dusted it as part of my cleaning duties at the menagerie.

A sudden understanding chilled me. "He is not just a statue, is he?"

"Nothing is what it seems," he echoed Radax's words to me.

The world of the menagerie was not just full of shadows. It crawled with lies.

The werewolf grew visibly more impatient the closer the noise of the *bracks'* tearing down the tents moved. "Can you unlock the manacles now, please? I'll have to get out before they come here."

I took the key out of my pocket but didn't unlock him yet, remembering I was dealing with a fae. "You haven't told me how to get to the portal. What is rule number two?"

"Right." He winced, stretching his neck and shoulders. "On your own, you can only cross back to the world where you came from. To travel to Nerifir, you'll need a fae or a *brack* to accompany you, someone who is native to that world."

"I won't be alone." I realized that since he'd been listening to my conversation with Radax, he must know about Kyllen already.

"I'll have Kyllen with me," I said. "I'm not leaving him here."

A loud noise of something heavy being dropped startled us both into silence. The noise was followed by *bracks'* yelling.

"Amira, please hurry," he pleaded, urgently rattling with his chains. "I'll talk as you unlock."

The time was running out. I dropped to my knees to release his ankles.

"Listen carefully," he said. "Once you make it to Paris, take the train to *Parc des Brouillards*, just outside of the city. It's a private property, be careful when getting in. There're guards." He winced, as if he'd met them personally and the memories still bothered him. "The portal only opens for about twenty minutes at three o'clock every morning. It's a small cloud of mist over the water of the pond, at the back of the park. It's very easy to miss, but it'd be pink, like the River itself."

Trying to commit his every word to memory, I unlocked his arms next.

He stumbled away from the frame, unsteady on his feet. I tensed, half-expecting him to lunge at me, now that he was free from the restraints. He was a tall man, looking strong even after all the tortures Dez had put him through. No longer a beast, he could still be dangerous.

Thankfully, he showed no interest in attacking me. He swayed, then got hold of the side rail of the frame, steadying himself.

"Is the portal there every day?" I asked.

"It should be. The flow of the River of Mists changes, but very slowly. It's been over forty years since I was in *Parc des Brouillards* last, but it would take centuries or even millennia for the River to alter its course enough for a portal to disappear."

"How do you know all of this?"

He released a long breath, glancing at the exit from the room. "Let's just say I spent some time with the goddess when she used to be a more benevolent creature, inclined to share things with me."

He was obviously talking about Madame. Though it was hard for me to imagine her ever being "benevolent." He must know her personally, and not just as her prisoner.

Not that it mattered. The werewolf upheld his part of the deal. He told me all about the portal. Now, I just needed to get back to Kyllen. Then, we could make a run for it.

"Be careful when crossing to Nerifir, Amira," the werewolf warned. "There's enough danger and hostility in that world, maybe even more than in this one."

What choice did I really have?

"I can't stay here."

He gave me a concerned look. Compassion floated in his clear gray eyes. "I wish I could come to Paris with you to help you get to the portal, but I can't. I have to stay in this country. The minute my escape is discovered, Ghata will send *bracks* to hurt an innocent woman simply because they believe I care about her. I need to make sure she's safe."

"I see." I nodded in understanding, well familiar with Madame's ways. "Don't worry about me. I'll manage." I had to.

He stepped closer and placed his hands on my shoulders. I flinched at the touch of a stranger but didn't move away. Maybe I trusted him too quickly, but he seemed like someone worthy of my trust.

"Stay with the menagerie until you get to Paris," he instructed. "I've sold all of my properties there but one." He gave me the address of what he said was a townhouse where he used to live. "In the main bedroom, under a loose floorboard under the bed, I have a safe box with some money. Remember the lock code." He slowly said the string of letters and numbers in the order that opened the built-in safe box, then made me repeat it. "Take as much as you think you'll need—all of it if you have to."

He didn't need to do that. Giving me money was not a part of our deal. But I didn't have a penny in this world or any other. Now, money meant freedom. Freedom to go anywhere. Freedom to run.

My heart tightened with emotion at his kindness.

"Thank you." I worried my lip between my teeth, mulling over an idea about what to do next. He'd been kind to me, and I wanted to repay him somehow. "You know, I can buy you some time to get to your woman."

"How?"

I ran to the canvas wall in front of his frame. The crate where the *bracks* were planning to transport him to London stood there, ready for him. It was nearly identical to Kyllen's. "Help me load your frame with restraints in here."

"Why?" he asked but did as I said.

Fae were inhumanly strong. But his time in restraints had obviously weakened him. His legs shook, and he still staggered on his feet. Together, however, we managed to drag the frame to the crate and shove it in.

"I'll throw some of these in there, too." I grabbed one of the sandbags piled up behind the canvas walls. The *bracks* used them to hold down the bottom edge of the tents' outer walls. The weight of the bags would make up for the missing werewolf inside the crate.

When the frame and a few bags were in there, I lowered the crate's lid back in place, closing it. "I'll hammer a few nails into it when you're gone. Then I'll tell them you've been loaded."

No one would know the werewolf was gone until we arrived in England. By then, it'd be too late. It would buy me some time, too. I can stay with the menagerie, travel to England at Madame's expense, and reunite with Kyllen.

"Will they believe that you managed to load me all on your own?" The werewolf's expression remained skeptical.

I nodded confidently. If there was anything I'd learned during my life in the menagerie, it was how the *bracks'* minds worked.

"Nerkan is with the group of *bracks* who are loading the truck outside of the main tent, and Vuk is with those who are breaking down the tents from the inside." I gestured in the direction of the shuffling, rustling, and clunking that had been steadily getting closer. "I'll tell Vuk that Nerkan loaded you. Then I'll tell Nerkan that Vuk did it. Both are too lazy to break into the crate to check. They'd just be too happy to know that it's done—less work for them."

His dark eyebrows rose. He seemed impressed. "Thank you for thinking of that."

The sound of voices and feet shuffling appeared to be coming from right behind the next partition now. We needed to leave before they discovered us here.

"They'll be coming here next," I whispered, creeping away from the noise along the canvas wall. "Come."

I slipped under a fabric flap, gesturing for him to follow. The strings of lights high under the ceiling of the massive tent struggled to illuminate this space, separated by several rooms and walls from the center.

"Here." I yanked up the fabric of one of the outside walls. Fresh air rushed in, chilling my feet. "The fair ended. There are no *bracks* or people on this side right now. But you'll have to climb over the chain-link fence to get out."

Even in his weakened state, I didn't think that would be a problem for a werewolf. Besides, he appeared to be getting stronger by the minute. Whether that was the effect of the *womora* gel I'd put on his wounds or the lack of the yellow powder in his system, I didn't know. Most likely, it was the combination of both.

He gently touched my hand. "Well, goodbye, Amira. Thank you for everything. Good luck, and may you find your happiness in Nerifir."

I nodded awkwardly.

"Good luck to you, too..." I hesitated for a fraction of a moment. "What's your name?"

I'd never asked that from anyone before Kyllen. Names meant friends. And one could not afford to have friends at the menagerie. But this was not the first rule I'd broken. The werewolf had been kind to me, and I didn't want to remember him as simply "a werewolf." I wanted to have his name.

"It's Lero." He smiled.

I nodded again. "Be careful out there, Lero."

He crouched by the opening that led outside. His bare backside came into my view.

"Um... Do you need any clothes?" I asked, wondering if I could steal a pair of *bracks'* pants for him.

"No." He chuckled, slipping under the canvas. "I'll have lots of fur to keep me warm soon."

Then I remembered. Tonight was a full moon.

As I stood inside the tent, listening for the sounds of *bracks* packing, a long howl rolled through the night from a distance.

The werewolf ran free.

The next morning, Radax was well enough to get up.

I waited by the *bracks'* trailer. Hiding around the corner, I watched them come out and head to the tents to finish loading the trucks.

When Radax came out, I rushed to him. "Radax!"

He turned to me, smiling. "Morning."

I took in every line and dip of his face, committing it to memory.

His full beard, his dark brown eyes, the red streaks in them barely visible in the morning light, the fine lines fanning in the corners as he smiled for me.

I touched his hand. "How are you feeling?"

"Fine," he easily replied.

A slight wince didn't escape my notice when he rolled back his shoulders, neither did the reproachful glance he tossed toward Madame's trailer.

Madame might control his mind enough to make him forget the whipping, but I didn't think she had the power to completely erase how he felt about it or her.

"You can't use his rage against me," she'd said. But I wondered if he'd use it against her himself one day. Sadly, I would no longer be here to see that.

The thought of leaving him was devastating. It crushed my heart, but I bit back the tears. Seeing me upset would make him ask questions, but he couldn't have the answers. The least he knew, the safer he would be.

"I love you, Radax." I rose to my tiptoes and gave him a big hug, the biggest I'd ever given.

He grunted in surprise, then wrapped his arms around me in response.

"I love you, too." He kissed my hair.

"I'll never forget you," I vowed in my mind.

Tears burned my eyes, but I blinked them away, shoving my emotions deep inside me. This was the only goodbye I could afford to have without risking putting Radax in danger. No one could suspect he'd helped me in any way.

I was ready. All I had to do was to get back to Kyllen. Then I would leave the only world I knew.

The idea terrified me, but there was no going back now.

Chapter Fifteen

KYLLEN

Despite Amira letting him know about the move, he half-expected Ghata to dump his crate somewhere, with him inside it. He'd made it clear he was not participating in her sick schemes. Obviously, she still harbored some hope of him changing his mind because she didn't discard him.

As Amira had warned him, a *brack* came by one day. The brute shook his crate, jolting him inside. Kyllen dutifully released a tortured groan to confirm he was still alive. A short while later, they loaded him into a vehicle and drove away.

He quickly realized Amira was not with them this time. For whatever reason, she stayed behind. Not having her around disturbed him more than she would ever know, and it wasn't just the water she brought that he missed.

Without ever laying his eyes on the woman, he'd grown accustomed to her company. Deprived of it now, he felt bereft—lonelier than he'd ever been in his life.

The need to hear her voice was so strong, he battled the urge to burst out of the damn crate and roam this world in search of her, even if that meant turning most of its inhabitants to stone copies of themselves.

Deep inside, however, he knew the quickest way to get Amira back was to stay put. Sooner or later, Ghata would assemble her menagerie in a new location, and he'd be reunited with his little human.

So, he waited.

The journey to the place they called England proved uneventful and mercifully quick. The temperature inside his crate went from unbearably hot to intolerably freezing. The air, however, remained consistently dry. Without Amira supplying him with water, thirst tormented him again.

That would be all he'd remember from this world—incessant burning thirst and Amira's refreshing presence.

His crate had been moved from one vehicle to another. He'd been jolted, shaken, and jerked inside it. From what he gathered, he spent a day or two, maybe longer, in a storage facility where it was dark, cold, and mostly quiet.

Patience was hard to come by as the time ticked away. The fact that only a flimsy wooden crate stood between him and freedom didn't make it easier. But he didn't simply want to get free of the crate. He wished to make it back home. And for that, he needed Amira.

She'd promised to find out about the portal, but he still hoped she'd join him in his escape, too. Obviously, he needed her in his life, since just a few days without her plunged him into complete misery.

The idea of leaving her behind, at the mercy of Ghata, left a disgusting taste in his mouth. He believed he could give Amira a much better life in Lorsan. And dammit, she deserved better.

From inside the crate, he could only go by the sounds reaching him to figure out what was happening on the outside. His crate had been loaded into yet another vehicle. When it stopped, the loud clanking of doors opening and the voices of *bracks* talking about unloading reached him.

He hoped this was their final destination.

The cacophony of noises quieted down as the *bracks* took some items and left. Then, the sound he'd longed to hear more than anything finally came—the familiar scurrying of a woman's light footfalls.

"Kyllen?" Amira's sweet voice called to him, and something inside him cracked.

She was here. And it was like a drop of water to his parched heart, a ray of light and a breath of fresh air in his dark, stuffy prison.

"Amira..."

Chapter Sixteen

AMIRA

I was restless the entire flight to London. Anxiety pricked me with tiny needles.

Lero was gone, and I fervently tried to predict when and how his absence would be discovered as well as how it might affect Kyllen, Radax, and me. Too many variables remained unknown. A lot could go wrong, and so much was at stake. If I made a mistake this time, I would certainly die. The two people I cared about the most in this life would suffer or even die, too.

The moment we landed, Madame left for a hotel where she was planning to stay while the menagerie remained in London.

I drove with the *bracks* to the facility Madame had booked for her exhibit. Because there were so many of us, we traveled in several vehicles, and I had made sure to get in the one without Radax. I stayed away from him as much as possible. The less we were seen together, the less there was a chance for someone blaming him for my escape.

He'd be better off without me, I kept telling myself. He'd have less to worry about and fewer responsibilities. Still, my heart ached whenever I thought about him.

Once we arrived at the venue—a large exhibition hall of sorts—the *bracks* broke up. Some went to work on setting up displays. Others headed to the loading dock to unload the exhibits from the incoming trucks.

I spotted Dez. He'd arrived a few days earlier and now was giving the other *bracks* the tour of our area inside the exhibition hall. I hid behind a partition, keeping out of view. If Dez saw me, he'd demand the key to Lero's restraints, but I had to find Kyllen first.

There was no sight of his crate anywhere inside the hall. I quickly made my way to the loading dock.

Two *bracks*, Leslo and Vuk, were unloading a wooden crate off the truck. It could be either Kyllen's or Lero's. Or maybe it held the dragon-man statue? It was hard to tell, as their crates were similar.

I waited until the *bracks* turned their backs to me, then snuck past them into the back of the tractor trailer. It was parked flush with the open doors of the dock for unloading. There was just one crate left inside. The question was, which one?

Hiding behind it from the *bracks'* view, I called softly, "Kyllen?"

"Amira..." came back in a whisper.

My heart leaped with excitement, then relief flooded me. "I found you."

"You did, my favorite little human." The rasp was more profound in his voice, once again reminding me of the wind rustling through a pile of dry leaves. He'd been without a drop of water for days; his throat was too dry.

The warm note of affection in his voice stroked with pleasure inside me. He sounded happy to hear me, and it felt nice to have been missed.

I couldn't help a smile. "I'm your favorite?"

"You're the only human I've ever spoken to, my dear. So, yes, you're my one and only, and my favorite by default." He was teasing me. By now, I'd grown attuned to every slight variation of his voice, capable of reading his moods from its intonations. I could tell he was smiling.

The sound of *bracks'* conversation moved closer. They must be returning for Kyllen's crate now.

"We need to get you out of this box." I slid my hands along the wooden planks nailed across the door.

"That I can do," Kyllen assured me. "You'll just have to tell me when, my friend."

He'd mentioned he could free himself before, but the crate looked solid and strong. "Are you sure you can open it from the inside?"

He scoffed, and I imagined him smirking. "Just say when, Amira."

The *bracks* were talking to someone just outside of the trailer. Next, they'd come here.

It was now or never.

"Now, Kyllen," I exhaled in one breath.

"Step back," he said with determination, then added with a hint of concern. "And Amira?"

I scurried to the far wall of the trailer. "Yes?"

"Close your eyes."

I should've closed my ears, too, as a crashing noise followed, shaking the truck. Pieces of wood shot in every direction, hitting the walls of the trailer. I hid my face behind my arms.

"Hey!" Leslo yelled.

I couldn't help a glance, lowering my elbow.

Brandishing a handgun, Leslo dashed inside the trailer.

"Stand back!" I screamed in warning.

A tall, hooded figure rose from the remnants of the crate. Kyllen stood upright, turned with his back to me.

"That felt good." He kicked a piece of wood with his boot.

Dressed in brown pants and a sage-green tunic, he had a dark hood drawn low over his eyes. The material undulated and shifted around his head. The ends of the hood draped around his neck and shoulders like a scarf.

"Who the fuck are you?" Leslo shouted. The end of his question trailed off. His features slacked with understanding.

Kyllen raised his hand and lifted the edge of his hood up, just a little. With Kyllen's back to me, I didn't see what made Leslo's expression turn to horror. Staggering back, the *brack* paled. His hand shook, dropping the gun.

Then… All color drained from Leslo. His skin, his eyes, his clothes, even the black lines of his tattoo—all turned gray. All fused into a solid, unmoving piece of rock.

Leslo was no more. Only a granite statue remained in his place, mouth agape, terror frozen in his dead eyes.

"Close your eyes, Amira!" A familiar voice warned.

Radax!

He rushed into the trailer.

Oh no. Not him.

Dread seized me. The world around me slowed down, sounds muffled by the echo of my thundering heart.

As if in slow motion, I watched Kyllen's torso shift. He was turning to face Radax.

In a moment, Radax would join Leslo as another lifeless statue.

"Radax, no!" I screamed, grabbing Leslo's gun from the floor.

My back to Kyllen, I lunged between Radax and him. But my height wouldn't be enough to break their eye contact. I had but a fraction of a moment left before it would be too late.

"I'm so, so sorry," I whispered, raising the gun. "I'll never forget you."

I pulled the trigger.

Shock flashed in Radax's eyes. Blood sprayed from the small round wound from the bullet in the middle of his forehead.

The veil of my tears hid his beloved face from view. Sobs tore from my chest, tearing at my heart with pain. I dropped the gun as Radax crashed to the ground. Dead.

"Amira," Kyllen's voice called to me through the shroud of horror that descended upon me.

Strong arms hugged my shoulders. "We need to go," Kyllen implored.

Other *bracks* shouted in the building. They'd heard the gunshot. They'd be here soon. They would shut the door to the trailer and trap us in here.

We had to go. Yet I couldn't bring myself to move away from Radax.

"I killed him," I sobbed.

"Not for long." Kyllen nudged me toward the exit. "He'll be fine. He's immortal, after all."

A human-made weapon couldn't kill a *brack*. I shot Radax to spare him the fate of Leslo. I saved him by shooting him before a look in the eyes of the gorgonian would kill him for good.

I saved him, but I had to hurt him for that.

Bile rose in my throat as Kyllen dragged me out of the trailer and into the building.

"Where to now?" he asked.

Lero's crate stood wide open in a small side hallway. Empty. In a matter of minutes, the *bracks* would get organized and go after us. We had no time to lose.

Kyllen's power was astonishing. But the *bracks* had captured him once before, and they could do it again.

I shook off the fear and grief, forcing my brain to focus.

"This way." I gestured at the glass double doors with the parking lot beyond them.

There were men out there—regular human men—probably the employees of the exhibition hall or truck drivers.

"Please don't hurt anyone," I pleaded with Kyllen.

He nodded, yanking his hood lower. From the corner of my eye, I could only see his chin, the hard edge of his jawline, and the very tip of his nose. He kept his arm around my shoulders.

Moving as fast as possible, but without running so as not to raise suspicions, we crossed the tarmac toward low-rise buildings beyond the lot.

"Now where?" he demanded.

"Um..." I had no idea. This was an entirely unfamiliar place to me, as it was to him.

A train rattled on the raised tracks just behind the buildings. I didn't know where it went or if we could get a ride.

"We need to get to Paris," I muttered under my breath.

"Where?" Kyllen turned back to the exhibition hall, checking the entrance over his shoulder.

"Paris. It's the capital city of France. That's where the portal is." I followed his gaze to the hall, sensing his worry. "But first we need to get much farther away from here."

I grabbed his hand and swerved onto a narrow path between the buildings.

We walked along the streets of London, keeping to the shadows. I'd been to this city before, long ago, as a child. Madame had toured Europe then. Of course, I hadn't gotten to see much of it and remembered absolutely nothing.

To get to Paris, we'd need transportation. To buy tickets, we'd need money. But first, I had to find a safe, quiet place to figure out a plan.

I'd asked one of the pedestrians, a middle-aged woman, where the train tracks led. She told me the trains ran to the city center. That was where we were going, following the tracks the best we could. Sometimes the streets followed them almost precisely. At times, they tangled in a mess that took some time to navigate.

As we were passing by two buildings with an archway in between, Kyllen pulled me under the arch and into a narrow alley.

"I don't think we're being followed," he said.

I poked my head out of the alley and scanned both sides of the street. There was no sign of *bracks* anywhere. With their size and tattoos, they'd be easy to spot.

"I think you're right. Maybe they didn't notice which direction we went." Or maybe they chose not to pursue us, seeing what Kyllen had done to Leslo. Sooner or later, Madame would make them search for us, though. I was sure of that.

He turned to me, his head bowed, his hood low. "You're tired." He took my hand in his.

We must've been walking for a couple of hours now, maybe longer.

The gray winter sky had turned a darker shade of gray meanwhile. It was evening. Night would come next, and I still wasn't sure what to do.

"You're thirsty," I replied. We had to get him some water before I could get any rest.

"I'll live." He placed his hands on my shoulders—a stranger with a so very familiar voice.

I stared at his wide chest, covered by the sage-green fabric of his tunic and crisscrossed by a couple of embossed leather belts. Kyllen had been but a disembodied voice to me. Now, the owner of that voice was towering over me.

Not quite as bulky as a *brack,* he was significantly taller than me. His chest was at my eye level. Judging by the way he'd blasted out of the crate, he must be much stronger than a regular human, too.

Mindful of his warnings, I resisted glancing up at him, studying what I could see without lifting my head, instead.

His clothes were wrinkled and worn—not surprising, since he'd spent months locked in the crate. However, there was not a trace of filth or unpleasant body odor. His scent was fresh, like the cucumber I'd fed him once, with a hint of wet moss and the smell of forest right after the rain. All the scents I rarely got to smell in my life.

"There you are," he murmured, and I realized he was studying me, too.

I immediately felt self-conscious. People usually found me odd—with the scarf I wore all year round, my baggy clothes, and my hair smoothed back, the long braid hidden inside my hoodie.

Weird. Ghost. Ridiculous. These were only some of the hurtful things I'd heard about myself from the fair crowd over the years. I closed my eyes, not wishing to recall all of them.

What would a fae lord think about me, the ticket girl?

Kyllen's hands traveled from my shoulders to my neck. He buried them in the folds of my scarf, but didn't search for my skin beneath it.

He leaned closer until his breath tangled in my hair. "My rescuer."

A tendril of pleasure sneaked into my heart at the gratitude in his voice.

"Thank you for breaking me out," he added.

I thought about the way he'd decimated that crate.

"Actually, you did all the *breaking* yourself." I hid a smile in my scarf.

He chuckled above me. "I'd fantasized about having my way with that crate for a very long time. It proved exceptionally satisfying to finally bring my fantasies to life."

I brought my hands between us, fidgeting with one of the leather belts over his chest.

"I need to get you some water." A long list of things to do was running through my head. The rescue wasn't over yet. "I need to figure out how to get to Paris. But first, where to spend the night—"

He stopped me by lightly pressing a finger to my lips.

"*We*," he corrected me. "*We* need to figure all of that out. Together."

Together.

The word had the comforting effect of a warm blanket. It reminded me that I was no longer alone. I tilted my head back, needing to see his face.

He quickly placed his hand over my eyes. "Careful!"

I exhaled a shaky breath, realizing the danger I'd so narrowly escaped just now. Chill of dread made me shudder. "Sorry..."

"Not your fault. It's difficult *not* to look. But please, try to be mindful. If something happens to you because of me, I..." his voice broke off.

With his hand still over my eyes, I felt his gaze on me. "You're looking at me."

"Hmm," he confirmed with a hum. "There's no harm in *me* looking at *you*, is there?" His voice turned soft, like a caress.

With one hand covering my eyes, he traced with a finger of the other along my jawline.

"Why have you never told me how beautiful you are?" The sultry note in his voice vibrated deep in my chest, ripples spreading through the rest of my body.

His touch tingled along my skin.

He exhaled a soft laugh. "I was a fool, fantasizing about the crate. When I could've spent more time envisioning you."

I never had a man speak to me like this or touch me the way he did. I froze, unsure of what to do. With my eyes closed, Kyllen looking at me might not carry the risk of either of us turning to stone, but it wasn't entirely harmless, I feared.

A loud noise of a door slammed open yanked me out of the trance-like state.

Kyllen's hand slipped away from my eyes as he turned around. He shifted forward, placing his shoulder in front of me to shield me from the man who had opened the door in the wall across the narrow alley.

The man casually shoved the door closed behind him, then leaned with his back against the wall. He took a pack of cigarettes and a lighter out of his pocket, giving us a narrow-eyed look.

He was a fairly ordinary looking man, probably in his forties, with closely cropped reddish-brown hair. Dressed in jeans and a t-shirt, he had a brown leather jacket thrown over his shoulders.

"None of my business." He shrugged, lighting his cigarette. "If you want to shag her here, go ahead. But I'm going to have my smoke."

I slid my hand down Kyllen's arm and wrapped my fingers around his. I could do that. I could hold his hand in public, and there was no one to stop me or punish me for the pleasure or comfort it gave me.

Kyllen tipped his chin at the wall behind the man. "What's this building?"

"A hotel." The man examined us more closely, spending more time on Kyllen.

With his richly embroidered clothes, his hood, and the bejeweled buckles all over, Kyllen looked like he'd come straight from a movie set, renaissance faire or...well, from a magical kingdom.

The man took a long drag from his cigarette. "Are you tourists? Need a place to stay?"

"Maybe." Kyllen inclined his head in a regal manner. "What does this establishment have to offer?"

I marveled at his audacity. We had no money for even a night in a shed, yet he acted as if he had a choice of luxury hotels lined up eager to welcome him.

"Depends." The man's eyes shifted up and down the alley as he hurriedly smoked his cigarette. "What are you looking for?"

"For accommodation for a night," Kyllen replied. "In a place that might be willing to negotiate on the price. If you know of something suitable, I'd like to make a deal."

The man shifted my way, giving me an appraising gaze.

Kyllen stepped sideways, almost completely blocking me from the man's view, clearly letting him know I wasn't a part of their negotiations.

The man spit on the ground. "I may have something for you. It comes with an entertainment option." He bared his teeth in a crooked smile.

"What kind of entertainment?"

The man shot his gaze up and down the walkway again. "Do you like gambling?"

Oh no. I squeezed Kyllen's hand in mine. "Let's go."

The man gave me a bad feeling. I'd seen plenty of his type at the fairs. They were always ready to strip a gullible person of their last penny. I had no desire to participate in whatever scheme he had in mind, even if I had money to spare, which I didn't.

"What kind of gambling?" Kyllen's voice picked up.

Was he actually considering this?

"Kyllen, no." I discreetly tugged on his hand.

The man's eyes flashed greedily. "Whatever you want. Blackjack, poker, roulette?"

I waved him off. "We don't know these games—"

"Roulette is good. Where is it?" Kyllen sounded excited.

He had told me that our worlds used to be one, long ago. Apparently, some things endured the passage of time—gambling, for one. He even knew of roulette.

I shook my head, battling a swell of worry rising in my chest.

The man tossed aside his cigarette and rubbed his hands together in the chilly late-January air. "Lovely, lovely. This way, mate."

"Kyllen..." I tried to stop him by squeezing his hand tighter, but he gently tugged me along.

"This will be fun." He flashed me a smile from beneath his hood. "Trust me."

Chapter Seventeen

KYLLEN

The shifty human walked them through the door inside a narrow hallway, then downstairs. At the bottom of the stairs, he turned around, offering Kyllen his hand.

"I'm Rourke, by the way."

Kyllen nodded, but didn't take the hand and didn't give his name in return. He'd accepted the man's offer to gamble, but that didn't mean he was willing to shake hands with him.

Rourke grunted, awkwardly putting away the unwanted hand. "Well, this way."

Not trusting the man, Kyllen paid careful attention to where he was taking them—down a wide corridor, then to a white double-door with a flimsy-looking gold-tone handle.

Despite them being in the basement of the building, it didn't look like a dungeon. The space smelled of cigarettes but was well lit. The wallpaper and carpet were plain and worn in places, but not filthy. It was also much warmer here than outside. That alone was worth staying, he decided with a shudder that chased the chill out of his muscles.

Voices filtered from behind the double doors. Rourke opened them, letting the noise spill out into the corridor.

The three of them entered a spacious room with a low ceiling. Though of different architecture, the room had similarities with any gambling hall in Nerifir. He recognized the tables with cards, even though not all games played looked familiar.

He'd spent a fair amount of time playing cards when he was younger. Most card games could be learned, which gave a player some sense of control and a chance to work out a strategy. However, the element of serendipity and luck was always there. It made a card game unpredictable and exciting.

Today, he wasn't interested in playing cards, however, because he couldn't afford to leave anything to chance. Carefully peeking from under his hood, he located the roulette table and beelined for it.

Several people lingered around the table. The wheel was spinning. He lifted his head enough to only see players' bodies up to their chests.

"So," Rourke rubbed his hands again, the gesture he found irritating. "What are you playing?"

"That looks like fun." He tipped his chin at the roulette table.

"That it does. That it does," the human repeated himself, which also grated against Kyllen's nerves.

Amira gripped his hand, but remained quiet, subdued in the presence of so many people.

The croupier greeted them as they approached. "Where are you from, folks?"

He could think of only one location in this world, the place Amira had told him she'd come from, "Middle East."

A soft gasp sounded from her direction, but she didn't contradict him.

People around the table shifted, probably gawking at him. Admittedly, his style of clothing stood out among their boring clothes. The *bracks* had taken away his weapons long ago. But he'd kept his bejeweled bracers and decorated leather sheaths.

Rourke nudged him with an elbow. "You can take off your hood here, mate."

Oh, the pesky human dared touching him, didn't he? It took all he had not to shove the man away. If he did, Rourke would've certainly crashed through the nearest wall, for he wouldn't hold his strength back with this man.

"No, leave the hood," Amira rushed to protest. "He has to have it on."

"I thought it's the broads that cover their faces in the Middle East, not the blokes," a man's voice blurted out from the group of the players.

She gripped his hand even tighter. "It's not that... He's just... He's not well."

"What's wrong with him?" Rourke asked suspiciously, taking a step back.

As much as he loved for the man to keep his distance, the last thing he needed was being kicked out of the game because of the locals' fear of some plague.

"I'm fine." He pried his hand out of Amira's little fingers and patted her arm in a soothing gesture.

"Nothing contagious," she assured the crowd. "It's...um, a genetic condition that he was born with."

"Is that why he's green?" a woman asked.

Green?

He inspected his hand. His skin was light brown, like his father's, with dark-green markings he inherited from his mother. In healthy and well hydrated gorgonians, the markings remained on the *senties* only, with some showing along their spines, too.

But he'd been perpetually thirsty in this world. His markings had descended down his body. The backs of his hands were covered in the distinct diamond pattern, faint but visible. Its dark-green coloring tinted his light-brown skin with green.

"Right." He fisted his hand. The dry skin on it stretched, threatening to split.

Amira cleared her throat.

"Are only people with a certain skin color allowed in this place?" Her voice sounded high with challenge.

She gripped his hand again. The woman risked breaking his fingers if she kept clinging on to him like that.

Rourke shrugged. "Fuck no. I don't care what color he is. Green or purple, whatever. As long as he's not contagious and has money to place the bets."

The croupier didn't appear to be concerned with his coloring, either. "How much do you have? The minimum bet is a hundred pounds."

"I'll use silver and emeralds." Gently freeing his hand from Amira, he unbuckled the bracer from his left forearm.

The leather of the piece had been embossed by the best artisans of Ellohi. The four silver buckles had darkened to pewter while he'd been rotting in the crate, but the emeralds glistened as bright as ever. To his knowledge, gem stones were an acceptable currency in all worlds of the River of Mists. This one shouldn't be an exception.

He tossed the bracer onto the table. "How much for this one?"

"Um." The croupier scratched his chest, looking somewhat stunned.

Rourke sneaked in from around him. "Are these real?" He inspected the stones in the buckles, then those set in the silver discs on the bracer.

"They don't look like much," the croupier scoffed.

Kyllen flexed his jaw, holding back a fiery rebuke that bubbled inside him. What would this peasant know about fine gems?

"I'll take them to the appraiser." Rourke shoved the bracer under his arm.

Amira stirred at his side. "Where is the appraiser?"

Rourke paused, staring at her, as if he'd already forgotten she was there at all. "Oh, we have one right here, in the house. Not all guests pay in cash..." his voice trailed off.

Amira shifted uneasily, obviously not entirely satisfied by the answer.

Kyllen wrapped his arm around her shoulders and drew her into his side.

"Go ahead," he said to Rourke. "We'll wait right here. Remember, I have more where that came from." He turned his right arm, letting the emeralds on his other bracer catch light and sparkle.

Rourke scurried away, but there was no need to worry. No matter how much he took, the weasel human would always come back for more. Kyllen knew the type.

A woman appeared at his side, wearing a dress barely held up by two thin shoulder straps. Her outfit was far closer in style to what the ladies at his father's court wore than any other clothing in the room.

"Can I get you something to drink?" she murmured as if offering something far more illicit than a beverage.

He would kill for a glass of water, but he didn't trust these people or whatever they might serve him. There weren't many foods that could harm a gorgonian back in Nerifir. The hag's ring on his right hand protected him from those that could. But he wasn't in Nerifir, and the effects of magical substances varied from world to world.

"No. We're good." He shook his head.

The woman left, and Amira leaned into his side, so trusting. Warmth from her body seeped through his tunic, which was especially pleasant in the cool air of this land.

He'd never met a human before her. He'd never even met a fae who'd seen a human before. Humans were exceptionally rare in the whole of Nerifir, not just in the Kingdom of Lorsan. Little was known about them. And even that knowledge came from sources like legends, fables, and myths, often contradicting each other.

What all the myths agreed upon was that humans were alluring. They held a special appeal.

Now that he had met a few humans himself, he could argue with that general statement. Highborn fae—rich, spoiled, and bored—appreciated everything new and different. Kyllen wondered if the fae fascination with humans stemmed from them being rare and exotic.

However, as far as Amira was concerned, he could certainly feel the appeal.

She was stunning. Even despite her ugly clothing that was at least twice her size, the signs of exhaustion on her face, and the lanky jerkiness of her movements, he found her beautiful. There was an irresistible attraction in her human fragility.

He carefully slid his gaze her way. Her small hands were clutched to her chest, and he suddenly wished to hold one of them again.

Rourke returned, holding a wad of neatly cut pieces of paper in his hand.

"Eight hundred quid for the cuff." He shoved the wad into his hands.

Kyllen turned the tightly wound stack of papers in his fingers. This must be the weird human currency he'd overheard the *bracks* talk about.

"No," Amira protested passionately. "That's not enough."

It probably wasn't. Each buckle of his bracer would easily pay for a boat or a horse back in Nerifir. He never expected Rourke to be fair. However, the amount didn't really matter right now.

"All right." He accepted the papers.

"Kyllen—" Amira started, but he silenced her with a one-armed hug and a kiss into her hair. The gesture was meant to show the rest of the humans that she was with him and under his protection. But it felt so good to hug her, he had to force his arm to let go.

"It'll be fun, my heart," he said with exaggerated enthusiasm and shifted closer to the roulette table. "How does it work again?" He drummed his fingers on the edge of the table.

The croupier slid a small stack of chips his way, swiping away the wad of paper money. "You can bet on the color—red or black, the number—odd or even. You can bet on one specific number..."

Kyllen listened with some attention to all the betting options and the pay-offs they came with. Overall, the rules were almost identical to those in Nerifir. Deep inside, the worlds truly weren't that different.

"Each chip you have is one hundred pounds." The dealer pointed at the eight black chips in front of him. "That's the minimum bet."

"How much are the others worth?" Kyllen gestured at the neat rows of chips in the tray in front of the croupier.

"Pink is two-fifty. Purple is five hundred. And gray is one thousand," the man explained. "There's nothing lower than one hundred."

That was a lie. He'd spotted chips of other colors in front of the players at other tables—yellow, blue, orange, and red. Maybe other tables had different rules, or maybe Rourke and his cronies were determined to drain him of his money as fast as possible.

Something must be missing in the gambling laws in this world, or maybe there weren't any at all. Judging by the appearance of this place and its inhabitants, however, Kyllen didn't think they obeyed many laws, anyway.

Not that it mattered.

"Are you placing your bet, sir?" the croupier asked.

"Yes." He placed four of the eight chips he had on a random row on the table.

Amira stiffened at his side.

"Wish me luck, sweetheart." He flashed her a smile. She probably wished to slap it off his face, but she said nothing.

The wheel spun, sending the little metal ball rolling. He watched, faking excitement and eager anticipation.

The ball landed on the wrong color and the wrong number. The dealer quickly collected his four chips. Kyllen made his shoulders drop, exuding disappointment.

Amira tugged his sleeve. "We should go."

She was right, of course. The four hundred they still had left might buy them dinner and accommodation for tonight. But then what?

Besides, his bracer cost more than what he got for it. He had to at least get its value back, even if in the silly paper money.

"All on this row!" He slammed the remaining four chips on the same row he'd just lost the money on.

Amira blew out a breath. "You've just bet on this one. And lost."

"Exactly!" he exclaimed enthusiastically. "But it has the lucky number seven, see? So, it has to win sometime."

The croupier grunted at his flawed logic, accepting the bet.

Rourke must already be eyeing his right bracer, or maybe the large emerald ring on Kyllen's left pointer finger. He doubted the plain river rock on his small finger on the right attracted any attention, even though it was far more valuable than the emerald where he came from.

The croupier spun the wheel. The little ball rattled and rolled.

Kyllen leaned in, as if watching it with rapt attention. He touched the edge of the table lightly, building the connection with the mechanics of the roulette—the bowl, the wheel, the bearings... The mechanism was simple, which was the point of the game, of course.

He sent a tiny tendril of magic, slowing the spinning of the wheel just a little bit sooner. It forced the ball to remain on seven instead of jumping over to eight.

The croupier announced the winning number, his voice stunned somewhat, then placed considerably more chips in front of Kyllen than he'd wagered.

"That pays five to one," the dealer explained flatly.

"Wonderful." Kyllen smiled brightly, resisting the urge to punch the man.

The payout should've been at least three times higher than that according to the odds of winning, but he wasn't here to teach these people the rules. Not when he had complete control of the game, anyway.

Amira leaned toward his ear again. "We really should be going now."

"Just a little longer, honey." He wished to at least triple the money he got for the bracer, and since the idiots were dead-set on ripping him off, that would take longer than if they played by the rules.

"Sure thing. You can't leave now," Rourke exclaimed with a fake enthusiasm. "You're on a lucky streak!"

Kyllen wondered what Rourke was getting out of it. Probably a cut from the sale of the emeralds. Maybe he had a stake in the whole establishment? Or maybe he got a portion of whatever each poor wrench he'd dragged in here would lose. Either way, the shady human showed way too much interest in Kyllen and his winnings.

To avoid raising suspicions, he let the game take its course for a little while. Placing small bets, he lost some and won some.

Once he was down by almost a half of his winnings, he made a bet that promised ten times the payout, according to their crooked rules.

"All or nothing!" He shoved all his chips, worth eleven hundred, on the number eleven, then turned to Amira. "You're tired, aren't you, my sunshine? We'll leave after this one."

He sent another small surge of magic, aiming for the ball to land in the pocket he needed.

That was exactly why roulette was outlawed in Lorsan. Anything with a ball and bearing counted as a mechanism, and gorgonians wielded power over any mechanism in existence.

For that reason, gorgonians weren't allowed into the gambling halls outside of Lorsan. That didn't stop some gorgonian travelers from sneaking into the halls in Sarnala, the land of the werewolves, or Dakath, the kingdom of gargoyles, to manipulate the game in their favor. Some of them won big and returned to Lorsan much richer than they'd left. Others were discovered and killed.

The most important rule when cheating in gambling was not to get caught.

He sensed it was time to quit.

"That's the last one, my sweetie pie," he promised to Amira.

"Eleven. Black," the croupier announced grimly. The man certainly wasn't impartial to the house losing. He must be getting a cut, too. In fact, Kyllen was surprised to find the table not rigged in any way. Well, maybe after tonight they would rig it in their favor.

"Yes!" He threw his hands up in the air, leaping up in excitement. "We won, my sugar plum!"

"Ten thousand pounds," the dealer counted out the chips in a hollow voice.

"That should be eleven thousand," Amira objected. Obviously, the multiplication rules didn't apply here, either.

Rourke froze for a few moments then jumped into action, quickly. "Hey, want to try some cards now? How about blackjack?"

Card games were Kyllen's favorite, but he couldn't leave anything up to luck tonight.

"No. Maybe tomorrow." He drew Amira to his side again. "The lady is tired." He kissed her on the cheek, mostly for show, but also because he really wanted to kiss her.

The skin on her cheek felt even softer than that on her hand. She smelled of earth and ocean. She even had the taste of the ocean, he discovered. The kiss left the smidge of salt on his lips. Then he realized where the salt had come from. She'd cried when she had shot that *brack*, Radax.

It was the salt of her tears he'd just tasted.

His heart tightened with a new sensation. Sorrow? Compassion? A combination of both? Either way, it wasn't pleasant. It hurt, as if Amira's unhappiness filtered through to him.

Curiously, he didn't regret the feeling. He didn't mind hurting for her. He just wished she would suffer less if he took some of her pain.

"We're leaving," he announced, wrapping his arm tighter around her. "Please exchange the chips for...whatever it is you call currency in these parts."

As could've been expected, that wasn't met with enthusiasm from those present. From beneath his hood, he saw men shifting closer. Even some of those he'd mistaken for patrons of this place now were closing in on them. With the establishment lacking uniforms, it was hard to tell who was a guest and who was an employee.

Rourke stepped forward. "The night is young. What's your hurry?" He spat through his teeth on the carpeted floor.

Kyllen let go of Amira and shifted her behind him slightly. "I said the lady is tired. We need to leave."

He really wished to avoid carnage at this late hour, but if they left him no choice, he had absolutely no problems resorting to violence.

Amira poked her head from around his shoulder.

"You said there's a hotel in this building?" she asked Rourke.

"So?" The man grunted.

"Well, can we stay the night? Then gamble some more tomorrow?"

Her quick thinking just saved these men their pitiful little lives.

Rourke sniffed, wiping his nose with his arm. "That could be arranged. Why not?"

"Splendid." Kyllen grinned at him. "Now get me my money, then lead the way to our accommodations, my hardly esteemed friend."

Chapter Eighteen

AMIRA

Rourke took us upstairs to the lobby of the hotel. Above ground, the place looked a bit more presentable, with red runners on marble floors and crystal chandeliers under the mirrored ceiling.

"You can have the best room we have," he chatted excitedly. "The top floor suite."

The price he named for it made my jaw drop.

Unfazed, Kyllen counted the bills from the thick stack of money he had gotten for his chips downstairs and handed them to the woman at the check-in desk.

She eyed him curiously, sliding the card key his way. "Enjoy your stay."

Rourke snickered. "Yeah. Have fun, you two. I'll see you tomorrow." He slapped Kyllen on the shoulder in a comradely fashion.

Kyllen said nothing, stretching his neck and rolling his shoulder back as if trying to shrug off the sensation of Rourke's touch.

Only when the two of us were in the elevator alone did I release a breath and let the tension drain from my back, neck, and shoulders.

A while back, Radax had arranged for a free rollercoaster ride for me with the carnie who operated it. I screamed my head off during the ride. The sensation of my insides rising to my throat then dropping into the abyss was unforgettable. Tonight reminded me of that very much.

"That was intense," I said. "Worse than a rollercoaster ride."

Kyllen chuckled. "That's the pleasure of gambling, isn't it? The thrill."

Maybe I wasn't cut out for gambling, but it'd been a bit too much excitement for me. I'd been ready to leave from the moment they had brought the money for Kyllen's arm bracer.

Once we reached our floor and exited the elevator, I leaned over to him and lowered my voice. "Just tell me one thing. Did you know you would win at the end?"

He brought his mouth to my ear. "Yes."

"Kyllen!" I recoiled from him, slapping his chest. "I was so stressed. I nearly had a heart attack every time you lost. Don't you ever do this to me again!"

He laughed, catching my hand. "Admit it, you had fun. Maybe just a little bit?"

"Fun? I'm a wreck." My insides hadn't settled yet, and my knees still felt like mush.

He grabbed me into a side hug while I slid the card key, opening the door to our room.

"I'm sorry, my honey cake," he murmured playfully, kissing my hair while dragging me in through the door.

"And don't you 'honey cake' me." I tried to summon some anger or at least annoyance to my voice, but it proved impossible to be cross with him when he cuddled me and purred silly nicknames in my ear.

I knew his using nicknames had been an act, for the sake of the others. Kyllen wanted them to believe we were a couple and had played the part.

It was time to drop the act, now that we were alone.

However, warmth tingled through me from being this close to him. This was the *thrill* I enjoyed. But it came with a chilling tendril of trepidation, too. These feelings were so new, so unfamiliar and overwhelming.

I stepped out of his arms and cast a glance around the room. It was nice, as far as I could tell. I'd been to hotels with Madame to help her unpack or to bring her things when she sent me on errands. I'd never actually stayed in one before.

Dark carpet covered the floor. A set of sliding doors separated the sitting area with a caramel-brown couch from the sleeping area with a bed under a cream-colored bedspread.

I opened the mini-fridge under the counter in the kitchenette area. "Water?"

Kyllen eagerly took the bottle from me and emptied it in a few hungry gulps. Tossing the empty bottle aside, he inspected the room with a nervous energy. He glanced behind the flat-screen TV, opened a closet door, then poked his head into the bedroom.

"Are you looking for something?" I asked, somewhat confused.

He turned to me, propping his hands on his hips. "Isn't a guest-house supposed to have a water feature? Even in this dry, cold world where water is packaged and distributed in miserly amounts?" He tipped his chin at the discarded water bottle.

A water feature?

"You mean like a fountain?" I clarified.

"A fountain, a waterfall, a basin... Something."

"Oh, a bathroom?" I opened a door near the entrance. "There it is."

I flipped the switch on to illuminate a large bathroom with a tub, a sink, and what looked like two toilets.

Kyllen glanced inside over my shoulder.

"The tub is empty," he stated disapprovingly.

"Well, let's fill it, grumpy pants." I headed to the tub and turned the faucet on. Warm water rushed out in a strong stream. "Here you go."

He stood next to me, watching it run. His arms crossed over his chest, he seemed calmer now.

"Are the bathtubs always full back in Nerifir?" I asked.

"I can't speak for all of Nerifir, but in Lorsan, the waterfalls never stop running. They're a part of the wetlands, as are our homes." He bent over to stick his hand under the stream.

"Is it warm enough? I can adjust the temperature."

"No. It's perfect." He unbuckled his belt.

I noticed it had an empty sheath attached to it. The two belts across his chest also had a sheath each on his back. These must've held weapons before. All were empty now, though.

He tossed the belts on the floor, toed off his boots, and yanked his tunic out of his pants.

"Are you joining me?" A teasing smile danced in his voice.

"Me?" I blinked, realizing I'd been watching him undress. "God, no!"

He laughed. "Is it such a repulsive idea to have a bath with me?"

I wasn't sure what exactly I felt at the idea of getting naked in the tub with him, but it was definitely not repulsion.

My face grew hot. My entire body felt too warm under my clothes. I buried my chin into my scarf and mumbled, "No... I'll take a shower after. The towels are right there." I gestured at the rack with a stack of clean towels and dashed for the door. "I need to go. Call me if you need anything...or no, please don't."

I shut the door, blocking the sound of his laughter, then leaned with my back against it.

We were sharing the room tonight. I both liked and disliked his proximity. I loved the feeling that fluttered inside me, heating my chest and belly, but it also unsettled me.

On one hand, being with Kyllen was like having a friend I'd never had. I could joke and laugh with him, feeling closer to him than I'd ever felt to anyone before.

On the other hand, with him around, awkwardness often stifled me and words left me. I had no idea what to say, or what to do, or even where to look.

I envied his confident manner. It wasn't even *his* world, but he behaved more at ease here than I ever could.

Pressing my hands to my chest, I walked over to the large window in the sitting area. Lights illuminated the dark street below. People rushed along the sidewalks. Cars hurried on the road.

I wasn't meant to see this view. Tonight, I was supposed to be finishing my chores then finding yet another place to sleep, only to get up before the sun the next morning and start running on the endless wheel of what used to be my life—every day a mirror copy of the one before.

There had been something comforting about the predictability of the routine. The unknown I was facing now was intimidating. But it was also exciting.

I might not know what tomorrow would bring, but for the first time in my life, I was free to make my own decisions. I'd accomplished something very important today. I'd left the menagerie against Madame's wishes. I'd released her prisoner, too. I had freed both of her VIP acts, Kyllen and Lero.

A long moan came from the bathroom with a splash of water as Kyllen must have submerged himself in the tub. I smiled, wondering how nice a bath must feel to him after months of being cramped in that crate.

I drew in a breath, straightened my shoulders, and unfolded my arms. The world seemed bigger than it had ever been. The life ahead of me was no longer a closed circle but an open road hidden in the mists of the unknown.

It was daunting to embark on this new journey, but I felt ready. And incredibly, I felt strong enough to face whatever lay ahead of me.

Chapter Nineteen

AMIRA

We decided against ordering the room service. Kyllen didn't trust the food from the hotel. Instead, I had sifted through the stack of the paper menus we found in the dresser under the TV. I figured out how to use the hotel phone and ordered our dinner from a nearby restaurant.

I even called the reception desk and asked someone to pick up toothbrushes and other necessities from the gift shop for us.

While waiting for our food order to arrive, I had a quick shower, then brushed my teeth and hair.

When the food came, I felt a ping of pride. We were making it. Kyllen and I were able to provide for ourselves out here in this strange outside world that neither of us knew much about. Just that morning, we'd been a prisoner and a servant. And now, we were free, eating pasta and fruit salad from cardboard containers.

I had the pasta. Kyllen declared it too dry, opting for the fruit instead. In addition to the food, I'd also ordered an entire case of drinking water for him, and he'd made it through a few bottles already.

We ate, sitting on the couch. I folded my bare legs under me, hiding them under the hem of my sweatshirt. It was as long as a dress on me, and I hadn't bothered putting on the pants after my shower.

Kyllen finished his fruit, opened a new bottle of water, then leaned against the sidearm of the couch. "Tell me more about the place where we're going."

He left his belts, boots, and the one remaining bracer back in the bathroom. Wearing only his pants, the long, tunic-like shirt untucked, and his hood, he was barefoot and looked relaxed and refreshed after his bath.

As he tilted his head to take a drink, the edge of his hood lay flat against his face, hiding the upper portion of it from me.

I chased the remaining few pieces of pasta in my container with a plastic fork. "Paris. It's the capital city of France. According to Lero, there is a place called *Parc des Brouillards*, not far from the city. The portal is above the pond there. It only opens for twenty minutes early in the morning."

"Every day?"

"Yes."

"Do you trust Lero?" he asked. "Who is he?"

"He is a werewolf. Madame held him captive, very much like you."

He blew out a breath, looking appalled. "She truly has no shame."

"No, she does not," I agreed. "I'm glad I got the chance to release Lero."

"What if he lied about the portal? For you to set him free?"

I took a moment to consider that. What did I really know about Lero? Not much. My trust came from the heart rather than reason or logic.

"He seemed nice," I said, fully aware of how naïve that sounded. "He gave me the address of his house in Paris and offered me to take as much money as we needed from there."

"So, he isn't a stranger to this world? How long has he been here and how did Madame get her greedy hands on him?"

"I...I don't know." I really knew nothing about Lero, nothing at all. The last piece of pasta proved hard to swallow. It nearly stuck in my throat.

Kyllen put his bottle on the magazine table in front of us and leaned toward me. "Amira. What if it's all a lie? Or worse, a trap?"

That was entirely possible. Only...I just didn't *feel* like Lero would do something like that.

"I have no solid proof he was telling the truth, but I believe he was," I said. "The *bracks* didn't abduct him from Nerifir. He came to this world on his own, so he remembered the location of the portal. He speaks with a French accent, which means *bracks* weren't the first people he met when he first arrived here. Every *brack* I know speaks English. And..." This was probably the silliest of my arguments, but it felt like an important one to me. "He has a woman he protects. That's where he went when I let him go. To her."

Kyllen rubbed his forehead through his hood. At least he didn't laugh at my logic or at my trusting nature.

"Well, we have no other options. We may as well go to Paris and see if the werewolf told you the truth. If he was Ghata's prisoner, chances are he'd be on our side, not on hers." He took a drink from his bottle, then licked his lips. The tip of his tongue came into view. *Two* tips.

I stared, my hand with the fork frozen in the air.

"Can I see?"

"See what?" He sounded confused.

"Your tongue."

Was my demand improper? Impolite? Probably. But curiosity got the best of me.

"You want me to stick my tongue out at you?" he asked flatly.

"Yes, please."

He shook his head, obviously not impressed, but slipped his tongue out between his lips. It descended past his chin. A little longer than a human's, a little narrower, it was still very much the same pink color as mine. But the end of it was split, like a snake's tongue. The two tapered tips moved independently.

"Wow." I dropped my hand with the fork into my lap. Of everything physically different between us, the tongue seemed the most astonishing to me. Maybe because I actually got to see it, unlike his *senties*, for example.

He withdrew his tongue, hiding it behind his lips.

"I don't think I've done that since I was a child," he said disapprovingly, reaching for his water bottle again. "Sticking one's tongue at people is exceptionally bad manners."

"I won't tell anyone," I assured him with a smile. "Here. I'll show you mine if it makes you feel any better."

I stuck my tongue out, wiggling its tip, though it didn't feel nearly as agile compared to his.

He tipped his head back to see the lower part of my face and suddenly choked on his water, coughing. Shoving the bottle aside, he leaned in, catching my chin between his fingers.

I quickly withdrew my tongue and shut my mouth.

He slid his thumb along my bottom lip. "I can't wait to find out everything that little tongue can do."

His voice was rough and low, making his words sound illicit. I sensed he spoke of things that belonged to that mysterious world of sex I knew so little about. I had no idea what role a tongue played in it.

"What do you mean?" I asked, holding my breath.

He exhaled, letting go of my chin, then shifted back, away from me.

"One day…" he said so low, it was unclear if he even meant for me to hear him, but it sounded almost like a promise.

Leaning back against the armrest of the couch, he picked up his water bottle and emptied it. Then, he opened another one and took a long drink.

Only then, he spoke again. "What else did that werewolf say about the portal?"

"The portal?" I scrambled to gather my scattered thoughts. "Oh… He said that when traveling between the worlds, one never lands in the same time or place."

"What?" Kyllen sat up straighter. "What did he mean by that?"

"Once someone leaves a world, either here or Nerifir, they won't come back to the exact same time or location when they return. Except for *bracks*, of course. Madame always drags them back to her, no matter what. You didn't know that?"

His shapely lips pressed into a hard line. "Should I have known?"

"Well, since Lero knew, I thought maybe they taught those things in Nerifir?"

"Maybe they do." He bit his lip. His canines were slightly longer and appeared sharper than those of humans, the points peeking out from under his upper lip.

"Maybe your tutors covered it in one of the many lessons you've skipped?" I suggested. "When you ran away with your friends to climb trees or ride water serpents?"

He looked subdued—a nearly eighty-year-old man, regretting his life choices.

"You should've done better in school, Kyllen," I said, half-teasing.

He blew out a breath, leaning back on the couch. "Well, that... That changes things."

It did, though neither of us could predict exactly how.

He slid his hand under his hood to rub his eyes. "A different place, I'm not so worried about. There're means to travel distances. But a different time... Did Lero tell you what time we could expect to arrive?"

"No. He said it's impossible to predict that. It could be centuries in the past, a month into the future, or the other way around. You can't tell until you get there."

He propped his elbow on the armrest of the couch and leaned his forehead on his hand. His silence concerned me.

"How bad can it be?" I prompted.

"Nerifir is an old world," he said. "Life doesn't change there quickly. We could end up thousands of years in the past, but I wouldn't find it much different."

That was what I figured from the stories he'd told me, but his obvious distress worried me now.

He took a drink from his bottle. A drop rolled down from the corner of his mouth. It skimmed the hard edge of his jaw before being absorbed by the soft material of the ends of his hood wrapped around his neck in a manner similar to my scarf. Normally, Kyllen was exceptionally careful not to waste any water. He must be truly distraught to let the drop get away.

"The main concern is my title." He flexed his jaw. "The window of time when the throne of the High Lord belongs to me by birthright is short. The further away from it I'd go in either direction, the higher are the chances of someone contesting it. Too far in the past, and one of my ancestors would be the High Lord of Ellohi. Too far into the future, and someone new would be on my throne. I may have the right, but the descendants of another bloodline may take over my position by then and would've made it their own."

"Is being the High Lord that important to you?"

He huffed a humorless laugh at that. "Oh yes, it is, my friend. It's my rightful place in my own home. It's my father's legacy." He fisted his right hand, nervously rubbing his fingers with his thumb. "Being the High Lord will also give me the means to support and protect you. You didn't want to come with me before, but you can't go back to Ghata after everything that happened today."

I hadn't told him about my decision to come with him all the way to Nerifir, but he'd assumed correctly.

"No. I can't go back." I'd burned that bridge and had yet to feel any regrets other than Radax... Sharp pain stabbed through my chest at the thought of him. I exhaled slowly, taking a moment to compose myself. "You don't need to worry about me, Kyllen. I don't need much." I shifted closer and touched his knee.

He smiled, covering my hand with his. "Oh, I know, my sweet pea. Only I wish to give you everything you deserve but have been denied in life. You rescued me. You earned my gratitude. I wish to dress you in the most beautiful ball gowns, decorate you with the finest jewels of Ellohi Court, and feed you the most delicious food Lorsan has to offer."

I didn't need any of that, but I enjoyed every drop of affection he spoke with.

"As a High Lord," he continued, his voice filled with strength. "I'd also have the power to annihilate anyone who'd even *think* about harming you. No one would dare so much as to raise their voice at you."

That was fierce.

"When you say I'll be safe, you really mean it, don't you?"

A corner of his mouth rose higher in a self-assured smile. "Why do things half-way?"

I stroked the top of his hand. His patterned skin felt much more supple after his bath.

"All I want is to be free, Kyllen."

His smile dimmed somewhat. "That's another reason I need to be the High Lord. Freedom is not guaranteed in Nerifir. One has to have the power to defend it."

I bit my lip, knitting my brows into a frown. Both Radax and Lero had spoken of Nerifir as a dangerous place. Even from Kyllen's stories, I'd gathered that deceit, rivalry, and wars were a part of life there just as beauty and magic. But I was prepared to deal with all of that.

He leaned closer, squeezing my hand in his. "More than anything, I want you to have a choice, Amira. Here is the one I can give you—you can stay here—"

I couldn't believe his words. Staying was not what I escaped the menagerie for. What I'd hurt Radax for...

I sucked in a breath, ready to argue, but he raised his hand, stopping me.

"You won't go back to Ghata, Amira. Never. But you can stay here, in this world. I'll be with you for as long as it takes for you to settle. We have some money, but I'll get you more—much, much more. You'll choose a house you like, anywhere in this world, wherever you feel free, safe, and happy. I'll make sure you'll never have to worry about Ghata ever again."

"And then what?" I asked. "Then, you'll leave?"

His chest rose as he inhaled deeply. "I can't stay here forever. Lorsan is my world. I'll have to go back and either take my rightful place or carve out a new one for myself."

The idea of separation cut like a knife. I shifted closer to him, fitting my knees between his.

"But couldn't you stay here instead? For good? We could choose our new home together. I heard Italy is nice. The pasta may be too dry for you, but they have lots of fruit. And wine. Do you drink wine?"

He smiled, but shook his head. "It's not about the wine—"

"I know, I know," I stopped him, desperately trying to convince him. "We can get a house big enough for two. You'll tell me goodnight stories. And I'll cook for you the wettest, moistest meals possible. Soups! I'll make the best soups ever for you."

I'd refused Radax's idea of protecting me outside of the menagerie because I knew that as a *brack,* he couldn't defy Madame. She would've found and killed us both.

But with Kyllen… She had no control over him. Maybe we had a chance? Only we needed to stay together. I didn't want to be alone, no matter how wonderful or safe a house we'd find. I didn't wish to part from him.

He slid his hands up my arms. "This world is not for me, Amira. I'll never feel happy here. I can't even get comfortable enough in it."

"Well, this is England. Some say it's one of the gloomiest parts of our world. And it's end of January, the coldest time of the year. But there are other places. Warmer, sunnier… We can live on the ocean somewhere, where it's more humid, too."

He shook his head, and I fisted my hands, fighting tears that threatened to overcome me. My head bowed, I stared at his chest, wishing I could look straight into his eyes. I would give anything just to be able to see his face.

"In this world," he said somberly. "I would never be able to take this hood off without risking killing innocent people. Don't you understand, Amira? I may no longer be locked in a crate, but I can never be truly free here."

The desire to be free, I understood way too well. He was right. If he stayed here, he'd be forced to spend his days wearing the hood. Going through life by peeking at the world from under it, constantly afraid of inadvertently killing people, hiding from them as a result—I couldn't force this life on him.

"Then take me with you," I breathed out. "Like you said you would."

His shoulders dropped.

"That was what I fully intended to do. But it'd be selfish of me. I can see it now. I don't know where I'd be taking you, Amira. Depending on *when* I'll end up landing, I may have no home, no place to stay, and no means to live."

"How would *you* survive, then?"

"I'm a gorgonian. Lorsan is my home. I'm also young, strong, and have some useful skills. No matter what, I'll find a way to make a living. I'm good with a sword and can become a mercenary. With the twenty-four self-centered High Lords in the Kingdom, there's always a conflict going on somewhere. I can join an army and wrap my name in glory, like I dreamed when I was a little boy."

A smile returned to his lips. His voice flowed, smooth and comforting, just as when he had been telling me one of his stories. Only this one could be real one day.

"I have skills too." I lifted my chin. That was true. I didn't spend my twenty-somewhat years for nothing. I'd learned quite a bit in my life. "I can cook, clean, take care of animals. I can drive... Well, you have no cars in Nerifir."

He curled his lip, directing a wave of a hand at the window facing the street. "Those smelly things? No, thank all gods, we don't have cars. Why would we turn our beautiful Wetlands into the hideous gray-stone nightmare that is this world?"

"Right. Well, but I also sew fairly well and can style hair beautifully. I've been serving a goddess all my life. I could certainly take care of a High Lady or a princess, or whoever else you happen to have in Lorsan. And..." I tilted my head for emphasis. "You know, I'll be able to deal with the moodiest, most temperamental women your world may have."

"I don't doubt you would," he said with a faint smile. There was pride in his voice, which made me feel warm all over. "You have enough grace and patience to rule a kingdom. But what if I have to leave you for months, maybe even years, to go to whatever war the king decides to wage?"

"Then I'll be waiting for you. And I'll make sure I have the best soup ever ready for when you come back."

He kept silent, a ghost of a smile playing on his lips.

Plucking at the soft material of his tunic over his chest, I twisted it in my fingers, worrying I failed to convince him, that he might be searching in his mind for the best way to leave me behind after all.

I had to try harder.

"You may end up in a time when no one knows you yet, Kyllen, or when no one remembers you anymore. You may be left completely alone in your own world. But if you take me with you, you'll always have a friend—someone who knows your story and shares some of your history. Because we have gone through things together, things that have brought us closer, haven't they?"

"Oh, my sweet Amira." He slid his hands up my arms again. "It's the noble part of me that's trying so hard to do the right thing and save you the uncertainty I'll be facing in Nerifir. The selfish and admittedly much larger part of me has long since decided to keep you. I like having you around, and I'm not used to denying myself what I enjoy."

I perked up with relief. "So, you want me to come along?"

"Is that what *you* want?" he asked slowly, adding weight to his question.

I might not always be sure about things in life, but I was certain about this one. "Yes."

"Chances are you'd be the only human in the whole of Lorsan," he warned.

That didn't bother me. Even with other humans around, I'd always felt the odd one out. "Not much different from the menagerie then, is it? I was the only human there, too."

He remained serious. "Do you have any questions about the world of Lorsan? Is there anything you want to know?"

My mind was reeling from convincing him. I couldn't gather my thoughts to come up with questions yet.

"You've told me so much about Lorsan. Sometimes I feel like I've been there already."

"Well, it's nice, warm, and humid, unlike this world." He scoffed with a shudder.

Weather was the least of my concerns.

"Just promise me one thing, Kyllen."

"Anything you want, my dear."

"Promise me that no matter what happens, we'll always be friends. Promise me, I can always trust you."

His hands on my shoulders, he brought his mouth to my ear.

"Staying *just* friends is not in my intentions, sweet pea." His voice gained that dangerously seductive note again, sending a charge of heat through my body in response. "So, I can't promise you that. But I will make you a promise."

He took my face in his hands, leaning so close, the edge of his hood skimmed the tip of my nose. His warm breath fanned along my skin, tickling my lips.

"I promise that no matter where I am or what I do, there will always be a place for you beside me. For as long as I live, I'll do everything in my power for you to have a roof over your head and food on your table. And should I die before you, you'll have the right to everything I own for the rest of your life." As he spoke, his voice hardened, gaining a gravity that sent chills down my spine. "May I spend the rest of my days impaled on a pole in the Garden of the Cursed if I break this promise."

Grave silence descended over us after the sound of his last words died. A feeling that we weren't alone came with it. The presence of something grand but dangerous swirled around us. Goosebumps prickled the skin of my arms.

"What happened?" I half-whispered. Speaking out loud suddenly felt like blasphemy. "Why does it feel so...intense?"

Still holding my face between his hands, he slid his thumbs along my cheekbones. "A fae cannot break a promise. I've just bound myself to you for life. That would be *intense* in terms of commitment, don't you think?"

The ominous feeling had finally lifted. With it, whatever had been present in the room had dissipated, too.

"So," I said in a lighter tone, trying to shake off the remnants of unease. "Does it mean you're planning to stick around then?"

"From now on, I really don't have a choice." A corner of his mouth curled up in a half-grin. "No one wants to die as a promise breaker, trust me on that." He shifted his hands higher, sinking his fingers into my hair. "Close your eyes," he suddenly demanded.

"Why?"

"I want to take my hood off. I need to see more of you than I can with it on."

Placing a hand over my eyes, he yanked his hood off with the other. He said nothing, but I sensed him staring at me, and I kept still.

The silence grew too long for me to handle, though. "What do you see, Kyllen?" I asked.

He placed the other hand on the side of my face, then slid both palms up, his thumbs over my eyelids to keep them closed.

"Can you smile for me, Amira? Please?"

He asked so sweetly, the smile that sprung to my lips was genuine.

"I've never heard you laugh." He sounded contemplative. "I waited to hear it when locked up in that crate. I tried to make you laugh, but you never did."

I didn't remember the last time I laughed. "I...I don't really do that."

"I think I shall add another part to my promise, then. I will make you laugh one day, even if that'd be the last thing I'd do."

Smiling wide, I parted my lips to reply, but didn't get a chance. Kyllen's scent moved closer. The air around me shifted, heating up with the warmth of his body. Then his lips touched mine.

He was kissing me!

I froze, unable to draw a breath. My body stiffened, even as my soul soared.

He angled my head a little, his lips moving faster, eagerly. Surely, he'd sense I had no idea how to kiss him back. I had to stop this before I embarrassed myself. But I didn't want this kiss to end. I didn't think I could move. Yet somehow my hands ended up fisting into his tunic, pulling him closer.

Something hot pulsed inside my chest. Maybe it was my heart exploding? Because it certainly felt like I'd died and was floating somewhere where there were no walls or ceiling, no top or bottom, just Kyllen's hands cupping my face and his mouth devouring mine.

His fingers held me firmly in place, his thumbs over my eyes. But then I felt another touch. Lots of touches. A dozen of...*fingers* stroked my hair, brushed the skin of my face, slid under my scarf to caress my neck...

I jerked my head back, gasping for air.

Kyllen leaned after me, refusing to let go.

Releasing his shirt, I propped my hands on the couch behind me.

"Kyllen..." I panted. "What was that? I need to see..."

His forehead pressed to mine, he rasped, "Just... Just give me a moment."

With a deep breath, he covered my eyes with one hand and used the other one to pull his hood back on. "You can't *see*, my sweet girl. I won't risk it."

He slid his hand from my eyes, then brushed with his thumb along my bottom lip. It felt hot and swollen after his kiss.

I pressed a finger to my lips. "So that's how it feels to be kissed."

For so long I had wondered, and now I knew. It turned out to be everything I'd ever thought it would be, and so much more. My heart was still racing, sending fireworks through my body.

"Amira." Kyllen sounded oddly guarded. "Was it your first kiss?"

Oh, no. Had it been obvious I had no idea what I was doing? Heat rushed to my cheeks.

Letting go of me, he slumped back against the couch, muttering, "Great Serpent, help me."

I twisted a corner of my scarf into a tight rope in my fingers. "Did I do something wrong?"

"You didn't..." Kyllen hesitated, which was unusual for him. Running a thumb along his jawline, he tilted his head. "You haven't been with a man, have you?"

"No. There are no men other than the *bracks* at the menagerie. You know that."

He got up from the couch. Sliding his hands inside his hood, he rubbed the back of his neck while taking a few random steps back and forth. He looked unsettled...no, outright distraught.

"Kyllen. What's wrong?"

He stopped abruptly, then sank to his knees in front of me. Clasping his hands together, he dropped them into my lap.

"You're right," he said, looking down as if talking to his hands. "I should've known. I just never really stopped to think about it. There are men *outside* of the menagerie. One or two of them could've been appealing enough for you to—"

"Kyllen, I'm sorry, but what on earth are you talking about? No, there haven't been any men for me—appealing or otherwise. You are the first one who has ever kissed me. And now—" I leaned forward and enclosed him into a hug, then quickly released him. "There, now you're the only man I've ever hugged, other than Radax. When it comes to men, everything is for the first time for me." I put my hands on his shoulders. "Do you think it's a problem?"

I liked him. Very much. But if my inexperience bothered him, there was nothing I could do about it.

He lifted his head, enough for me to see his mouth. "I'll tell you what it is. I'm seventy-eight years old—"

"You look good for your age," I quipped, making him smile, which was the point.

"I've had many...encounters. Fae, in general, are pleasure-loving creatures. We don't run away from it. I certainly never have."

"I wouldn't expect you to." I held no illusions. Kyllen had lived in this world three times longer than I, and he'd be alive for centuries after I was gone. He didn't pledge me his heart, just his care and protection. "I'm not asking you for anything more than what you've already given me. All I want is a friend I can trust."

"Oh, but you see, I most definitely want more than just a friend in you. Sooner or later, I'll want more than just a kiss, too."

My lips still tingled from his last kiss, but I already wouldn't mind having another one. I was definitely not opposed to "more," whatever he meant by that.

"Why is that a bad thing?" I asked softly, hoping that with his hood on, he wouldn't notice my fervent blushing.

"Bad? No... I..." Kyllen obviously struggled for words, which I couldn't recall him ever doing before. "Listen. Virginity is not something my people keep for long. There is no reason to hold on to it. I lost mine to one of my mother's ladies-in-waiting. I was in my teens, and she was...well, older than me. After her, there were many others. The people at my father's court love to party and...well, to fuck. I've never been with a virgin. I don't think I've even seen one of age. I certainly have never been anyone's first kiss, or first touch, or first anything. There had always been lots of others before me."

"And? Why is it such a big deal for you to be *my* first?"

"Because I don't know what to do!" He threw his hands up in the air dramatically. "It feels like a huge responsibility. What if I mess it up for you?"

I laughed.

The problem wasn't me, it was him. Kyllen had finally encountered something that knocked him off balance and shook his confidence.

"Then there's something new in it for both of us," I said.

Frankly, it was a relief to see him like this. He had his own insecurities to deal with, which in a way made us equal.

I hugged his wide shoulders and gave him a peck on the cheek. He rested his head on my shoulder.

"At least I finally made you laugh," he mumbled.

I couldn't help another burst of laughter. "That you did."

Chapter Twenty

KYLLEN

Amira hid a yawn while cleaning the small table after their dinner. They'd had a long day, and she obviously was exhausted.

It's been tiring for him too. This new world proved overwhelming with its incessant noise, cold air, and foreign smells. The vehicles here, not powered by magic, produced stench and deafening rattle. Everything was generally loud and obnoxious, including people. Only the colors remained boring and dull.

"Time to get some rest." He headed to the bedroom area.

Apparently, humans slept in beds—a rectangular one stood in the middle of the sleeping area. This wasn't entirely unfamiliar to him. Highborn werewolves in Sarnala lived in castles, constructed from rock and mortar similar to the human dwellings in this city, and slept in raised rectangular beds.

The bed was large enough for both of them to have a restful night. Amira remained standing by the couch, however.

"Is something wrong?" He paused.

"You go ahead." She waved him off. "I'll be fine here, on the floor...

or the couch."

Well, that wouldn't do.

He sat on the foot of the bed, staring at her through the open doors. Without seeing her face, understanding her was difficult at times. "I'm afraid I need an explanation, sweet pea. Is it the bed or the idea of sharing it with me that repulses you?"

"I'm not repulsed... I'm just." She wrung her hands, obviously distressed, which disturbed him greatly.

He wished to grab her into a hug and make whatever was upsetting her go away. Except that grabbing her might not be the best course of action in this situation. He risked distressing her even more, he feared.

"I don't sleep in beds," she said.

"Oh, I know very well how you sleep, dearest." He got up and sauntered her way. "You spend a night next to me, while I tell you a story. Every now and then, I pause to make sure you're still listening, and you ask me, 'And then what?' So I continue telling it to you until eventually all I hear is your deep breathing when you finally fall asleep."

He came close enough for their toes on the carpet to touch, then lifted his head to see all of her up to her nose. She was biting her lip. When he touched her hand, however, she didn't take it away.

"Tonight doesn't need to be any different from all those other nights we've spent side by side, Amira." He tilted his head. "Please don't tell me you prefer I were in a crate."

"No. No, I don't want the crate," she protested passionately. "It's just the bed... And the covers. I don't use bedding. I need to keep my clothes on..." She reached for her shapeless pants on the chair.

"Who says you can't keep them on?" He took the pants and handed them to her.

He would've loved to have her naked. The idea of her sleeping next to him without the wooden wall of the crate between them tickled his chest with excitement. To his delight, the sensation spread lower than his chest, too, this time.

A faint spark of lust had finally flickered low in his belly when he'd kissed her. It now glowed stronger, making his cock twitch. He finally felt hydrated enough to be fully a man, once again.

But tonight was not about his lust. He wished for Amira to feel comfortable around him just as she used to be when he sat in that stupid crate. And he was willing to wait as long as it took.

She taught him patience, something no one had ever been able to do before.

Amira clutched her pants to her chest.

"Come." He led her to the bed. "Sleep dressed. On top of the covers, if you wish. I'll definitely get under. It'd be too cold for me otherwise."

She plopped down to sit on the bed. Keeping her head down, she quickly pulled on her pants and socks.

He sat beside her and bounced on the mattress a couple of times, testing its softness.

"This bed isn't that comfy, anyway," he complained. "Honestly, it's probably not much different from the pile of rags you used to sleep on."

A smile touched her lips. She placed a hand on the mattress between them. "It's softer than anything I've ever slept on before."

"Great." He grabbed her legs and turned her, putting her feet on the mattress.

She squeaked, hugging her knees.

"There you go." He crossed his arms over his chest, admiring the sight of her in his bed. "It's not so bad, is it?"

She shifted, drawing her knees closer to her chest. "It's alright." She sounded calmer now, her posture more relaxed, which pleased him.

He realized he cared about this woman enough for his enemies to use her as a weapon against him. If Ghata sent her *bracks* after them, his biggest worry was them catching Amira. Because there was little he wouldn't do for her freedom and happiness.

Of course, he remained the biggest threat to her himself.

"Can I have your scarf, please?" he asked.

"What do you need it for?"

"I'll have to tie your eyes closed, just in case."

He knew nightmares frequented her. He'd heard her sobbing and whimpering in her sleep before. She'd wake up abruptly with a gasp, then would toss and turn afterwards, sometimes for hours. Her sleeping fully dressed, he guessed, wasn't just about modesty. She had no home to feel safe, no place to belong. Her clothes had become both her safety shield and her comfort blanket.

Like a pea had her pod, Amira had her layers of baggy shirts and her scarf to hide from all horrors real and imaginable.

"My hood may not stay on when I'm asleep," he explained. "If we both wake in the middle of the night, I want to make sure we don't accidentally look at each other."

"Oh, okay." She unwound one end of the scarf from around her neck.

Taking it from her, he tied it over her eyes, leaving the rest of the scarf around her neck the way she usually wore it.

"That's better." He yanked his hood off, unfurling and stretching his *senties*. Keeping them curled in a knot at all times had been unnatural and straining.

Amira remained in the sitting position. She was a picture to behold —her head tilted back, her pink lips slightly parted, her eyes tied. Blindfolded, she was completely at his mercy.

Her trust in him floored him. In his world, trust often was a currency, never given freely. He hadn't met anyone who trusted as easily as Amira.

Yet instead of taking advantage of that, he felt fiercely protective of her. A woman like her would need a strong protector in a place like Lorsan. More than anything, he wished to be worthy of her trust.

Her lips practically begged for a kiss. He pondered stealing one, sensing she wouldn't object. But he wasn't lying when he'd said he had no idea what he was doing with someone as inexperienced as her.

For him, making love was as natural as breathing. And until now, he'd always been on even ground with his partners. Sex was like a dance. Someone might lead, but in each of his encounters, the other side always followed confidently through every step.

What happened when one of the partners didn't know the steps? In dance, there'd be stumbling, stepping on each other's toes, tripping over feet, and finally falling into a tumble.

He didn't want to fall with Amira. With her, he wished to soar. But how could she tell him what she wanted from a man when she'd never been with one before?

So, he kissed her forehead and guided her down to the pillow, fully dressed as she was. He didn't force the blankets on her. Maybe she found the covers restrictive. Maybe they made her feel trapped. Whatever it was, he let her be.

"Kyllen," she said. "Would I have to keep my eyes closed at all times in Lorsan?"

"At the beginning, yes. But not forever." He couldn't force her to spend her life blindfolded. "There are means for you to see us."

"Like mirrors?"

"No. Something better. I'll get it for you right after I've made sure we have enough food and a reliable shelter." He went to his side of the bed and sat down.

He selfishly wished to keep her, no matter what. But he had to be honest with her. She needed to be fully informed to make her own decisions. She had to know what to expect.

"It will be a veil, Amira," he confessed.

"What do you mean?" She turned to face him, even as she couldn't see him.

"A veil made from spider silk from the Sky Kingdom. Our best artisans weave their magic into it to allow others to see us unharmed. Veils are used mostly by merchants and foreign dignitaries." He stripped out of his clothes, then climbed under the covers. "It will be a veil. You'll have to wear it day and night until the day you die."

He wanted to keep her, but he couldn't trick her into the life she might resent.

"I could never take it off?" she asked. "Not even when I'm alone?"

"Even when you think you're alone, you may not be. Someone may glance at you through a door or a window. A small mistake can cost you your life. As long as you remain in Lorsan, it'll never be completely safe for you to remove it."

She rose on her elbow propped on the pillow. "Well, then I'll wear a veil."

He shifted closer to her, for warmth more than anything else at that point. The bedding was chilly—dry and cold like the rest of this world.

"Are you sure you can do it? You'll see the world through the fine mesh of silk at all times."

A smile ghosted her lips as she lay back on the pillow. "I've been watching life pass me by from the dusty canvas of Madame's tents. A silk veil would be an improvement, don't you think? I can live with it, as long as I'm free."

She reached over the covers for him, and he met her hand half-way, lacing his fingers with hers. They stayed like that for a few minutes. She didn't appear asleep, and he wondered what she was thinking about.

"Kyllen?" Her voice was small, barely audible, and filled with so much hurt, it alarmed him. "How long does it usually take for a *brack* to...wake up?"

She was worried about the *brack* she had shot. She said he was something like a family to her, as if a *brack* with no mind of his own could be a family to anyone. Loneliness could facilitate the weirdest of attachments, it seemed.

"He'll be fine," he assured her, then added, sensing she needed more than that, "He won't remember anything from the time he was 'dead.' It's like being in a deep sleep. He may have a headache for a while after. But that's all."

Gorgonians couldn't drown, but they reached a near dead state when left under water for a prolonged period. He'd been trapped on the bottom of a river once and knew exactly how that felt.

"He will forget me." Her voice trembled, and he tightened his fingers around her hand.

The *brack* most definitely would forget her. It was a miracle he'd felt in any way partial to her to begin with. But Kyllen had to console her.

"Isn't it better that way?" he asked. "Isn't it better for him to forget than to miss someone he'll never see again?"

She heaved a long, heavy sigh. "I suppose it is better. For him."

He stroked her knuckles with his thumb as she went quiet again. After a while, her breathing evened out.

His eyelids dropped closed, too.

"Are you too tired to tell me a story, Kyllen?" she asked, making him open his eyes again.

He stifled a yawn. "Maybe a short one? What do you want me to tell you about?"

"I want to know more about that woman. The lady-in-waiting who took your virginity."

"Um..." The request rendered him speechless. That encounter

happened too long ago and obviously hadn't been that impressive since he didn't remember much. "Why? What do you want to know about her?"

"Did you love her?"

"What? No." He shifted uneasily, the stiff sheets chafing against his skin uncomfortably. "Listen, how about a nice funny story about me learning to shoot a bow instead?"

She yawned, covering her mouth with her hand.

"Okay," she agreed, thankfully not insisting on a "love story" from him. "Can you shoot a bow?"

"I can if I have to, but it's not my favorite choice of weapon. Let me tell you why."

They both were tired and needed some rest. It had to be a very short story. Thankfully, it wouldn't take him long to tell her how he had accidentally shot his very snotty aunt in her backside. The woman had so many skirts on, the arrowhead had never even pierced through them all. That didn't stop his father from punishing Kyllen by locking him in his room for two days straight, which would've been a real torture had he not climbed out of his window the minute the door had been locked.

"Under one condition," he warned.

"What condition?" She sounded so adorably sleepy.

"You'll have to cuddle with me," he said and added quickly, "For warmth. It's freezing in here and, you know—"

She chuckled, not letting him finish, and lifted her arm in an inviting gesture. "Come here, Kyllen."

He hugged her, and she snuggled into his chest, their arms around each other. He under the covers. She on top of them. He in the nude. She fully clothed.

And he already knew this night was about to beat his old record for his best night in this world.

KYLLEN

He woke up but kept his eyes closed. Amira lay next to him, his arms around her.

The throbbing pressure between his legs announced a morning erection—something he hadn't experienced for a while. He obviously had drunk enough water last night for this to happen. Taking a bath had certainly helped, too. He shifted his hips, but the rubbing against the cover only made it worse.

He carefully extended one *sentie* all the way to the headboard, then made it open its eyes.

A *sentie's* field of vision was small. Using just one of them was like illuminating the room with a flashlight instead of turning on the overhead light. But it was enough for him to see that Amira's scarf was still firmly tied around her head, keeping her eyes closed. He rose on his elbow and studied her.

Even with that gray scarf hiding a big portion of her face, she was beautiful. She had no idea how gorgeous she was, and that might be a big portion of her appeal. She was genuine, someone he would've never encountered at his father's court.

She stirred. "Kyllen?"

"Hm," he hummed softly.

"You're staring at me, aren't you? I can hear your breathing right over my face." She grinned, and he couldn't control himself.

He leaned closer and kissed her lips. Self-control had never been one of his strongest qualities. And around her, it had been tested greatly.

She met his kiss with a soft gasp, but didn't slap him or pull away.

His *senties* trembled with his eagerness to put them on her, but he held back, remembering how she'd reacted when he'd let them touch her before.

Amira ran her hands up his arms to his shoulders. She cupped his nape, then trailed her fingers to the back of his head. Her hands brushed by the base of several *senties*, sending a jolt of arousal to his groin. And he couldn't hold back anymore. He let his *senties* loose.

They sank into her hair, filling his senses with its fragrance and the sensation of its silky texture. He coiled the *senties* around her fingers and hands, tasting her skin. He slid one along her check and inside her scarf, gliding the tip along the warm, delicate skin of her neck. The scent of her was the strongest there, and he savored every tendril.

She let go of his head, and he broke the kiss, afraid he'd startled her.

But she didn't move away. Her lips still parted and glistening after his kiss, she trailed her fingers down one of his *senties*, spreading pleasurable shivers along his skin. He stifled a moan.

"Is that what you're hiding under your hood?" Her voice held no fear or repulsion, just curiosity. She was a curious little thing.

"*Senties*," he explained. "That's one of the twenty-four I have."

She coiled it around her wrist, her fingers stroking another one. It was the most sensual thing, Amira playing with his *senties*. He moaned again, this time openly.

"Does it feel good?" she asked.

"Very much so." He thrust his hips her way. He was so hard, it surely could be felt through the covers.

"Oh." She let go of his *senties*, freeing her wrist. "Sorry... I didn't know."

Great Serpent, he didn't want her to let go. He wanted her to keep toying with his *senties*, to let him explore her body with them, inside and out. But she had already moved away and was now getting out of bed, holding on to the wall to guide her in her blindness.

"Wait." He leaped out of bed, too, then tossed his tunic on over his head and donned his hood. "You can open your eyes now. It's safe." He neatly coiled his *senties* inside the hood, forcing them to calm down.

"Okay." She took the scarf from around her head and stood on the other side of the bed, facing him. "Oh." She cleared her throat, and he realized she must be staring at his crotch.

The tent he had going on there was probably big enough to house Ghata's entire menagerie. There was nothing to do about it but to stuff it into his pants, which he did, his erection, the tunic, and all.

Amira got busy by making the bed. "We should be going. It's not a good idea to stay in the same place for too long when the *bracks* are surely after us."

She made a good point. Not that he planned to linger in this hotel, anyway.

"We can get breakfast in the city," she said. "Then figure out the best way to get to France."

He looked longingly at the bathroom door. It had felt divine submerging his entire body into a tub of water last night. He wished he could do it again, instead of facing the biting winds outside. But Amira was right. The sooner they started on their way, the quicker they'd reach their destination. The baths in Lorsan were by far superior to anything this world had to offer, anyway.

"You're not planning to gamble today, are you?" Amira asked quietly when they left their room.

"No. We have enough money. Right?" He had a stack of the paper money stuffed in each of his boots. Amira hid the rest in the pockets of her sweatshirt that seemed bottomless. "Besides, I don't think they would let me play roulette again, and I can't manipulate card games for a sure win."

"Then we probably should sneak down the stairs instead of taking the elevator."

He heard concern in her voice, and fear. She was afraid of the pathetic human men who tried to con him last night. Of course, they'd be disappointed that he deprived them of a chance to weasel his money from him. There was a chance they would try to stop him from leaving the premises.

Not that he cared. But Amira was worried.

"All right. Let's take the stairs." He let her lead him to a set of stairs, then down to the same door they had entered through with Rourke last night.

When he placed his hand on the handle of the door to the alley, another door opened down the hallway.

"Hey, mate, leaving already?" Rourke hurried their way. He wasn't alone. Three equally sketchy individuals flanked him on both sides. "Didn't you promise to play cards with us today?"

Promise was a strong word. He didn't make promises lightly because for a fae the penalty for breaking them was too great. He never really made a promise to Rourke. He might have misled him into believing he was going to give him a chance to get his winnings back, but he certainly had no intentions of doing so.

"I lied," he said simply.

Rourke spat onto the floor. "Well, that wasn't very nice of you, was it?"

Kyllen shrugged, not dignifying the man with a verbal answer.

"I guess we'll have to get our money back another way, then." Rourke tipped his chin at his accomplices, and they moved onto Kyllen and Amira. "In addition to the cash, I'll take that other cuff of yours." Rourke smirked. "As a compensation for my disappointment." He guffawed.

Kyllen cringed at the sound, then punched the first man lunging his way.

The man flew back a few paces, hitting the wall with force. Kyllen hadn't held back his strength. Why would he? He was too irritated to play nice. It was their fault—annoying him before he'd even had breakfast.

"Shit." Rourke gaped at his friend sprawled on the floor. Tossing the side of his leather coat back, the human yanked a knife from his pocket.

Another one snuck up behind Amira.

"Do as Rourke said!" the human yelled, grabbing her. "Or she'll pay."

Amira gasped in horror. The man gripped her throat, cutting off all sound from her. His other arm seized her around her middle, pressing both her arms to her torso.

Kyllen's annoyance sparked into white-hot rage. The low-life dared putting his hands on what belonged to him.

The human deserved to die.

"Close your eyes, Amira," he gritted through his teeth. "Keep them closed, no matter what you hear."

She squeaked a strangled sound in agreement and shut her eyes.

He yanked his hood off.

But he didn't just want to kill the scum. He wished to terrify the life out of them.

He spread his *senties* in a wide halo around his head—wild and undulating. Tipping his head down, he glared at the one holding Amira. Jerking his *senties*, he directed their eyes, all forty-eight of them, at the offender, too.

Fifty deadly, golden gorgonian eyes stared directly into the human two. Color bled out of the man's irises, pale blue replaced by granite-gray. The gray spread, leaching into his skin, hair, and clothes. A living, breathing person fully became dead stone less than a second after meeting Kyllen's eyes.

Slowly, he moved his lethal gaze over to Rourke next.

"What the—" The words froze on Rourke's lips as his tongue solidified into rock.

"Hey—" Another one.

"Ugh—" And another.

One by one, all four of them were dead. None had run. People usually ran from danger *after* taking at least a glance at what the danger was. And a glance was all that Kyllen needed.

Anger still coursed through him. Throwing punches might've released some of it. Killing with a look wasn't nearly as satisfying. But they had dared to threaten Amira. He had to deal with them quickly.

"Amira?" He coiled his *senties* quickly and pulled his hood back on.

She was locked in the unbending arms of the statue. Her eyes shut so tight, the skin around them crinkled and paled from strain.

"Good girl," he thought fondly.

"Keep your eyes closed, my sweet pea." He made his voice sound soft and soothing, coming closer.

The cold, gray fingers of the statue tightly gripped her throat. She could barely swallow against them.

He broke them off one by one, wishing the human was still alive and could feel each of his digits breaking.

"*How dare he?*" Kyllen seethed inside. *"How dare this pathetic excuse of a man touch her delicate neck?"*

"Thank you..." She gasped for air the moment he freed her throat.

He ripped the entire hand off, then broke the arm that held her around the middle.

"Amira..." He yanked her to him.

In a flare of anger, he kicked what remained of the human who'd trapped her. The statue crashed to the floor, exploding into dust and pieces on impact. The stone might look like granite, but it was more brittle than most rocks found in nature. Flesh didn't make for a solid material, even when it hardened to rock.

Amira was breathing rapidly, sucking in air in quick, shallow gasps. Her heart thundered against his chest pressed to hers.

"Are they...gone?" she panted.

He kissed her hair above her temple. "Yes. You can open your eyes now."

Keeping one arm around her shoulders, he led her between the bodies of men frozen in death. She clung to him, hiding her face in his sleeve.

Brutally cold wind greeted them outside, rushing through the thin material of his tunic. A violent shiver ran through his body.

"There must be a place in this city where they sell coats," he muttered under his breath.

"Do you want to go shopping?" Amira's voice trembled a little.

"What use is money if you can't spend it?" He hugged her closer.

For one, holding her kept them both a little warmer.

And two, he'd promised her a place at his side, and he was beginning to think that was exactly where she belonged.

AMIRA

I asked the taxi driver for a place to have breakfast and for a clothing store. He took us to Oxford Street, promising us both. On the way, I asked him a few questions about the best way to get to Paris, and he helpfully listed the options from a plane, to the train, to the ferry.

The clothing stores turned out to be still closed. So we decided to have breakfast in a small café, waiting for them to open.

The waitress threw a curious glance at Kyllen, pausing at his hood.

"He can't...um, look, you know," I muttered an excuse for him. It wasn't a lie. Kyllen couldn't look at her. If he did, she'd be dead.

Compassion warmed her kind face. "Oh, I see." She nodded, leading us to our table. "Would you like a menu in Braille?" She clearly assumed he was blind.

"Oh no. Thank you. I'll just order for him."

When she brought us our drinks a little while later—a coffee for me and a teapot with a cup for Kyllen—I asked her a few questions about the transportation, too. Since I had no phone or Internet access, I used helpful strangers to get information. Thankfully, the world was full of kind people ready to help. The café wasn't overly busy, and the woman seemed happy to chat.

When she left, I leaned across the table to Kyllen, "I think a train or a ferry would be better than a plane, but there are complications with either."

"Like what? What are the complications?"

"Well, we're crossing the border to another country. They'll be asking us for IDs, passports, some kind of travel papers." I had none. Madame never had issues transporting her establishment to any country she wished, including me. I suspected she used magic for that.

"A plane is a flying machine?" he asked.

I nodded.

"Then I suggest we take a train." Kyllen didn't sound overly concerned. He sipped his tea, both hands wrapped around the cup for warmth. We had to get him some winter clothes the moment the stores opened. The poor man was clearly freezing.

"Why the train?"

"Because if I manipulate a train's engine, I don't risk plunging it out of the sky like a plane or sinking it like a ferry." That was a very convincing argument in favor of the train.

"I'm worried we may not even get onboard for you to manipulate anything at all."

"Why is that? We have enough money to buy the tickets, don't we?"

We certainly did. The issue wasn't the money but the lack of documents.

"They check the passengers' travel papers, I believe. Passports and such. They do that when people cross the border of another country."

"How do they check?"

"I'm not sure how, but I don't think you can manipulate anything in that process. It's not as simple as the roulette wheel."

"Why not?" He raised his chin in challenge. "As long as there's any kind of mechanism involved, I can make it work the way that suits me."

"Most of the devices used nowadays are electronic, not mechanical. They operate by sending electrical signals, not by springs and levers."

He set his cup down and leaned back slowly, spreading his shoulders wide. He looked as if I'd just personally offended him, and he was about to launch a defense.

"Look, I didn't—" I started to explain, but he didn't let me.

"Give me an example of an electronic device."

"Well..." I looked around the room. "The two girls at the table by the window over there." He turned in that direction, following my gesture at the two teenagers with cell phones. "They're using smartphones, which are electronic." I knew very little about the actual workings of a smartphone. I never owned one myself. Neither did I know much about the differences between mechanics and electronics. But I knew they weren't the same.

Kyllen turned his head, sweeping the café with a gaze from under his hood.

"How about that thing?" He tipped his chin at the machine the waitress handed to a customer to process a credit card payment. "Is that electronic?"

"Sure," I said, not too convincingly. I'd never used a credit card. Madame found cash easier to track and control.

When the waitress came back with our order—an egg sandwich for me and a bowl of fruit and yogurt for Kyllen—he pointed at the payment machine in the pocket of her apron.

"May I look at this device?" he enquired politely.

She blinked at him with a shocked expression, and I felt exposed as a liar for allowing her to believe he was blind. Silently, she handed the machine to him, keeping an eye on it.

"Hm." He twisted it between his fingers. The screen of the device briefly lit up, then went off again. "Interesting." He gave the machine back to the woman, who left promptly. "A curious thing."

I dropped my shoulders, feeling deflated. Madame's *bracks* might be after us. By now, the "fossilized" bodies of Rourke and his buddies must be discovered. What if someone connected their deaths to Kyllen? We might have Rourke's people on our heels, too. Maybe even the police.

We had to get out of this city, but how?

"See." I said to Kyllen. "Electronic devices are different."

"They are." He sipped his tea, reclining in his seat. "They're much easier."

“Easier?” I gaped at him. “How?”

“There are no parts to manipulate. All I need to do is send signals. No wonder electronic payment machines don’t exist in Nerifir. They’d be useless with how easily they can be manipulated by everyone.”

“But how do you know what signals to send?”

“I don’t. I just know what I want it to do, and I make it happen. Our bill is paid, by the way.” He grinned.

“What bill? The café bill? For breakfast?”

He nodded, plucking a strawberry out of his bowl, then tossing it into his mouth.

“But with what money?” I wondered.

“No money.” He shrugged. “I just marked it as paid. Can’t you see now how stupid these electronics are?”

“But the café management will figure it out.”

“Maybe. Eventually. When we’re long gone.”

I chewed on my lip. “That’s wrong.”

He huffed. “Fine.” He produced two fifty-pound notes from his boot and tossed them on the table. “Will this make it right?”

It was better than stealing food.

“Okay.” I nodded and bit off my sandwich, pacified.

He finished his yogurt quickly, then ordered a second pot of tea. Though his eyes remained hidden beneath his hood, I sensed his attention was on me by the way his head was raised, as if he tried to see as much as possible of me, below the eye level.

“Why are you hiding your hair?” he asked unexpectedly.

“Why does it matter?” I muttered, caught off guard by his question.

“I’m curious.”

No one had ever asked me this question before, but I knew the answer. It was because I hid everything I could of myself, including my hair. Most of the time, I wished I could hide the rest of me, too.

Of course, I couldn’t tell him that without risking him thinking of me as a weirdo, like so many people did.

“It’s long.” I said instead, drinking my coffee. “It gets in the way. Especially when I work.”

“How long is it?” There was something in his voice that made my cheeks warm, and I dropped my gaze to my coffee mug.

"Long." I swallowed.

He wouldn't give up. "Can I see all of it?"

"Now? Here?"

"I never saw hair up close before I met you. Never touched any, either."

"Really?" That shouldn't be surprising. Gorgonians didn't have hair. Just *senties*, whatever exactly those were. "Well..."

I glanced around to make sure no one was watching us. The few people at the tables in the cafe were busy with either their phones or their own conversations.

"Alright." I tugged at my braid, pulling it out from behind my scarf and my hoodie. When braided, it reached a little past my waist. Unbraided...well, I never wore my hair loose.

"May I?" He leaned across the table and took the end of the braid from me.

Yanking the elastic off it, he unraveled a good third of the braid. Naturally wavy, my dark hair retained the crinkled shape of the braid I'd made when it was still damp after the shower last night.

He ran his long fingers through the strands. "It's so much softer than a horse's mane."

That made me smile. "I sure hope so. Does it feel weird?" It was completely new to him, after all.

"It tickles... In a rather exciting way." He grabbed the ends in a fist and twisted his wrist, winding the braid around his forearm. He yanked at it, bringing my face closer to his.

"Kyllen," I exhaled against his lips.

"I love it," he rasped in a coarse whisper.

I tilted my head, increasing the pull at my roots. My scalp pricked and burned slightly. It felt oddly...exciting, just as he said.

"Do you like it?" he murmured, as if we were all alone in the room. "Do you like it when I play with your hair?" He moved his arm, making me turn my head the way that suited him.

It was bizarre being completely at his mercy like that, like a marionette on a string. At the same time, I felt more in control than I'd ever been before. I'd spent my life led by the will of others, having no say in what was happening to me. With Kyllen, it was different. I knew no matter what he did, he cared about what I thought and felt.

"Let me go," I said softly, just to test if he would.

He relaxed his fist, releasing my hair. My messed-up braid unraveled from around his arm and dropped to the table.

"Did I scare you?" He flashed me a self-assured grin. "In a good way, I hope."

Was there a good way to be scared?

I supposed there was, but only because I trusted him. The echo of the tiny prickles to my scalp spread down my neck and arms in ripples of pleasure.

He toyed with the ends of my hair on the table between us. I watched his deft fingers quickly braid it into a neat plait again.

"For someone who hasn't seen or touched hair before, you're pretty good at braiding it."

"I'm good at many things," he boasted, without shame. "This is just one of the ways to make a rope." He snapped on the elastic to secure the ends, then waved the braid in the air between us to demonstrate his work. "See?"

"Thanks." I slid my finger along his knuckles. The dark mesh pattern on them had almost disappeared. Only traces of it were still visible when he turned his hand to the light in a certain way.

"Your skin feels softer," I noted.

"Hm," he agreed. "The bath helped last night. No matter how much I drink, the air is too dry in this world to keep me properly hydrated. Soaking in the tub allowed me to drink enough for once."

"To *drink*? Do you mean you drank the bathwater?"

He laughed at my bewilderment. "Yes, through my skin that absorbs moisture from the air. It sucks it in like a sponge, which makes our skin supple and soft." He stroked my fingers with his. "It allows for a much better perception by touch, too."

"It does?" I breathed out, mesmerized by his caress.

"For us, touch is even more important than sight." He wrapped his fingers around my hand, pressing it gently. "My hands often can tell me more than my eyes."

"How? What can you tell by touching my hand?"

"Right now? That you're cold." He brought my hand to his lips for a quick kiss. "Which is not surprising at all. It's freezing here, even inside."

"Alright." I took my hand from him to tuck my braid back into my hoodie. "Let's go get you some warm clothes. I can't stand you being this miserable."

Chapter Twenty-Three

AMIRA

We spent some time in a men's clothing store, searching for just the right cashmere sweater and wool coat for Kyllen. Once we'd found and bought what he liked—a soft-as-a-cloud, olive-green sweater and a light-brown, long coat—he dragged me to a women's clothing boutique nearby.

I grabbed the first plain black coat and was ready to leave, but Kyllen wouldn't let me.

"I don't need anything else," I argued. "I'll be warm enough in this."

"You may not *need* anything else, but is there anything you *want?*"

"Want?" I glanced around the store hesitantly. Soft fabrics, shimmering trim, gentle pastel colors—so many desirable things. "What's the point, Kyllen? I can't take any of these with me."

He rested his hands on his hips.

"Unless you're planning to cross the River of Mists in the nude—which I wouldn't object to, by the way—you will wear something. Why not let it be clothes you like and choose for yourself?" He gestured at my baggy outfit discreetly. "Something that fits you better than this."

I took a critical look at my reflection in the mirror between two aisles. A scrawny person, unclear whether male or female, stuffed in a shapeless pile of black and gray cotton, glared back at me.

"Fine. I guess I could change," I conceded.

"Splendid." Kyllen's lips spread in a satisfied smile. He then leaned closer to whisper in my ear, only for me to hear. "Remember, we have lots of paper money that will be useless anywhere else but here. Go, sweet pea, find something you like." He waved a hand at me, leaving me in the care of the super enthusiastic saleswoman.

Shopping for myself didn't prove easy. Other than getting bras and panties off the rack, I'd never bought clothes before. I had no idea what "body type" I was, what "style" I wore, what was my preferred "color pallet" or any other equally confusing things the salesperson kept asking me. I didn't even know what size I was. We had to figure that out by trial and error.

When we finally put together an outfit for me, I felt winded and drained.

My new clothes consisted of a pair of black velvet pants and a sweater. The pants seemed dressy, for special occasions, but they were so soft and comfortable, I could wear them all day, every day. The sweater was cashmere and in the same olive-green color as Kyllen's.

I exited the fitting rooms and twirled in front of Kyllen, who reclined in an armchair. "What do you think?"

He lifted his head, taking me in from my old, comfy running shoes, which I'd refused to change, up to my chest. With the edge of his hood shielding his eyes, he couldn't see higher than my chin.

"How about this?" He lifted a wide strip of blush-pink material that had been draped over his knee.

The saleswoman nodded approvingly. "Oh, that's a pashmina scarf. So beautiful."

"You want me to change my scarf?" I fisted my hands into the familiar gray fabric wrapped around my neck.

It was fairly new. I'd only been wearing it for a couple of months and only because the black scarf I'd had before got so old and ratty, it resembled a rope when coiled around my neck.

Hanging the pink pashmina over one shoulder, Kyllen got up from the armchair and strolled my way.

"All I want is for you to try and see how *you* like it." Placing his hands on my shoulders, he walked me backwards into the fitting room, then spun me around to face the mirror. "May I?" He took the end of my gray scarf between his fingers, with a clear intention of removing it and exposing my neck.

I hiked up my shoulders, bracing my spine.

He didn't move, patiently waiting for my permission.

The last time someone had removed my clothes, it was the *bracks* just before they whipped Radax and me. The helplessness, shame, and fear I'd felt then rushed over me anew. My heart raced, and my hands turned clammy.

"I..." I dragged in a heavy breath.

"Shh." His voice came like the sound of a breeze in tall grass, calming and comforting. His lips gently skimmed the shell of my ear. "It's just me, Amira. I won't harm you. I'll never do anything unless you let me."

Kyllen would rather walk this world half-blinded by his hood than risk harming me. He wasn't a *brack*.

"Okay, Kyllen," I gave him my permission.

Slowly, as if giving me a chance to stop him at any moment, he unwound my old gray scarf from around my neck and tossed it to the floor. Instead of replacing it with the pink one, however, he gently trailed his fingers up the sides of my neck.

The air felt cool against my exposed skin, his touch light like a brush of dragonfly wings.

"Mmm," he half-moaned, burying his nose in the place where my neck met my shoulder. "I love this spot," he murmured against my skin, breathing in deeply. "This is where the scent of you is the strongest. I feel like I could taste it."

The fabric of his hood shifted as something twitched underneath.

A wild thought hit me, bursting through my chest with anticipation and thrill. Madame had used a mirror to look at him. I was standing in front of a floor-to-ceiling mirror right now, with him right behind me.

"Kyllen, can I see your eyes?" I'd been dreaming about him. In my dreams, his eyes were black and empty sometimes, like holes into the abyss. Other times, they were impossibly bright like two stars. "It's safe for me to look at you in the mirror, isn't it?"

I wanted to see his face, if just this once.

He jerked his head up. A smile quivered his lips, as if he'd just thought about it too.

"Yes, it's safe."

"Please." I held my breath.

He raised his hand to his hood, then pulled it back a little, just up to the middle of his forehead.

His eyes met mine in the mirror, and my heart all but stopped.

They weren't black like the abyss or white-bright like the stars. They were gold, but their depth and shine could be easily compared to the stars. A slim vertical pupil cut the iris in the center. He had no eyelashes or eyebrows, but the tan color of his skin thickened to green-black along his brow ridges, with the barely discernible diamond pattern like on his hands.

Black color edged his eyelids, too, extending past the corner of the eye like winged eyeliner. It looked at once elegant and masculine. So beautiful, it made me think of the ancient Egyptian paintings.

His skin appeared to glow along his sharp cheekbones, on the straight ridge of his nose, and on the proud rise of his strong chin.

I recalled the glow that had surrounded Zeph, the siren, when he was still in Madame's water tank. Or the faint shimmer that had emitted from Lero, the werewolf, as he was shifting from his beast form. The magic of the fae made them look ethereally beautiful.

"Your eyes are the same color as your hair," he said softly, and I realized Kyllen had been studying me, too.

I tried to look at myself through his eyes. There was nothing magical in my weary expression. My skin seemed dull in comparison. Instead of a shimmer, I had dark circles under my eyes.

"Yes," I released a breath. "Not much variation there."

"It's beautiful. So...unusual." He slid a hand down the side of my face, then leaned to kiss my temple.

A thick curl dropped from under his hood. It hung in front of his face, reaching past his chin. Then it unfurled, stretching down to his chest.

I gaped at it, my eyes opened wide, as the diamond-shaped tip of "the curl" lifted. I inhaled a shaky breath, met with a pair of golden, beady eyes staring at me in the mirror.

A snake!

Tan-colored on its belly, it had the dark-green mesh pattern on its back, with a golden shimmer along its spine. It slinked its split tongue out from its mouth, turning toward my exposed neck.

I stiffened, raising a shoulder to shield my neck.

"Sorry." Kyllen caught my horrified expression in the mirror. "I tend to lose control around you."

The snake promptly disappeared under his hood, as if someone yanked it back by its tail.

"Was that—"

"One of my *senties*. Did it scare you? Shock you? Repulse you, maybe?" he asked carefully. "Not all fae like gorgonian appearance."

I got along well with the bird-snakes from Nerifir at the menagerie. They were three to four feet long, covered in feathers, and could fly. Earth snakes, however, were not my favorite animals. I once ended up spending several nights sleeping on top of a cargo trailer because the *bracks* had caught a rattlesnake in one of the tents.

But this wasn't a snake, was it? It was a part of Kyllen...somehow.

I swallowed hard and managed a smile. "It surprised me. That's all."

Reaching back, I cradled his cheek in my hand. His eyelids dropped. A tender smile played on his lips as he leaned into my touch.

"Can I see it again, please?" I let go of his face, spreading my fingers wider. "You can touch me with it."

"Are you sure?"

"Yes. If it's a part of you, it won't harm me." I truly believed that.

"As long as you don't look straight at it," he reminded me.

"I won't." I kept my eyes on his reflection in the mirror.

The small diamond-shaped head tentatively poked out from under his hood.

"Come on, little one," I coaxed, wiggling my fingers. "Don't be scared."

Kyllen snorted a laugh. "You realize you're talking to a part of my body, right? It's like if I was talking to your finger."

"It doesn't have its own brain?"

"Of course not. What do I need a headful of sentient appendages for?" He chuckled.

"Well, but they have eyes." I pointed at the pair of shimmering golden beads on each side of the "head."

"Which are connected to *my* brain. I'm the one with the fifty eyes, remember?"

"Don't they have a tongue, too? I think I saw something."

"Yes, they do." A slim ribbon of forked tongue flicked out of the open mouth at the end of the "head." "They have mouths, too. But I make them open. See?"

The little mouth opened wide.

"There are no teeth," I noted.

"No. They don't eat."

I noticed there was no throat inside the mouth, either. Instead, the top and the bottom parts fused inside like a mouth of a sock puppet, with the tongue sticking out from the middle.

"Why do they need the tongues?" I asked, fascinated by this part of his anatomy.

"*Senties* are sensors. Like fingers, they can touch."

The little head moved closer to my cheek, brushing my skin, then gently slid down to my neck.

"The tongues are even more sensitive. With them, I can smell." The tongue flicked out, coiling like a spring next to my skin. "I can taste." The fork of the tongue touched my neck.

Kyllen's chest expanded at my back. A muffled groan vibrated deep inside it. He tipped his head back, half-closing his eyes, as if savoring a sip of fine wine.

"I've been dreaming of tasting you." He leaned his forehead to my temple.

More little touches came from everywhere. Slipping out from under his hood, the *senties* wound around my neck, slinking under the neckline of my sweater, burrowing into my hair to rub against my skull.

It was like being touched by twenty-four gentle but insolent fingers. I felt one of them sneak into my bra and raised my hand to slap it, but paused. I could always stop it later. But what would happen if I let it go for just a little bit longer?

How far could this tingling sensation along my skin grow?

How hot can the warmth in my lower belly get?

What would happen when I couldn't stand the teasing any longer?

What if I needed more?

A woman cleared her throat behind us. "I beg your pardon, but are you buying any of the clothes?"

The voice of the saleswoman yanked me out of the warm, shimmering dream that Kyllen's touch had plunged me into.

He half-staggered as if coming out of a trance, too. Yanking his hood down, he turned to face the woman. "We'll take them all."

"And the pashmina?" She wished to know.

He took the pink scarf off his shoulder and draped it gently around my neck. "What do you think?"

It felt like a kiss against my skin. I sank my hands into the scarf, nuzzling into the material, which was as soft as a cloud I imagined would be. I closed my eyes and moaned.

"Yes," Kyllen said to the woman. "We're taking the scarf, too."

I left my old clothes at the store, letting the salesperson dispose of them however she felt fit. The only thing I wished to keep from my old life was the dragonfly barrette Kyllen had made for me. I clipped it into my hair, just above my right ear.

When we finally left the shop, I buried my nose into my new scarf and took a furtive glance at Kyllen.

In his coat, he almost looked like any regular guy now. Taller than most and wider in the shoulders, he walked in a confident swagger few could master, but he no longer stood out like a visitor from a magical kingdom.

I noticed people no longer threw curious glances my way, either. Now, we both blended in so much better. Even Kyllen's hood didn't stand out too much among so many other hoods of sweatshirts and jackets pulled over people's heads against the wind.

Kyllen shoved his hands into his pockets, and I hooked my arm into his.

"You never said whether you liked my new outfit." I nudged him with my elbow.

"Do *you* like it?" he asked.

I snuggled with my chin into my new scarf. "I love it."

"Then I like it, too." He smiled.

"That's it? You like it if I do?"

He slowed down his steps. "Sweetheart, I liked you well enough in those dreadful things you wore before, and I'd take you dressed in a burlap sack. It doesn't matter to me what you wear, as long as you're happy." He tilted his head. "Did wearing the *bracks'* clothes make you happy?"

I frowned. So many memories came with those old clothes, hardly any of them were worth remembering.

He nodded. "Didn't think so."

Chapter Twenty-Four

AMIRA

Boarding the train proved easier than I thought. After lunch, we bought the tickets, then snuck on the train in the early evening, avoiding customs. Kyllen worked his magic, and it only took a few doors to open at exactly the right moment when they were supposed to be locked, and a few turnstiles to move against the direction they were supposed to.

Once on the train, I dropped into my seat next to his, feeling exhausted.

"Tired?" Kyllen caught on to my state. "Come here." He wrapped his arm around me and brought my head to his shoulder. "We have two hours of being locked in this tube of a vehicle. You may as well have a nap."

On the surface, it had been a rather relaxing day. We'd had breakfast, gone shopping, then had lunch, and boarded the train in the evening.

In reality, I was cuddling with the man who had killed four people that morning, and he'd done that by simply looking at them.

In a way, Kyllen was even more dangerous than Madame.

He had snakes growing on his head. I should be running away from him. Instead, I snuggled closer. Being next to Kyllen relaxed me. It made me feel safe. His voice comforted me. And the "snakes..." Their touch excited me, instead of making me repulsed or terrified.

I'd never spent so much time with anyone before. I'd never had a friend I could go out for breakfast or clothes shopping with. Things that people did all the time and took for granted were new and exciting to me. And having all of them at once, like today, exhausted me.

"But we're going to travel underwater," I mumbled, fighting to keep my eyes open. "I don't want to miss that."

"From what I gathered," he said. "It's going to be a dark tunnel. You won't miss much."

I never found out if he was right. I ended up falling asleep within minutes and slept until the end of our trip.

When we got off the train, it was already dark.

"We should get a hotel, rest a little, and look for the portal the day after tomorrow," Kyllen suggested. "Or do you want to find Lero's house instead? Would he mind if we spend the night at his place?"

We'd left the station, and I found myself on the street of yet another unfamiliar city. Only this time, I was also surrounded by people whose language I didn't understand.

I felt restless, suspended in transit with the final destination almost in sight already. I didn't think Lero would mind if we stayed at his place for the night, but I was anxious to keep going.

"We need to go to the park," I replied. "Lero said the portal opens around three o'clock every morning. It's only ten-thirty. We can cross when it opens next, in four and a half hours."

By the time the sun rose, I could already be in the place that would become my home for the rest of my life. Maybe I could finally belong somewhere.

"Is that what you want?" Kyllen asked. "To cross tonight?"

I nodded. It had been a hard decision to leave. But once I'd made it, I didn't want to linger any longer.

He turned to me, placing his hands on my shoulders. "I want you to think about this very hard, Amira, one last time." I couldn't see his eyes, but the intensity in his voice was unmistakable. "After this, there is no coming back. You'll never be able to return."

"I know."

"You will never see Radax again." His voice softened. "He'll never know what happened to you."

At that, my heart pinched painfully.

Leaving Radax hadn't been easy. By bringing me to the menagerie he'd taken the role a *brack* was never meant to play—taking care of a child. And he'd managed it well. He'd taught me everything I knew. He'd been my support, my comfort, my safe place for years.

But it cost him. His life would've been so much simpler without me.

When I'd hugged him the last time, it felt like a piece of my heart had chipped away. I knew I'd never get it back, but it brought me comfort to know that Radax gained some freedom, too. He was now free of any responsibility for me. Madame could no longer hold me against him to manipulate either of us.

She had no reason to suspect him of helping me escape. He'd refused to tell me anything about the portal. Even if she searched his brain, that would be all she would find. He knew nothing about my plans. And if that wasn't enough, I'd shot him...

The pain in my heart grew unbearable, burning my eyes with tears.

I stifled a sob and steadied my breathing before replying. "Radax is far better off without me. He's immortal. I'm but a tiny fleck on the endless road of his existence. He'll forget me soon enough."

Kyllen stood in silence, his hands on my shoulders, his thumbs rubbing my muscles through the coat. Maybe he just wanted to give me some time to listen to my heart before I made the final decision—I was so new to being in control of my life. Or maybe he was thinking about what it meant for him, too.

No matter what, the life as we both knew it was gone. No one could tell us what would find us on the other side of the River of Mists.

Kyllen dropped his hands off my shoulders. "Let's do it, then. We'll have time to get dinner, then I'll find someone to take us to *Parc des Brouillards.*"

We stood on a busy street. Despite the late hour, a steady stream of pedestrians rushed by us. Life throbbed all around, and it was hard to imagine that in a few hours we would no longer be a part of it.

By the time we found a place to eat and had dinner, it was past midnight. When we got into a taxi, however, the driver refused to drive all the way to *Parc des Brouillards.*

"It's too far," he said in heavily accented English. "Best take the train in the morning."

"But we need to go now," I pleaded.

"How much?" Kyllen enquired calmly. "What would it take for you to drive us, now?"

The man squinted through the rear-view mirror at Kyllen and named a sum that made a breath stick in my throat.

"Fine." Kyllen took a stack of bills from the wad he kept in his boot. "Here." He handed the whole thing to the driver. "Take us. Now."

The driver stared at the money, clearly dumbfounded. "That's British pounds, not euros."

"Isn't a pound higher in value than a euro?" I wasn't entirely sure myself. I'd had no chance to look into that yet and probably never would now.

"Here." Kyllen threw a few more bills his way.

I cast a cautionary glance his way. Sure, we'd have no use for this money where we were going, but I worried the driver would get suspicious with Kyllen tossing bills at him like candy wrappers.

Thankfully, all that rain of money convinced the driver to take us. After a long but beautiful drive through the nightscape of the City of Paris and then through its suburbs, we arrived at the park.

"It's closed for visitors at this hour," the driver warned as we exited his vehicle. He waited for a minute, maybe to see if we'd change our minds having seen the place closed with our own eyes. Kyllen waved him to go, and the taxi drove away.

The two of us were left standing in front of the wrought-iron gate built in between two stone columns. As far as my eye could see in the darkness, the iron fence ran in either direction from the gate. Lero had mentioned that *Parc des Brouillards* was a private property. The owners obviously valued their privacy, even if they had the place open to the visitors during the day.

I recalled the time from when I'd last glanced at the clock on the dashboard in the taxi. "We have less than twenty minutes before the portal opens."

"That's not much." Kyllen headed to the fence on the right of the gate. "We'll have to find the pond. Can you climb this? Come, I'll give you a boost."

He placed his foot on the stone foundation. I climbed on his knee, then over the fence, carefully trying not to impale myself on the spiky ends of its metal posts. Once I was on the other side, Kyllen easily scaled the fence to join me.

We walked swiftly along a stone path between the neatly trimmed hedges powdered with snow. The crisp winter air smelled fresh. I tried to commit to memory the scents of my home world, but these scents were foreign to me.

The smells that would forever be tied to this world for me were those of dusty canvas walls, animal enclosures, and the stale air inside trucks and train cars that were either too cold or too hot to travel.

"There." Kyllen pointed up ahead after a while.

The light of the setting moon reflected in the surface of water in the distance.

"That's a very big pond." I'd imagined something much smaller and far less freezing than the large body of water up ahead. That looked like a lake.

A wooden dock held a painted sign in French and English, advertising rental of pedal and paddle boats, though no boats were anywhere in sight. They must've been put away for the winter. It hadn't been cold enough for the water to freeze. Just a thin lace of ice had formed along the shore overnight. It would surely melt in the morning.

A sudden thrill of a whistle sliced through the air. Someone yelled in French.

Two people were running to us from the small building on the side of the lake. A man and a woman, both dressed in black uniforms.

Kyllen turned to me.

"Must be security," was the only explanation I had.

I quickly scanned the surface of the pond. There was no sign of any portal. Maybe Kyllen had been right in his suspicions, and Lero had lied. But I wasn't ready to give up yet.

"Can you stop them?" I asked Kyllen, gesturing at the quickly approaching guards.

He raised his hand to his hood.

"No!" I grabbed his arm. "Not like that."

Horror echoed through me. My hands shook. I couldn't let him do it. I couldn't watch more people die. Rourke and his gang might've deserved what he did to them, but the security guards were just regular people doing their job.

"Could you just...punch them or something?" I asked. That would hurt, but at least they'd stay alive.

He shrank back from me, seemingly appalled. "Are you asking me to hit a woman? Who do you think I am?"

"You were about to kill her," I pointed out the obvious.

He shook his head. "That's different."

"How is punching her any worse than turning her to stone?" Frustration rose in me.

The shouting grew louder. The guards were coming closer.

"Well." I shrugged out of my coat. "If you insist on being a gentleman, then we'd better run."

I spun on my heel and took off away from the guards. Kyllen easily caught up to me, taking his coat off, too, on the way. We sprinted along the shore. But the shrills of the whistle and the screaming of the guards sounded closer. The guards were gaining on us.

I ran faster, pumping my arms.

"Amira, look!" Kyllen pointed at the pond.

A small cloud of mist rose over the path of moonlight that reflected on the surface. It would look not much more than evaporation over the water—steam rising in the cool air—if it wasn't for the tendril of pink shimmer in the very core of it.

"Oh my God, it's true!" I nearly tripped over my feet. "The portal is true, Kyllen!"

There was no other reason for the pink color to appear. The night was still black with bluish-silver moonlight and not a hint of sunrise yet.

This had to be the mist of the magical river that connected the worlds. It had to be.

The female guard grabbed the end of my scarf. She yanked me back, shouting in French.

"No!" I twisted out of my scarf, leaving it in her hands.

I was so close. Nothing was stopping me now.

"Run!" Kyllen swerved off the path toward the pond, dragging me along.

Ice crunched under our feet. The freezing water rushed into my shoes. My breath hitched, my skin going numb. I gasped, the cold air invading my lungs.

Cold. It was everywhere. And the portal was still a distance away.

"Can you swim?" Kyllen yanked at my arm.

I shook my head, taking short, shallow breaths as the ice-cold water rose higher and higher up my legs with every step we took.

The dumbfounded guards remained on the dry land, shouting even louder and blowing their whistles. They obviously had no idea what was happening, and probably would report two people drowned in the pond the next morning.

None of it concerned me anymore. There was just the dark night and the black as ink, freezing water.

The bones in my legs ached, as if turning to ice.

"Hold on to my shoulders," Kyllen commanded. "Whatever happens, don't let go."

I could hardly hear his voice over the chattering of my teeth. But I nodded. He turned with his back to me. I hooked my arms around his shoulders. He dove forward. And the water engulfed us.

Cold I had never known before seeped through my clothes, my skin, and my flesh to my very bones. It deprived me of the ability to move. Even breathing became a nearly impossible task.

I locked my arms around Kyllen's neck from behind and propped my chin on the back of his head, struggling to keep my face above water.

Somehow, he managed to swim. His strong arms cut through the ripples of the moonlight on the surface, stroke after stroke.

The silver mist surrounded us, taking a gentle tint of pink, and...we sank into it. The water closed over our heads, like an icy sarcophagus. But it was no longer dark.

Light filtered through my closed eyelids. It shimmered and danced as if playing in the leaves on a tree or the ripples on a pond.

Some feeling returned to my muscles. My skin prickled as if poked with a thousand needles.

The current ran by me, stroking my face. But it no longer felt like the water of the pond. It was much softer, gentler, warmer.

And I could breathe in it.

I opened my eyes.

Kyllen and I were suspended in the silky pink shimmer. It streamed all around us, but its movement had a direction. And we floated in it, being carried by it.

"Close your eyes." Kyllen's voice drifted through the mists to me. He turned in my arms, taking me into a hug. "Whatever happens, don't let go of me."

I flexed my arms tighter around his neck.

He kissed my cheek, then gently pressed my face into his shoulder. "Hold on to me, Amira. Don't let go."

I opened my mouth to reply, but the mist around us suddenly turned denser. It rushed into my mouth and into my lungs. I coughed, choking. My chest burned. My throat closed.

Kyllen's arms held me tight like in a vise.

I thrashed against him, desperate to get to the surface wherever it was. I needed air. I couldn't breathe.

Only there was no surface. No up. No down. Just suffocating water.

My mind swam, life drifting out of me with the stream.

Chapter Twenty-Five

KYLLEN

The River of Mists released them.

And the waters of Lorsan received them.

Caught in their torrent, he had no idea where the surface or the bottom were. Holding Amira tight in his arms, he kicked his feet. His boots encountered something solid. He shoved against it, propelling them in the opposite direction, which happened to be the *up* he'd been searching for.

Breaking through the surface, he gasped a lungful of air. His hood had been shoved off his head by the current. Jolted by panic, he pressed Amira's head to his shoulder to keep her eyes closed.

She had stopped fighting his grip a moment ago. Her body slacked in his arms.

Alarm lanced through him. Did he kill his rescuer by dragging her between the worlds?

A strip of land stretched in front of him, the familiar expanse of yellow-green. He headed in that direction. When the water got shallow enough for him to walk, he shifted Amira over his shoulder and waded out to the dry land.

Each step jolted her. His shoulder pressed into her chest. By the time he dropped to his knees on the sandy shore, she sputtered and coughed —choking, but alive. For that, he thanked every deity he knew.

Shedding his new sweater, he yanked his tunic out from his belt, then ripped a long strip of fabric from its hem.

"Keep this on. At all times." He tied the strip around her head over her eyes. "It's not just me you have to worry about here."

She gripped his hand.

"Are we in Lorsan? Kyllen, did we make it?"

He drew in a long breath. The air was warm and thick with moisture, filling his lungs with the familiar scents of golden duckweed and fuzzy willow, wet moss, and mushroom strings. He didn't need to closely examine the place they'd landed in to know for sure that this was home.

"Yes, sweet pea. We made it."

They truly did.

Spreading his *senties* wide, he let his body bask in the rich, nourishing air of his homeland. Excitement rushed through him. He was home, and it was all because of her.

Amira sat on the riverbank, blindfolded and looking lost. He leaped to his feet and scooped her into his arms.

"We are in Lorsan, my little human friend!" He gave her a twirl through the air, needing to hear her laugh. "We're free!"

She smiled finally, wrapping her arms around his neck. He couldn't fight the need to kiss her and took her mouth with his. She returned his kiss, shyly.

"Kyllen." She tilted her face to him when he let go of her lips. "Tell me where we are."

"In Lorsan, my darling."

"Yes. But *tell* me what it looks like. Please."

A pinch of regret twitched in his heart. He wished for her to see his homeland. For a moment, he contemplated taking the blindfold off, so she could take a quick look for herself. But he immediately discarded that idea.

It was tempting. As it always would be. Just a quick look, the briefest of glances. What could possibly happen in a second or two?

But a glance could cost them her life. Here in the land of gorgonians, it wasn't just he they had to worry about. Someone could show up unexpectedly. And then...

No. A glance was not worth her life. Nothing was.

She rolled her shoulders back, tugging at the neckline of her sweater. "It feels warm."

He reined in his excitement and the urge to keep moving. She needed some time to adjust, and he wanted to give that to her.

He sat on the ground, then drew her into his lap. "It's the green season now. Summer."

"Is there a winter, too?"

Hugging her from behind, he placed his chin on her shoulder. "Kind of. We call it the golden season. It's when the trees turn yellow. Some leaves fall. Some wither and dissipate into the wind, only to be reborn when the green season comes back."

"So, there are leaves on the trees now? Grass on the ground?"

"Yes. The grass is the warmest shade of green. It's tall. It would reach to your waist if you stand up and take two paces either right or left from where we are, along the riverbank."

"It doesn't cover all the ground, does it?" She tilted a bit to pat the sand next to where they were sitting.

"Almost all of it, really. There're just a few sandy patches left bare. This is one of them where we're sitting. The tall grass comes all the way to the water along most of the river bank. It grows in the stream too, where it's shallow. The wide blades spear through the sheets of golden duckweed that rim the water's edge. Like most rivers in Lorsan, this one is wider than it is deep. It sprawls through the forest, often flowing between the trees. The sandy-golden water is lazy and warm."

She gripped his hand. "It scared me so much when we were in it."

He kissed her temple. "It scared me, too. Because it was unexpected. But water itself is not much of a threat in Lorsan."

"What is?"

"The things that live in it, for one. Most dangerous, however, are the people who live in these lands."

"The gorgonians?"

"Hm." He nodded. "Fae are treacherous folks, Amira. You can't trust anyone. I know a werewolf showed you some kindness back on Earth, but it doesn't mean other fae wouldn't want to harm you when they meet you. You have to be wary of everyone."

He had to be frank with her. She had to live in this world now, and she had to do that practically blind. The least he could do was to arm her with knowledge.

"Well, you've been kind to me, too, not just Lero," she pointed out.

"My kindness has been self-serving. Whatever I've done for you ultimately benefited me, too."

She remained quiet for a few heartbeats, then got off his lap. "Thank you for the warning."

"Amira." He leaped to his feet, too.

He loved having her close. He liked the way her soft, pliable body fit into his arms, how neatly she could fold herself in his lap when sitting or curl against his chest when sleeping. And despite his own warnings, he loved how trusting she was with him.

He wanted her armed and guarded against the world. But he detested her distancing herself from him.

He caught her from behind, drawing her back into his chest. "If there's someone you can trust here, it's me."

She pressed her mouth into an unimpressed frown. "You've just told me—"

"I know." He nuzzled the side of her neck. She'd lost her scarf, and he loved having her delicate skin exposed like that for him. "But I've also given you a promise, remember?"

"Promises don't always mean much." She shrugged her shoulder, as if trying to shake off his caresses.

He wouldn't let her, though, pressing his lips in the place where her neck and her shoulder met. Oh, how he loved that spot. The sweet scent of her mingled with the fresh smell of the river water.

"Not for fae," he murmured against her skin. "If we break a promise, we lose our mind and shortly after our life. That's why I never make promises in the first place."

"You don't?"

"No, my sweet little pea. The promise I gave you was my first one ever. I really hope it will be the last one I'll ever make, too. Promises carry a huge obligation to keep them. And I find any obligation annoyingly restrictive."

She didn't make another attempt to push him away. Instead, she spread her arms in front of her, feeling the space. Her fingers brushed a branch of a nearby tree.

"Fuzzy willow," he told her the name of the tree.

She caught one of the long leaves between her slim fingers. The leaf was dark-green and glossy on top and soft silvery-green on the underside.

"Its trunk is about fifteen paces to the right of us." He tried to make up for the loss of her eyesight with his descriptions. "It would take both of us to hug it, that's how thick it is. And the branches are long enough to trail in the water."

She heaved a sigh. "Thank you. It helps to know where I am."

"Come." He kissed her cheek and released her from his arms, getting hold of her hand instead. "I believe we were lucky enough to land in my father's domain. This is one of his hunting grounds right here. Now, we just need to figure out *when* we are."

Chapter Twenty-Six

KYLLEN

Hiking through the wetlands was tricky. The river split and branched into smaller arms that merged some distance downstream only to split again. In addition, independent creeks and ponds interspersed the land. Some were shallow enough to wade through. Some required a real effort to cross.

Kyllen wasn't thoroughly familiar with this part of his father's estate, but he had enough general skill and knowledge about navigating wetlands on foot to find a passable path without much difficulty. Even with the practically blinded Amira in tow, he moved at a decent speed.

Amira kept up without a complaint, but he knew she must be getting tired. They both needed food and rest soon.

He'd chosen to go downstream because if the river was Elgrall, as he believed it was, then the High Lord's palace would be in the direction of the current. It lay in the spot where the Elgrall River bloated into Layahi Bay, which shouldn't be too far away.

Chances were, of course, that no one at the palace would know who he was. He didn't expect to be welcomed "home" with open arms, but he hoped to find some food and shelter there, at least for a little while.

He didn't have much to bargain with, but there was always a chance to strike a deal.

A faint sound of music drifted over the water.

He strained his hearing.

It was a flute. A stringed instrument accompanied it, possibly a lute. The wetlands weren't the best place for a group of musicians to practice their craft. Unless they were a part of a travel party, playing for the entertainment of someone affluent enough to pay for their talent and skill.

He hurried along the river bank, staying hidden behind the trees.

The music got louder as the travel party got closer.

Peeking from behind the trees, he saw them enter the river from a wide side arm. An entire flotilla of paddle boards surrounded several larger vessels. The last one carried a carcass of a river moose, already gutted but not skinned.

The biggest boat held a seat draped in hunter-green velvet embroidered with the Ellohi coat of arms. The man sitting in it looked eerily familiar.

Kyllen needed to get closer.

"Amira, darling, you'll have to stay here for a little while." He led her to a large willow tree at the water's edge and helped her sit down on one of the gnarly roots arching above the wet ground.

"What's happening, Kyllen?" she asked quietly, matching his lowered tone.

"I'll need to go talk to that fancy hunting party over there. But I don't want them to see you. Not yet." Not until he knew exactly who these people were. "Just stay here and be as quiet as I know you can be. I'll come back for you soon."

"Okay." She folded her hands in her lap obediently, and he kissed her cheek.

"I won't be long."

Without Amira in tow, he easily caught up to the hunting party and got ahead of them, all while remaining unseen by them. Climbing on a fallen tree that had tipped over the stream, he strolled along its trunk to meet the flotilla head on.

"Greetings!" he shouted, spreading his feet wide for balance and propping his hands on his hips.

Spotting him, the guards paddled back to front, fighting the current that slowly carried them toward him. That slowed the flotilla down. With a stroke of a paddle, a guard on a stand-up board advanced forward. He wore the palace uniform in the colors of sage and gold.

"State your name and business," the guard demanded.

The man was not someone Kyllen recognized, and he was no fool to give his name just to anyone.

"I'm a traveler. Returning to Lorsan after a long absence. I'd like to offer my services to the High Lord of Ellohi."

"Your name," the guard insisted.

Behind the group of guards on the boards, a movement on the main boat caused a commotion. The man in the seat of the High Lord rose to his feet. The people in his boat rushed to his side, grabbing his arms for support.

"Kyllen." The name rasped in the air like a rustle of dry leaves.

The guards slid aside with their boards, parting to let the main boat through.

Kyllen peered intently at the man standing upright in the boat, supported by his people on both sides.

Could it be? Could he be so lucky as to not only return to his father's lands but also to the time when his father was alive?

The boat moved closer.

The face of the High Lord bore the clear signs of aging. The dark-green pattern of dehydration was sharp and prominent both on his *senties* and his hands, leaching onto his face, too. The mortal drought of aging had set in.

The man's face bore Kyllen's family features, but it wasn't his father.

"Kyllen. Brother." The High Lord spread his arms. "You came back."

"Udren?" His little brother, who had been only sixteen years old when Kyllen was taken, was now an old man, clearly standing at the threshold of death already.

A much younger man at the High Lord's side glared at Kyllen. "Brother?"

Udren swept his hand between the two of them. "Bherlon. This is Kyllen. Your uncle."

Uncle? He had a nephew, now?

The High Lord turned to his guards. "Let him come here."

With another stroke of a paddle, the boat slid close enough for Kyllen to jump from the tree trunk into it. He landed right in front of his brother.

"You haven't changed a bit." The old man smiled. "Just as fast and agile as you've ever been."

"Udren..." He stared at his brother, lost for words.

Centuries had passed in Lorsan, taking a toll on Udren. He was an old, fragile man now. His entire life had passed while Kyllen was away.

"Father and mother?" he asked, not harboring much hope.

"Both are long dead," Udren replied.

He expected this answer. Yet the pain of loss seized his heart nevertheless. He genuinely loved his mother and respected his father. He dreamed of living up to their legacy and hoped to make them proud one day. Now, that day would never come.

He still had to consider himself lucky to land close enough in time to catch someone from his family alive, someone who still remembered his name.

Emotions overwhelmed him, and he reached for his brother.

"Udren." He took the old man in an embrace.

"Brother." The frail arms wrapped around him in return. "Welcome back."

When the High Lord released him, Bherlon, the nephew, gave him a brief nod in greeting. Udren slid his gaze down Kyllen's frame, undoubtedly taking in the sorry state of his clothes.

"I can't wait to hear where you've been, brother." He then turned to his entourage, raising his voice, "A big celebration is in order. My brother came back from the faraway land of humans."

Kyllen arched a brow ridge. "How did you know it was the human world they took me to?"

Udren faced him again. "I saw the men who trapped you, Kyllen. Bald, with Ghata's tattoos on their arms. They were her monks, the werewolves she converted to *bracks* to serve her. She'd escaped this world long ago, as you know, but her *bracks* show up in Nerifir now and then, trading for her. We knew where they took you, but we never hoped to see you again. This is a glorious day." He waved his hands at the guards. "Let us go. Let the palace know Lord Kyllen has returned."

"Wait!" Kyllen stopped them. "I'm not alone."

"Who are you with?" Bherlon cast a guarded glance along the shore, as if expecting an ambush.

"A human woman helped me escape. She came with me."

"A human?" Udren and Bherlon exclaimed at once.

Udren shook his head. "But why? She won't last here long."

"I'm intending for her to *last* as long as her natural lifespan will allow, which is about a hundred years," Kyllen said loud and clear for everyone to hear. He wasn't going to let them treat Amira's life as something less precious than that of a gorgonian.

Udren turned towards the shore, squinting his eyes. "Where is she?"

"I'll go get her." Kyllen jumped onto the board of the closest guard.

"May I?" He took the paddle from the hands of the man, who looked somewhat stunned by his audacity.

"Let him." Udren waved his hand, then heavily lowered himself back into the chair. "I know my brother. If you don't give him the board, he'll swim for it. And there are purple leeches in this part of the river."

Judging by the look in Bherlon's pale yellow eyes, his nephew wouldn't mind for the purple leeches to suck his uncle dry. Kyllen made a mental note to keep an eye on his nephew as he dipped the paddle into the stream. The guard jumped into the High Lord's boat, leaving the board in Kyllen's full control.

Shifting all the way to the back end of the board, he raised the front out of the water, then turned the entire thing sharply with one powerful stroke of the paddle.

The High Lord chuckled from the boat approvingly. "He taught me how to do that."

With long strokes, Kyllen easily overpowered the lazy current, steering back to the place where he'd left Amira. Slowing down, he plowed through the tall grass and beached the nose of the board on the wet ground.

"Amira," he called, propping the paddle into the river bottom to steady the board.

"Kyllen?" Her quiet voice came from behind the tree where he'd told her to wait for him.

"Come here, my sweet pea," he coaxed. "It's safe to come out, but keep your blindfold on."

She felt her way around the tree trunk.

"Just follow my voice," he guided. "I'm in the water on a paddle board. You'll have to go through the patch of tall grass. It's wet here. Your shoes may take in some water. Don't be scared."

"I'm not." Keeping her hands in front of her, she walked toward him in small, hesitant steps.

She trusted him, fully and literally blindly. It would never cease to amaze him, her endless capacity of trust. The ease with which she could be fooled made him feel like doing the opposite—protect her at all costs.

"That's a good girl," he murmured as the toe of her shoe nudged the edge of the board.

He could extend the paddle for her to grab on to. But he didn't want to startle her with the unfamiliar object. Instead, he shifted closer along the board and offered her his hand.

She found it by touch and clung to his fingers like to a lifeline.

"There you are." He led her onto the board. "Now sit down right here. No, there's no chair here. You'll have to get all the way down and sit on your pretty bottom. Right. Just like that. And try not to make any sudden movements. I'm a bit rusty on the board after all those long months in the crate. You don't want us to tip over."

"Where are we going?" She asked, sitting down.

"To the palace of the High Lord of Ellohi. Udren, my younger brother, has taken the throne."

She gasped softly, but said nothing more.

Gliding the board over the murky waters of the river, he quickly caught up with the flotilla and lined up his board with the boat of the High Lord.

"You both are welcome to join me in here," Udren offered, casting a curious glance at Amira.

The guard Kyllen had misplaced by taking the board rose to his feet, ready to trade places, but Kyllen didn't move. In the boat, he'd have to sit at his brother's feet, looking up at him if they wanted to talk. While standing on the board, his head was higher than that of the High Lord. He preferred this position.

Besides, it felt good to be on the board once again. There had been times while he had sat in that cursed crate when he didn't think he'd ever get to do this again.

Amira tilted her head back, breathing deeply. Deprived of her eyesight, she appeared to let her other senses guide her in the exploration of this new-to-her world, including the sense of smell.

"This is my brother, Amira," he said. "Udren, the High Lord of Ellohi."

She straightened her back and turned to face the boat.

"Nice to meet you," she said sweetly, her voice polite but guarded.

With a gesture at her, he introduced loudly for the entire flotilla to hear, "This is my Amira."

That was a public claim. The word "my" was a warning to everyone to keep their hands away from her. And judging by the intrigued stares tossed at her from every direction, the warning was badly needed.

"Welcome to Ellohi, Amira." Udren tilted his head. "I hope you'll like it here."

She smiled and bowed her head—the gesture full of grace. She sat closer to the front of his board with her legs crossed, visibly calm. But by how perfectly straight she held her back and how white the skin over her knuckles turned as she gripped the edge of the board on each side of her, he could tell she was nervous, out of her element, and probably outright stressed.

He wished he could pull the board over to the river bank, gather her into his lap again, and calm her down with hugs and kisses. But the High Lord's palace was already visible up ahead. And the kisses had to wait.

Chapter Twenty-Seven

AMIRA

I almost didn't need to *see* the palace to know where we were when we arrived. Kyllen had described his home so perfectly in his stories to me, I could envision it well in my mind.

A giant royal marsh tree housed the central portion of the palace, with rooms spaced evenly between the wide branches. It was surrounded by seven younger trees. All were interconnected by hanging bridges on every level.

Thick roots grew deep into the ground, raising the tree trunks out of the water of Layahi Bay. High in the middle of the central tree would be the great court of the palace where all the major gatherings took place.

I wondered if that was where they took us upon our arrival. Noise of a large crowd descended on me like a suffocating blanket the moment we got off the paddle board. It grew even louder as we climbed up some stairs and ascended inclined paths. Afraid to trip on the way, I kept clinging to Kyllen's arm.

"Ahhh," he exhaled at my side. "This is just as I remember it." I wasn't sure whether he was referring to the place or the crowd surrounding us. Probably both. "Not much has changed. How long has it been? Four? Five hundred years?"

That was the "when" we had landed in. These many centuries would mean some drastic changes on Earth. But in Nerifir, Kyllen had said before, life flowed slowly, with few visible changes from generation to generation.

His words drowned in the ocean of voices—the ocean that seemed close to consuming me.

How many people were around us? Hundreds? Thousands?

They surrounded us. I could feel their stares with my skin that crawled with unease. Every now and then, a phrase would leap at me from the cacophony of noises, lashing like a slap.

"Human? How curious..."

"What's the lord going to do with her?"

"Fuck her. Or trade her. Humans are rare. She would fetch a good price."

"Is she a trophy or a prisoner?"

"If she was a prisoner, why didn't he just execute her?"

"That would've been a mercy. She won't last long, anyway..."

Their comments didn't scare me. I trusted Kyllen not to hurt me, not on purpose, anyway. The invisible crowd, idly chatting about my execution, seemed far more menacing. I gripped Kyllen's sleeve tighter, pressing my side to him.

More voices sounded all around me. Now they were talking about him.

"Is the lord going to reclaim his position, do you think?"

"Well, he's the eldest son. It's his birthright."

"But Udren has been our High Lord for centuries. He committed no crime by taking his father's place."

"Dinner is served!" someone announced over the noise of the crowd.

"Hungry?" Kyllen whispered into my ear.

"No," I replied quickly. I'd lost whatever appetite I had.

Sitting at a table with all these people, feeling like their stares were burning through my blindfold... I couldn't do it, not when I was exhausted by the lack of sleep and the long hike through the wetlands of

Lorsan. I felt too overwhelmed by the new world that had crashed over me so suddenly and so...intensely.

"My lord," Kyllen said loudly. "Please allow us a few minutes to change our clothes. We don't want to disgrace your fine company with our ragged appearance."

"Don't linger, brother," Udren demanded. "We all are eager to hear about your adventures in the land of humans."

As Kyllen led me aside, someone joined us. "I'll show you to your rooms."

"I know how to find *my* rooms," Kyllen snapped.

The man cleared his throat and continued uncertainly, "Well, Lord Bherlon is currently occupying your former rooms, my lord, with the adjacent apartments being taken by his wife, Lady Igaed."

"Of course they'd be taken." Kyllen didn't sound surprised. "By my *nephew*," he added pointedly.

It wouldn't be easy for him to slip back into his life at the palace. It had been taking its course without him for so long.

"We have other beautiful rooms to offer for accommodation to you and your...um, human friend," the man suggested.

"Do you now?" Kyllen replied flatly. "Well, lead the way, my fine man."

The gorgonian led us to a room he said was for me. He then wanted to take Kyllen up a few levels to a room they had prepared for him, but Kyllen refused.

"Find me one right here, next to hers," he demanded. "I'll help her settle meanwhile, while you're getting it ready."

The moment we were left alone in my new room, I turned to Kyllen. "I don't want to go to dinner. Please. Not even if we get changed. I can't..."

He petted my arm. "I gathered you wouldn't. It's too much, isn't it?"

"Yes," I exhaled in relief that he understood.

"I'll have to go, though. It's important that I attend." He sounded rather grim.

I squeezed his hand. "I know. It's fine. I'll wait here."

"I'll send you some food."

I shook my head. "Don't bother. I'm so tired, I'll probably fall asleep before it arrives."

How long had it been since my last sleep? Or meal? Did the time in the River of Mists count? Or did it stand still?

I just knew that I was too tired to eat.

"Let me help you familiarize yourself with this place a little before I go." Kyllen took my arm.

Walking me slowly around the room, he placed my hand on each object, explaining its purpose.

"Table and two chairs. I'll shove them closer to each other so you'll have more space and less chance to trip over them. Window. Stay away from it. It's large enough to walk out of, with only a few branches trained to grow across for a railing. The water is deep enough to possibly survive the fall, but the impact would be hard—we're quite high above the surface here. Bathing basin. It's always full in Lorsan." I heard a smile in his voice. This was a clear reference to the empty bathtub he had found in the hotel room back in London.

A trickling of water reached my hearing.

"Waterfall?" I asked.

"Exactly. Touch it." He took my wrist and extended my hand for me.

A warm stream pleasantly rolled over my fingers.

"Good to drink and bathe if you like. The toiletries are here on the ledge to the right." He then opened another door. "Waste room. It's quite small."

The noise of another waterfall rushed from inside the small room.

"Does the waste get flushed straight down into the Bay?"

"Of course not." Disgust tinted his voice. "It gets processed and sanitized first."

"How?"

"I'm not sure." He closed the door, and the sound of the waterfall disappeared behind it. "I never had the interest to study the specifics of waste processing, but if you absolutely need to know—"

"No," I stopped him. "Definitely not tonight."

"Alright. Your nest is here." He took me to the other side of the waterfall with the bathing pool.

"The nest?"

"The bed," he explained. "You call it 'the bed.' Werewolves often say 'the lair' or 'the den,' depending on the region of Sarnala they're from. And gargoyles refer to it as 'the perch' sometimes. But it's all the same with small differences—the place where you sleep. It's right here, behind the screen."

With one hand on the wall of polished wood, I followed his lead to a recess in the wall. A screen of silky material stretched over a wooden frame hid a soft mattress that appeared to be placed right on the floor.

"The nest is round, not square like your beds." Kyllen continued to serve as my eyes, describing the things I couldn't see. "It's not raised, but it's so thick, you'd never feel the floor."

I bent over to examine it by touch. The edge of the mattress was about three feet high. A thick soft cushion roll circled the edge, which would make it look very much like a nest, I imagined.

A knock on the door sounded. The man who had brought us here came to announce that Kyllen's room was now ready.

"It's on the same branch as this one. I sent a maid to fetch a dress for...um..." He clearly was at a loss on how to address me.

"Amira," Kyllen set him straight. "*Lady* Amira to you."

"I'm no lady," I muttered under my breath.

"You are now." He drew me into his side. "It's easier that way. They need to know where to place you." He then spoke to the man again, "The dress won't be necessary tonight. Lady Amira won't be coming to dinner. She wishes to rest instead."

"As you wish, my lady," the man said. "Your evening clothes are laid out in your room, my lord."

"I'd better go." Kyllen placed a kiss on my forehead.

My heart dropped, letting him go, but I forced my fingers to unclench from around his hand. He wasn't here to babysit me. His entire life had just been re-organized, and he had to sort it out.

"Sweet dreams." He wished me before leaving.

A few moments later, someone knocked on my door again.

"Yes!" I perked up, hoping against all odds that Kyllen had returned, that he would spend my first night in the new world with me.

The door opened.

"My lady," a feminine voice sounded instead of Kyllen's. "My name is Geltar. I was sent to help you get ready for the night."

"Help? But how?" And why? What was I supposed to do to go to sleep? Other than lay down and close my eyes? Not even that, I realized with a smile. My eyes were already closed by the blindfold.

"Um...well." The poor woman sounded discomfited. "I'll have to brush and braid your hair, take off your clothes, and put on your nightgown."

Was she concerned I wouldn't manage all that on my own?

"Oh. Thank you. But I can do it myself." I wasn't entirely incapacitated, even with the blindfold on.

"But..." The woman hesitated, making me feel sorry for her.

"Is there a problem?"

"A lady needs a maid to get ready for sleep," she said softly but with conviction.

It dawned on me that was what Kyllen meant when he'd said that people needed to know where to place me. There appeared to be a hierarchy here at the court of the High Lord. Each role came with a set of rules, with rights, obligations, and privileges. A lady apparently needed a maid, and since Kyllen told them I was a lady...

"Well. How about you come in the morning and help me get dressed instead? I'm too tired to be...um, *helped* right now. Will that work?" I kept my voice as gentle as possible. The last thing I wanted was to offend anyone when I'd just gotten here. It was impossible to accurately judge people's reactions without seeing their faces.

"Oh, all right. As you wish. I'll leave the nightshirt right here, then, on the screen frame."

"Thank you, Geltar."

She left, closing the door behind her. I came to the door and inspected it by touch, searching for a lock. Not finding one, I propped a chair against the door and made a mental note to ask Kyllen about the lock tomorrow. He was the one who'd told me not to trust anyone.

I briefly contemplated sleeping in my clothes like I normally would. But they were still damp from our dunk in the river. The long pants and the sweater were also too hot for the mild, humid climate of Lorsan. I couldn't wait to take them off.

Keeping my arms stretched in front of me, I found the screen and the nightshirt that Geltar had left for me. The material felt paper thin and light, like a spiderweb in my fingers. I quickly peeled off my wet clothes, including the bra and panties, and changed into the long, sleeveless nightshirt. The light, airy garment felt pleasant against my skin.

Next, I used the waste room, then washed my face and brushed my teeth in the main waterfall in the bedroom.

All of that could've been accomplished easier had I taken the blindfold off. I'd thought about doing that. There was no one else in the room. I could at least peek from underneath it a little to get a visual of my surroundings.

But that would be the problem then, wouldn't it? I would always try to sneak "a visual" whenever I'd think I had a chance. But what if I wasn't alone? What if, like Kyllen had once said, someone glanced at me through the window or walked in unexpectedly?

I'd be dead, and there'd be no second chance.

If I couldn't look at anyone, it was best to train myself not to see at all. Maybe it'd be best not to know what I was missing? Besides, there were enough new smells, sounds, and textures for me to process for now.

Exhausted, I stumbled toward "the nest" and climbed in. It was unbelievably comfy—soft and warm with cool, silky sheets. At first, I lay on top of them. But without my scarf and wearing only the thin nightshirt, I felt too exposed and uncomfortably naked.

Peeling the top sheet off, I got under it.

Kyllen had made my blindfold from a piece of his shirt, and it still smelled like him. His comforting scent of moss and rain cradled me as I drifted to sleep.

Chapter Twenty-Eight

AMIRA

The noise of the chair legs scraping against the floor woke me up with a start.

It was dark. No light filtered through my blindfold, whatsoever. The screeching of the chair was followed by cursing said in a hushed but familiar voice.

"Kyllen?" I sat up.

"Close your eyes, Amira."

"They are closed." My heart slowed down from the wild race that the sudden awakening had sent it on.

He climbed onto my "nest." His hands on each side of my head, he found the blindfold.

"Good girl," he murmured. "Did you put that chair there?"

"Yes. There's no lock."

"Smart." He kissed the tip of my nose.

"What happened, Kyllen? Why are you here?"

"Oh. That's a very good question." He found the end of the top sheet and climbed under the cover with me. "You see, after the dinner, I went to the room they gave me. Had a bath, got undressed. Then, I lay in the nest and wondered, 'What by the Garden of the Cursed am I doing here? Alone? When my little human is just next door, and there are no chains or crates keeping me away from her?' So, I got up, sent the guard I'd placed at your door away, and came here." He scooted closer and shifted a bit, making himself comfortable. "And I'm glad I did. It seems, they gave you a much comfier nest than mine. I feel much better here."

I smiled. "I like having you here."

"That is very fortunate, my dear, because I think I'll be staying here from now on."

I didn't mind that one bit, leaning into the now familiar warmth of his body.

"How was the dinner?"

He took a moment before replying. "Interesting."

"Tell me."

"No," he said. "I need to *think* about it first, before I can *talk* about it."

He could be overwhelmed too, maybe not as much as I was, but it couldn't be easy to skip centuries on a timeline.

"You must be tired," I said.

He'd gotten less sleep than I had. Since we woke up in the hotel in London, he hadn't even had a nap.

"I'm simply exhausted," he admitted.

"Let's go to sleep, then." I curled against his chest, only to shrink back again. "Oh, you're naked." There was no thick comforter between us this time.

"So? That's how I always sleep." He skimmed my hip with his hand. "You, on the other hand..." He rose on his elbow. "By the power of Great Serpent... Amira, what are *you* wearing?"

He yanked the sheet off me. I rolled to my back to grab it, but it was too late. He'd already exposed me down to my knees.

I had no idea how much coverage the fabric of the nightshirt provided. Judging by the charged silence from him, it wasn't much. The night must be not as dark as it seemed to me with the blindfold on. He saw...something.

"Gods take me..." he groaned. "What is this garment? It's *barely* there and leaves you so delightfully *bare*."

"A maid brought it." I gave up fishing for the sheet and used my arms and hands to try to cover myself. "She said it was a nightshirt."

"Great Serpent, bless the maid." He leaned down and kissed the hand I'd placed over my left breast.

Incredibly, being exposed to him like this didn't make me feel helpless or ashamed. On the contrary, the appreciation in his voice and the reverence in his touch made me feel powerful.

"Oh, let me touch you, Amira. Please. I need this tonight." He kissed my collarbone, then my neck, making his way up to my lips. His *senties* trembled around my head and shoulders, their touch tender, like a brush of rose petals against my skin.

A teasing flicker of heat sparked deep inside my belly, needy and tantalizing.

"Kyllen..." I breathed against his lips as he covered my mouth with light, tender kisses.

"Yesss? My sweet, sweet girl," he hissed softly, shifting his hips closer to mine.

One of his *senties* skimmed my collarbone and slid down between my breasts. The other nudged its diamond-shaped head under my hand on my breast. When I let my hand fall away, the *sentie* promptly slid lower, under my shirt. The thin, slithering tongue flicked against my nipple, then the small mouth closed over the hardened bud. Its firm, tiny nibbles sent a shudder of pleasure through my body. Heat tingled between my legs.

"What is it?" I asked the question that had been unanswered for years. "What is happening to me? What do I feel?"

"Oh, sweetheart." Kyllen cradled my head between his hands, sinking his fingers into my hair. "It's pleasure, Amira. Call it 'sex' or 'making love,' it's all fine, as long as it feels good." He kissed me again, then flicked my right hand from my other breast. He cupped it through my shirt, rubbing the nipple with his thumb. "Does this feel good, my sweet?"

The tip of my breast tingled, tightening. Ripples of heat spread lower, making me restless. I needed...something.

"Yes, Kyllen," I moaned, arching my back. "So…so good."

"What a good girl you are." He slid the shirt off my shoulder, exposing my breast.

His familiar voice soothed me. His touch excited every nerve in my body. His *senties* caressed my neck as he palmed my breast, pinching the pebbled tip between his fingers.

"Oh God, Kyllen, yes." I sucked in a breath, surrendering to the swells of pleasure that rolled through my entire body.

"Let me make you feel good tonight…" His voice floated over me, musical and enthralling, as his hands hiked up the skirt of my night-gown. He trailed his fingers up my inner thigh, igniting a new wave of thrills. "This is where you want me, isn't it?" He pressed a finger to something right between my thighs and my legs jerked, pleasure bursting through me like fireworks.

"Oh…" was all I could manage, blinded by the sensation and craving more of it.

"Let me give you what you want, my darling." He rubbed lightly, swirling the tip of his finger in circles.

I whimpered, raising my hips. "More… Oh, please Kyllen, a little more…"

He leaned over me, whispering in my ear, "Like this?" He pressed harder, rubbing faster. "How does it feel?"

I had no name for this feeling. Even if I did, I could no longer say anything. Words deserted me. My entire being seemed to narrow down to the tip of that one finger of Kyllen's and the spot where he pressed it to me.

"Does it feel like you couldn't possibly take any more?" he spoke for me, his whisper hot and urgent as he moved his hand ever faster. "Like you would explode into pieces if I continued? Yet you'd rather die than make me stop?"

I moaned something incomprehensible in reply, writhing my hips under his hand. I rolled my head on the pillow, and he caught my mouth in a kiss. His *senties* played with my breasts, coiling around them. Two small mouths closed over both of my nipples, nibbling and rubbing.

Sharp charges of pleasure rolled in bursts through my chest down to my lower belly. It tightened and wound in the spot right under Kyllen's finger on me.

"Let it explode, my sweetest," he murmured. "Let it go."

And I did.

I couldn't contain it any longer. I let it happen. Floodgates opened inside me somewhere and pure bliss coursed through me. Uncontained.

The unknown need that had been sparking in me through the years had finally come to completion. This was what I had wanted. This one body and mind shattering moment, when I fell apart, and couldn't care less if I'd ever be whole again.

"Just like that." Kyllen took me through it all. He slowed down, then removed his finger from me. Instead, he cupped me between my legs with his hand. The slight pressure he applied reaped a few more shudders out of me, each gentler than the one before, until my muscles quieted. Inside me, something still quivered slightly, like aftershocks of an earthquake of pleasure.

"What..." I panted, struggling to catch my breath and to find my words again. "What was that?"

"Orgasm." Kyllen nuzzled the side of my face, smiling against my skin. "Was it your first?"

"You know it was."

He rose over me. "I know that no man has ever touched you. But haven't you done it yourself?"

"I..."

What could I say to that?

That I had never had any time for myself? That I'd lived in a constant state of alert, expecting someone to yell for me any minute? That despite being lonely all my life, I'd never been left alone. I had no privacy. I'd never felt safe or relaxed enough to explore my body without a threat of invasion or interruption, and possibly punishment.

I released a breath, then said something that in a way encompassed all of the above.

"I never had my own nest before."

I kept my voice light, expecting Kyllen to laugh at that. He always laughed so easily, even when he was a prisoner locked in a crate. But he didn't laugh this time. Instead, he gently cradled me to his chest.

Something hard, long, and shaped very much like the cucumber I'd tossed at him once pressed to my side. I made a move to lean back and explore what it was.

But he kept holding me to him, not letting go. "Shh. Sleep now."

"But—"

"You're tired. Don't worry about that. It can wait. We'll have plenty of time together."

Oh, how I wished it was true. And maybe it was?

Madame wasn't here to threaten me or people I loved. There was no need to fear. I relaxed against his chest.

A handful of his *senties* caressed my cheek, then rested peacefully on the side of my neck.

I'd never felt like I belonged in the world that I'd left. Neither could I be sure yet that Lorsan would ever accept me as its own.

But right here in Kyllen's arms, I was more at home than I'd ever been before. I felt like I finally belonged.

MARINA SIMCOE

PART 2

THE RIVER OF MISTS

Chapter One

AMIRA

Lady Igaed poked her needle through the embroidery she was working on. Her canvas was stretched so tight in the frame, I heard every single stitch she made.

"Is Lord Kyllen coming home tonight?" she asked, laying stitches in an uninterrupted battery of pokes.

At the sound of Kyllen's name, my heart leaped and skidded. It was the fourth day since he'd been gone, but it felt like an eternity.

"Yes." I clutched the cup of tea in my hands. "He said he'd be home tonight."

There wasn't much else for me to do at the palace but eat and sleep. With the blindfold on, I couldn't even join Lady Igaed in needlework to kill time until Kyllen's return. I agreed to meet with her this morning only because sitting in my room alone had started to feel way too much like hiding behind a crate in Madame's tent.

"Did he say where he was traveling?" Lady Igaed inquired for the second time since we'd gotten together after breakfast.

We were sitting on a patio of sorts. The way the High Lord's palace was constructed, living spaces blended with the outdoors seamlessly.

Bedrooms were carved into the thick branches of the great royal trees, with walls and partitions added where needed. Halls and common areas often remained under the open sky, shaded only by the leafy canopy above.

A breeze caressed my face. Lights filtered through my blindfold in an ever-changing pattern as sun rays must be playing between the leaves above us. Geltar, the woman assigned to be my maid, had told me that Lady Igaed had invited me to join her in her drawing *room*. Yet here we were, in the breeze and sun, under the leafy canopy. This wasn't "a room" in the sense that I was used to.

"No. Kyllen didn't tell me where he was going when he left," I replied, keeping my head down.

I hadn't expected him to leave me alone so soon, barely a day after we first arrived in Lorsan. Before he left, he'd kissed me and given me a long hug that still hadn't felt nearly long enough. Then, he'd placed something on my ring finger.

"This will protect you while I'm gone."

"What is it?" I felt the object carefully. It was a ring with a stone that had a hole drilled in it. I remembered he wore it on his pinky.

"It's a hag's stone. Magic flows through it, carving a passage. Right here." He took my hand and pressed one of my fingers to the smooth funnel of the hole. "It'll protect you from curses or from the effects of anything they may decide to add to your food."

"Don't trust anyone," his words sounded in my head again.

Holding the teacup with my fingers overlapping, I traced the smooth edges of the hole in the stone on Kyllen's ring. It felt warm and, in a way, comforting.

"Hmm." Lady Igaed kept energetically stabbing the canvas with her needle. "Lord Kyllen has been rather secretive, hasn't he?"

She hit a nerve. It bothered me that he left without telling me where he was going and why. I trusted him implicitly, but he chose to keep secrets from me.

My thoughts rushed to the day he left again. We'd had breakfast together. He'd wished to know which eggs I liked better, fish eggs or pickled frog eggs. He'd ordered both for me to try. I'd told him I still preferred chicken eggs, which made him laugh.

Oh God, I missed that laugh. Longing speared through my chest so strong it hurt. I wrapped my fingers tighter around the teacup, trying not to fall apart, not in front of Lady Igaed.

I willed my voice not to shake. "I'm sure he has his reasons."

"Does he?" she echoed. "I don't see what they could be. We're all his family here. We welcomed him back. The High Lord was planning a big celebration to mark his return. And he just left..."

She let the end of the last sentence hang in the air, as if inviting me to explain.

Only what could I say other than Kyllen probably didn't want to talk about his travel plans because he didn't want anyone to know? Maybe he didn't trust his family, just like he obviously didn't fully trust me.

When I'd asked him where he was going, he'd told me to wait and see. The waiting part was killing me now even more than my inability to see.

"Men," Lady Igaed huffed, and I imagined her shaking her head. "It's best for a woman never to rely on one."

It was a curious statement coming from the woman who was married to Lord Bherlon, the son of the High Lord of Ellohi, and who was expected to rule these lands alongside her husband one day.

"Are you and Lord Bherlon bonded mates?" I blurted out.

She chuckled. "Oh no, sweetie. Finding your fated mate is so rare, one can spend their entire life searching and waiting in vain. It's hardly worth it. Most fae unions are not bonded. And frankly, it's easier that way."

"Easier? How?"

"A bond requires a strong emotional involvement. To the point that if one of the mates dies, the other one quickly follows. It's sad, really." She heaved a sigh. "Whereas a practical, arranged union allows a woman to keep a lot more of herself—her heart, her soul, even her body in some cases."

I tried not to sound naïve but couldn't fight my curiosity. "Isn't sex required in a marriage?"

She giggled softly.

"Not necessarily. A state marriage really only requires your mind and your wallet, or whatever status and property each partner contributes to the union. My father, High Lord of Stevali, transferred a great portion of his prime hunting grounds to Ellohi as part of our marriage arrangement. Lord Udren had signed an alliance with him in return."

"Oh..." I took a sip of my now tepid tea.

I had so much to learn about this new way of life. Now, that I had more free time than ever before, I wished I could find books to read about it. Except that with the blindfold on, it would be impossible to read, anyway.

"But *you* don't have to concern yourself with any of that, my dear," Lady Igaed pointed out. "Humans don't become either spouses or bonded mates to fae. At least, I've never heard of that ever happening."

Her dismissive tone stabbed through me like her needle through the canvas in the frame.

"What do they become?" I asked with apprehension.

"There haven't been many of your kind in Nerifir. I haven't heard of one ever coming to Lorsan, for obvious reasons." She clearly was referring to the necessity of my blindfold. "Legends from other kingdoms of Nerifir say humans make for great lovers. They're also easy to breed. Your birthrate is much higher than that of fae, despite your shorter lifespan, or maybe because of it. Also, a child born to a human is always a fae. That's convenient to have in a lover, especially if one has no legitimate heirs."

I set my cup down on a side table. If I tried to take another sip, I'd probably choke on it. There was also a real danger of me dropping it as my hands trembled. I fisted them, hating that Lady Igaed could surely see the distress her words had caused in me. I'd never been good at hiding my emotions.

"There is no need to worry, sweetie," she cooed. "As long as you're young and pretty, you'll be able to find a lord anywhere in Nerifir to take care of you."

I wasn't sure if her words were meant to console me, but they did nothing of the sort. I'd come to Nerifir to be free. Not to become someone's mistress or...a breeder.

The tight bodice of the dress that Geltar had laced me in that morning seemed to get even tighter. I bent my head, but there was no scarf for me to hide in. The dress didn't even have a collar, leaving my neck and shoulders exposed. It felt like my very soul had been exposed, too, bare and vulnerable.

Someone walked out onto the terrace where we were sitting.

"Oh, morning, darling," Lady Igaed murmured to the person. "You're up."

By the intimate tone of her voice, I assumed the newcomer was her husband.

"Up and looking for you," he said, and I realized it was not Lord Bherlon. The voice belonged to another man, though I didn't know to whom exactly.

His words were followed by the sound of a kiss and a giggle from the lady. Another kiss, then the rustle of clothes and the creak of her chair.

Did they think that because I was blindfolded, I wouldn't know what they were up to? Or did they simply not care?

"You have to go, honey. I'm having a conversation with Lady Amira. Can't you see?"

"Morning, Lady Amira." The man changed his tone to a slightly more formal one. "Pardon me for interrupting."

I nodded in his direction, unsure what to say. Neither of them had bothered to introduce us. I didn't know his name.

His footsteps disappeared in the distance, announcing his departure.

"He's one of the personal guards of the High Lord," Lady Igaed explained, though I hadn't asked for an explanation. "He's also one of my lovers."

"And Lord Bherlon..."

"Knows, of course," she finished for me. "But he doesn't care. Lord Bherlon has a number of courtiers, male and female, to keep him company in his nest, too. Like I said, a highborn marriage is a political union, first and foremost. Other than my husband's scheduled visits to my nest, hoping to conceive an heir one day, I'm free to decide whom to reward with my attentions. My heart remains mine." She must have leaned my way because her voice sounded closer. "If you're a smart woman, Lady Amira, never give your heart to anyone at all. Without land, name, or a title, your heart is your most precious possession—your *only* possession. Keep it." She leaned back again, her voice lifting. "It's the best way to avoid a heartbreak. Besides, one man can never give a woman everything she desires, even if he tries. So, why settle for just one?"

I had no idea how to reply to that question. Did she even expect an answer?

Probably not, because she kept talking, "Anyway, when Kyllen tires of you—"

"He won't." I stopped her, unwilling to hear the end of that sentence. "He promised me—"

She scoffed. "Fae don't make promises if they can help it, my dear. Sometimes, it may sound like we do, but words can be easily twisted."

"Kyllen didn't twist anything," I argued. "He promised loud and clear. He made a vow." For that was how his promise had sounded to me back when Kyllen had made it in that hotel room in London—like a vow.

"What exactly did he promise?" she enquired casually. In fact, it appeared she made a great effort to sound uninterested.

I had no idea how Lady Igaed could benefit from knowing the exact words of the promise that Kyllen had made to me or whether that could harm him, but his warning about not trusting anyone rose in my mind again.

"I think it's best if you ask him," I said firmly. "It's *his* promise, after all. It's up to him to disclose it."

"Or not," I added in my head.

When I finally made it back to my room, the words of Lady Igaed kept haunting me.

I flipped the new lock closed that Kyllen had installed on my door before he left. Then I paced the room, lost in thought.

It had been so easy to bask in Kyllen's affections while he held me in his arms. So easy to keep my eyes closed—literally and figuratively—to the world around me and to ignore the court life and the people who surrounded me.

Not paying attention would cost me, though, wouldn't it? This was supposed to be my new home. I had to figure out where I fit into the court's life.

But how exactly did I want to fit in? Where would my ideal place be?

I wasn't entirely sure on that, either.

I wanted to be with Kyllen, but was it realistic? We hadn't spoken about marriage. I'd never even thought about it until the conversation with Lady Igaed. The marriage itself didn't matter to me. As long as Kyllen and I were together, I didn't care in what capacity it happened.

But it mattered to others. In Lorsan, status determined everything.

If I couldn't be Kyllen's bonded mate or his wife, how would I feel if he decided to get married one day? The idea of him being intimate with someone else didn't sit well with me. Even if those were just "scheduled visits" for the purpose of procreation between him and his future wife, I couldn't fathom sharing him with anyone else.

On the other hand, I understood I had no right to demand anything from him. He didn't make any promises to me beyond taking care of me. And maybe that should be enough. But it wasn't. I wanted more. I wished to have him in my nest every night, just the two of us.

What was I to him, though?

Kyllen loved having fun and excitement. He enjoyed new things. He found me in another world and decided to keep me as his own—like a kid would do with a shiny new toy.

Possessive as he was, he wouldn't let others touch his favorite plaything. But that didn't mean he wouldn't have more lovers to play with himself. Nothing stopped him from showering his affection on as many people as he liked. Especially since it was the norm at his brother's court.

Maybe Lady Igaed was right when she advised me not to give my heart to anyone. However, I feared her advice might've come a little too late.

Chapter Two

KYLLEN

With his forearms enclosed in leather bracers, he moved the tall sharp blades of amber cattails out of his way. Both boards, his and that of his companion, were magically enhanced for added speed. Each sure, long stroke of their paddles sent them flying ahead along the surface of the river.

Despite the thick grass in this part of the stream, the boards slid along nicely, keeping a steady pace. The sharp blades of the tall grass nicked his clothes. If it wasn't for the bracers, the skin on his forearms would've been shredded.

"Just around this bend, my lord." Hapon gestured at the patch of land that cut into the lazy waters of the Gex Creek, one of the many arms of Layahi Bay. "We'll be at the palace by dinnertime."

Kyllen didn't need Hapon to tell him that. He knew by heart the mouth of every stream flowing in or out of the bay. But he allowed Hapon to lead. The man clearly enjoyed being useful, and he had no heart to set him straight.

He'd chosen Hapon to accompany him for the same reason he had put this man to guard Amira's door on their first night back in Lorsan.

When he first saw Hapon, the man reminded him of Sedren, one of the few loyal guards his father had. He later learned that Hapon was Sedren's son, which made it easier to trust him.

That didn't mean, of course, that Hapon wouldn't betray him if given a chance. But so far, he'd proven to be a great travel partner.

It didn't hurt that Hapon's mother came from the small village near Lorsan's border with Olathana, the land of the sirens. It had taken them almost two days to reach the place. But Hapon knew the village well and had helped Kyllen find what he needed quickly.

They turned around the bend where the stream merged with Layahi Bay. The grassy patches retreated to the banks. Their boards now glided on the clean surface smoothly, unimpeded.

Water boards were the best mode of transportation for their party of two with little baggage. Many parts of the wetlands were impassable by horse, no matter how magically enhanced their horseshoes happened to be. Traipsing the wetlands on foot would take weeks one way. He'd hate leaving Amira alone for that long.

As it was, he and Hapon had covered the entire trek to the border and back in less than four days. Their boards needed just a little push of magic here and there to make it through some grassy patches.

The brightly lit royal tree of the palace glimmered in the distance. It used to be home. From the day he was born, all of Ellohi was meant to be *his* one day, but it had slipped between his fingers.

He should be ecstatic about returning to Lorsan so relatively close to the time when he'd left. But it wasn't that simple.

Udren was the only person he knew. The only one who remembered him. Other than his brother, the palace was full of strangers.

During the dinner he'd had with the people who were now his family, he'd learned that Bherlon was three hundred and twenty-three years old. All these years, his nephew had been groomed to become the next High Lord, and he showed no intentions of giving it up now.

No one had expected Kyllen's return. They had mourned and put him to rest, literally—there'd been a funeral with a symbolic urn of dirt placed on the final resting mound beneath the roots of the palace tree.

After that, Udren, his brother, had taken his place in every way. The little scoundrel had even married Kyllen's betrothed, Lady Eiphed. Not that Kyllen was upset about losing his bride. He hardly knew the woman and had absolutely no feelings or even a firm opinion about her.

He couldn't blame Udren for taking over. The world couldn't have stayed still for almost five centuries while he was gone. Udren didn't break any laws by taking the place vacated by Kyllen's abduction.

But the place always remained Kyllen's. He was the rightful High Lord of Ellohi, and he'd be damned if he stepped aside now in favor of the nephew he'd never met until a few days ago.

The golden lights of the palace blended with the brilliant pink and orange of the sunset on the horizon. The beauty of his homeland took his breath away. He couldn't wait for Amira to *see* this, too.

The thought of being with her soon added strength to his weary arm muscles. Hers was the only face he wished to see after the long and exhausting journey. She had been his one ray of sunshine during his imprisonment by Ghata. And she remained his guiding light now, in the place that should be his home but no longer felt like one.

He and Hapon approached the palace, weaving between the hundreds of other boards, rafts, and small boats. Kyllen gestured for Hapon to steer to the side, instead of the busy main passage.

They maneuvered between the trunks and roots of the nearby trees, docks, and other vessels. He slid his boat closer to the royal tree. Amira's window was quite high up. He could only see the glow from the light from her room up above them.

There were no branches past the thin growth right over the water. The smooth expanse of the royal tree trunk stretched high and wide.

"My lord?" Hapon sounded hesitant.

"Can you take my board back to the main dock?" Kyllen slid his paddle into the slot on the side of the board, then uncurled the length of rope attached to the nose of it. The rope was used to tie the small lightweight vessels when not in use.

"How are *you* planning to get inside, my lord?" Hapon frowned. The man's reddish *senties* stirred agitatedly, betraying his unease.

"I'll climb." Kyllen tipped his chin at the tree.

Hapon glanced up at the trunk. "It's my duty to inform you that climbing the walls of the palace is impossible. In addition to the magic wards, the tree is smoothed and polished on purpose, to keep the High Lord and his family safe from intruders."

"I know, Hapon."

"The wards may not stop you, since you are of the High Lord's blood, but even without them... It's just physically not possible, my lord."

Kyllen hid a smile. Hapon sounded so much like his father. Sedren had scolded Kyllen many times for climbing this very wall when he was a child.

As Hapon had said, the wards didn't concern Kyllen. The blood of his ancestors would allow him to get past them. However, the lock he had installed on Amira's door before he left could only be opened from inside her room. Of course, he could knock on her door and wait until she opened it for him. But that was the problem—he just couldn't *wait* any longer.

"It's faster this way." He kicked his boots off, dismissing Hapon's concerns with a wave of a hand.

He used the underbrush to climb the first section of the trunk. Once he reached the smoother surface, he slowed down a little, searching for the tiny, barely noticeable protrusions in the bark.

Using his fingers, toes, and even *senties*, he rediscovered the familiar path, steadily climbing up.

Many changes had taken place in this world during his absence. But it was a pleasure to discover some things had stayed the same. The royal tree hadn't changed at all.

AMIRA

By dinner time, I'd worn myself out with worrisome thoughts. I felt restless, needing to move. Heck, I would even clean something to get rid of the nervous energy that buzzed through me.

Geltar came to help me get dressed for dinner. I needed help, and it wasn't just because of my forced blindness. Getting into the evening gown that Geltar had brought proved much more difficult than pulling on a t-shirt and a hoodie.

There was no corset, thank goodness. But the double-layered bodice was tight on its own and was laced up the back with a ribbon. The light, flowing skirt had a high slit on the side that exposed my right leg every time I took a step.

My neck, arms, and shoulders remained bare. The breeze from the window chilled the expanse of skin I'd never exposed before.

Geltar circled my upper arms with metal armlets. Long scarfs of the same flowy material as my skirt were attached to them. The light fabric streamed down my arms to the floor.

"What color is this dress, Geltar?" I asked, stroking the soft material of my skirt. Despite its many layers, it felt weightless.

"Oh, it's the gentlest shade of mint-green," she cooed. "It tints your skin green a little. So lovely."

She sounded like she was giving me a compliment.

"Do gorgonians like the color green?"

"Oh yes," she replied enthusiastically.

I thought of the pattern on Kyllen's *senties*.

"Do all gorgonians have green in their coloring?" I asked, trying to imagine the crowd I'd be surrounded by tonight.

"No. Not all." She helped me into a chair, then started brushing my hair. "Green is beautiful. But it's usually just displayed in the markings on people's backs and *senties*. Our skin comes in many other colors, from pale sand, to reddish clay, to every shade of blue and gray, to beige or bronze. The markings have even more variety—green, burgundy, black, purple, gold, pink... Colors are beautiful—" She cut herself short, possibly realizing that I didn't have much to boast in terms of color. "Your hair is lovely, my lady. And if you like, I'll bring you a pallet of powders. We can tint your skin in any color you want. I can also find someone to paint markings on your back. We have many talented artists in Ellohi."

I untied my blindfold but held it to my eyes while she braided my hair. "Thank you, but that's all right. I'll just keep the skin I have, plain as it may be."

No matter what I did to my appearance, I sensed, it wouldn't make the Court of Ellohi accept me any faster. For a while yet, I would not feel comfortable in my own skin, regardless of what designs I'd paint on it.

Geltar deftly parted my hair into sections and braided them in plaits. There were twenty-four of them, she said, chatting about how she learned to style hair while growing up in a family of merchants who traveled along the border to trade with sirens and werewolves.

She secured the ends with snake-like clips by twisting them in spirals around each braid, then tied the blindfold back in place for me.

"You look beautiful, my lady." By the sound of her voice, she appeared to step back, possibly to admire her work.

"Thank you, Geltar." It was beyond bizarre to have another person dress me and brush my hair when I'd done the same for somebody else all my life. “Would you mind adding this to my hairdo as well, please?”

I handed her the dragonfly barrette, the only thing I’d brought from my old world, not counting the discarded pants and sweater.

“Oh, this is cute.” She took the barrette from me. “Looks rather plain, though. The box with jewelry that the High Lord has sent for you tonight has much better pieces. I can choose—”

“No.” I had enough trinkets decorating my arms, fingers, and neck already. Their cool, hard metal chilled my skin wherever Geltar had placed them. “I just want this one. Please clip it on any of the braids you’ve made.”

She did as I asked, then offered, “Would you like me to take you to the dining room now?”

I shook my head. “I’ll wait for Kyllen.”

“But what if Lord Kyllen is delayed?”

“Then…” The idea of sitting at the High Lord’s dining table alone, surrounded by strangers, terrified me. But I couldn’t continue hiding in this room. Blindfolded or not, I had to keep learning more about my surroundings. “Well, if he’s delayed, then you can come get me just before the dinner starts.”

When Geltar was gone, I sat in one of the chairs at the table and tried to collect my thoughts.

How did one prepare to face a crowd of people they couldn’t actually see? Would all of them be like Lady Igaed, dressing up insults to pass them on as helpful advice? Was my skin thick enough for me to survive it unscathed?

A rustling of leaves and snapping of branches yanked me out of my troubling thoughts. I jumped from my seat and grabbed the first thing I could possibly use as a weapon—the chair I’d been sitting on.

“Who’s there?”

The familiar chuckle reached me from the window.

“Oh, my sweet Amira, how sexy you look brandishing that chair.”

“Kyllen…” I dropped my arms down. The chair slipped from my fingers, hitting the floor with a thud. “You’re back.”

I took a step toward the sound of his voice, and he caught me in his arms. He smelled like forest and the river, and everything wonderful that had ever happened in my life.

I slid my hands up his chest and took his face between my palms. He slunk his *senties* between my fingers, wrapping them around my wrists to anchor me to him as he kissed me.

"Were you really going to whack me with that chair?" He smiled against my lips.

"I didn't know it was you." I snuggled against him. A shiver of pleasure ran through my body at the contact. "Why the window? What's wrong with the door?"

"I missed you, and it was quicker that way. Besides, you were a true vision with that chair, ready to hurl it at my head."

I lacked the gorgonian strength to be hurling furniture, but I just shook my head at his teasing. Pure happiness spread through me at having his arms around me once again. I'd missed him, too. So much.

"You scared me." I pressed my nose to the tunic on his chest, breathing in his familiar scent.

"I didn't mean to." He kissed my hair. "I missed you so much for the past four days. I really couldn't wait another minute. Do you believe me?"

"I do."

He exhaled a laugh. "But you see, *I* can't believe it myself. No one has ever had this hold over me before, Amira. I couldn't care less about being away from the palace. But I couldn't stand being away from you."

Not many people remembered him in this world. Kyllen and I had some shared history that would forever connect us. But I sensed there was more than that. I hoped there was.

I wrapped my arms tighter around him, leaning closer. I wished to align every part of myself with every part of him, and just stay like this—warm, comfy, and at peace.

"It's so good to have you back," I murmured into his chest. "Where have you been?"

"Oh, right." He stepped out of my embrace. "I've got something for you." There was a rustle of fabric; he must be rummaging in the travel bag he had slung over his shoulder.

"What is it? Another present?" Anticipation fizzed inside me with warm effervescence. "You know you risk spoiling me."

"You're long overdue for some gifts and pampering, my sweet pea. But this is not just a frivolous gift." Pride rang in his voice. "I wanted to get it for you the moment we were back in Lorsan, and now I did. Here."

He placed something on my head. It felt like a circlet, firm but flexible enough to fit snugly around the crown of my head.

"Now let me take this off." He untied my blindfold.

I kept my eyes closed, surprised by his actions. "What's going on?"

With a finger under my chin, he tilted my head up. "Look at me, Amira."

Look at him? After he had repeatedly urged me to keep my eyes closed ever since we met?

"Don't worry," he assured me. "It's safe. I tested it on a siren."

"Tested what?"

"The veil."

Something light caressed my face, sliding down my bare shoulders with a whisper of a breeze.

"Look at me, Amira. Let me see those gorgeous eyes of yours once again."

The desire to see him conquered fear. Slowly, I raised my eyelids.

His face was right above me, his golden eyes twinkling with excitement, a smile playing on his lips. But a milky-white haze framed the image.

I touched the side of my face, my fingers coming in contact with a delicate material.

"Spider silk," Kyllen explained. "All the way from the Sky Kingdom."

The white, cloud-light veil dropped down to my knees, shrouding me. I touched the circle of the diadem on my head.

"The headband is gorgonian made," he said. "It'll stay on your head without falling off or bothering you. You can even sleep with it."

I turned around, taking in the room I'd spent several days in but hadn't even taken a look at until now. "I can *see*."

The woven-grass rugs on the floor had a beautiful floral pattern. The waterfall and the space around the basin of the pool below were laid with yellow, green, orange, and gray river rock. The bedding on my nest was in pale lavender. And the frame of the silk screen, the door, and the window railing were painted with colorful vines of flowers interwoven with golden swirls.

"I can see." I turned back to Kyllen. Despite all the beauty of the room, he was the most gorgeous sight of all.

Pride of accomplishment shone in his eyes, weary after his long journey. His *senties* moved slightly with his barely contained excitement. The lighting in the room highlighted the golden streaks of their dark-green markings.

"Thank you." I placed my hand on his cheek. "Was that why you were gone? To get the veil for me?"

He nodded. "I wanted you to have it as soon as possible. It couldn't be fun to have two perfectly good eyes and not be able to use them."

It hadn't been fun, but I'd known how it was going to be before I got here.

"I didn't mind."

"But that didn't mean you liked it, right? In this world, you have to use all the eyes you have. I'll protect you from any known danger, Amira, but you need to watch out for yourself, too."

"Thank you. I will." I could neither stop smiling nor stop looking at him.

He stared at me, too. "Oh, I just love seeing your gorgeous eyes again." He kissed my right eye, then the left one. The veil was so thin, I could barely feel it between his lips and my skin.

"I have a question," I said as he trailed his kisses down the side of my face to my neck.

"What is it?"

"What happened to the siren you tested the veil on?"

"Oh, he lived," he dismissed casually, placing another kiss, this one on the corner of my mouth. "That's how I knew it was safe."

"But what if he didn't? You could've killed the poor man."

"If he died, I would've gone back to the merchant who sold me the veil and demanded my sword back. Next, I would've used that sword to teach the old crook a lesson."

His tone of voice remained light and casual, but the hard glint in his eyes left no doubt he meant what he said. I was glad the veil turned out to be the real thing, after all, and both the siren and the merchant were still alive.

"You traded a sword for it?"

"Udren let me have my weapon collection back." He shrugged. "Not that it could be of any use to him anyway, not even when he was younger. Swordplay has never been my brother's thing."

A puff of breeze floated from the window. The evening was warm and refreshing. I glanced out at the landscape that until now had been only a picture in my imagination.

As it turned out, the picture didn't really do justice to the reality. The golden sunset tinted both the lake and the sky in warm sepia colors. The sunlight rippled on the surface of the water, making it look like liquid gold.

A group of large, winged creatures flew across the sky, visible between the branches of the palace's expansive canopy. As high as the creatures were, they still appeared massive.

"What are they? Dragons?" I asked, mesmerized by their majestic forms.

"Gargoyles," Kyllen replied. "The males can shapeshift into dragons whenever they wish."

"Are they coming to Lorsan?"

"Not likely. They don't land here often, for obvious reasons. Gargoyles turn to stone every night, but they have no desire to be put in that form permanently by us. They're probably just flying to Olathana, to trade with sirens, or maybe to fight them. Gargoyles like a good squabble. They're often at war either between themselves or with others."

The creatures slid through the sky, their movements light and graceful despite their size.

Kyllen took his leather satchel off his shoulder. "You look stunning in that dress, and I've spent the past four days mostly on the paddle board or wading through the marsh. I need to take a shower and get changed before we go to dinner."

"They brought some clothes for you." I gestured at the stack of gold-trimmed, emerald-colored fabrics on the table.

"Splendid." He ripped his tunic off over his head, then shoved his pants down on his way to the waterfall. "I'll be quick."

I could turn away and give him some privacy. But why would I? He hadn't asked for it. Now that I could see again, I wished to watch.

He stepped over the edge of the pool into the water that reached just above his knee. Hard muscles rolled under his skin. Fresh air and sun had laid a new layer of bronze glow on his back and arms.

A ribbon of snake-skin pattern ran along his spine. It fanned out over his shoulders just below his neck. The edges of the pattern blended into his skin, only visible if the light fell at the right angle. It looked beautiful, as if etched by light. No painting could ever replicate this.

Kyllen slid his hand up the river rock on the wall next to the waterfall. A spout lowered out of the wall, diverting a portion of the stream over his head like a shower.

Taking a handful of soap paste from the jar on the ledge of the basin, he lathered it between his palms. With the water running over him, he spread the suds all over his torso, arms, and legs.

I followed his hands with my gaze, taking in every dip and curve of his body, learning by sight what I'd loved to learn by touch.

Tilting his head back, he spread and stretched his *senties*. All twenty-four of them. The longest ones reached down below his waist on the back. The one in the front dropped like a thick curl over his face. When stretched all the way down, the end with the golden beady eyes reached below his chest.

Every line of his body carried power and grace. Not a part of him was unsightly or out of place. I could just stand there and ogle him all day.

Forcing my stare away, however, I walked over to the chest by the waterfall and took out a towel for him.

Sliding the spout back into the wall, Kyllen turned, and...I was faced with his erection, bobbing between his legs.

I tried to avert my eyes again, but it wasn't easy. That appendage of his, almost as thick and long as the large cucumber I'd once whacked him in the eye with, commanded attention. I'd felt it pressed against me before, but this was the first time I'd gotten to see it in all its glory like that.

It jerked higher under my attention, then higher still. In fact, the longer I stared, the thicker and longer it got, now pointing straight at me.

Was I supposed to say something? Or ignore it and turn away?

All I really wanted at that moment was to reach out and touch it.

"Towel?" I thrust the towel at Kyllen's chest, finally tearing my eyes from that fascinating body part of his.

My eyes met his, and I knew I'd been caught staring. My face heated so much, I didn't think the veil could hide the blush.

"Do you like what you see?" he asked.

I glanced aside. "I didn't mean to stare."

"Oh no, my dear." He waded across the pool to me. "Please stare. If I wanted to keep you blind to the world around you, I wouldn't have gotten you that veil."

"The veil is priceless," I muttered under my breath. "I've never been as grateful for the ability to see as I am right now."

He chuckled, stepping out of the basin and coming to me.

"I couldn't possibly have you deprived of this beautiful sight for too long." He gestured at himself, with a cocky grin.

"The *sight* is truly beautiful," I said without a hint of flattery, simply stating the truth.

He took the towel from me, patting his *senties* with it lightly. The water that glistened on his body was slowly absorbed by his skin.

My hands moved to him, as if on their own. With the tip of a finger, I traced a path left on his chest by a droplet of water running downwards. I followed it all the way to the first dip between the hard squares of his abdomen.

His erection bobbed in response, and I yanked my hand away.

He caught my wrist then pressed my hand to his flat belly. "You can touch, Amira. My body is yours to explore, to do whatever you wish with, as long as it brings you pleasure."

I swayed on my feet a little when he stroked my cheek through the veil.

"Whatever thought has made you blush like that, I want to hear it later. I wish we had more time for all of it right now. But we can't miss the dinner." He heaved a long breath. "I need to find out what has been happening in this snake pit while I was gone."

"A snake pit?" Was that what he really thought of the palace?

I sensed there had been some tension with Kyllen's return—I was not the only one having trouble with fitting in. But Kyllen referring to his family home as a snake pit indicated even bigger problems than I thought.

"Don't concern yourself with any of this for now," he said. "But I do want you to keep your eyes open."

He gathered up the bottom of my veil and draped it over my shoulders, allowing it to fall freely down my back. The soft folds around my neck brought the sensation of comfort, like wearing a scarf used to do. I buried my chin in the silky material.

"Feels good?" He kissed me through the veil.

"It does. Thank you for this." I trailed my fingers along the barely-there fabric.

"Are you ready to face the Court of Ellohi?" he asked.

I nodded. With Kyllen at my side, I could face anything.

Chapter Four

AMIRA

Being around too many people had never been easy for me. Finding myself in the center of everyone's attention as Kyllen and I arrived at dinner was torture. Being able to see every detail of tonight's festivities, though important, didn't make it easier at all.

The only thing that kept panic at bay was the warm sensation of Kyllen's hand in mine. I held on to him with the desperation of a drowning woman clinging on to a lifesaver and kept my gaze straight ahead.

We entered onto a large open platform located high between the branches of the giant palace tree. Illuminated by the clusters of soft, yellow lights suspended in the leaves above, the place was filled with people. They mingled around a long table set in the middle. Rows of smaller, round tables stretched along the edges of the platform.

Slow music floated between the branches. I searched for the musicians but couldn't find any. They remained out of sight, making it appear as if the tree itself emitted the music.

The High Lord sat at the head of the long table, conversing with courtiers who congregated around his high-backed chair.

Despite having spent a few days at the palace already, I couldn't recognize anyone other than the High Lord. And even him I knew only because of his position in the chair and the extra attention he received. I couldn't even guess which one of the beautifully dressed ladies was Lady Igaed. I'd had a conversation with her, but I'd never *seen* her.

People rushed to us, eager to greet Kyllen and gawk at me. With a polite greeting and a nod here and there, Kyllen masterfully maneuvered us through the crowd, laying a course toward the main table.

As revealing as my dress appeared to me at first, the outfits of the others could be considered outright scandalous by how little they concealed. And that applied to both men and women.

Even Kyllen wore no shirt. Instead, he had a wide scarf draped over one shoulder. The front end of the scarf was tucked under a bejeweled belt around his hips. The other end flowed freely behind him like a long, embroidered cape.

"Brother." Kyllen bowed his head to the High Lord, getting his attention. "What a lovely evening."

"Kyllen. You're back!" Udren perked up.

It was hard to believe this was the young boy whom Kyllen had saved from the *bracks*, risking his life and losing his freedom. The man in the chair looked so much older than Kyllen.

Most of Udren's body was concealed by a long robe, leaving only his head and hands exposed. The beige tone of his skin had been almost entirely taken over by the dark green. The diamond pattern had spread from his *senties* onto his head and face, leaving just small patches of skin clear. His hands were entirely covered by it, making them look as if the High Lord was wearing textured mesh gloves.

It reminded me of Kyllen's hands when he was in the crate, suffering from severe dehydration. Something similar was happening to the High Lord. He was drying out, dehydrated, even as he was surrounded by water and surely had enough of it to drink.

"Where have you been?" the High Lord demanded from Kyllen.

"Shopping. After five centuries of being absent, I found myself in need of a few things. Thank you for asking, *my lord*." Kyllen bent his head in a bow that I couldn't help but think was more mocking than respectful.

A woman in an outfit made of black-and-silver chains, tulle, and gemstones fingered the end of my veil.

"Oh, how lovely," she said, and I recognized Lady Igaed's voice. "He went to get you this, didn't he?"

"Yes." I nodded.

The High Lord paid us little attention, speaking to Kyllen. "They said you took but one man to accompany you. Why didn't you ask for more?"

"More would've slowed me down." Kyllen shrugged. "I would've been late for dinner tonight. It'd be awkward if I didn't show up for my own celebration, don't you think?"

"It's hardly safe to travel with so little escort," Lady Igaed intervened.

Her light, pearly-gray skin glowed softly. Some of the glow was natural, like that of all fae. But some came from the golden powder she had generously applied to her cheeks, collarbones, and her breasts, concealed only by the cascading silver chains and black beads. Other than the clusters of jewels and chains, her outfit consisted of a long, puffy skirt that shrouded her legs like a black cloud.

Kyllen slightly inclined his head her way. "I'm fully aware of the perils of travel, my lady."

He didn't elaborate on his reasons to travel light. But maybe he didn't bring more people along and hadn't told anyone where he was going—not even me—because he truly didn't trust anyone. And maybe it was wise to be cautious.

Kyllen's family appeared happy to see him after the long absence. His brother was giving this lavish dinner in celebration of his return. But not all was as smooth and cheerful as it appeared on the surface.

"Well, let us all sit down." Udren waved both hands, summoning everyone to the table. "Bherlon." He gestured to the right of his own chair. "Kyllen." He gestured to the left.

The place at the table must hold a meaning. Bherlon smirked, taking the seat to the right of his father. The coloring of Kyllen's nephew looked remarkably like his uncle's. He also had tan-colored skin with a dark-green pattern on his *senties* and back. Except that Bherlon's eyes were lighter—lemon-yellow like Udren's instead of Kyllen's dark gold.

Kyllen's jaw muscles flexed as he sat down on the left of the High Lord. Lady Igaed confidently strolled to the chair on the other side of her husband's.

I hesitated, wishing there'd be place cards or a sitting map indicating my place. Meanwhile, a woman with a dark-orange pattern on her *senties* took a step toward the seat on Kyllen's left.

He draped an arm over the back of the chair and gestured for me. "Amira."

The woman glared at me but silently retreated to another chair down the table as I sat down next to him.

Once everyone had taken their seats, a flock of servants appeared, bringing out the drinks and trays laden with dishes.

One of the servants leaned over my shoulder, with a dish in one hand and a serving spoon in the other. "Frog eggs, my lady?"

"Um, no, thank you," I replied quickly.

Kyllen's soft chuckle sounded to my right. "I'll take some." He gave the servant a sign to come closer.

Gorgonians drank considerably more than they ate. Each guest had a large stein with a long handle standing in front of them. Servants with giant carafes on their shoulders constantly refilled the steins with water. In addition, each setting included a tall glass for wine and a wide cup with two handles for soup.

A servant with a crystal decanter filled with dark blue liquid bowed at my side next. "Fruit wine, my lady? It's made with oranges and blueberries."

I hesitated, wondering if alcohol might be good for me in this situation.

"Would you like some wine, Amira?" Kyllen asked.

I nervously scratched my nose under the veil, leaning his way. "I've never had wine before."

"Never?" He stared at me like I'd just told him I ate live lizards for breakfast.

"No. Even if there was some at the menagerie, Madame certainly never served it to me."

A smile spread across his face. "Give me that." He took the decanter from the servant and poured a little of the blue liquid into my glass.

"Here you go, my sweet pea," he murmured, handing me my glass. "I love giving you all your *firsts*."

He chuckled at my gasp. Blush warmed my cheeks, when I thought back to our first night in Lorsan and my very first orgasm that Kyllen gave me.

"May there be many more." He clinked his glass against mine in a toast.

The way he stared at me over the rim of his glass while taking a sip, I knew he had not been talking about the wine. His eyes narrowed. Heat flashed in the dark gold of his irises. His look held a promise, sending a swirl of anticipation through my belly.

Udren lifted his wine glass.

"To my brother," he declared loudly. "Let's thank the Great Serpent for bringing Lord Kyllen back to us safe and sound."

Everyone at the table raised their glasses. I lifted mine, too. The wine was sweet and fragrant. It slid down my throat smoothly.

The soft yellow lights suspended in the leaves above us kept moving. A few of them came close enough for me to see that they were insects—moths and dragonflies with glowing wings.

It was such a beautiful place up here in the giant tree above the placid bay. The warm, pleasant evening would've been easy to enjoy had it not been for the tension hanging over the High Lord's table like a thunder cloud.

The courtiers studied me, some furtively, others more openly. When I mustered enough courage to meet their stares, I saw curiosity and calculation in their eyes. Some had undisguised hostility and resentment on their faces. None of the expressions seemed warm or friendly. I dropped my gaze, but their attention prickled at my skin like needles.

I emptied my glass of wine quickly. A servant appeared at my side, ready to refill it, but Kyllen waved him away.

"It's best to space it out, sweetheart, especially since this is your first time drinking." He slid a cup of cattail root soup my way, instead. "Drink this first. You must be hungry."

The wine shrouded my awareness with fuzzy nothingness. It made it easier to deal with the battery of stares shot at me from every direction. A part of me wished I could lose myself in the effervescent indifference of the intoxication completely. But Kyllen was right, I had to remain alert. I lifted the cup of soup to my lips under the veil, sipping the warm liquid.

Bherlon raised his glass of wine.

"To you, Uncle!" he announced loudly before emptying it.

The man sitting on my left chuckled softly. He appeared more relaxed and easy-going than most of the people present.

I dared asking him, "What's so funny?"

"He called him 'uncle,'" the man snorted. "He's older than Lord Kyllen by centuries!"

"Surely, that happens often with fae?" With their long lifespan and an almost as long fertility period, the lines between the generations would be fluid.

The man shrugged. "It does. But in this case, the uncle was born way before the nephew. So, he should be much older, but he's not. That's funny." He snickered, making a silly face at me.

The way he held himself prompted me to ask, "How old are you?"

"I'm nineteen. Why?"

That might explain his goofy attitude and carefree manner. I hid a smile. It was unexpected to find someone younger than me at the table full of fae who'd lived for centuries.

"What's your name?" I asked.

He puffed his chest out. "Lord Qayren. The heir to the Krevai Estate."

"Nice to meet you." I bowed my head. "I'm Amira."

He squinted at me. "I've heard."

By now, everyone must've heard who I was—the only human at the table, the only one with the veil.

He chugged his entire glass of wine at once.

"You know why else this is funny?" He tipped his chin at Bherlon. "His mother was supposed to be Lord Kyllen's wife."

"Oh, did Lord Udren marry Lady... Sorry, I forgot her name."

"Lady Eiphed, the daughter of the High Lord of Prusim. Yes, she was our High Lady."

"Was?"

"She died of old age."

"I see." I glanced at Kyllen, who was now engaged in a conversation with Udren. They were talking about the latest hunt of the High Lord. Apparently, hunting was Udren's favorite pastime. He refused to give it up, even as he spent the hunting trips in a chair now.

Did Kyllen know that Udren married his bride-to-be? Did he care? From what he'd told me back at the menagerie, he held no special feelings for the woman who was meant to be his wife. However, knowing his possessive nature, I wondered if it irked him that his brother had taken his betrothed, too, while he was gone.

Lady Igaed turned to Kyllen.

"What are you planning to do now that you're back, Lord Kyllen?" She asked the question I sensed was on the minds of many people present.

Kyllen flashed her a smile. "Make my father proud, of course."

The High Lord leaned forward and said quietly enough for only the five of us at the head of the table to hear, "Useless endeavor, brother. I spent centuries trying to impress our father while he was still alive, and I failed. Don't waste your life trying to do the same now that he's dead."

Kyllen silently raised his glass to his lips for a sip of wine.

Lady Igaed flicked her fingers, clicking the many rings she wore against each other. "The best way to honor your ancestors is by keeping this family united."

Kyllen set his wine glass on the table. "I have no intention of tearing it apart."

She narrowed her eyes. "Intentions matter, but it's your *actions* that will have consequences."

"The wise thing would be for you to wait your turn," Bherlon blurted out.

By that, Bherlon clearly meant for Kyllen to get behind him in the line of succession to the High Lord's throne.

Kyllen leaned back in his chair and casually popped a couple of frog eggs into his mouth.

"My turn is now," he said matter-of-factly.

Bherlon's eyes flashed with a hot temper, sending a chill down my spine. Other than that one spark, however, the lord's expression remained cold. Calculating. Which seemed even more menacing than an outburst would've been.

"You will not displace my father." Bherlon's words sounded like a threat.

"Some things may be negotiated." Kyllen shrugged.

Despite his easy manner, tension stretched between him and his nephew like a string ready to snap. The air crackled with it like electricity before the storm.

Udren shifted uneasily. "Later. All of that can be discussed and decided later." He raised his wine glass, his hand shaking either from age or nerves, or both. "Tonight, we'll celebrate."

Chapter Five

AMIRA

Kyllen's perfect composure had waned by the time dinner ended. Not waiting for the dancing to commence, he thanked the High Lord for a "warm welcome" and took his leave, whisking me away, too.

"Was it wise to let them know of your intentions?" I asked when the two of us were finally alone, back in my room. *Our* room, really. Kyllen had hardly spent any time in his own bedroom.

"There isn't much to hide." He yanked the silk embroidered scarf from his shoulder and tossed it over the back of one of the chairs. "I'm expected to take my rightful place. Anything else would be a disgrace."

"How are you planning to do that? The High Lord—"

"Udren can stay where he is." He rubbed the back of his neck, stretching his shoulders. "I'm not in a hurry to displace him. He doesn't have much time left before the Great Serpent recalls him and the Lorsan Wetlands take him. He's been the High Lord most of his life, and he deserves to die as such."

"That's not what you said to Bherlon." He'd only let his nephew know there might be room for negotiations.

"I expect Bherlon to fight me. In which case, I'd like to have as many negotiation chips as possible in my pocket."

"What exactly do you mean by him fighting you?" I had no doubt Bherlon would oppose Kyllen taking over, but I desperately hoped it wouldn't come down to a physical battle.

He heaved a breath. "Well, there're several options to resolve this matter honorably. Either way, however, I'm in the right here."

"Are you sure?"

He ran his fingers through his *senties*. "I'll need to find evidence to support my case. There are plenty of books on ancestry and succession in the archives below the palace. I dodged reading them in my youth, but I'll need to go through them now and build my case to present to the king if I have to."

"Can the king decide on this matter?"

"He could rule on it, yes, which would help. But there will likely be a tournament, too."

"A tournament?" Worry spiked inside me.

"Yes. The strongest one wins."

"And what happens to the weakest one?" From Kyllen's stories, I knew gorgonian tournaments weren't mere exercises of sportsmanship. They didn't end well for all participants.

"The loser usually dies," he said.

I blew out a sharp breath, feeling like I'd been punched in the stomach.

"Amira." He took me in his arms. "A tournament is actually the desired outcome in this case. It takes place in public. Its results are indisputable. You know I've won enough tournaments to have a good chance at winning one more."

Kyllen was younger than Bherlon, but it didn't mean he was faster or stronger. On the contrary, Bherlon had the advantage of the longer experience in life.

Their physical age didn't mean much to fae. Their youth lasted for centuries. Unlike that of humans, who not only had much shorter lifespans but also spent their entire lives aging.

"I hope it won't come down to a tournament." I slid my hands up his bare chest. "There has to be a way to resolve this without trying to kill each other. Wouldn't the king's ruling on the matter be enough?"

"Maybe it would, maybe not." He exhaled a long breath, as if trying to let go of the worries with it. "There is nothing we can do about it tonight, can we? It'll have to wait until the morning." He leaned his forehead to mine. "You don't have to concern yourself with this. Tonight, I just need you..." He breathed in deeply. "Gods, I missed you so much."

He slid his hands under my veil. Crumpling it, he lifted it past my nose and pressed it against my eyes to keep them closed.

"Kissing you always makes the world feel like a better place," he murmured, lowering his mouth to mine.

Wasn't that the truth? My concern lifted somewhat. All problems felt so much easier to deal with when Kyllen was with me. Tomorrow, we'd figure something out. As long as we were together, we could do anything.

Kyllen's forked tongue slipped between my lips, then curled around mine in a kiss that felt both sensual and intimate.

His *senties* dove into my hair, then trailed down my neck and into the bodice of my dress. Like dexterous fingers, they stroked and caressed, dancing along my skin and making my body sing with desire.

He tugged at the ribbon lacing my dress, loosening it. Shoving down the fabric, he bared my body for him. Curling a *sentie* around one of my breasts, he made its mouth tug and nibble on the tip. My nipple beaded, turning hard. Arousal rippled through my body, pooling hot between my legs.

Now that I knew exactly *what* he could do to me, the need for him flared stronger. I moaned as he palmed my other breast, his thumb playing with my nipple.

"You like that, don't you?" He trailed hot nibbling kisses down my neck. "You like my hands on you."

His hands, his lips, his *senties*... I liked them all on me. I wanted all of him.

A low growl vibrated deep in his chest as he yanked me closer. His hardness pressed against my lower belly.

He shifted down my body, taking a nipple between his lips and grazing it with his teeth. I gasped, intense pleasure flushing my veins. But I wouldn't let him distract me this time. I reached down between us, palming the hard length bulging in his pants.

He sucked in a breath, making a sound I had no word for—a half-roar, half-groan.

"With your hands on me, I won't last long," he warned, jerking his hips away from my touch.

I wouldn't give up, finding his length with my hand again. "You've teased me long enough, Kyllen. I want to see it."

He groaned into my shoulder, "I could climax just from those words alone, Amira."

But he opened his pants for me, his hands trembling. I promptly slid my fingers inside, wrapping them around his hard length. He felt hot, hard like a bone, but also so very delicate.

I tried to shove his pants further down. "Let me see."

"You'll be the death of me, woman," he muttered, helping me take off his pants.

His erection sprang free—long, hard, and thick. The silky skin stretched tightly over it. Like his *senties*, it had a hint of green, though without the snake-skin pattern.

"It really looks like that cucumber I tossed at you," I said, taking him in my hands.

"A cucumber?" He huffed a deep laugh. "Now, that's something I haven't heard yet."

"You haven't?" I asked, genuinely surprised. "But the similarities are so obvious. It's almost as long. Might be a little thicker, though." I turned and stroked him in my hands as I spoke, circling his girth with my fingers to measure it.

Leaning toward me with a groan, he propped a hand on something behind me, which happened to be the silk screen. It crashed to the ground with a loud noise as he'd shoved too hard against it. He shifted his weight, managing to keep his balance. Though, he looked rather unsteady on his feet.

"You make me weak in the knees," he gritted through his teeth. "Literally."

"Let's go to the wall, then." I smiled, leading him by his erection.

He followed, so delightfully obedient, it made my head spin. All it took to make this strong, magical man follow me like a puppy was getting hold of his hard-as-rock penis.

How marvelous was that?

I leaned with my back against the wall by our nest. He towered over me, both hands propped on the wall over my head.

I slid my hands up and down his "cucumber." He moaned, his eyelids dropped, his jaw slackened. I figured he liked what I was doing.

"I want to see you orgasm, Kyllen. What do I have to do to make it happen?"

"Oh, my sweet, innocent girl..." he croaked, pressing his temple to mine. "You have no idea you're doing it already."

Was I? I kept sliding my hands along his length, squeezing it slightly. When I circled the tip, he hissed, his eyes rolling back into his head. I did it again, hoping to see him lose control completely.

"Amira..." he breathed out my name like a prayer, thrusting into my hand.

The chiseled squares of his abdomen flexed, tightening. His breath hitched. His length jerked in my hands. Spurts of creamy substance shot from the opening in the tip that I'd had no idea was there. They landed on my skirt.

I slowed down a little, remembering how he had touched me the last time we were together. Loosening my grip on him, I pumped my hand a few more times, milking a few more shots of his release. He heaved a long breath with a deep, tortured sound, and I let go.

One arm still propped onto the wall behind me, he wrapped the other one around me, hiding his face in my shoulder.

"Amira," he whispered. "My sweet, precious darling. What have you done to me?"

Tenderness swelled in my heart. I gently raked my fingers through his *senties* in a soothing motion.

"Are you okay, honey?" It occurred to me that the groans and growls he'd made could've been from pain just as much as from pleasure. Had I read him wrong? "I didn't hurt you, did I?"

"Oooh, no." He lifted his head. A lazy, satisfied smile stretched his lips, allowing me to exhale in relief.

"Was it good then?" He looked rather happy, but I had no experience to compare. I needed to hear it from him. "Could I've done it better?"

"I don't think I've ever had it better, sweet pea." He studied my face through the veil. "There is no magic in you, yet being with you still feels magical, and I can't figure out why."

He stared at me in wonder, as if I was some kind of a miracle or an enigma he couldn't explain. I flustered under his intense stare. Dropping my gaze to his chest, I started tracing little circles on his skin with my finger.

"It's certainly not because of any special skills on my part," I said with a smile. "You're the one and only man whose...um, 'male equipment' I've ever seen or touched."

"It's not the skill, Amira. It's *you*." He kissed my hair, then exhaled a soft chuckle. "I have a feeling you could use my cock as a rolling pin, and I would still enjoy myself immensely."

I snorted a laugh at the visual his words created in my mind.

He shoved my dress down past my hips, and it sank to the floor in a puffy heap. "You're like no one I've ever met before." He took me in his arms, lifting me out of my dress. "Being with you is a different kind of pleasure—gentle and real, like a breath of fresh air or the caress of sunshine on my face. It's irreplaceable. When I'm deprived of your company, I suffer."

I moved aside that one stubborn *sentie* that kept falling in front of his face. "Please, don't leave me behind again. Next time, take me along. Wherever you'll travel, I'll come, too."

He climbed into the nest, bringing me with him. "It's dangerous out there in the wetlands."

"It's hardly safer here in the palace."

"True." He laid me down on the soft, silky bedding, then sat back on his heels, sliding his gaze down my naked body.

"I can *see*, now," I implored. "You won't have to watch over me every step of the way. I can take care of myself, and I can help."

"Traveling with you would be infinitely more pleasant," he said, not promising anything.

He leaned over to kiss between my breasts. I tried to envision going on a trip with him. The destination didn't matter. It'd be great to see more of Lorsan than was possible from the palace window.

With Kyllen's mouth on me, however, focusing on that thought was getting harder by the minute.

He shifted down my body, trailing his kisses between my breasts, past my belly button and...lower.

"What are you doing?" I rose on my elbows.

He slid a *sentie* between my legs. Its tip brushed against the same spot he'd rubbed when he'd made love to me before. I gasped and whimpered from a sudden surge of pleasure. The *sentie* nibbled on it next, sending me back into the pillows with a moan of bliss.

Shifting lower still, Kyllen peppered the inside of my thigh with light, invigorating kisses. His breath hit between my legs, just before he... dragged his tongue between my folds.

"Did you just lick me?" I jerked up, gaping at him in shock. "*Down there?*"

He lifted his head, his hands holding my thighs on his shoulders.

"Another *first?*" He flashed me a lopsided grin, a brow ridge arching gracefully.

Was it normal? Did people really lick each other? There?

"Is that... Who does that?" I mumbled.

"I do." He kept grinning unapologetically. "I'm really good at it, too."

Sticking his tongue out, he twirled the forked tip around the tight little bud at the apex of my thighs. My desire spiked, making me fist my hands in the sheets.

"Oh, Kyllen..." I exhaled with a moan.

It felt so incredibly good, I suddenly no longer cared what was "normal."

One of his *senties* circled my opening, then worked its way inside me. It swirled against my inner walls just past the entrance as Kyllen's tongue danced on the most sensitive part of me. I writhed with pleasure that rolled through my body in waves.

Pressure built low in my belly, coiling like a tightly-wound spring. With another twirl of his tongue, it unfurled, flooding me with ecstasy.

Kyllen held my hips, licking and nibbling, coaxing every last shudder of my orgasm out of me. Until I stilled in the sheets. Spent.

He chuckled, sliding up to my head on the pillows.

"I told you I was good." He gave me a cocky smile.

Hooking one arm around his neck, I pulled him in for a kiss. He rolled to his side, taking me with him.

"You can say whatever you want, Kyllen, and I have no choice but to believe you," I teased. "You're my one and only. You know I have no other man to compare you to."

"And that's how it's going to remain," he said firmly. "There'll be no other man, my sweet pea. You're mine." He took my chin in his fingers, staring at me through the veil. "*Only* mine."

Goosebumps skittered down my arms at the intensity in his voice.

"Are you sure? Monogamy isn't common at the High Lord's court, is it?" I tested the waters to see where I stood with him and how deep I'd be sucked in before it was too late.

But maybe it was too late already? He already could break my heart in so many ways.

He rose over me, propped on his elbow. "Am I not enough for you, Amira? Do you want more?"

As confident as Kyllen was, when it came to me, he appeared to have his own insecurities.

I cupped his cheek. "You're everything I could ever dream of, Kyllen. But...will I be enough for *you?* Life is long. Don't fae get bored with just one partner?"

How many lovers did Lady Igaed have? And what about her husband? She'd said he had quite a few, too.

Kyllen's features relaxed a little. "Oh, is that what it is? My little sweet pea doesn't like sharing, either?"

I kept my eyes on his.

"What am I to you, Kyllen? What will I ever be?"

"What do you mean, Amira?" Sunny sparks still danced in his golden eyes, but the rest of his expression turned serious. "I made you a promise. You'll always be with me."

"But there really is no place for me, is there? There is no appropriate position for a human in Lorsan."

"Then, I'll *make* a position." Grabbing my shoulders, he sat up in the nest, taking me with him. "Amira. No one forced me to make that promise to you. I made it because I wanted to. Fulfilling it is not a burden. I want you in my life, by my side. I need you..."

"But why? Just because I'm *different?*" I exhaled a humorless laugh.

"Oh yes, you are different. In more ways than you know. With you, I don't feel like I need to watch my back. Only with you, can I be myself without reservations." He sat back as if the realization had just hit him. "You're the only person in this entire world whom I feel I could trust. Implicitly."

He stared past me into the distance somewhere, with a pensive expression. As if the very idea of implicit trust was so novel to him, he needed some time to rearrange his entire way of thinking around it now.

"Fae have partners, allies, family," he said, turning to face me again. "You're more than any of those to me. What you and I have gone through together, in your world and mine, will forever connect us. No one would ever understand me as completely as you do. No one could give me *everything* the way you have."

"No man could ever give a woman everything," Lady Igaed had said. But she was wrong. When I was with Kyllen, I wished for no one else.

"I trust you, Amira. I cannot say that about any other person in this place."

"Yet you didn't trust me enough to tell me where you went when you left to get the veil." The earlier disappointment echoed through me.

He shook his head.

"That wasn't because of *you,* but because I didn't trust the people around you. You're so new to this world, to this court. There are so many of those who could trick you, even hurt you, to get what they want. I made sure you had nothing to reveal." He tossed a handful of *senties* over his shoulder. "I couldn't risk anyone knowing even the direction in which I'd traveled. It would've been so easy to attack the undesired heir out in the wetlands and make it look as if he'd never returned at all."

Dread seized me at his last words. "Could they really do that? Would they?"

He shrugged. "If anyone wished to get rid of me, that would've been the best place and time to do it, out of sight. The wetlands provide plenty of excellent places to hide a body. It'd be absorbed quickly and without a trace. The news of my return hasn't traveled that far yet. It'd be as if I'd never come back. Which would be preferred by some, I'm sure."

I sat back, frozen in horror at how easily the man who meant so much to me could be erased from existence.

"No..." I shook my head. "Don't leave ever again. Please. I know you had to make that trip. I know you did it for me, and I'm very grateful for the veil. But if something happened to you..." My voice broke. I refused to imagine the world without him. "I need you, too, Kyllen. I need you in my life."

"Come here, my sweetest." He pulled me to him. "I'm not going anywhere. Definitely not tonight."

I twined my arms around his neck, and he used his *senties* to tie me to him.

"Stay with me," I whispered against his lips as he kissed me.

"As much as it is in my power, I will never leave you again."

For now, it was enough. It had to be. Tonight, all I wanted was simply to be with him, just like this, wrapped into each other's arms.

Lost in Kyllen's touch, I barely heard the quiet knock on the door.

"My lady?" Geltar called from behind the door.

Kyllen tore his mouth from mine long enough to growl, "Go away!"

"But..." the maid insisted. "I have to help Lady Amira get ready for the night."

Heat pulsed low in my belly. Pressure was building up between my thighs, demanding Kyllen's attention.

He slid his hand between my legs and groaned approvingly, kissing my neck. "Oh, the lady is perfectly ready for the night I've planned for her."

"I've brought her nightshirt..." Geltar pleaded.

Feeling sorry for the poor woman, I reluctantly let go of Kyllen. "I'll get it. It won't take long."

Untangling myself from his limbs and *senties*, I climbed out of the nest.

"What's the use in a nightshirt?" Kyllen grumped, obviously deeply annoyed by the interruption. "I'd take it off you, anyway."

"She's just doing her job, following the court's norms. Etiquette? Protocols?" I shrugged. "Whatever you call it."

Yanking the top sheet from him, I wrapped it around myself to cover up. That left Kyllen exposed and gloriously nude.

Reclining on the cushions, he rested a forearm on a bent knee. I couldn't resist sliding a long look down his strong, beautiful body. His erection bobbed eagerly at my attention. My skin tingled in anticipation.

"Just...um, hold that thought," I quipped and hurried to the door.

The gears of the intricate lock Kyllen had put on the top part of the door slid and shifted under my fingers, their bearings smoothed by magic.

"Thank you, Gel—" The name of the maid stuck in my throat.

There was no nightshirt.

Geltar's head was tipped back, her *senties* wrapped around Bherlon's wrist, their ends clamped in his fist. Her warm-orange eyes were open wide in horror. In his other hand, Bherlon held a knife to her throat. At least a dozen guards surrounded them.

Shocked, I leaped back, trying to shut the door.

"Get her!" Bherlon ordered.

Chapter Six

AMIRA

A guard stuck his foot out, stopping me from closing the door. More guards barged into the room, shoving me aside. One of them grabbed me around the middle.

Bherlon released Geltar, and she ran away, sobbing.

"Kyllen!" I yelled to warn him as soon as I got my voice back.

But he was on his feet already. The guards cut him off from his sheaths with daggers and swords he'd left on the chair by the table.

He kicked a sword out of the hand of the closest guard. Spinning on his heel, he stabbed another guard in the chest with it. Whipping around, he faced the next one, then...shrank back, startled.

"Hapon? You?" Kyllen's voice filled with bitter disappointment. He hesitated for a fraction of a moment, his hand with the sword paused in the air.

Using the moment, another guard lunged at Kyllen from behind, slashing across his back with a dagger. The blade came back, dripping with blood.

Kyllen arched backwards, roaring in pain.

"No!" I fought against the rough hands gripping me.

Bherlon grabbed a handful of Kyllen's *senties.* A guard kicked my man in the back of his knees. They buckled, sending him down to his knees. Yanking Kyllen's head back, Bherlon raised his knife, aiming it at Kyllen's throat.

"No. Please!" I cried in horror, tears streaming down my face. "Please, don't."

The guard dragged me through the door, but I grabbed the frame. Holding to it with everything I had, I scratched the wood, breaking my nails.

"Kyllen!" I screamed.

The guards held him down. They weren't humans. Their strength rivaled his. And there were so many of them.

Cold moonlight reflected off the raised blade in Bherlon's hand.

"Close your eyes, Amira," Kyllen croaked against the guards' hold. He didn't want me to see what they were about to do to him.

Bherlon lowered his hand. The blade slashed through the air on its way to Kyllen's neck.

"No!" I screamed.

The guard yanked me out of the room. My fingers scraped the frame uselessly, letting go.

"Let me go! Let me go to him. Please," I screamed.

I cried.

I pleaded. "Kyllen!"

A hand slapped against my mouth. "Shut it!" the guard hissed in my ear.

He dragged me down the giant branch of the palace tree, then down a small staircase that ended with a ladder hidden in the shrub at the bottom of the trunk.

There were more of Bherlon's guards here. One tossed me over his shoulder while climbing down the ladder. He then threw me on the bottom of a boat.

"Take her to Ufaris," a voice said in the darkness as several men jumped into the boat with me. "Tell them she's a gift to King Zeldren from the High Lord of Ellohi. We all know, our High Lord will need the king to turn a blind eye to what has happened here tonight."

Someone pushed the boat away from the dock.

"Let me go!" I scrambled to my feet.

"Down!" one of the guards yelled.

"The stupid wench will flip us over," another warned.

The boat swayed side to side precariously. I fought the rough arms, clawing at the guards' uniforms. "Let me go to him!"

I had to be with him. My place was with Kyllen, come what might.

"Enough!" A punch landed heavily in my jaw, knocking me to the bottom of the boat. Pain rang through my skull. My face went numb.

"Hey! That will leave a bruise," someone hissed. "If you mess up her face, it'll bring the price down."

"What price?" the other replied. "She's a gift, isn't she?"

"You know how much she's worth? It's stupid to *gift* her. Lord Kyllen is gone. The others will have their hands full, cleaning up after his death. There's no one to stop us from doing whatever we want with her now."

Paddles went into the water with hardly any splash. Darkness enveloped us as the boat slid along the smooth waters of Layahi Bay, taking me away from the golden lights of the palace and into the night.

I curled in on myself on the bottom of the boat. It felt like my life ended back in our bedroom, with Kyllen brought down to his knees and destroyed. My heart had been torn out of my chest, with nothing but a raw, gaping hole left in its place.

And it hurt.

So much.

The agony of loss numbed all other feelings and emotions, including the ache from the blow to my face.

"Lord Kyllen is gone."

The words made no sense. How could this world exist if Kyllen was not in it? What was this place without him?

Tears didn't come, ripping me apart from the inside instead. Darkness pressed heavily on me, and I wished it would just crush me. I wished to be nothing but a shadow, like I was always meant to be.

Chapter Seven

AMIRA

Ufaris, the palace of the King of Lorsan, wasn't housed in a single tree or even in a group of trees. It took up an entire forest.

The giant royal trees grew in the placid waters of Ufaris Lake that sprawled as far as the eye could see. Golden lights illuminated the branches, competing with the silver moonlight flooding the night.

Wisps of fog rose in the air from the surface when one of the guards yanked me up to my feet.

I didn't know exactly how long it'd taken us to get here. I'd spent nearly the entire journey curled up on the bottom of the boat, unmoving. Daylight had warmed me, nights had chilled my skin through the bedsheet I had wrapped around my body. Someone must've fed me and given me water because I was still alive. But I had no recollection of eating or drinking.

The boat lurched side to side with the guards' movements. I struggled to stay upright. Someone stepped on the sheet wrapped around me. It slipped from me, pooling at my feet. I remained covered only by my veil down to my knees, but I had nothing left in me to care or even feel ashamed.

"Well." A guard smirked, giving me a leering once-over. "She's pretty, but nothing special. I don't get the nobles. What do they see in her?"

"Humans are rare," the other one explained. "She's exotic. Which is enough to get the lords' cocks up and wagging." He snickered. "What do we care, as long as they pay?"

The other one chimed in, "Is she supposed to get the king's shriveling cock up? He's dying, I've heard."

"Why would the king even buy her?" someone else asked from the back of the boat. "The Great Serpent is about to take him. The king doesn't need her or anyone else, anymore."

"Oh, don't you worry. I already secured a buyer, and he's ready to pay a fortune for her. This little human is literally worth her weight in gold. Aren't you, precious?" Grabbing my chin, he lifted my face to his. "That fucking bruise is still visible, asshole!" He kicked the guard sitting in the boat at our feet. "If it ends up costing me money, I'll rip your *senties* out and boil them in a fucking soup."

I listened to their conversation with an odd detachment. My body was there, but my soul had been suspended in another place ever since my last glance at Kyllen on his knees. I didn't care what they did to me now. The worst had already happened.

The boat smoothly glided through the fog. We were surrounded by at least a dozen more guards on paddle boards. It was quite an entourage to deliver "the gift" to the king.

As we got closer, the lights of a giant royal tree shone brighter through the tendrils of fog. Its trunk was lifted slightly over the water, supported by the thick, gnarly roots, each the size of a thick tree itself. A maze of interconnected docks and pathways spread from them in every direction.

A dark figure stood at the end of a dock section that was shaded by underbrush and hidden from the water traffic that was busy despite the late hour.

"Cover her up," the guard who seemed to be in charge ordered the other two in the boat with us. "No one is gawking at her without paying first."

The two picked up the sheet from the bottom of the boat. The fabric that used to be the color of pale lavender was now dusty and muddy after the days of traveling. They attempted to wrap it around me.

On the dock, the tall figure, shrouded in a dark cloak and moonlight, lifted a hand.

"Leave it," a male voice commanded. "I want to see what I'm buying."

"Listen to the man," the leader of the guards told them hurriedly. "You see that bag at his feet? I bet it's filled with gold and jewels. I told you she's precious."

The guards removed the sheet again. The leader grabbed on to one of the dock's support pillars, bringing the boat to a stop.

"Is she really a human?" the man on the dock enquired.

"She sure is."

"Where did you get her?"

The guard shifted from foot to foot, looking uncomfortable. "As I said through the man I sent to the palace yesterday, the young lord returned to Ellohi from the human realm last week. He brought her with him."

"Why?"

The guard shrugged. "For his pleasure."

"Why is he selling her, then?"

"He's dead. His nephew is the one selling her. Lord Bherlon knows a rare thing like her should belong to the king, no one else."

The cloaked man shoved his hood back. The moonlight hit his pale face and dark *senties*. It bounced off with a silver-blue shimmer, making him look like an ethereal being.

"Lift her veil," he ordered.

"If I do, she'll die," the guard replied.

The man jerked his head in a gesture of frustration. "I didn't tell you to kill her. Lift it up to her neck only. The veil casts a glow on her skin in the moonlight. I wish to see her body without it, to make sure she's human as you claim she is."

Following his orders, the guards hiked up my veil. Now, there was absolutely nothing between the stranger's scrutinizing stare and my body. I didn't bother to try covering myself with my hands, letting him stare instead. My soul was dead, and shame had died with it.

"She's rather quiet," the stranger observed, curling his lips in misgiving. "Listless."

"Obedient, my lord," the leader of the guards rushed to reassure him. "She knows her place. As she should."

The stranger gestured at the dingy sheet in the guards' hands. "Is that all she has for clothes?"

"Well," one of them started to explain. "We were in a haste—"

The leader shoved an elbow into the speaker's ribs, cutting him off.

"Yes. That's all she has," he replied instead.

The man in the cloak watched me in silence for another moment.

"Let her cover up, then. I'm taking her," he said. "This is yours, as agreed." He kicked the large bag at his feet. It made a clinking sound. He then stretched his hand my way. "You're coming with me, human."

Throwing the sheet over my shoulders, the guards shoved me toward the dock. The boat swayed. I grabbed on to the stranger's hand for support. He yanked me in his direction, and I stepped up on the dock, climbing out of the boat.

I didn't look back at the people who'd just sold me. After days of traveling in their company, I didn't know their names and would not remember their faces. They didn't matter.

Nothing did.

The man with the dark cloak and the face that glowed like moonlight brought me up a set of carved stairs to one of the lowest branches of the castle. He opened a small door and shoved me through it.

"Tonight, you rest," he said. "Tomorrow night, you'll be presented to the king." He shut the door.

I was left standing in the middle of a small, round room with smooth carved walls and a grate high under the ceiling. A pile of blankets made a small, messy nest. A metal chamber pot stood nearby.

With a clunk, the door locked behind me.

I was not a guest in Ufaris. I was a prisoner.

Chapter Eight

AMIRA

Being locked in a cell didn't feel much different from being tossed on the bottom of the boat. To me anyway, it didn't.

I lay in the nest of tattered rags, staring at the wall in front of me. At some point, I must have slept, though it felt as if I blinked, and the sky in the tiny opening above me was now bright and golden instead of dark and silver. Day had replaced the night.

Someone brought me a tray with food and water. I closed my eyes, not caring who it was.

As the sky in the opening grew dark again, two gorgonian women came.

"Time to get you cleaned up," one of them said, helping me up.

The two half-led, half-carried me out to a small platform between the branches. A waterfall streamed from the leaves above, pooling in a small basin carved into the wood below.

The women took my dirty sheet away from me. Hiking up my veil, they led me into the basin of tepid water.

After the humid heat of the day, the water felt refreshing against my skin. For the first time since I had last screamed

Kyllen's name, I felt some shred of emotion as I sank into the bath.

The women got busy, scrubbing my arms, back, and shoulders. I let them, as I had let things happen to me in the past few days.

Taking refuge inside my head, I let life take its course around me, not taking a part in it myself. I'd done it before as a child and later when going about my days at Madame's menagerie. I gave up control, simply drifting along. It felt safer this way.

"Raise your arm," one of the women said.

I obeyed while she scrubbed my side.

"Now the other one," she instructed, and I silently did as she said.

My body was theirs to do with as they pleased. Like an observer locked in a room, I watched what was happening to me through the slits between my eyelids.

Why bother to feel, to think, to try to change anything if I had no control?

I had no choice.

"We need to wash her hair." The second woman wrinkled her nose. "It stinks."

The first one sighed. "Having hair is a messy business. It's so much harder to keep it neat and clean than *senties*." She leaned to my ear, saying loudly as if afraid I had weak hearing, "We'll need to take off your veil. Close your eyes."

"Close your eyes, Amira!" the echo of Kyllen's voice rang through my memory.

I closed them while the women worked out the diadem from my mussed, tangled hair to remove the veil.

Suddenly, it dawned on me, I did have a choice. I'd always had one. All I had to do was lift my head and look straight in the eyes of either of these women—and all of it would end. There'd be no more pain. No excruciating feeling of loss crushing me. The numbness would turn absolute, and I would become stone.

"Close your eyes, Amira," Kyllen's voice urged me in my head. *"Keep them closed."*

He'd wanted me to live. He'd wished for me to have a full, vibrant life, too. One of the first things he'd done upon returning to Lorsan had been getting this veil for me. He'd wanted me to see, to learn, and to make my own decisions.

He hadn't just brought me to Lorsan. I'd made the choice to come here on my own.

Kyllen had called me strong. Could I find a way to make it through just one more day? My life had always been about survival. Maybe I could muster the strength to survive for just a little bit longer.

I kept my eyes closed.

The women lifted me out of the water and wrapped me in towels. They dried and braided my hair—twenty-four plaits with a metal snake wound in a spiral around each.

One of them fussed over the faint bruise on my jawline. The spot still ached a bit when she pressed on it. With a sponge, she applied something to cover it up. They then placed the diadem back on my head and lowered the veil over my face.

Only then, I opened my eyes.

"Stand up, now." One yanked me up by my arm. She didn't seem unkind, just busy and hassled.

With the veil gathered around my neck, they powdered my breasts, hips, and buttocks with gold shimmer. A heavy bejeweled belt went around my waist. A cascade of silver chains and crystal beads concealed a narrow strip of my front below the belt.

One of the women rubbed my nipples with fragrant oil, then placed two soft-tipped clips on each. Thin silver chains dangled from the tiny bells attached to the clips, connecting them to each other. Another set of chains went from the clips on my nipples to the wide armbands that the women had circled around my biceps.

Fastening sheer ribbons in pink and lavender to my armlets, one woman said, "You're very pretty, you know?"

"Now, when you're clean and smell nice," the other one added with a giggle.

Next, they put a necklace with dozens of strands of clear crystal, pink quartz, and green jade around my neck. A pair of sandals with soft soles and strings of multi-colored jewels went on my feet. Rings, bracelets, and anklets, set with gemstones and tiny bells, were put on my fingers, wrists, and legs.

"What's going to happen to me?" My voice came out raspy. I hadn't used it for days. I almost surprised myself by speaking now.

Silence had always been my natural state. Until Kyllen... He'd made me talk and smile. He taught me how to laugh.

"Close your eyes, Amira..."

Once again, I obeyed his voice in my head. I closed my eyes tight, but tears still found their way out, rolling down my cheeks. Pain stirred anew, cutting sharp, and I missed the numbness of not caring.

"Oh, sweetie. Don't be sad." One of the women petted my cheek, smearing my tears over my veil. "You belong to the king, now, the most powerful man in the whole of Lorsan. He'll take care of you."

"You'll have pretty clothes to wear and lots of food to eat," the other woman joined in. "You'll be safe. No one will ever dare to hurt the king's pet."

The first woman patted my head. "All you have to do is make the king like you."

Soft rustling came from the distance. It blended well with the whisper of leaves on the branches above us. I wouldn't have noticed it, but both women snapped their backs straight, jumping to attention.

The man from the dock entered onto our small platform. He no longer had a cloak on. Instead, a shirt of pearly-white silk stretched over his shoulders, wide sleeves draping loosely around his arms. Dark pants hugged his hips tightly, held by a leather belt with a short sword in a sheath.

"Lord Adriyel." Both women bowed their heads in supplication.

He didn't bother returning the greeting.

"How is the human girl?" He gave me a long, appraising look.

In the warm light of the sunset supplemented by the yellow glow of the fire moths under the branches, his light-blue skin glowed with pale gold. The snake-skin pattern on his *senties* shimmered with midnight blue. Even without the moon, he appeared to be awash in moonlight.

"She's ready, my lord," both women said at once.

He circled me slowly. I almost felt his gaze travel along every curve of my body. When he stood in front of me again, heat burned in his gaze. I recognized the expression. This man wanted me in every way Kyllen had pleasured me and more.

"Lovely." He smirked. "You have everything needed to charm the king. Let's hope you'll do it."

Spinning on his heel, he took off.

"Go." The women nudged me to follow him.

So, I did. I followed Lord Adriyel up a wide staircase carved in the side of a branch as thick as a large building on Earth, then along another slightly inclined branch that was as wide as a two-lane road.

This must be one of the main passageways in this part of the palace. Gorgonians hurried along it, some carrying trays or clothes. Others seemed to simply be strolling by, hand in hand with a companion. All paused to cast curious glances my way.

Dressed in little more than beads and jewels, I felt exposed under their stares. Many women here wore hardly more than what I was wearing. But people's attention made me feel naked and insecure, whereas the others were protected by their status and confidence.

Lord Adriyel took me through a set of double doors inside the tree trunk. A wide staircase was carved in the middle of a spacious hall.

"This way." He headed up the stairs.

I hurried after him, trying to ignore the scrutinizing stares of the people in the hall. The heavy belt pressed on my hips, scratching my skin. The clips on my nipples tugged with every step. Chains swayed. The tiny bells trilled, announcing my presence to anyone who cared to know. The courtiers followed me with their eyes all the way to the top of the stairs.

Lord Adriyel turned right into a section divided from the main hall by a wall. I released a breath, glad to finally get away from the crowd.

The court's intense attention and my discomfort at it hadn't escaped Lord Adriyel.

"You're a novelty," he explained. "We learn about humans only from myths and legends. You must forgive our people for forgetting their manners when seeing someone like you in person."

"No one cares for my forgiveness," I muttered under my breath. He gave me a long look but didn't argue.

Stopping in front of another set of carved double-doors guarded by two gorgonians in green and gold uniforms, he said sharply, "Lord Adriyel, heir to the High Lord of Mevon, to see King Zeldren."

The guards stepped aside, letting us enter.

Inside the spacious room with glassless, floor-to-ceiling windows, the king sat on his throne.

Other than the golden crown with turquoise spikes of precious stones placed over his *senties*, he looked like an ordinary gorgonian man, his hands and face darkened by age and dehydration. "The throne" was just a wide chair with a tall back. But the way the king held himself was nothing but regal. It would've made any chair he sat on look like a throne.

"Your Majesty," Lord Adriyel announced in a formal tone. "This is the only human in the whole of Lorsan. And she's yours. A gift from me to you."

Chapter Nine

AMIRA

I'd lost track of how many times I'd changed hands, who'd sold, bought, or gifted me. Now, apparently, I was the gift from Lord Adriyel to King Zeldren of Lorsan.

"Is she really a human?" the king gazed at me skeptically, an empty goblet dangling in his fingers.

"Yes, Your Majesty." Lord Adriyel took my hand and slid the veil up to reveal my bare arm.

The king leaned forward, studying the skin on my arm that was dull and matte compared to the glow of the fae.

"Interesting." He took my hand from Lord Adriyel.

The snake-skin pattern on the back of his hand was dark brown. The rest of his skin was the color of golden sand with the glow of magic pulsing through it. My hand seemed like a piece of pale clay in comparison—plain, dull, and rather *un*interesting.

The king kept turning my hand in his, clearly intrigued. "This is remarkable. So...earthy looking. Is it true that humans are completely void of magic?"

Lord Adriyel looked pleased with the king's interest in me. "Yes, Your Majesty. They are."

"What can she do, then?" the king asked, as if I was a curious mechanical toy presented to him. "Can she dance?"

Lord Adriyel glanced at me, and I shook my head.

"No, Your Majesty," the lord replied for me. "She doesn't dance."

"Sing?"

Another glance of the lord to me. Another shake of my head.

Lord Adriyel narrowed his silver-gray eyes at me, and I wondered if he already regretted his purchase. "No. She can't sing, either."

"So, what good is she for?" The king tilted his head.

Lord Adriyel stepped behind me and placed his hands on my shoulders. "Isn't she lovely, Sire? Humans don't live long. They age quickly. Their youth lasts years instead of centuries. This is her prime, but it will pass quickly. It's like catching the river orchid bloom before it withers and dies. Fleeting and rare. Enjoy her for as long as she lasts."

He skimmed his hands down my arms. The king's gaze followed the lord's gesture down my body displayed under the veil.

The look in the king's amber eyes grew heavier. It paused on my breasts, then on my hips.

"Leave us," he ordered.

Lord Adriyel inclined his head in a bow. He peeled his hands from my arms slowly, almost reluctantly. With one long look at me, he departed, closing the doors behind him.

"Well," the king drawled. "You should be good at something. Let's see what you can do." He thrust his empty goblet my way. "Get me some more wine."

I took it from him. It was large and heavy, inlaid with colorful gemstones. The crystal decanter he gestured at stood on a small three-legged table by his chair. I filled the king's goblet, then passed it back to him.

"Here you go."

He raised his eyes to me. "You didn't grow up in a noble court, did you?"

"No."

"It shows," he scoffed, taking a swig of wine. "You've no idea how to address your king."

He set the goblet on the table and leaned back in his chair, then opened his red-and-gold robe to expose his velvet-clad crotch.

"Well, since you can't dance or sing..." He unclipped his belt, then opened his dark velvet pants. "Come here, sweet thing." He gestured for me to come closer. "Lift that veil up to your neck. I may as well play with your tits while you suck my cock."

I stood there, rooted in place.

Suddenly, something mattered to me again. And it mattered very much.

People could look at me naked all they wanted. But touching was different. No man had touched me but Kyllen. The memory of his hands on me was the only one I wished to have. No one would soil it. Not even the king.

If he wanted me to lift my veil, I'd do it. But I'd lift it all the way up. If he forced himself on me, cold stone would be the only thing he'd get to touch tonight.

"So?" He stared at me expectantly. "What's the matter? Isn't that what you came here for? To pleasure your king?"

I didn't come here on my own. I'd been taken, dragged, and led. I'd been caught like a dry leaf in a current, tossed and twirled. And I let it all happen to me because nothing had mattered. But now, it did. I cared about what happened to me next.

The king gestured at me impatiently, urging me to come to him. I stepped closer to his chair, but didn't lift my veil, disobeying his order. He grabbed my hand and yanked me down, making me drop to my knees.

I crossed my arms over my chest, shielding my breasts. My heart beat frantically in the place that held nothing but a dark empty void until now. Fear jolted me, bringing me back to life.

"So, are you going to use your mouth, human?" the king demanded.

He slumped back in his chair, his knees spread wide, his pants undone. He seemed relaxed, but there was a droop in his shoulders and a dullness in his eyes.

The king was dying. In addition to the strikingly dark pattern taking over his skin, there were other signs that confirmed it. Stiffness crippled his body in the same way I'd seen in Udren, the High Lord of Ellohi, Kyllen's aging brother.

"I can do many things with my mouth," I croaked.

"So you say," he snapped, yanking his pants open wider and exposing himself to me. "Yet I'm still waiting."

The king's penis was shriveled and limp. The dark diamond pattern seized it, covering it whole. In its flaccid state, the king didn't even reach a quarter of Kyllen's length or half of his girth. But then again, Kyllen had never been flaccid when naked with me.

"Well, show me what you can do with your mouth void of magic, little human. Can you raise the dead?" he chuckled, though somewhat somberly.

I cleared my throat, hugging my arms tighter. "I have never done what you're telling me to do."

His brow ridges shot up in surprise. "Never?"

I shook my head.

"Are you a virgin?" He blinked at me incredulously.

I nodded. Kyllen and I hadn't made it that far... Taking a deep breath, I shoved away the dark feeling of loss that thinking about Kyllen threatened to plunge me into again.

"I believe I could be much more useful to you in other ways," I suggested.

"Like what?" The king now looked exhausted. And bored.

"I can offer you something more interesting than my body. Something more engaging that would entertain you far longer." His brow twitched. Was he intrigued? "I can tell you a story."

"A story?" he scoffed, grabbing his goblet from the table again. "What could you possibly tell that would entertain someone like me? I've commanded the world's most victorious armies, forced powerful men to bow to me, known the pleasure of the most beautiful women of every kingdom in Nerifir."

I chewed on my bottom lip, considering my options. Negotiating with the king was a gamble. But what did I have to lose? There was always the option to die. No one could take that from me. I gambled for one more day to live.

"The story I'm going to tell you isn't epic. But it may make you smile. Your mind will rest while you listen. And it may help you fall asleep without numbing yourself with wine." I tipped my chin at the goblet in his fingers.

He flexed his hand, his mouth turning into a thin, hard line. His stare rested on me, pressing on me heavily.

I refused the king. I poked his ego. Maybe I deserved to die for that, but I waited to see what he'd do.

His *senties* flared into a halo around his head...then rested upon his wide shoulders.

"What is it about? The story that you think is worthy of my attention?" There was a clear interest in his voice this time, and I ventured to take a longer breath.

The king shifted in his chair, yanking his robe closed to conceal his undone pants and his motionless member.

Emboldened, I reached for the knitted orange-and-green throw that was folded over one of the armrests of his chair. "May I, please? If you're not using it."

He lifted his arm, staring at the throw as if seeing it for the first time. Frowning, he took it off the armrest, then handed it to me.

Turning away from him, I unfolded the blanket, then quickly wrapped it around my practically naked body. Reaching inside, I discreetly yanked the silly clamps off my nipples and tucked the chain with them in my belt.

"Ahhh." I turned to face the king again. "This feels much better." I gave him a smile in response to his curious stare.

"Well, what do you know?" he muttered under his breath. "She can smile."

His brow was furrowed, but he didn't seem upset. He looked...expectant.

I sat back on my heels, snuggling into the soft blanket.

"I'll tell you a story about a little boy," I said. My voice shook, but I steadied it. "The boy was born and raised in a palace, but his mischievous nature often got him in trouble. It also led him to many adventures. Tonight, I'll tell you about the time when the boy snuck out of his bedroom, climbed down the great royal tree of his father's palace—"

"It's impossible," the king interrupted with a growl. "The great royal tree trunk is too smooth and way too wide to climb."

"Oh, but the little boy was nimble as a monkey. He often skipped his classroom lessons to the chagrin of his parents and tutors, but he was smart in other ways. You see, he never agreed with the bedtime his parents set for him. So, he figured out a system that allowed him to escape even the highest room in his father's palace. He practiced it every night—"

"What kind of system?" the king interrupted. "Because unless he had the arborist equipment, with all the ropes and pulleys..."

I pursed my lips, pinning him with a glare. "Who is telling the story, you or me?"

He blinked, raising both eyebrow ridges at my audacity—I dared reprimand the king. He could order me beheaded if he wished.

Having nothing to lose, however, gave me courage. I held his stare until he snorted a laugh with a shake of his head.

"Fine. What happened next?"

"Well..." I continued.

Back at the menagerie, Kyllen's stories had given a reprieve to both Kyllen and me. To me, they had held everything new and exciting in my dull life of mind-numbing labor. To him, they were a distraction from the despair of his imprisonment.

Now, telling one of his stories helped me survive the night. I still had a body made of flesh, not of stone. For a human in Lorsan, that alone was an accomplishment.

The king chuckled, shaking his head.

"That kid! He reminds me of myself when I was little. I never shied away from an adventure, either. And if an adventure didn't find me, I'd search for one myself." He shifted eagerly in his chair. "So, what happened next? After he and his friends stole the paddle boards from the dock at the tavern?"

"Oh, that is a whole new story. But it's kind of late now, don't you think? You should get some sleep."

I'd been talking for probably close to an hour. My legs had fallen asleep while folded under my butt. I couldn't remember the last time I ate or drank anything. All I really wanted to do was to lie down and pass out for the rest of the night.

"Nonsense!" The king raised his goblet. "Night is wasted on sleeping. Night is the time when life really happens."

Maybe it was that time for him, but I felt physically exhausted and emotionally drained.

"I'm afraid I can't talk much longer without losing my voice completely," I argued. "And then where would we be? No more stories at all."

He made a face but conceded, "Fine. I can wait until tomorrow. After all, patience is a royal quality."

"Okay." I got up from the floor in front of his chair, clutching the blanket to my chest. Blood rushed back to the muscles in my legs, making them feel like they were pierced with hundreds of needles.

"Okay?" He tilted his head. "What does it mean?"

I shook my legs out, one after the other, chasing away the prickling pain. "Oh. It means 'sure,' 'I'll do it,' or 'I agree.'"

"Or *'yes, Your Majesty*?'" he corrected, giving me a pointed stare.

I blanched, momentarily embarrassed by my lack of manners. I was talking to the king, after all. It came with a set of rules. An etiquette. But with everything that had happened lately, the honorifics had left my mind.

"Right," I mumbled. "Please forgive me, *Your Majesty.*" I bowed. But when I straightened to meet his eyes again, he didn't appear pleased by my apology or by my courteous manner. He looked pacified, but bored again.

I recalled everything anyone in Lorsan had said about humans so far. The fae lords considered us 'exotic,' 'different.' And that apparently was where our appeal to them lay. My conforming to the norm must make me sound boring and mundane to the king.

Well, if it was 'different' that he craved...

I raised my chin, tossing him a look.

"I mean, '*Okay*, Your Majesty.'" I gave a slight nod instead of a bow and a smile that was somewhere in the middle between cheeky and sweet.

It worked. He threw his head back and laughed, looking as pleased as could be. Navigating the court of the King of Lorsan promised to be as easy as balancing on a razor blade. This time, however, it appeared I succeeded. For now, anyway.

"Get me another glass of wine!" the king ordered, thrusting his goblet my way.

I took it, pausing my gaze on his hand. The dark mesh of the snakeskin pattern covered the top of his hand, including his fingers.

"How old are you?" I blurted out.

The king's eyebrow ridges jerked up in shock once again. Then a spark of amusement flashed in his burnt-orange eyes.

"How old do you think I am?" He smirked.

"I can't tell." I shook my head. "Age is difficult to gauge with your kind."

"My kind?"

"The fae," I explained. "You mature as quickly as humans do, but your appearance remains unchanged almost until the day you die."

He dropped his hand back on the armrest, leaving the goblet in my fingers. "You know how long fae live?"

"Five hundred years, I've been told."

"Right." He heaved a breath so heavy, it appeared to carry a weight of several lifetimes. "I'll be six hundred next year. That is, if I live for another seven months."

"Six hundred?" I gaped at him.

He nodded. "Almost a full century of life borrowed. It's time to repay the debt soon."

Propping his hands onto the armrests, he rose heavily from his chair. The king was as tall as Kyllen, but broader. Where Kyllen was agile like a leopard and graceful like a serpent, the king was solid and wide like an old oak tree.

The pants that he'd left undone slid down to his knees, tripping him. He swayed, losing his balance.

Dropping the goblet and the blanket, I grabbed his arm to steady him, then led him over to the raised nest piled high with olive-green cushions and sheets.

He groaned, sitting down on the edge of the nest, and stretched his legs in front of him. I swiped my blanket from the floor and wrapped it around me again. He had caught a glance of my naked breasts but with less interest in his expression than before.

Picking up the goblet from the floor, I walked across the room to the elaborate water feature at the wall across from the nest. I rinsed the goblet in one of the fountains, then filled it with clean water from one of the waterfalls.

The king curled his lips in distaste when I offered the water to him. "That's not wine."

"Water may be better than wine for you at this hour," I suggested.

"Are you telling the king what to do, human?"

"I wouldn't dare, Your Majesty." I curtsied clumsily, which made him snort and shake his head. "If I were to make choices for the king, I'd order a glass of warm milk from the kitchen or better yet—a cup of herbal tea."

He winced.

"You're talking like my caretakers." He stretched his patterned hand in front of him. "This dehydration is not caused by lack of water, you know that, right?"

The king was dying, and no amount of fluids would cure it. Staring at his dry skin, I drank the water from the goblet myself. An hour of talking had made me incredibly thirsty.

He watched me drink without objection.

I set the goblet back on the small table nearby. "What brings you comfort, Your Majesty? What makes you feel at peace? What helps you rest at night? Is it wine? Because if it truly is, then I'll get you some."

He stared at me for a long moment, then took off his crown and set it on the side table. Then, he lay back in the nest, saying nothing.

I crouched down to free his feet from his pants, then helped him turn to put his legs in the nest, too. As I tucked the luxurious blankets around him, the king gave me a cheeky smile that suddenly made him look centuries younger.

"A virgin, are you?" he murmured. "Here, in my nest."

I shot my gaze to his face with alarm and clutched my blanket tighter to my chest.

He smiled dreamily. "Had I met you a few years earlier, I would've fixed that quickly. I would've kept you up all night. When I rut, I pound hard. I used to fuck at least a dozen times a night. You wouldn't be able to walk for days after I'd been done with you."

I released a shaky breath, giving a silent prayer to whatever deity was watching over me for not letting me arrive in this world a few years earlier.

"You're staying here tonight," the king mumbled sleepily, closing his eyes. "But not in my nest—that's my space. Grab some pillows and make yourself a nest over there, on the window seat."

"*Okay*, Your Majesty."

The king chuckled. A minute later, his rumbling snores rolled through his chamber. He was asleep.

Chapter Ten

AMIRA

The king fell asleep quickly, but I lay awake in my narrow nest by the window.

I buried my face into the silk-covered pillow I'd taken from the king's bedding. It retained his scent, unfamiliar and wrong. I missed the scent of another man. I missed having Kyllen next to me.

Loneliness wasn't a stranger to me, but until Kyllen was gone, I realized I'd never known the true meaning of being completely and utterly alone. The excruciating emptiness of it crushed me. The memories of the night he was taken from me came back, stabbing me from the inside with the pain too strong to bear. Tears bubbled hot in my chest, then finally erupted to the surface. I curled into myself and cried.

I cried for Kyllen. For everything he had survived in my world at the hands of Madame only to be killed in his home, by his own family.

I cried for my love for him that now had no purpose and no anchor, leaving me adrift in this strange new world.

And I cried for myself, unable to find any footing in the black twister of grief, loss, and pain.

"You said you'd never leave me," I whispered into the pillow. "You promised..."

"A fae can't break his promise," the familiar voice sounded behind me, jolting me with shock.

His arms twined around me. His body pressed to my back.

"Kyllen..." I gasped, turning in his arms.

His smile greeted me, along with the glint of his familiar dark-golden eyes.

"Kyllen... You're here? You're alive." I touched his face, his chest, his shoulders. His body felt real, the warm skin with the hard muscles underneath. Bone and flesh, not some ethereal entity.

He was here.

"But how?" My head was spinning.

"Shh." He placed a finger to his lips. "It's night here right now, is it not?"

"Yes." I blinked, puzzled by his question. Was he not sure it was night? Could he not see it for himself?

"People may be sleeping where you are," he said. "Let's not wake them."

I glanced over to the king's nest. I knew it should be there, but I couldn't quite make it out in the darkness that shrouded everything beyond my nest. The king's snores had remained out there in the darkness, too. I couldn't hear them anymore.

Kyllen was real. However, the rest of the world wasn't quite what it should be.

"What's happening?" I searched his face for answers.

He smiled. "I'm not quite sure."

"Are you really here? Where are we?"

"So many questions." He caressed the side of my face. Lifting one of my braids, he moved it over my shoulder. "You've always been such a curious little thing, my sweet pea."

The sound of his nickname for me made my heart squeeze with longing.

"Oh, Kyllen... I..."

"I know." He kissed my eyes, one then the other. "I feel everything you do, my darling."

His kisses were more real than ever.

Because there was no veil between us.

"Oh, no..." I breathed out with a jolt of terror, touching my face. "How am I still alive?"

"Because you are a survivor, Amira," he said, not talking about the veil. "Every day of your life, you've been fighting for survival in your own quiet way."

"But what for? What is the point?" I drew in a shuddering breath. "I thought I could change things by being brave. I left everything behind, hoping for a better life. And what did I find here? I changed nothing, for either of us." Sorrow gripped my heart, twisting it with so much pain, it hurt to breathe. "I only made it worse."

He stroked my back, kissing my hair.

"I don't think I can do it, Kyllen... I can't keep going. I'm just..." I cried.

But it wasn't the same as crying alone. The glide of his hands on my body soothed my grief, drying my tears. There was so much comfort in his strong arms around me.

"I know you're scared," he said when I'd calmed down enough to listen. "You're hurting and you're alone. You're screaming inside, and it's deafening." He winced as if in pain, too.

"I'm screaming?"

"Not on the outside. You're quiet for everyone else, but *I* can hear you. I feel your pain. And I can't stand it. That's why I'm here. To make it all better." He ducked his head in search of my eyes. "I make you feel better, don't I?"

I sniffled. "You always do."

He flashed me a cocky grin. "I knew it."

I released a long breath. Some of the pain seemed to let go with it, dissipating into the darkness beyond my nest.

"Will you stay with me, Kyllen?"

"Of course I will. I'm not going anywhere."

"But how are you here at all?" The logic escaped me. At the same time, I didn't want to think about it too hard, afraid that if I questioned it too much, Kyllen might vanish as suddenly as he had appeared.

He was here, now. It was all that mattered.

"Think of it as a cucumber," he said.

"What?" I smiled in utter confusion.

"Remember the cucumber you threw at me? That alone didn't exactly save my life, but it gave me the nourishment to be able to think, to cope, and to hope. It's my turn to toss you a lifeline, Amira. I can't let you drown in your sorrow and grief."

"You want me to hope?"

"I want you to think. You need a clear mind to survive. Now more than ever. You have been my light in the darkness. Let me be that for you."

"You've been that for me, Kyllen, and more—my anchor, my purpose."

"Well, there you go." He grinned happily. His chest expanded with a deep breath. "You need to rest. Let me hold you while you sleep."

He drew me to him, and I buried my face in his chest. His familiar scent enveloped me like a comforting blanket. For the first time in days, I was able to breathe freely.

Chapter Eleven

AMIRA

Warm sunlight landed on my face, waking me up. The shadows of the night were gone, and with them, the sensation of Kyllen's arms around me. Panic struck me. I didn't want to open my eyes. Because I knew, I knew that I was alone in my nest.

The king's snoring reverberated through the room. The whisper of the veil caressed my face again. This was the real world. And Kyllen was no longer in it. He stayed in the dream that had vanished.

Grief gripped my throat. Tears threatened to suffocate me again.

"You are a survivor..." Kyllen's words from my dream echoed in my head.

The dream was gone, but his words stayed with me, as did the memory of comfort I felt through the night.

He was right, I survived. That was what I did. And I did so by taking it one day at a time. When even a day seemed like too much to tackle at once, I made it through hour by hour, minute by minute.

All I had to do now was make it through another minute, just a few breaths in and out. And the next minute...

The next minute, the doors to the room flew open, and a group of men marched in.

"Good morning, Your Majesty!" The one in the front announced brightly.

He carried a tray laden with food. The others started tidying the bedroom. There were quite a few of them, but it was hard to tell exactly how many. They moved so quickly, I kept losing count.

Someone picked up the king's discarded pants. Another one rinsed his goblet and refilled it with water. They straightened the furniture, trimmed the vines around the windows and the plants around the waterfalls, wiped down the marble of the washbasins, and filled the room with a flurry of activity.

"Time to wake up, Your Majesty," the man with the tray said in a sing-song voice. He placed the tray on the side table next to the king's nest.

The king's snoring stopped abruptly. He rolled onto his back with a loud groan. "Kiris, may the Great Serpent eat you."

Kiris didn't seem offended by the king's rude greeting. On the contrary, he smiled.

"Maybe one day, Your Majesty," he said. "But until then, you get your breakfast, a massage, and your herbal tea brewed by the healer."

The king winced in the morning light, then rubbed his eyes. "On second thought, the Great Serpent would probably spit you out. You're impossible to stomach."

Kiris laughed. "I'm glad to see you in a good mood this morning, Your Majesty. You slept well?" He bent over the king, helping him to sit up in bed.

"Right up until you showed up," the king grumped. His gaze crossed with mine as I sat up in the window seat, his orange-green blanket wrapped around me. A lopsided grin spread across his face. "I could've used some more sleep this morning. After getting busy with my new toy last night."

Kiris shot me a slightly annoyed look from under his green-brown *senties*, as if I were a nuisance, like a cat that misbehaved.

"Keeping a daily routine is important to your health and balanced disposition," he said to the king.

"Shoving you out of this window would do wonders to my disposition," the king muttered under his breath as Kiris placed the tray in his lap.

"I doubt that'd be of any benefit to you," Kiris retorted, not skipping a beat. "No one would take better care of you than me." He lifted a wide, two-handled cup from the tray. "Tea, Your Majesty."

"Only if you leave me alone once I drink it." The king took the cup from Kiris and emptied it in a few big gulps. "Here." He shoved the empty cup into the other man's hands. "Now get lost."

Kiris gave the cup to one of the men cleaning the room, then lifted the covers to expose the king's legs. "I'll massage your feet while you eat your breakfast."

The king yanked the covers back over his legs.

"Leave," he gritted through his teeth.

Kiris blanched. The king's previous grumpiness hadn't affected him. However, the last order was given with added power. The king's tone of voice promised consequences if disobeyed.

"Get out of here." The king waved his hand in a dismissive gesture.

Kiris bowed and called off his team. "We'll leave you to enjoy your morning, Your Majesty."

"Let me eat in peace," the king added, in a little less lethal tone of voice. "And send a maid with some clothes for her." He gestured in my direction. "After breakfast."

With another deep bow, Kiris departed, taking his helpers with him.

The king leaned back against a pile of cushions and closed his eyes.

I wondered if he would fall asleep again, and if I should take the tray off his lap before he turned and knocked it over. I also wondered if he would rather I didn't bother him. Maybe he wanted me gone, too, like Kiris? I would leave if I had a place to go.

"Come here." The king patted the place next to him in his nest.

I did as he said, bringing my blanket along.

He opened his eyes, watching me climb into his nest and sit next to him.

"Hungry?" he asked.

I nodded. My stomach felt so empty, I could possibly fit the entire Great Serpent in there, no matter how big he might be.

The king shifted the tray from his lap into mine. "Eat."

"Thank you." I grabbed a boiled duck egg topped with black caviar and shoved it in my mouth.

The king gave me a wide mug next. "Drink?"

I nodded, taking the mug from him while also stuffing my mouth with more duck eggs, crispy lizard sausage, and slices of blue orange.

"Slow down." The king chuckled. "I don't want you to throw up all over my nest."

I took a long, slow drink of cattail root broth from the mug.

"Sorry. I don't remember when I ate last." I sat back. Picking up a small bowl of gooseberries drizzled with lily honey, I ate them with a spoon in a slightly more dignified manner. A pleasant heaviness settled in my stomach with the satisfaction that came from a good meal.

The king scoffed. "Was Adriyel more concerned with dressing you up than feeding you?"

To be fair, I had gotten some food delivered to the cell where Lord Adriyel held me. I just hadn't had any appetite or even the presence of mind to eat at that time.

"Are *you* hungry?" I took an alarmed look at the nearly empty tray. I'd almost eaten the king's entire breakfast.

He picked up a cucumber slice from the plate of cut-up vegetables and chewed on it slowly. "My appetite is no longer what it used to be."

I stared at the remaining slices on his plate.

"Think of it as a cucumber..."

Kyllen's words sounded in my mind, his voice light with humor and full of life.

It had been so real... More vivid than any dream I'd ever had.

I glanced at my nest by the window. A long terrace ran along the tree trunk under it from the outside. It stretched all the way to the next window that also served as the door out to the terrace.

"What's stopping someone from climbing up the tree from the outside?" I asked the king. "To get in here?"

He halted his chewing, clearly confused about the reason for my question.

"The royal tree is impossible to climb." He shook his head. "No one is going to come and steal you. If that's your concern."

"But what if the person *could* climb it?"

The king smirked. "Kind of like the boy in your story?"

I nodded, stilling my breath. "Kind of like him."

"Even if he managed to climb all the way up here somehow, he wouldn't be able to come in. The wards on my windows wouldn't let him. They keep away anyone who is not of the royal blood. And since I am the only one of my bloodline," he chuckled, "you and I are absolutely safe from any intrusion here."

My hope dwindled and died. The crazy notion that Kyllen had somehow survived Bherlon's attack, then traveled to Ufaris, naked and unarmed, to climb the tree to visit me last night was just that—crazy.

Without hope, however, there was nothing but pain.

The king shifted in the sheets uncomfortably, his face twitching into a grimace.

"Is there anything you need?" I asked, glad for the distraction from my dark thoughts. "Do you want me to call Kiris again?" I moved aside the breakfast tray.

The king waved me off. "Kiris will be back soon enough."

"He said something about massaging your legs. I can do it for you if it helps."

He smirked, giving me a measuring stare. "Isn't your purpose here to massage my cock?"

I glanced away, feeling my face warm with a blush. He chuckled, touching my burning cheek through my veil.

"So innocent. Words make her blush," the king murmured as if to himself.

I cleared my throat.

"I have very little experience to adequately deliver for *that* purpose," I said, choosing my words carefully. "But I have worked for years, serving others. I can take care of people. Wouldn't you rather have a skilled caretaker than a clumsy lover?"

"I already have a palace full of caretakers." Moving his fingers under my chin, he lifted my face to his, then slid his thumb along my bottom lip. "In her prime..." His eyes were hooded by his eyelids in a dreamy expression. "Rare like the blossom of the river orchid." He heaved a breath. "Had our paths crossed just a little earlier, I would've delighted in making a skilled lover out of you. The things I would've done to you. You'd scream for mercy, but eventually you'd beg me for more."

My heart made a thud in my chest. Gaining the favor of a powerful man like King Zeldren could make the difference between life and death for someone like me—a human woman with no family, no friends, and no means to support myself.

I feared, however, that gaining his favor might come with the price I couldn't pay. I decided to make it clear, even if it might cost me my life.

With my chin in his hand, I stared straight into his eyes through the milky haze of the veil between us.

"I will not let you touch me, Your Majesty," I said, my voice quiet but firm. "I'd rather die."

Shock flashed in his eyes. I braced myself for his hand to slide down to my throat and squeeze. Hard. But he tossed his head back, erupting with a thunder of laughter while slapping his thighs.

"There were times when women would die for a chance to be fucked by me. Yet you would die to *avoid* that honor? That's new!" His laughter tapered down, then ended with a heavy sigh. "Obviously, I've lived for too long."

"I didn't mean to offend you."

He pinned me with a stare. "Of course you didn't, but your intentions don't matter. Any offense to the king, deliberate or not, is punishable by death."

"I'm sorry, Your Majesty." I dropped my gaze into my lap.

"Watch your mouth next time," he said somberly. It was a warning, not quite a threat. "I won't have you speak like that to me, especially if we are in the presence of others. I've killed for less before."

"I'm sorry." I apologized for the insult my words had brought but not for what I'd said. If I had to repeat my words, I would.

He dismissed my apology with a wave of a hand.

"Don't worry. Your virtue is safe. I'd rather keep the glorious memories of my rutting into a woman so hard these walls shook instead of replacing them with some feeble attempts to resurrect what's now clearly meant to remain dormant."

He turned away from me. I had a feeling he would've loved to storm out of the room, slamming the door loud enough for the noise to reverberate through the entire palace. But he couldn't. All he could do was glare. That in itself was heartbreaking. To see this man, who once might've been able to crush granite in his hands, being helpless to even express his rage the way he wished.

I fidgeted with the edge of my blanket.

"I can be useful still," I said softly. "There are many things I can do for you. I can fetch you food, water, or wine. Or shield you from Kiris and his housekeeping posse when you need peace. Or I could help them take care of you if you wish. I could also tell you more stories when you feel like being entertained."

To survive, I needed a place and a role at the king's castle. I could be useful if he needed me in any other capacity than his lover.

But I also spoke out of compassion. He was clearly suffering, and I hoped my company might distract him from his pain.

Maybe easing his pain would help me deal with mine, too.

He turned back to me, still glaring. "I don't need another caretaker."

"Okay. But how about a friend?"

He sneered. "I've never had a need for those."

So much was obvious—the king didn't seem like the friendly type.

"It's never too late to make a friend. I'd love to be yours." I wouldn't give up.

He threw me another glare from under his heavy brow. "The title of a king's friend has to be earned."

"Then give me a chance to earn it. Would you accept me on...um, a probationary period?" I gave him the sweetest smile I could manage. "You could have me keep you company in the evenings, instead of nursing a wine goblet here alone. If it doesn't work out, you can tell me to leave anytime."

He shifted under the covers again, looking uncomfortable. "Well, I'll have to call Kiris back now. Unless you can prove to me you're really as good at giving massages as you say you are."

Had I said I was good at giving massages? I didn't remember. But I had massaged Madame occasionally and lived, so I couldn't be completely useless at that.

After securing my blanket around my chest, I removed the breakfast tray from the nest.

"The oils are there." The king gestured at the battery of vials, bottles, and jars lining the wall shelves next to the waterfalls.

I examined the collection. "Which one do you prefer?"

"I don't care." He shoved the covers aside. "Start with the legs."

Grabbing a random bottle off the shelf, I sat at his side. I put some of the fragrant substance from the bottle onto my hands. It smelled like almond, and anise, and something else I had only smelled in Madame's herb collection.

The king stretched his legs in front of him. Thick and muscled like tree trunks, they were crippled by the thick, dark mesh pattern. His skin felt as dry as tree bark, too, the snakeskin markings raised and textured. It quickly soaked in the oil, like the desert floor would absorb raindrops. I added more. This time, I didn't bother putting it on my hands, pouring it directly on his leg.

The king watched me spread the oil along his shin with my hands then gently rub it into his dry skin and stiff muscles underneath. Seemingly satisfied with my performance, he leaned back onto the cushions, letting me proceed on my own.

"How does it feel?" I asked.

"You want to know what it's like to be drying out alive?"

I wanted to know what he thought about my massaging technique, but if he wished to speak about his sufferings instead, I wasn't going to stop him.

"The skin hardens and pulls with every movement." He closed his eyes. "It used to be thin and dry like paper, cracking every time I turned. At least it's hard enough to stop breaking now. My muscles are drying out, too. I can't walk, save for a couple of paces here and there. Soon, the mortal drought will spread to my vital organs. Then, my spirit will leave, and my body will turn to dust. Ufaris Lake will absorb what's left of it. The Lorsan Wetlands will take back their magic, and the Great Serpent will carry my spirit into the afterlife."

I drew in a long breath, subdued by his words. "I'm sorry."

"Why? Don't you feel sorry for me, little one. Whatever is waiting for me in the afterlife is surely better than this." He glared at his legs with disdain.

I moved on to massage his other leg, and he put his head back on the pillows again, staring at the ceiling.

"I never thought I would go this way. Slowly drying out in my nest." He no longer appeared to be speaking to me, just saying his thoughts out loud. "I was meant to perish in battle, slain by a sword. What a glorious death that would be! See, my little human?" He flicked his gaze to me again. "Being the ultimate winner didn't turn out that great at the end. I've killed so many, and here I am now, envious of all those who have lost to me."

He chuckled without humor.

"See that sword?" He raised his hand, pointing at the massive weapon mounted on the wall above the nest. The metal was dark, almost black. Large blotches of rust stained the long blade. "I used to wield it with one hand, slicing the heads of my enemies as if they were heads of cabbage during harvest. Now..." His chest rose and fell with a deep, sorrowful sigh. "Now, I don't think I could even take it off the wall if I tried."

Sadness gripped my heart at his words. I sat with my hands in my lap after having finished massaging his legs.

He glanced at me.

"Hey!" He sat up. "What's that frown for? Did I make you sad, my pretty river orchid?" Finger under my chin, he lifted my head. "There is no need to feel sad or sorry for me. My death might be rather pitiful, I have to agree. But my life has been nothing like that. I've had it all. I've done everything I ever wanted and much, much more. Any man would've cursed his own mother to have the life I've had. Trust me, there is nothing to be sad about."

I nodded, giving him a reassuring smile. "I'm not sad."

"Good." He looked at his now well-oiled legs. "Well, you've done a decent job here. But there's more." He shrugged out of his robe. "Help me take the tunic off, would you?"

Sliding his thin, cream-colored tunic up, I helped him free his arms from the sleeves, then took the garment off over his head.

Left completely naked, he lay on his stomach over the sheets.

"Let's hope you'll be as good to my ass as you've been to my legs," he joked as I started massaging his back, his skin rough and textured under my palms. "What's your name, by the way? Did Lord Adriyel ever tell me?"

"He didn't." Lord Adriyel didn't know it himself. He'd never asked. "It's Amira."

"A lovely name, just like you. Well, tell me, Amira, what happened to that little boy in the story?"

My hands paused, as if on their own. "You want to know more about him?"

"Well, when I speak, I make you sad. I'd rather let you speak. It amuses me to listen to the boy's adventures. The rascal has just stolen some paddle boards with his friends, hasn't he? That's what you told me last."

"Yes." I smiled, resuming my work.

"I can't believe they tricked the barmaid into giving them the key to the lock. Did they ever get caught? By the way, does the boy have a name, too?"

"He does." I lifted my hands from the king's back as my fingers began to tremble. I fisted them and closed my eyes before saying his name. "Kyllen."

Tears burned behind my eyelids, and I shut my eyes tighter, holding them in.

"Kyllen? It sounds familiar somehow. Is he real or did you make him up?" The king's voice remained light. Lying on his belly, he couldn't see me, and had no idea what effect saying that name out loud had on me.

"He's real." I swallowed a thick lump in my throat. "*Was*. He's...no longer here."

"He's dead?"

Dead.

The word just couldn't apply to someone like Kyllen. He'd always been so full of life even when on the verge of death at the menagerie.

"Well, that's too bad," the king drawled. "I would've liked to have known him."

I nodded, keeping my eyes closed. "I'm sure you would've loved him. Kyllen was so easy to love."

AMIRA

In the weeks that followed, I lay in my nest every night, tightly hugging my pillow. My eyes closed, I waited for the sleep to take me, secretly hoping to dream about Kyllen again.

Sometimes, I thought I felt his arms enclosing me into a hug just before I'd fall into a deep, restful sleep. And then...it'd be morning. I slept, but I didn't dream, or at least I didn't remember dreaming.

At daytime, the king and I had fallen into a routine.

Kiris and his men would wake the king up. They brought him breakfast and cleaned up the room.

I gave the king a full-body massage after breakfast, then entertained him by telling stories or playing board games with him until lunch, unless there was a Royal Council meeting that morning. In which case, the king would wheel his magically enhanced mechanical chair to the council meeting room. Despite his condition, he was still the ruler of his kingdom and had a lot of decisions to make.

In the afternoon, Kiris and his helpers usually gave the king a bath, and I was free to explore my new home.

By now, the courtiers had gotten used to my presence somewhat.

Instead of chains, beads, and those scandalous nipple clips, I wore regular dresses, which helped attract fewer stares. Instead of gawking openly at me, people just threw furtive glances my way when I passed.

I still learned the intricate layout of the palace, which wasn't easy. The location of rooms and corridors didn't follow any logical grid but the pattern in which the branches of the palace trees grew. In addition, sections of the palace often moved, using magic and mechanics, to suit some new purpose. That created new rooms and passageways, undoing what I'd already learned.

I loved studying the beautiful artwork that decorated every surface inside the palace of Ufaris. Some were paintings, others carvings, some a combination of both. There were portraits of past kings, depictions of epic battles, and scenes of hunting with fantastic beasts.

One day while the king was in his bedroom receiving a bath and bickering with Kiris, I stood in the main hall in front of yet another depiction of an epic battle. This one was made with a combination of bright glossy paint and colorful wood inlays. It was a huge picture, taking up most of the wide, slightly curved wall of the hall in one of the seven main trees of the king's palace.

A warm sensation tingled the skin on my back, rushing up to my nape then down my arms.

"Kyllen?" I whispered.

I wasn't asleep. Yet I *felt* him.

His presence remained elusive, like the golden mist over the lake at sunrise. It caressed and warmed my heart, but slipped through my fingers no matter how hard I tried to hold on to it.

I stilled, afraid to breathe.

"Come to me, Kyllen. Please, let me see your face again." I wasn't even sure if I said it out loud or if the words simply formed in my head without passing my lips.

A chuckle vibrated at my back.

"My face? It's a handsome one, I've been told. But I far prefer looking at yours." A kiss landed on the side of my neck, gentle like a brush of a dragonfly wing.

"You're here!" I whipped around as he nuzzled the side of my neck.

The moment I faced him, his lips landed on my mouth. His kiss was everything I remembered. The illusion didn't muffle the sensation of his lips against mine, neither did it make my response to him any less vivid. My blood heated with the awareness of his naked body next to me—naked as the night he was murdered...

I jerked my head back, breaking the kiss.

We were in the grand hall of the King's Palace in Ufaris, but I could no longer see the artwork on the walls or the courtiers mingling around. All of that had sunk into shadows. Only Kyllen remained.

"Where have you been?" I panted, catching the breath his kiss had stolen.

"Where? Here, with you." His gaze roamed over my face. He'd been clearly dying to see me, too, greedily taking in my features.

I shook my head. "Where do you go when you're *not* here, Kyllen?"

He flinched. "I don't know."

"Do you exist outside of this place?"

His expression fell. "It certainly feels like I don't. I am truly myself only when I'm with you, sweet pea. You are my only purpose now."

Now.

"Do you remember what happened?" I asked. "The night when you..."

Died.

I didn't want to say that word out loud, afraid the finality of it might break whatever magic had brought him back to me.

"The night when we got separated," I said instead.

He scoffed, shaking his head. "No one can separate us, Amira. You and I are two parts of a whole."

"Are you watching over me from the afterlife? Is that what it is?" If so, I was not going to be the one to send him back. "Stay with me. Always."

"Of course." He grinned. Everything would be so much better if I could just see that smile from time to time. "You look well." He cupped my face. "There is less darkness inside you. You're no longer screaming, driving yourself frantic and me insane. But you're still lost."

"That's nothing new." I sighed. "I've never had a place to belong."

He stroked my hair, trailing his fingers along one of the braids. "Doesn't mean you don't deserve to have such a place, one day."

One day.

"Do you still think there is something better for me out there?"

"Of course there is," he said with conviction. "No sorrow can last forever. Pain is not as enduring as people think. Even the darkest clouds recede and pass with time."

"Are you telling me to move on and get over you?"

"What?" He leaned back, staring at me with shock. "Why would I say that?"

"Isn't that what people usually say? Move on. Let go. Get over it."

"Nonsense." He scoffed. "I wanted you to climb out of that pit of despair you've been floundering in. But I don't want you ever letting go of *me*. Why would you even think that?" He looked genuinely upset, even hurt, now.

"That's what they said in the books I've read," I tried to explain. "They'd tell me to search for happiness elsewhere instead of pining after you for the rest of my life."

He squinted at me. "Then, you should probably find something else to read. Archives hold plenty of books. Some may be too boring for my taste, but you have much more patience than I do. I'm sure you'd find something there that hopefully wouldn't advise you to *forget me*."

The way he wrinkled his nose in distaste made me smile.

"How could I ever forget you, Kyllen?" I released a brief laugh.

He watched me, a smile forming on his lips. "I feared I might never hear the sound of your laugh again."

He had taught me how to laugh. And now, he was making sure I didn't forget how.

"Did the picture make you smile?" a voice burst from the shadows. It popped the bubble of light around Kyllen and me.

I blinked, finding Lord Adriyel at my side.

He inclined his head, gazing at me with curiosity. "Or did you have a vision?"

Kyllen was gone. The regular life of the palace resumed, with its usual noise, color, and movement. I was awake, fully dressed, standing in front of the same picture I had admired earlier. Had Kyllen been here at all? Had I spoken to him?

Momentarily forgetting whether the protocol demanded I bow or curtsy to Lord Adriyel, I did both, which seemed to amuse him.

"What is a vision?" I asked.

He shook his head with a ghost of a smile. "I said it in jest. Because of the way you looked—stunned or day-dreaming. Only hags can bring visions, and we haven't had a royal hag at the palace since King Zeldren banished the last one for daring to criticize his actions."

"If there was a hag who brought a vision, could one see another person in it?"

He looked intrigued. "Have you seen someone?"

"Never mind..." I shook my head. The last thing I wanted was to discuss something so personal with a man I hardly knew.

"Sometimes, visions are used to connect with those who've passed away," he said. "Spirits can be coaxed from the afterlife for brief visits."

"The spirits of dead ones?"

"Yes. In order to travel, the spirit needs to be free of the body, and the body cannot live without its soul."

"Of course..." I turned back to the picture on the wall, pretending to study it.

I needed a moment to adjust to reality again and to the fact that I had just been visited by a ghost that looked, felt, and kissed just like the man I knew and loved.

The battle depicted in the image on the wall was taking place at a junction where one wide stream merged with another. The warriors on both sides were gorgonians. Some rode giant, midnight-blue snakes with plumes of either fins or feathers on top of their diamond-shaped heads. Some used short, easy-to-maneuver paddle boards to navigate the turbulent waters that were tinted red with blood of the wounded and dead.

"The Battle of Two Rivers," Lord Adriyel said. "You seem fascinated by it. Do you like the picture?"

"Honestly, I'm not sure." It was masterfully made, no doubt. But the realism of it was off putting, considering this was a battle scene, with people being murdered. "People are dying here, drowning..."

"Gorgonians can't really drown," he noted.

"How about this one?" I pointed at a warrior with an arrow sticking from his neck. His mouth was opened wide in a silent scream. Only his head and arms remained visible above the foamy water as he fought the dangerous rapids in the wake of the serpents' tails around him.

"This one has an arrow in his neck." Lord Adriyel pointed with his finger. "But that's not the wound he will die from. There is another one, from an iron sword right under his last rib. Once he stops fighting to stay afloat, he'll sink. Then, he'll bleed to death while lying on the bottom of the river."

"That's...horrible." I moved my gaze from the picture and stared at the embossed leather belt across the lord's chest, instead. The black leather stood out in contrast to his white silk tunic.

"That's war," he said.

"Have you ever been to war?"

"Many times. The truce we're currently enjoying only happened because the king is no longer able to personally lead an army. And, as is typical for him, he doesn't trust anyone else to lead it for him."

I ventured a glance at his face. It was a handsome one, beautiful in its midnight glow. His dark blue *senties* rested upon his shoulders, which was unusual for gorgonians. Normally, their *senties* were always in motion, their eyes scanning the room, their tongues tasting the air, especially when the person was in public, surrounded by others.

Lord Adriyel either felt absolutely comfortable at the king's palace or he wanted everyone to believe that he did.

"Well, the king has other things to worry about right now, doesn't he?" I said.

He tilted his head with a slight squint of his eyes. "What are the things the king is occupying himself with nowadays?"

His silvery-blue eyes displayed polite interest, so I gave him the benefit of the doubt, answering sincerely, "The king is dying. He's fighting a lot of pain every day."

"He has a lot to repent for." Lord Adriyel clearly misunderstood me. I was talking about physical pain, but he appeared to mean an emotional burden.

Curiosity prompted me to ask, "Like what?"

Lord Adriyel studied my face for a moment. "Do you feel sorry for him? If so, you don't need to. King Zeldren has led a long and brutal life bathed in blood. Maybe looking death in the eye now has calmed him down, but make no mistakes, my dear. Had he not been crippled by mortal drought, you would've become just another casualty of his by now."

I couldn't argue with that. The king was cantankerous and grumpy at times, but from the glimpses of his true nature I got, I believed he'd been much worse when he was younger.

"Is that why you *gifted* me to him?" I asked. "To watch him destroy me?"

His lips stretched into a predatory smirk. "If I wanted you destroyed, little human, I could've done that myself." He shook his head. "You're too precious for deliberate destruction. I brought you to him to ease the sufferings of a dying man, nothing more, and it seems to be working." He leaned my way, the focus in his eyes sharpened. "You are relieving his sufferings, are you not?"

Judging by his tone and expression, he was suggesting the "relief" I provided to the king was sexual in nature. He stared at me, waiting, only I didn't know what for. Did he expect me to tell him all about the sex I was supposedly having with the king? Or did he want me to reassure him the king hadn't touched me?

I said nothing, moving my attention back to the picture. I hoped he'd leave, but he remained standing next to me.

"Do you know that King Zeldren impaled one of his lovers for betraying him?" Lord Adriyel said unexpectedly. "He then placed her in the Garden of the Cursed and left her to rot to death among the promise breakers, even though she had given him no promises and therefore didn't break any."

I snapped my gaze back at him in shock. "That is so..."

"Horrible?" He brought his hands together. "Yes, it is. He married another one off to a lower lord in Sarnala when he found out she was pregnant with his royal child. The poor girl had her eyes gouged out and her *senties* cut off before the werewolf lord even agreed to marry her. Her baby was murdered the moment she delivered it—so fearful were the werewolves of the look of its gorgonian eyes."

I listened in horror, my clasped hands pressed to my chest.

"But why would the king let it happen to his own child? Aren't pregnancies rare among fae? And aren't all babies precious?"

He inclined his head. "They are. So much so that even bastard children are usually taken into palaces and raised alongside legitimate heirs. There are plenty of examples where the bastards succeeded their parents in inheriting the title when no legitimate children were born."

"Why didn't King Zeldren keep his child, then?"

His jaw ticked, and his *senties* twitched but settled down again quickly.

"Because King Zeldren believes *no one* is worthy of his crown," he said with force. He drew in a long breath before fully regaining his composure. "The king has searched for his bonded mate for centuries but never found her, which happens quite often. Bonds are rare, even more rare than babies."

That I knew. Finding a true mate seemed like winning a lottery—everyone wished for it, but only the lucky few had it happen to them.

Lord Adriyel's stare grew more intense. His eyes heated, the silver in them appearing to melt.

"Bonds are rare," he murmured. "But not nearly as rare as humans."

He slid the back of his fingers down one of my braids that had fallen over my shoulder. He followed its curve over my breast.

I took a step back, evading his touch. "Why didn't the king marry someone else when he failed to find his bonded mate? Most marriages aren't bonded, anyway, are they?"

"Because no one but a true mate is worthy of our great King Zeldren," he replied with heavy sarcasm. "He would not pass his crown to a bastard child. Yet he would never marry to sire a legitimate one." He inhaled deeply. "So, here we are now. With a king about to leave this world, and no one to succeed him."

"What will happen then, when the king is no longer here?"

He spread his arms, palms open. "A tournament if we're lucky. A war if we follow in King Zeldren's steps."

"Was that how *he* became a king?"

He nodded in affirmation. "He stabbed the rightful king with his iron sword." He turned to the picture again. "During the Battle of Two Rivers."

"Oh..." I stared again at the image of the wounded man who hopelessly fought the churning waters, arrow in his neck, his *senties* up and rigid in fear, the mortal wound from the sword hidden from view. The weapon that inflicted it must be the one I saw hanging over King Zeldren's nest.

"You seem upset," Lord Adriyel said, looking at me instead of the picture. "But isn't it always better to know the truth, no matter how comforting the lies may feel?"

Things weren't always what they seemed; I'd learned that long ago. But did I want to learn the whole cruel, bloody history of this place to discover the truth?

The more I knew about this world and its people, the better I might understand it. Kyllen was no longer here to create a position in this world for me. I had to find my place on my own.

"Where can I read more about this?" I asked Lord Adriyel.

He arched a graceful eyebrow ridge. "You want to read?"

"I'm new to Lorsan. I have a lot to learn. Where can I find more information? Is there such a place?"

A smile graced his shapely mouth once again. "There is. As a matter of fact, it's closer than you may think. Right between the roots of this tree lie our Royal Archives."

Archives.

Kyllen had just spoken about that place, too, in my vision.

"If you're not in a hurry, I can show you the way right now." Lord Adriyel offered me his arm.

"Well, I..." I glanced at the massive mechanical clock that occupied the entire wall above the first landing of the grand staircase.

The face of the clock was a piece of art on its own. It was a mechanical map of Ufaris, complete with the waters of Ufaris Lake and the seven great royal trees that comprised the core of the palace. The details were incredible, as were the many movable parts—people on paddle boards, fish in the water, birds in the branches. Even the leaves on the trees appeared to be alive and moving with a breeze.

According to the clock, I still had at least thirty minutes while the king would be occupied by Kiris and his bathing routine, maybe longer if he took a nap afterwards.

"I have some time." I placed my hand in the crook of Lord Adriyel's elbow. "I could at least take a look."

I thought about Kyllen again. He did tell me to find something else to read in my vision. The thought of him warmed my heart, bringing a smile to my lips.

Lord Adriyel took me down a smaller staircase on the side of the hall. Then we walked outside to a branch that twined down along the main trunk like a narrow pathway toward the water. Instead of dipping into the lake, however, the branch curved around one of the thick roots that supported the royal tree above the water like gigantic pillars.

The lake flowed between the roots and under the tree. The bottom of the trunk caved in the middle, creating a dome ceiling over the water.

Vines draped between the roots on the outside. Water plants floated on the surface around the roots, but there were none directly under the dome. Sun didn't reach here. However, the dome ceiling glowed with faint green light, reflecting in the dark water below.

In the very center under the tree, a high mound rose from the lake. Its edges were laid with large river rock to prevent erosion. The rest was covered with dark-green grass—so dark it appeared black, absorbing all light, including the glow from the ceiling above.

"What is that?" I asked Lord Adriyel, gesturing at the hill in the middle.

"The Funeral Mound," he explained somberly. "The final resting place of Lorsan kings."

"Is that where they're buried?"

He shook his head with a brief chuckle. "No. Gorgonians don't bury their dead in the dirt. The fallen kings are laid atop the Mound. Once their bodies dry completely, the Mound absorbs them, and their magic is reunited with that of the Lorsan land."

I gazed at the dark Mound, wondering how many kings it had absorbed, with all their sins and virtues.

"It's a special place," Lord Adriyel said. "The land's magic lingers here. The Archives hold the knowledge of generations. It's preserved in scrolls. The magic of this place protects them." He directed me to a metal-clad door in one of the root-pillars. "The entrance is right here."

He slid his fingers over the gears visible through the cut-outs in the metal, and the heavy door opened noiselessly.

Stairs spiraled along the wall inside the root column, leading down and underground to a wide, arched entrance.

The space here was awash in a pale green glow. Shelves lined the walls from the mosaic floors to the vaulted ceiling as far as the eye could see. Clusters of scrolls hung from the ceiling, attached to a track system with little ceramic tags dangling from each scroll.

The wide support columns, I realized, were the roots of the royal tree above us. The space for the Archives had been excavated between them, with many rooms branching out from the main one where we stood.

"This is incredible." I twirled, but the place was too big to take it all in at once.

Lord Adriyel watched me with a smile playing on his lips.

A subtle rustling came from one of the adjacent rooms, then a man appeared from behind a root-pillar.

"Councilor Delahon?" Lord Adriyel greeted the newcomer with a slight tilt of his head. "I should have known we'd find you here."

"This is where I spend most of my time." Councilor Delahon spread his arms aside as if to encompass the entire space of the Archives. His bright magenta *senties* stood in striking contrast to his onyx skin. "Greetings, Lord Adriyel and..." He turned to me, making the pause hang in the air like a question mark. "I beg your pardon, we haven't been introduced."

Lord Adriyel turned to me, too. Waiting silently. He couldn't introduce me to the councilor because he didn't know my name, either.

"I'm Amira." I gave Councilor Delahon a courteous bow. "It's nice to meet you."

"Amira..." Lord Adriyel repeated in a soft whisper. "How beautiful."

"A lovely name for a lovely girl," the councilor agreed. "What brought you here?"

"Amira would like to learn more about our history," Lord Adriyel replied for me.

"Why?" The councilor appeared confused.

"Lorsan is my world now," I explained. "Sadly, I know very little about it."

The councilor rubbed his chin in thought. "Well, maybe I can help. I won't claim to have read every scroll in this library. No one could do that. But I do spend a lot of time reading. Counseling the king on how to run the kingdom requires a lot of knowledge and thought. What in particular are you interested in, child?"

"The Battle of Two Rivers," Lord Adriyel spoke for me again before I even opened my mouth.

"To start with," I added.

The councilor clasped his hands in front of him. "Oh, yes. The battle that laid the start to our current dynasty—the dynasty that, it appears, will include just one king." He touched the nearest shelf, and the entire room seemed to come into motion.

With a soft whirring sound, the track system above us moved, the suspended scrolls swayed. The shelves also shifted, merging into ever-changing patterns, like pieces of a kaleidoscope.

When it all stopped, the councilor lifted his hand to a scroll right above us and checked the round ceramic tag dangling from it.

"That's the one," he said. "A summary and analysis of the battle. Clear and concise, perfect for a beginner. Now, are you planning to read it here? Or would you prefer to do it in your...um, in any other place in the palace?"

Despite its size and location, the archive room was warm and cozy. Striped, compact nests had been placed on the floor in every room, looking soft and inviting. It was quiet.

Reading here would be ideal. But the king must be done with his bath soon. And if he didn't take a nap that afternoon, he'd grow bored on his own. When the king was bored, he turned cranky. And when the king was cranky, he made people around him miserable.

"I'm afraid I can't stay here," I said to the councilor. "I'd like to take it with me."

He let go of the scroll suspended over our heads.

"All original scrolls are warded against damage or theft. They cannot be removed from the Archives. But you can take an exact copy of it." He took a book bound in bright fabric from the nearby shelf. "This one you can read anywhere."

"Thank you." I accepted the book from him and pressed it to my chest.

The councilor gave me a curious glance. "You're very welcome. You can find me here almost every day if you have any questions. Of course, first you'll need to learn what to ask." He chuckled. "Asking the right questions makes all the difference. Though, it also needs a fair deal of knowledge."

I thanked the councilor again before Lord Adriyel led me away. As we walked back up the stairs, my new book tucked under my arm, he took my hand.

"You're way too trusting, Amira." Lord Adriyel said my name slowly, as if testing the new sounds on his tongue.

I glanced at him, unsure what he was up to.

He didn't meet my eyes, staring straight ahead instead. "Today, you followed me all the way to the Archives, never questioning it even once."

"I don't understand. You offered to take me. And you did."

"But I could have led you anywhere else instead, and you would've followed me just as easily, until it was too late."

Chills slithered down my spine in a cold trickle of fear.

Chapter Thirteen

AMIRA

"Why would you want to hurt me, Lord Adriyel?" I walked faster, not wanting to be alone with him.

When we finally entered the main hall, I exhaled with relief, glad to see the groups of courtiers mingling here and servants gliding between them.

"What I meant was that you should be careful." Lord Adriyel reached to touch Kyllen's ring with the hag's stone on my finger. "This ring won't protect you from every peril in existence. There are many people in this palace and beyond who may have ill intentions in regards to you."

He stopped at the base of the grand staircase, concealed from the others by the pillar on its side. I stepped aside, too, to better see his face in the shadows.

"Who are those people? And why would they wish me ill?"

"Your favor with the king makes you a target."

"The king hasn't granted me any special favors," I protested. My position was hardly better than that of a pet. Any servant at the palace enjoyed more rights and freedoms than I had.

"You sleep with the king. You take private meals with him. You are the only person in centuries to share his bedroom for longer than a night. You have the king's ear. People will attempt to use you to further their agenda. Some may see you as a threat to the established status quo. You need to be careful."

"Trust no one," I repeated the words I'd heard so many times.

"Right." He slid his hands up my bare arms, turning me with my back to the pillar. His palms felt warm on my chilled skin. A shudder rushed over me, and I tucked my chin into the gauzy folds of the veil gathered around my neck, just like I used to hide it in my scarf before.

He lowered his head to mine so close that our temples nearly touched. "In Lorsan to be safe, a human woman will always need the protection of a powerful man."

I inhaled a lungful of his scent—sweet citrus and cool mist, pleasant but that of a stranger to me. My back pressed to the pillar, I couldn't get away, not without physically shoving him aside. I wished my strength could rival his.

"I have a powerful man to protect me," I replied. "The most powerful man in the kingdom—the king."

"But how long will he be there to keep you safe?" His breath fanned over my ear. "The king will die way before you do. What will happen to you then?"

I closed my eyes, afraid to think about that.

Yet Lord Adriyel kept talking, forcing me to think. "The king will die without naming a successor. A war will break out. Do you really think a vulnerable human woman like you has any chance at surviving a gorgonian war? Alone?"

I had no answer to that. It'd been so hard just focusing on surviving each day, I'd hardly thought about what the next day would bring.

"You're nothing but a plaything for the nobles, Amira," he proceeded, revealing the ruthless truth. "A novelty, a curious toy to grab as soon as your current owner is gone. The best thing, the *only* thing, for you to do is to secure a new protector. Someone who can take care of you and defend you from all the others."

He slid his hand up my shoulder and under my veil. His fingers connected with my bare neck.

"You need a man who is strong and powerful enough to become the next king," he said in a hot, coarse whisper. A pure, undiluted hunger shone in his cool silver eyes—hunger for power and...for me.

He slid his other hand up my side, cupping my breast, covered only by the thin silk of my powder-blue dress. My nipple hardened at his touch, pushing against the flimsy material. Desire zapped through my body, making my next breath shaky and weak. I'd been hungry, too, famished by grief and starved for affection. But not from him...

He smirked at my body's reaction, kneading my breast through my dress. The heat in his eyes surged higher. Cupping my neck with his hand, he yanked me to him.

My book slipped from my fingers, falling to the floor.

"You'd make the strongest of men lose control, little human." He took my mouth in a kiss through my veil.

The sheer material offered no protection from his bold invasion, no escape from his heady taste. His strong arms crushed me to his chest, knocking the air out of my lungs and lifting my feet from the floor.

My arms trapped between us, I made no attempt to free them or to hug him back. My mind reeled. My thoughts went spinning into a twister. I felt like I was spinning, too, caught in a hurricane, dangerous and deadly.

My lungs burned with a desperate need for air. I trembled in his arms, and he mercifully loosened his hold on me, breaking his kiss.

"You need a *real* man, Amira." He roamed his hands all over my body. One slipped into the deep cut-out of my dress on my back, cupping my backside. With his other hand, he shoved the dress strap down my shoulder, exposing my left breast.

He groaned, ducking his head to suck the tip of my breast into his mouth. I exhaled sharply as his fangs scraped my nipple. The sting of pain felt oddly invigorating.

"You need a man who knows exactly what to do with this tight, hot body of yours," he growled against my skin. Trailing a finger down my spine, he slid it lower, between my butt cheeks. "A man who can give you exactly what you need. Not that dry log you've been spending your nights with."

I had to end this, somehow. I *needed* to end it.

Gathering all my strength, I shoved against his chest, but he wouldn't budge. The muscles in his arms locked, trapping me.

"Tantalizing, delicious little human," he muttered, oblivious to my struggles. "Say the word, and I'll be your protector."

I managed to shift aside, away from the pillar behind me. I then jerked back and out of his arms. He lurched after me, with a feral expression, his *senties* undulating wildly—a tangled mess around his moon-blue face.

"I-I need to go, my lord."

I grabbed my book from the floor and made a mad dash for the stairs. Running up the grand staircase, two steps at a time, I straightened my dress.

My heart thundered wildly when I returned to the king's bedroom. The king was napping. His loud snoring reverberated between the walls.

I paced the room, unable to calm down.

Afraid to wake the king. I slipped into his wardrobe room, adjacent to his bedroom. Here, behind the closed doors, I could pace to my heart's content between the carved trunks filled with fine linen and the lavishly embroidered robes hanging along the walls.

My mind was reeling. Desire still pulsed through my body, awakened by Lord Adriyel's uninvited touch. For the first time since Kyllen, a man had stirred it in me. Instead of excitement, however, a dark, gaping hole of despair grew inside me.

Lord Adriyel could never fill the emptiness Kyllen had left behind because being with Kyllen had never been just about physical desire. It'd been so much more.

Yet Kyllen was no longer there, was he? All that remained was a shadow of him, coming to me in my unexplained visions and dreams.

A strong arm caught me around the middle, and I stumbled into an embrace.

"Kyllen?" I recognized his scent, his strength, his presence that filled the room, making the rest of the world fall away. If this couldn't be a vision, it also wasn't a dream. "I'm not sleeping."

"Oh no. You're fully awake, now." His hot whisper fanned along the side of my face. "All of you. Your soul, your mind, and your body. You're living again, Amira."

Only it wasn't *he*, who had awakened my body. Another man did...

"I don't want to feel this." I lifted my face to his. "I don't want this without you."

"I'm here." He kissed my face.

There was no veil between us. This *was* a dream.

And what a beautiful dream it was!

He was naked, like always since the last time I saw him alive. He slid my dress off my shoulders, kissing every inch of my skin he exposed. My body sang under his touch, without restraint.

Freeing my breasts, he kissed them. I hugged him around his neck, burying my hands into his *senties*.

"Take me, Kyllen. I don't want it to happen with any other man, but you."

Heat flashed in his eyes. "There could never be another man."

Hiking up my skirts, he pressed my back against the wall, lifting me up. I wrapped my legs around his middle. Holding me under my backside with one hand, he slid the other one between us, finding the spot where I needed him the most.

"No one would ever stand between us, sweet pea. It's me and you, no one else."

Oh, how I wished for this to be true. To be real.

He grinded his hips against me. The press of his fingers was like his words, hard and unyielding. I needed this so badly. I wanted him to erase every trace of that other man touching me.

"More..." I rode his hand, gripping his shoulders.

Desire and longing blended in a bitter-sweet mix of pleasure and pain. I felt him in my heart, in every part of my soul. I needed him in my body, too.

"Take me, Kyllen. I want to be yours like I was meant to be."

"Mine..." he echoed, pressing his erection against me.

I halted my breath, waiting for his invasion, needing it, craving him to claim me. But he stopped, his determined expression wavering with confusion.

"What is it, Kyllen? Please..." I reached down, finding his erection. It was hard as rock, pulsing in my hand with tremors of need running through his body. Yet when I tried to guide him inside me, I felt nothing—even the sensation of him in my hand disappeared.

I felt his confusion. But I believed I also knew the explanation. There was a point past which Kyllen and I could never go anymore. He existed only in my memories, now. And I had no memories of him ever being inside me. My imagination couldn't possibly recreate the sensations I hadn't felt in real life.

Only how could this feel so vivid if it wasn't real?

All of it was a new kind of torture.

"There is a barrier between us I cannot breach," he said, with a crestfallen expression. "A place where you can't meet me."

The barrier between life and death?

I dropped my feet to the floor, letting my skirts drape down to cover my legs.

"Where are you, Kyllen? Please don't tell me you're here because you're not. This is a dream, an illusion. Magic? I don't know. But are you out there somewhere? If so, please come back." I held tight to him. "Come to me. Be with me. Always, not just in my dreams."

"I can't," he exhaled, pressing his forehead to mine. "I'm trying, but...I'm no longer whole."

This was the first time he'd acknowledged he wasn't actually present, that this was just a part of him, no matter how solid and real it might feel.

I cupped his face, leaning back to meet his eyes.

"Then take me with you." My heart beat fast against my ribs. "Where you go, I'll go, remember? I'll go to the afterlife with you if that's where you are."

Pain crumbled his handsome features.

"There is nothing but darkness and agony here, Amira. I wouldn't bring you here even if I knew how." He took my face in his hands, sinking his fingers into my hair. "You deserve so much better."

I blew out a breath, closing my eyes for a moment.

"You're the only one in this entire world who thinks I deserve anything at all."

"Oh, Amira. Please, fight the darkness. Don't let it take you." He lowered his mouth to mine. It was a long, poignant kiss, filled with longing. It stole my breath, but it didn't stop there, consuming all of me.

It tore me apart to break the kiss, but I couldn't let it go on. It felt as if my very being would dissolve into sadness and cease to exist if I kept holding on to him.

I would become my grief.

"Then go." I pressed my hands into his chest. "Leave me because..." I took a step sideways along the wall, moving out of his embrace. "I can't continue living for the tiny shreds of memories of what it used to be. Let me go, Kyllen. Then maybe...maybe you will find some peace, too."

"Never." In one fluid movement he was in front of me again. Leaning over me, he propped his hands onto the wall behind me, caging me with his body. "If peace means leaving you behind, then I don't want it. We're two parts of a whole, remember? If I leave, it'd tear us both to pieces. You won't survive."

"But this is not a life, either. Every time I dream about you, I come back to life. And every time I find myself alone once more, I die inside, over and over again."

"Do you think this is how I want it to be?" He searched my face with his gaze, his *senties* undulating agitatedly, reaching for me. "I have no choice, Amira. I keep coming here because without you, I can find no rest. There is nothing but darkness and pain around me. They pull me away from you, and I have to search for you again and again—and every time, I find you. Because you're all I have. Next to you is where I'm meant to be."

I released a shuddered breath. Strength deserted me. My back to the wall, I slid to the floor. He sat next to me, and I leaned against him.

"How many times do I have to lose you before I learn to live without you?" I whispered, gripping his hand.

He didn't give me an answer. Because there simply wasn't one.

The king found me asleep on the floor of his wardrobe room. I was fully dressed. And alone.

"That's an odd place for a nap," he commented, but didn't demand an explanation. As an exotic pet, I supposed, I was allowed to behave in an unusual way at times. "Come, I started a new game."

I followed his mechanical chair to the bedroom, where he had the table set with game pieces already. Passing by my nest, I quickly stashed under the pillow the book I'd brought up from the Archives, then took my place at the table across from the king.

I did my best to play well enough to make the game entertaining for him. But my thoughts remained elsewhere.

Kyllen and I came to this world together. And together I thought we would be. I'd lost myself in him, and it had been a wonderful place to be. But now, I was alone.

Somehow, I had to learn to survive without him.

Lord Adriyel's warnings had been mostly self-serving. I saw through them, but he wasn't wrong. One way or another, the king's death would upset the current balance of things. I couldn't let it catch me unprepared. I had to secure my place in this life, even if the purpose of my life remained only survival.

I had no magic, no real power, but there was a weapon available to me—I had to arm myself with knowledge.

After dinner, when the king settled back into his nest for the night, I took my place in the window seat. Leaning back against the interwoven vines that served as a window frame, I opened my book.

The intricate characters on the page looked unfamiliar, but their meaning was clear in my head. Just like Kyllen could speak English in my world, I had gained the ability to speak and read his language when I crossed into Lorsan.

For too long, I'd relied on what others told me about Lorsan. It was time to learn its laws and its history on my own, straight from the source. Then maybe I could find my place in this world and figure out the best path to get there.

I had to stop being tossed around by the will of others and take the course *I* wanted to take.

Chapter Fourteen

AMIRA

A few weeks later, the king touched a figurine on the board of the game the two of us were playing. It was a complicated strategy game called Reign and War. The first round we had ever played had taken the king less than ten minutes to win, despite my studying all the rules for hours prior. But as I'd been learning the tricks and nuances of the game, the rounds we played had gotten longer.

This time, I had planned and mounted a defense that had allowed me to deflect the king's attacks for three days now. He was no closer to winning now than he'd been when we started.

He tapped another game piece on the board but didn't move it. Jerking his hand away, he cupped his chin in thought instead.

"So, tell me, what has our boy Kyllen been up to lately?" he asked.

My heart squeezed painfully at the sound of that name. I'd regretted revealing it to the king many times since.

Ever since that time in the wardrobe room, I hadn't seen Kyllen again. Maybe that meant I'd been healing from my loss, and my mind no longer needed to conjure his image to keep me sane. Though, I wasn't ready to let go of him, either.

Instead of his vivid visits that had been both torture and bliss, his presence in my mind had become more subtle but also more constant somehow. Even without seeing or talking to him, I often felt him with me, day and night. The sensation was warm and comforting, and I desperately hoped it would last.

Maybe his spirit truly couldn't leave me, as he'd said. Or maybe, I never wanted him to leave me at all, even when I begged him to. As painful as it felt, I'd rather have a part of him than nothing at all.

I swallowed hard, waiting for the stab of grief to subside before asking the king, "You want me to tell you another story?"

"Yes..." He rubbed his chin, his attention on the board. "Or maybe not. I've heard plenty of stories about the boy. Tell me about the man."

"The man?" I breathed faster.

"I know you said Kyllen is dead. But did the boy live long enough to become a man? Or did he die young?" He chuckled. "I wouldn't be surprised if he didn't make it into adulthood, the mischievous rascal that he was."

I removed my hands from the board and fisted them in my lap, not giving him a chance to see them trembling.

"Kyllen lived until the age of seventy-eight," I said in a low but firm voice.

"Not long. Do you know how he died?"

I held my head up, staring straight ahead.

"He was killed by one of his family."

The king nodded unfazed, as if that kind of murder was a common thing.

"What was the reason?" he asked, then shrugged. "*Was* there a reason?"

I shifted in my seat, unsure of how long I could continue with this conversation. Every question felt like a knife twisted in a wound that wouldn't heal. Over two months had passed now, but the night of Kyllen's murder remained as fresh as ever in my memory.

"Succession," I replied softly. "He was murdered over a title."

"Ooh." The king sat back in his chair. "That happens all the time. Did he challenge the rightful title holder and lose? Wouldn't it be just like that boy to aim for a place that wasn't his?" He laughed wholeheartedly. "Unfortunately for him, not everyone can pull that off successfully."

The last words were said with pride. The king obviously referred to how he came into the possession of his crown.

"The title was Kyllen's to begin with," I argued.

One of the books I had stored under the pillows in my nest was about succession laws of Lorsan. Though fluid and often bent by crude power, the law was on Kyllen's side. I knew that for sure, now.

"Kyllen was born the legitimate heir to the High Lord of Ellohi," I told the king. "He was abducted and held captive in the human world. At home, they thought him dead. His younger brother inherited their father's throne. By the time Kyllen returned, the brother had a son, his nephew. Kyllen's plan was to have a peaceful transition. A tournament if it came down to that. He was also going to petition you for support. The nephew must've known that Kyllen would win, so he attacked him at night like a coward. And..."

I dropped my head and tried to blink away the tears that threatened to burst again.

This time, my distress didn't escape the king. "Kyllen was your lover, wasn't he? Albeit not the best one, obviously, since he left you a virgin."

I looked him straight in the eye. "Kyllen was my *everything*. The love of my life. My only one."

Sorrow seized my heart, swelling thick in my throat. I loved him—I still did—even if it took me a while to recognize the feeling for what it was.

"Did they make you watch him die?" the king asked casually. I wondered if that would be something the king would've done or...had done before.

I shook my head.

It hurt, but for the first time in months, I recalled the details of that night. "I saw the blade raised, aimed at his neck. I heard it stab through his flesh..."

There had also been that sound that I tried to block from my memories—the strangled gasp men made before life was ripped out of them. I'd heard the *bracks* make it when Kyllen had turned them to stone. Rourke and his men had done the same. The sound had been there that night, too. It was the last I'd heard from that room before they had dragged me away.

"So, you didn't see him die?" the king confirmed.

"No. I was taken away, brought here, and sold."

"Do you know for sure that he's dead, then?"

Oh, how tempting that sweet hope was. But I nodded, biting my lip. "If Kyllen were alive, he would've come for me." Not just in my dreams. He'd be here in flesh and blood, I had no doubt about that. He would've never abandoned me. By now, the news of the human woman living in the king's palace must've reached every corner of Lorsan and beyond. If only he were anywhere in this world, he would've found me already. "He made me a promise."

"He did?" the king sounded surprised, just like Lady Igaed had been.

"He promised to always have me at his side." Maybe the need to fulfill that promise was what had brought his spirit back to me?

His soul was tied to mine one way or another. The connection didn't break, no matter how much time had passed. It only grew stronger.

"He would've come," I repeated with conviction.

The king frowned. "I don't recall any reports about him."

"Because there weren't any. I've gone through all recent communication from Ellohi in the Archives. All letters and recordings are signed by Udren, the High Lord, with no mention of Kyllen or his return. They got rid of every trace of him, as if he perished in my world and never came back."

The king sat in silence for a few moments, resting his chin on his hand.

"Udren has been the High Lord of Ellohi for centuries," he said slowly. "I've met him on a few occasions. "

"He's Kyllen's younger brother. Udren's son, Bherlon, was the one who murdered Kyllen."

The king scratched his jaw with a rough, grating sound against his dry skin.

"Something as big as the heir returning after a long absence would definitely be news normally shared with the king. Unless there was a plan to get rid of the heir, of course." He shrugged. "Unfortunate but not unusual. The law may be on Kyllen's side, but if the nephew was raised to believe the High Lord's throne was his, I'd expect him to fight for it."

"To *fight!*" I fisted my hands tighter. "To openly defend it in an honest dispute would be an honorable thing to do. But to cowardly ambush a member of his own family..." I closed my eyes, battling the sickening feeling rising in my throat. "To murder in cold blood..."

"That was a crime," the king agreed calmly.

I met his eyes. "Shouldn't Bherlon be punished for what he's done?"

He tilted his head, gazing at me with interest. "Is that what you want, my little pet? Revenge?"

Punishing Bherlon would not bring Kyllen back. Forgiving and forgetting might be a noble thing to do. However, everything inside me burned with thirst for retribution. Kyllen deserved that. He deserved justice. And I might have the power to make it happen.

Like Lord Adriyel had said, I had the king's ear. The most powerful man in the kingdom might be inclined to do me a favor. I'd never asked him for anything before, but for Kyllen, I would.

"Yes." I squared my shoulders and raised my chin. "I want Lord Bherlon detained, tried, and punished for the murder."

The king stared at me with a new expression in his eyes, as if he'd just met me and tried to figure out what kind of person I really was.

"Would that make you happy?" he asked. "If I made him pay?"

"Happy? No." I shook my head with a humorless laugh. Happiness wasn't possible for me in this world without Kyllen. But punishing those responsible for his death would give me some satisfaction. "It would bring Kyllen justice. And for me... Well, maybe I would get a modicum of peace from that."

He nodded. "I'll send a commission to Ellohi to do a formal investigation and to arrest those found responsible."

"Thank you." I pressed a hand to my chest and bowed my head in gratitude.

He sprawled in his chair in a more comfortable position. "Meanwhile, instead of telling me a story about the boy today, why don't you tell me something about the girl?"

"What girl?" I blinked, confused.

"This one." He tipped his chin at me.

I sat back. "You want me to talk about myself?"

A faint smile played on his lips. "Yes. You've been sleeping in my bedroom for two months. Yet all I know about you is your name. Tell me, where are you from?"

I hesitated. "From nowhere, really."

That was true. I had no roots. In the world where I was born, I'd been nobody. Everything that I would ever become would have to start here, in Lorsan.

"I... I really don't know what to tell you." I spread my arms.

"Tell me about your world. Where were you born? Where is your family? Where did you grow up? How exactly did you get to Nerifir? And how did Kyllen make you fall in love with him that fiercely?"

"Oh, I..."

I was about to insist that there wasn't much to tell, that my life hadn't been anything special, that I hadn't done anything that would interest the king. Because really, how could my twenty-somewhat years of cleaning animal cages and brushing Madame's hair compare with the centuries of waging wars and ruling a kingdom that had been the king's life?

But I stopped myself, thinking about the answers to all the questions he'd just asked.

There had been tragedies in my life, and there had been beautiful, magical moments. I'd met some remarkable men who'd helped me along the way. I'd known love, loss, and true friendship. I'd gone against the wishes of a goddess and crossed the River of Mists.

Maybe I did have a story of my own to tell, one that might captivate the king.

"Okay, Your Majesty." I smiled at him. "I'll tell you about myself, but under one condition."

"A condition?" The familiar spark flashed through his dark-orange eyes. The king was intrigued.

"Yes. My story isn't free. We'll trade. For every part I'll tell you about the girl, you'll tell me something about the king. Deal?"

He laughed heartily.

"You want me to talk about myself? Be careful what you ask for, my girl. I may never stop." He rubbed his eyes, shaking his head. "Really, you can read all about it. There are hundreds, thousands of scrolls down in the Archives, documenting every glorious moment of my life. I know you go to the Archives daily." He gestured to my nest by the window, the pillows raised with the books hidden under them. "I've seen you read. What books interest you?"

I tried to read during when the king was busy and didn't need me. But I hadn't tried hard enough to hide it from him, either.

He didn't appear angry right now, just curious.

"History books, mostly," I said. "Also, some about current laws and governance."

His brow ridges shot up in surprise.

"Why those? Surely, we have plenty of much lighter reading, more suitable for a young girl like you."

"I want to know everything gorgonians know about their homeland," I replied.

"Why?"

"Because Lorsan is now my home, too."

He squinted his amber eyes at me. "I see."

I'd read some of the scrolls about his life, too, but I wanted to hear his own accounts of that. I especially hoped he'd tell me the parts that weren't documented that well, or possibly hadn't been recorded at all.

"I'd love to hear about your family, Your Majesty. And about how you decided to become the king. You weren't born into the line of succession."

He huffed a laugh.

"No, I was not. But I always knew I was destined for greater things than just being one of the lower princes in Ufaris. There are many lords in the Kingdom, but only one king. I wasn't born as the successor, but I knew I was meant to wear the crown one day."

I propped my elbows on top of the game board and rested my chin on my folded hands. "I want to hear all about it."

"Well, it's a deal, then. A story for a story."

Chapter Fifteen

AMIRA

Another month later, the king and I were finishing our dinner when the sound of a light patter hitting the leaves came from outside. I raised my head, wondering about the source of the noise.

The king lifted his *senties*, spreading them wide. Their little heads turned toward the windows, their tongues flicking in and out rapidly.

"Rain!" the king exclaimed with the excitement of a child. "It's raining, Amira."

I remembered Kyllen telling me how much gorgonians appreciated the rain. Again, the sensation of him being close came, as if he stood right there, next to me. I knew I wouldn't find Kyllen in the room, even if I searched. He wasn't in any particular place. He was *everywhere*.

I pressed my hand to my heart, where I felt his presence the strongest.

"Well." I smiled at the king. "Let's go outside, shall we?"

I lowered the footrest on his mechanical chair and tucked his blanket around his legs.

"There you go." I stepped aside. Not possessing the gorgonian magic, I couldn't operate the chair, but all the king had to do to move it was to touch it.

He placed his hands flat on the armrests, and the chair rolled along the floor toward the terrace outside the windows. I moved the vines of the frame out of the way, allowing his chair to pass. He rolled it out at the exact moment when the slight pattering of the raindrops turned into a real deluge.

Tipping his head back, he turned his face up to the streams of water rushing from the sky. With his eyes closed, the expression of utter bliss settled on his drought-worn face.

Rain pounded down hard on the king, soaking the blanket in his lap and streaming down his *senties*. Yet the king seemed absolutely happy.

The lake below quickly filled with people. Using boats, paddle boards, and anything that would float, they paddled from under the branches of the great royal trees into the open area where nothing impeded the rainfall.

Many swam. Treading the water of the lake, they turned their faces up to the water falling from the sky.

"Come, Amira." The king noticed that I remained inside the room. "Come on out."

The magic wards would allow me to leave the room. The king would lead me back inside through them after. But I shook my head, leaning against the window frame. "No thank you. I'd rather stay dry."

"Really?" He looked befuddled. "Humans are funny creatures."

I laughed. "Why? Because we don't like getting our clothes wet?"

He gave me a once-over, pausing on my chest. The humidity in the air, combined with the few raindrops that had landed on my front, made the flimsy fabric of my dress cling to my body, highlighting every dip and curve.

He wiggled his eyebrow ridges. "That's a shame you don't like wet clothes, because they sure look good on you."

I smiled, taking his words as a compliment. By now, I knew the king's attention wouldn't go any further than the occasional harmless flirting. The appreciation in his gaze was more flattering than alarming.

The downpour had slowed a bit. The king held up his hand, watching the drops fall into his palm that was now also heavily patterned. The raindrops gathered in his palm, then ran down the sides of his hand between the raised ridges and deep grooves of the pattern on his skin.

"You know I'm not proud of everything I've done in my life," the king said suddenly.

Shocked, I raised my eyebrows. That was the first time he'd ever admitted anything of the sort.

For a month now, we'd been exchanging stories of our lives. So far, his accounts hadn't differed much from what I'd read in the Archives—boastful, flattering articles that showed the king in the best light possible. That seemed to be the trend with the documents in the Archives. Anything critical of the past kings could only be found after their deaths.

From the king's words now, I gathered, he'd been assessing his life from a slightly different perspective.

Sliding down the frame, I sat on the windowsill and stretched my legs in front of me. "Do you have regrets?"

He nodded without looking at me. "I do. And some are deeper than others."

"Would righting the wrongs help deal with them?"

He laughed—a loud but humorless sound.

"Those I've wronged have long turned to dust, my little human. There's no one left for me to make amends to. That is if I wanted to make any," he added with his usual self-assurance.

"You don't?"

He leaned his head to the side, stretching his neck. "Admitting I have any regrets at all is as far as I'd go in this life, Amira."

That was already something, I supposed.

He shifted in his chair to face me better. "Tell me something."

"What would you like to hear?"

"Anything." He was obviously looking for a distraction from his dark thoughts, of which I guessed there must be many. "What are you reading now?"

"The summary of the most recent Council decisions by Councilor Delahon."

"Oh, that scoundrel." The king made a face.

"Is he really a scoundrel? I talk to him often, down in the Archives. He seems nice, honest, and just. If a bit set in his ways."

The king moved his shoulders, looking uncomfortable.

"He's all about law and order. Always giving me a hard time when I try to do anything."

I could see how that would happen. Councilor Delahon was a very knowledgeable man, with high respect for the established order and the kingdom's laws. And the king... Well, the king preferred to make his own laws, doing whatever he pleased.

Of course, these two would clash a lot.

"Is that what interests you? Council meetings?" The king winced, as if he'd just bit into something sour. "They're dreadfully boring even if one attends them in person. I can only imagine what a headache-inducing read the councilor's account of them would be."

I smiled but agreed. "It is a pretty dry read at times."

"Why are you reading it, then? What do you want to know?"

The more I learned, the more I realized how little I knew.

With help from Councilor Delahon, who delighted in structure, I'd worked out a system for my studies. Yet, a lot remained unclear. Operation of a land as vast as Lorsan, patched together with individual holdings of High Lords, was a complex machine with many moving parts and the position of the king as the heart of the engine.

"Everything," I said. "I want to learn everything there is to know."

My initial goal had been to gain some general knowledge about my new world. But it drew me in much deeper.

"Do you want to come to the council meeting with me tomorrow?" he asked. "You'll get to see what you've been reading about."

That would be something I hadn't even dared dreaming of.

"Am I allowed?"

He shrugged. "Why not? If I had a pet lizard, I could bring it with me anywhere I wished. Why not a human girl? Besides, I'm the king. I do whatever I want. My word is the law."

From what I'd read, that wasn't entirely true. The king's "because-I-said-so" could only go so far. The law performed best when it was aligned with the will of the people and was supported by them.

But I said nothing, of course. My current place, apparently, was not higher than that of a pet lizard. So, I acted accordingly, keeping my mouth shut.

I had many questions about the hierarchy, structure, and palace life in general, though. Not all the answers could be found in books. The king seemed to be in a lenient, talkative mood today, and I decided to take advantage of that.

"Can you tell me more about your courtiers, please?" I asked.

He scoffed. "What about them?"

"Lord Adriyel, for example. What's his role at your palace?"

He exhaled a derisive laugh. "Ha! Him?" There seemed to be no love lost between the king and the man who so fervently wished to take his place. "Adriyel has no role. Not in my palace, anyway. He's the heir of the High Lord of Mevon, which is located next to Ufaris. His land is so close to mine, it allows him to practically live here, now, waiting for me to drop dead so he could grab the Crown of Lorsan as soon as it rolls off my head."

"Can he really do that?"

"Not if the others have something to say about it." He rubbed his hands, a wicked spark of excitement flashing in his eyes.

"Who are the others?"

"The twenty-three other High Lords. All of them are jousting for the place closest to the throne, each waiting to drop his ass in it the moment I vacate it."

"Why wouldn't you just choose one of them as your successor?" I asked.

He smirked. "Why would I deprive myself of the pleasure of watching them fight over my throne from the afterlife? Not one of them is worthy to be the next king, anyway. The High Lords are just power-hungry cowards. Why would I hand over the king's crown to any one of them? Why make it easy for them? Nooo," he cackled, rubbing his hands together again. "After I leave here, I want them to fight like a pack of rabid jackals while I'm laughing at them from the afterlife. Oh, what a show that will be!"

A show that might plunge the kingdom into a bloody war, possibly resulting in years or even centuries of violence and costing thousands of lives.

"Can a spirit watch over the living from the afterlife?" I asked.

He shrugged. "I haven't seen anyone come back to confirm that. But who can say for sure that it can't be done?"

The rain had ended. Only the occasional fat drops of water still splashed from the leaves.

I got up, shaking out the leaves and tiny twigs the wind had blown into my skirt. "Shall we go back inside? It's getting dark."

"There's still some time to start the next round of Reign and War," the king said with hope in his voice.

"We can do that."

"I need another chance, since you won the last round."

I smiled, satisfaction spreading thickly in my chest. It had been a hard-won but clear victory on my part, and I was proud of it.

"Is it all that reading you've been doing that made you this good at strategizing in the game?" the king asked.

"Actually, I've learned that particular line of defense and attack from you."

"From me?"

"Yes. I based the whole thing on a series of your own moves. I've memorized them over the past games we've played. Then, I adjusted them a little, to suit me." I jumped back into the room. "Come. I'll show you the combination I used."

He appeared stunned and...impressed.

"All right."

Wheeling his chair to the table with the game board, he stared at the pieces piled on the side after my last victory.

"I tell you what. Show me how you won the last time," he said. "Then I'll tell you how my game strategy can be applied to win a battle in real life. Deal?"

I nodded eagerly. "Deal."

Chapter Sixteen

AMIRA

I followed the king from the council meeting room down a wide branch that led us to the great hall. His chair whirred softly, cushioned by air to glide over any bumps on the way.

"They sure got mad back there," I muttered to myself, processing what had just happened.

The king chuckled. "You did ruffle some *senties*."

It had been two months since I started coming to the council meetings with the king. By now, I'd caught up on the processes and all the major issues discussed. I had my own ideas and opinions, too, but as a good pet, I'd kept silent. Until that morning.

The Council had been concerned about the increase of werewolf attacks along the border. The peace with Sarnala was protected by a trade agreement, but only for as long as trading was possible. However, during the green season, the flooding of the travel routes between the two kingdoms forced the trade to stop, which lifted the restrictions of the treaty.

When that happened, gorgonian border towns suffered from frequent raids. Wearing veils like my own, or even blindfolded, werewolves viciously destroyed gorgonian property and looted the towns' resources. Murder happened, too.

The magistrates repeatedly petitioned King Zeldren to mitigate the attacks. He agreed to send an ambassador to negotiate a possible extension of the treaty period. I'd asked to be considered for the position of the ambassador. Of course, the councilors didn't take it well.

When I'd spoken, the shock on their faces was as if a piece of furniture had suddenly come to life. Then, all hell broke loose. Some had laughed, others yelled, but no one had given me the chance to explain.

The king maneuvered his chair up the grand staircase.

"I don't think I've ever managed to get them as agitated as you did today." He sounded amused and even somewhat envious.

I felt deflated. "I should've kept my mouth shut."

"Why would you?" The king shrugged, turning into the hallway to his bedroom. "Generally, sending you to Sarnala makes sense. Werewolves are always wary of gorgonians. Negotiation would go more smoothly, I imagine, if both parties could look each other directly in the eye."

"Yet the Council would never support sending me now, just because the suggestion came from me."

He didn't argue with that.

"The position of a Royal Ambassador is highly coveted by many," he said. "No matter what, there'd be competition. Regardless of the Council's decision, though, I wouldn't send you, anyway."

I whipped around to face him. "Why not?"

He shrugged casually. "Why would I risk one of my most precious possessions being stolen by a bunch of dirty werewolves?"

That summed up my position at the Court of Lorsan. I was the king's current favorite toy. A precious one, maybe, but still just "a possession."

I pursed my lips. "That's a shame. Because I also have an idea for improving the trade with Sarnala. Year round."

Lifting my chin, I marched ahead.

"What kind of idea?" The king sped his chair after me.

I didn't reply, as we came within earshot of the guards by the door.

After we'd entered the royal bedroom, I closed the doors and leaned against them.

The king turned his chair to face me.

"Speak up, Amira. What are you talking about?"

Well, at least I still had "the king's ear." He looked ready to hear me out.

"The trade with Sarnala stops because of the floods, right?"

"Yes."

A flood would never prevent gorgonians from traveling wherever they wished, but werewolves disliked water. They wouldn't venture far into Lorsan without passable roads.

"Sarnala needs dry roads for the werewolves' wagons and horses to travel, in order for the mutual trade to continue."

"Right," the king agreed.

"I studied the map of the Ahonne River, and I believe at least one of the roads could be saved from the flood. The one that runs along its north bank."

"Saved? How?" He seemed intrigued.

"By building a levee."

The king blew out a breath, shaking his head. "We don't do anything that would restrict the natural flow of water in Lorsan. It'd be akin to blasphemy."

"A levee wouldn't be really restricting, just redirecting it. Think about it. Wouldn't it be worth it? A dry road year-round would facilitate the trade and automatically extend the treaty, which will save people's lives and property."

He didn't look convinced. "The Council's recommendation is to increase armed patrols along the border."

"I know." I sighed. "Gorgonians tend to rely on force in conflict resolution. Werewolves do too. But things could be solved without aggression and violence. In this case, at least."

He rubbed the back of his neck. "The construction can have its own problems."

"True. But that's where thorough planning is important. Werewolves have built quite a few levees in Sarnala. Their land is so flat in some places, they'd have wetlands, too, had they not contained the floods. Instead of negotiating the treaty extension, you could have the ambassador pitch the levee idea to the werewolves and acquire their assistance. Here."

I grabbed a book from under my pillow and opened it on the page I'd bookmarked.

"See. This is the map of one of the arms of the Ahonne River in the territory of Sarnala. The levee here was constructed just sixty years ago, and it's been working amazingly well."

He cast a glance at the book in my hands.

"What if it causes a drought in my lands?"

"I don't think it will, but of course, we'll need to consult much better experts than myself. However, with the werewolves' expertise and gorgonian magic, a lot can be accomplished."

"Let me see." The king rolled his chair to the table. Moving the current board game aside, he placed the open book on the table and leaned over it, studying the map.

"And here..." I placed another book next to the one he had. "This is the map of the flood area along the northern bank of the Ahonne River, with the trade road running through it."

He squinted at both of them, studying the maps for a minute.

"Well, this may work. The Grand Master and his apprentices will have to assess it, of course. He oversees all construction projects of this scale. You'll have to present it to the Council—"

I stopped him, shaking my head. "They'll never even look at it if they know it came from me. You'll have to tell them it was your idea."

"But if it does prove executable and beneficial, don't you want the credit for coming up with it?"

"No." I huffed a laugh. "The levee will never be built if they know the idea for its construction came from the king's human pet. There are more important things than my pride or any credit. If it does get built, both kingdoms will benefit from it. Lives may be saved. I don't care if I never get the recognition."

He rested his gaze on me. "You put the interests of the kingdom before your own. That's admirable. But you should care about your interests, too."

I waved a hand, stifling a sigh.

"There is no point. For the councilors and the High Lords, I'm nothing but a king's plaything. I might as well have played the part and kept the bells on my nipples."

He laughed. "Those were delightful!"

I rolled my eyes but then smiled back at him. As the drought claimed more of his body, the king's merry moods became rare. This time, too, his laughter didn't last long. A serious expression settled over his face, now completely covered by the dark, raised pattern of diamond shaped mesh.

"You're right. That's all you are to them," he said somberly. "They will rip you apart and eat you alive after I'm gone. The pack of jackals," he spat through his teeth.

That was the reality I faced if I stayed in the palace after his death.

"I can't stay here without you," I said. Unsure about my true place in Lorsan, I already knew it couldn't be in Ufaris after the king had gone. "I'll need to leave."

He shook his head. "No matter where you go, they will hunt you. You're too tempting a prize to let you be, my little human, a tasty morsel to be possessed and consumed, a status symbol. They'll fight over you just as they will over my crown."

Deep inside, I feared that, too.

I had enough skills and knowledge to perform a variety of jobs from a lady's maid, to a tutor, or even to an apprentice of a keeper at the Archives. If I found employment at a lord's court, I could make a living and support myself.

Except that the nobles wouldn't leave me in peace.

My being a human made me unemployable anywhere in the kingdom. I was chattel, a rare property. And as the king's pet, people knew about me. Hiding would be difficult if not impossible.

"I'm thinking about moving to Sarnala." I'd been reading about the neighboring kingdom. That was how I came upon the information about the levees, in the first place. "At least when living among the werewolves, I wouldn't need to wear the veil."

The king didn't appear to like that idea. Frowning, he rubbed his chest through his richly embroidered silk robe. "The werewolves have teeth sharp enough to literally tear you apart, Amira."

"That's why I thought that going to Sarnala as the Royal Ambassador would be ideal. The status would offer me protection."

"It won't be enough," he dismissed. "You'll need a much higher level of protection, the highest I can give you. I'll have to marry you," he added unexpectedly.

"You... What?" Surely, I'd misheard him.

He directed his eyes at me. They once were deep amber but had dulled and paled in color during the past months. The expression in them, however, remained as sharp as ever.

"The only way you would ever have a fighting chance after my death," the king said, "is if I passed my crown on to you. As my wife, you will become my successor."

"Wow... Hold on. You want to... It would never work." My mind was reeling at his words. He couldn't possibly be serious.

This was huge. This was...insane.

I wasn't his mate.

I wasn't even a gorgonian.

Yet the king appeared determined.

"When I'm gone, Amira, the crown will give you the protection I'll no longer be able to provide to you."

"But how? The nobles are already suspicious of me," I pointed out. "They'll rip my head off that much faster if you place the Crown of Lorsan on it."

We would never get away with that.

He tapped the golden circlet decorated with polished spikes of gemstones that was nestled among the *senties* on his head. "The wearer of this crown holds power. If it's passed publicly, it'd be hard to contest or remove. The High Lords will have to swear fealty to you as my successor. They'll give a vow, which if broken, would condemn them to the Garden of the Cursed. Come here." I kneeled in front of his chair, and he placed his hands on my shoulders. "If you play it right, child, the crown will help you keep your head on your shoulders."

I closed my eyes, listening to his words. In my mind, they started to make sense. This could be my chance. In my heart, however...

"It's just so...unexpected."

This would be a marriage in the name only, but I'd be his wife. If there had ever been a man whom I could imagine as my husband, that man was now dead.

"Amira." Taking my hand, the king helped me up to my feet, then pulled me down into his lap. His thighs were so hard and solid by now, even with the robe covering them, it felt like I was sitting on a wooden chair. "If it is a past commitment that holds you back, let it go," he said sternly.

I dropped my gaze to my folded hands. True to his word, Kyllen had never left me. By now, his presence settled so deeply in my heart, I had no doubt we really were two parts of a whole. There was no life for me without him, even in death.

The king stroked my arm. "A message arrived from the commission I sent to Ellohi."

"When?" My attention snapped back to him.

"Yesterday. Kiris delivered it while you were in the Archives."

"And you're just telling me about it now?"

"I was trying to figure out the best way to tell you." He shifted slightly. "There is no good news."

I'd tried hard not to let hope take root in my heart. Yet it had wormed its way in anyway. And now, it was crushed all over again.

"Kyllen is confirmed dead," the king said.

The emptiness inside me grew bigger than ever, shutting away any remnants of light inside me. I closed my eyes as the world around me kept spinning out of control.

"How many times do I have to lose you?"

There was no limit. The torment never ended.

The king petted my knee. "The full report is in the Archives. You can read it when you're ready."

My head swam with dizziness. For a moment, I forgot how to breathe. The pain never stopped, never waned.

Then, an all-consuming need for revenge bubbled to the surface.

"Has Bherlon been arrested?" I wished to see that man suffer at least a fraction of the pain I was feeling. He had to pay for what he had done.

The king pressed his lips in an odd expression.

"What is it?" I demanded. "Please don't tell me he got away."

"Lord Bherlon was also reported dead."

"What? It can't be true. He's dead? How?"

"Killed, apparently. Though the circumstances are still unclear. That's why I didn't recall my investigators. The commission remains in Ellohi for the time being."

I fisted my hands in my lap. The king placed his large, rough palm over my fist.

"Either way, you'll have to forget about Kyllen, Amira. He is your weakness. Even the memories of him make you upset and vulnerable. A ruler cannot afford to have any weaknesses at all."

"A ruler..." I echoed, growing numb inside. "I am no queen."

"You will be. I'll announce our betrothal immediately. We'll wed tomorrow. As you know, my dearest bride, I don't have much time left to enjoy our marriage. We need to act fast."

Was he making a huge mistake? Would I be a fool to go along with this?

A crown could give me a chance. But it could also become the cause of my demise.

He saw the doubt on my face. "I'm doing it to protect you, child, to give you a weapon strong enough to oppose the lords and their power. But make no mistake. Taking the crown is just the first step. Keeping it is the real challenge. I wouldn't give it to you if I didn't feel you have what it takes to keep it." He squeezed my hand. "You have the thirst for knowledge. You have a strong mind and a noble heart. You've gained the confidence to speak up. The crown on your head will simply make everyone pay attention next time you speak."

I leaned against his chest. "Thank you."

The king might think I was thanking him for the crown. But there was so much more I was grateful to him for—for seeing a person in me when no one else in Ufaris did, for believing in me, and for teaching me. Because that was exactly what he'd been doing all this time—by discussing the strategies with me, by telling me about his past, by explaining to me his decision making process—the king had been teaching me how to govern.

He stroked my cheek through my veil. "I believe you'll do just fine, little human."

Chapter Seventeen

AMIRA

I'd heard women dreamed about their wedding day from when they were little girls. But it hadn't been like that for me. Back when I worked at the menagerie, there'd been no time or energy left for daydreaming. Neither had there been anyone I could even remotely imagine as my future husband.

Even after meeting Kyllen, I hadn't fantasized about marrying him. All I'd ever wanted was simply to *be* with him.

The night before my wedding to the king, I couldn't sleep. As his snoring filled the room, I climbed out of my nest and sat in the window. Hugging my legs, I watched the occasional paddle board pass by on the dark lake far below.

Kyllen had never asked me to marry him when he was alive. Yet my marrying the king still felt like a betrayal somehow. If there truly was an afterlife for gorgonians, then Kyllen would know how I felt, even in death. He always was so acutely attuned to my emotions when he was alive.

I wished I could speak to him again, that I could see his face once more. I'd dreamed about him almost every night. But those were just regular dreams, not the vivid visions of before.

Closing my eyes, I drew in a long breath. I *felt* him. The connection between us was so strong, even death couldn't break it. I felt his affection, and I embraced it, letting it fill me with warmth.

I didn't need to learn to live without Kyllen after all, because he never really left. He'd never been further than a thought away from me.

Placing a hand next to me, I curled my fingers. It took just a few heartbeats before I felt the sensation of his warm, strong fingers lacing with mine. It never lasted long, just a second or two, before the feeling of his touch would slip away and the warmth would seep through my fingers like the morning mist.

"No matter what, I'll always be yours," I whispered. "Don't let me go. Don't ever let me go."

I might be marrying another man tomorrow, but there would never be a place for anyone else in my heart. Wherever he was, I longed to believe Kyllen sensed it, too.

I sat there, listening to the familiar sounds of the Ufaris night.

In just a few hours, I would marry King Zeldren and become the Queen of Lorsan—the role I had never dreamed of taking and felt like an imposter for accepting it.

Normally, people had a lifetime to prepare for something like that.

I had hours.

There'd be courtiers, lords, and councilors to deal with. Every one of them would judge and appraise me. In my role as the king's pet, I hadn't been expected to speak. Silence helped me observe and analyze. By now, I knew these people much better than they knew me. That could give me an advantage if I used it properly.

King Zeldren said the crown was just a weapon. But it was a mighty weapon to have. I had to learn how to wield the power he was giving to me. Then, I could hope to keep my head on my shoulders and live another day.

The leaves on the tree moved gently with the breeze. The roots of the great royal tree sucked the lake water up, then sent it down its branches in waterfalls. Some had been diverted to fill in the water features in the many rooms of the courtiers. Some were allowed to flow freely. The trickle of the water added a calming sound to the peaceful night.

Soft lights of the glowing insects living in the tree reflected off the smooth lake below. Music from the taverns in the distance traveled over the surface. Somewhere close by, life burst with energy. But on this side of the tree, all was quiet.

I sat awake for hours, enjoying the night, until the sky grayed with the rising sun, and the stars twinkled and paled.

Instead of music, distant voices sounded over the water. Merchants' paddle boards glided busily over the surface with baskets of bread or produce tied to them.

Teams of arborists appeared on the trees. Using intricate systems of ropes and pulleys, they could get to any branch, trimming and training twigs or patching cracks in the bark.

The busy life of Ufaris had become a familiar picture to me. The sounds felt comforting.

This had been the longest I'd ever stayed in one place, and I loved it here. Every little, mundane thing made me feel at home. I loved having more than one change of clothes and enough space to store them. I enjoyed knowing where my next meal would come from and where I'd sleep each night.

Whether I planned for it or not, Ufaris had become my home, and I didn't want to leave it.

I was ready to fight to keep it.

As the sky grew lighter, I came back to my nest and got an hour or two of sleep before Kiris and his small army of caretakers appeared.

Right after breakfast, an equally energetic group of maids and ladies-in-waiting arrived to whisk me away into the adjacent quarters meant for the queen.

These rooms had rarely been occupied during the reign of King Zeldren. He'd never had a queen before. I'd read that important dignitaries had stayed here on a few occasions. Other than that, the rooms had been vacant.

Until now.

Practically overnight, the queen's apartment had been cleaned and dusted. Fresh, blush-pink sheets graced the luxurious nest. New grass mats covered the floors.

The maids bathed me and brushed my hair. The ladies-in-waiting I recognized as wives and daughters of the lords and courtiers who had rarely spoken to me before now chatted animatedly. They fluttered around the room and filled the space with activity without being particularly useful.

I was dressed in an apple-green gown. Due to the constraint of time, the Royal Wardrobe Master and his team of tailors and seamstresses had just taken one of the dresses I already had, attached the longest, most luxurious piece of lace they could find for the train, then added matching sleeves, almost as long as the train. In the remaining time, the seamstresses had added as many fresh-water pearls and gold thread to the entire garment as they could.

The result was breathtaking. I'd never worn anything this elegant before. The gold and pearls shimmered in the daylight. The delicate lace of the sleeves hugged my upper arms, flaring from the elbows all the way down to trail on the floor.

The maids left my hair undone for today. In the humid air of Lorsan, it immediately sprung up into its thick natural waves. In lieu of the crown, they attached a wreath of yellow water lilies to the circlet holding the veil on my head.

The ladies-in-waiting produced dozens of chests filled with priceless necklaces, rings, bracelets, and anklets. Once they were done with me, it felt like I had the entire king's treasury on my person. My arms felt heavy, with the golden snake bracelets spiraling from my wrists to the elbows. There was at least one ring on each finger. My legs ended up decorated from my toes to my thighs. And a multi-tiered necklace heavily weighed on my chest, the strands of pearls, crystals, and gold cascading all the way past my breasts.

"You look gorgeous," the ladies-in-waiting cooed.

"Let's just be done with this," spun through my mind. With this much weight on me, I wondered how long I'd last.

Walking out of the room was unnerving. Both the corridor and the hallway behind it were filled with people gawking at me. The urge to run away and hide in some small, dark place itched inside me. But I took a deep breath and raised my chin.

I was about to become their queen, and a queen wouldn't run. A queen would meet any challenge head on and deal with it. She would handle the attention with grace, too.

Plastering a huge smile on my face, I held my head high, meeting their stares instead of cowering from them. They bowed to me in return.

King Zeldren waited for me at the top of the grand staircase in the main hall. His chair had been adjusted to bring him to my height, shoulder to shoulder.

"You are a vision, my bride," he greeted me.

"Thank you." I smiled. "You look dashing yourself."

The king's long, hunter-green robe, embroidered with gold and gemstones, complemented his regal posture. The rich material draped over the chair, largely hiding it from view.

My breath caught in my throat as I turned to face the crowd gathered at the bottom of the stairs. The main hall I had wandered often, studying the artwork on the walls, was now filled with people. The wood-inlay floor was no longer visible under the feet of so many courtiers and the trains of the ladies' gowns.

All attention immediately switched to us. The impact of so many stares landing on me was almost physical. I gasped softly.

The king chuckled.

"They're here to see you, Amira. Greet them."

They were here to watch their dying king—who they must believe had lost his mind—marry his "exotic pet." But I did as he said. I smiled and waved my hand in greeting, as a queen would.

Something clanked inside the staircase. The top landing jerked slightly, then smoothly moved forward, taking the king and me across the hall.

I gripped the side railing as the staircase rearranged itself, first folding into a straight vertical column, then unfolding into stairs again, only leading in the opposing direction now. The top platform connected with the wide balcony across from the grand clock.

The High Priestess and Councilor Delahon waited for us there.

The king took my hand in his, his rough skin scratchy and dry, his fingers stiff when bending around mine, but his smile was as wide as ever. He took me to the edge of the balcony, all the way to the railing of the intertwined tree branches.

Thousands of cheers erupted from the lake below. They fused into an explosion of noise, rising from the water to the highest branches of the trees.

The sight of the crowd took my breath away. Not a patch of water could be seen. Every inch of the lake had been taken by boats, paddle boards, or simply people floating in the water. Their hands up in the air, they shouted, clapped, and cheered.

These couldn't be just the residents of Ufaris. Word about the king's wedding didn't have much time to travel. However, some gorgonians must've come here from the nearby lands overnight.

I raised my hand to wave in greeting, and the crowd responded with another eruption of noise. Not all of them were happy about me marrying their king, I was sure. But a wedding was a cause of celebration. The overall energy of the people was positive.

What meaning did this marriage hold to them? As much as Lorsan lords loved war and conflict, the regular gorgonians cherished the period of peace and prosperity that marked the past few years of King Zeldren's reign. With me at the king's side now, there was hope for a smooth transition, without a new war breaking out among the High Lords.

A smooth succession, hope for future stability, and peace—all of those were good causes for celebration.

The High Priestess lifted her arms. The breeze from the lake caught the sleeves of her long, golden robe, billowing them like two wings in the air. She started the ceremony.

Her strong voice carried over the lake, easily drowning the noise of the crowd below. Two tall devices, positioned on each side of the balcony, caught and amplified the sound of her voice, making her words loud enough to be heard by everyone in Ufaris.

When it was the king's turn to say the wedding vow, he squeezed my hand a little tighter.

"Amira, I promise you my trust and loyalty until the day the Great Serpent takes me."

A wave of magic twirled around us, sealing his words. It was accompanied by the sounds of awe and shock from the crowd, amazed by the king's words.

Like any promise, breaking a wedding vow resulted in damnation and death in Lorsan. Love was not something easily controlled. Therefore, gorgonians never vowed to love each other. Instead, they pledged the things they could actually give.

The king's unconditional trust and loyalty were precious gifts no one in the kingdom had—except for me, now.

Human promises didn't carry the same weight as the fae's. I didn't face the same consequences if I broke my vow. But I felt it deep in my heart when I said, "You'll have my trust and loyalty, too, Your Majesty. I will stand by your side for as long as you are with me. And I will keep you in my fondest memories until the day I leave here, too."

It was not just a wedding vow but a goodbye in some way. My eyes filled with tears, and I blinked rapidly, trying to get rid of them.

The king looked touched by my words. He took both my hands in his, then placed a kiss on my lips through my veil. This was the only kiss we'd ever shared.

The crowd cheered.

I might have just married the King of Lorsan, but my lifelong commitment was to them, to the people of the kingdom. They were the ones I had to pledge my loyalty to, and I had to work hard on earning theirs in return.

I longed to put it all into words for them. Yet when confronted with the thousands of faces turned up to me, I froze. The words deserted me. All I could do was just wave and smile again.

Councilor Delahon sealed the record of our marriage to be added to the records of other royal unions in the Archives. After that, we all ascended to the outdoor terrace, located in between the tree's main branches.

Here, I was officially crowned as the Queen of Lorsan. The wreath of yellow water lilies was removed from my head and the identical copy of the king's crown was attached to the circlet of my veil.

My crown held no magic like the king's did, but wearing it held power. I was no longer the king's toy, someone to gift, steal, or dismiss. I was the queen, and I felt the full weight of the crown on my head acutely the moment it was placed.

"Will Her Majesty address the court now?" Councilor Delahon asked the king, who turned to me.

"I don't know. We shall ask *Her Majesty* herself."

That was me. They addressed me as the queen. It was my duty to act accordingly even as my chest hollowed with trepidation at the idea of speaking to the thousands of people crowding the terrace.

Raised on a dais over them, I swept the place with my gaze. Faces of the courtiers met me, so many faces, framed by colorful, lavishly decorated *senties*. The eyes of some glared with poorly disguised hostility. Others appeared friendly. Most seemed expectant.

They all waited for me to speak, even as some wished for me to fail.

I drew in a lungful of air.

"People of Lorsan—" My voice broke, and I cleared my throat.

The courtiers weren't the true representation of the people of Lorsan.

I turned to Councilor Delahon.

"I need to see them all." I gestured widely, beyond the terrace, beyond the main royal tree of the king's palace.

Crushing the silk of my skirt in my hands, I lifted the hem and walked off the throne platform. I crossed the terrace, the courtiers stepping aside, the crowd parting for me like the sea. I stepped to the railing on the very edge of the terrace to see the people on the surface of the lake below.

It looked even more crowded now. Strings of rafts laden with food and drinks stretched from one tree to another. Merchants on paddle boards squeezed through the throngs of vessels and people, selling refreshment to the crowd that wouldn't disperse. People had gathered here for a celebration, and celebrating they were.

Some noticed me standing by the railing.

"The queen!" they shouted, gesturing up. Thousands more cheers and shouts followed as others tilted their heads, staring up at me.

I gestured for the voice amplifying devices to be moved from the dais to the railing. When that was done, I spoke.

"People of Lorsan. I promised my loyalty to your king, but I want to make a vow to you, too."

A roar rolled over the lake in response, resonating with the shock of the crowd. It was unprecedented for a ruler to make promises to the entire kingdom. For any gorgonian, such promises would be impossible to keep because of so many different opinions and interpretations.

As a human, I simply spoke from the heart, meaning every word I said.

"I promise to rule this kingdom with your best interests in mind. I'll always strive to make the life of everyone in Lorsan better. I promise to be fair, just, and kind. I promise to take every opportunity to learn how to become the queen you deserve—*your* queen."

Words like that had never been heard from any of the kings or queens of Lorsan before. People seemed stunned. Only a quiet rumbling scattered above the surface of the lake.

Everyone knew human promises were easy to give and retract. Speaking to a crowd of thousands, however, I had thousands of witnesses to hold me accountable to every word. I meant what I said, and I was ready to deliver on my promises.

The meaning of it slowly settled in the minds of the gorgonians, and...they cheered. Waving their arms, *senties*, and paddles in the air, they balanced on their boards, climbed onto merchants' food rafts, or clung to the low growing branches of the nearby trees.

The cheers weren't just for me. Some were for the king. Others shouted congratulations on the wedding. But regardless of what they screamed, they wished well.

I laughed, waving energetically with both hands.

Councilor Delahon appeared at my side.

"Very good, Your Majesty. Let's go back to your throne now."

"I wish I could be down there, on the lake." I kept waving at the people gathered under the royal trees.

"It's impossible. And dangerous. Your place is next to your husband." He got hold of my elbow and gently but firmly maneuvered me back to the throne on the dais.

The king patted my hand when I took my place at his side.

"Just like the crown, people's approval is easier to gain than to keep," he warned. "But for now... Well done, my queen."

It was late into the night when the king and I finally returned to our respective bedrooms.

My new maids and ladies-in-waiting stripped me of my gown, bathed me again, braided my hair, and dressed me for my first night with my new husband.

They giggled and teased in good humor while rubbing me with fragrant oils, then decorating me with flowers and strings of beads, as if I really had a night of passion ahead of me.

Once they opened the doors to the king's chamber, I entered his room and closed the doors behind me. Then, I quickly shed all the ornaments and decorations they had put on me like on a Christmas tree.

The king was already in bed. I quietly padded to my little nest by the window and put on my simple nightgown.

"Tonight, you'll have to spend in my nest," the king rasped in the dark. "It's a tradition. They will expect to find you here in the morning."

I walked over to him and climbed under the covers. Well aware that the king detested sharing his personal space with anyone, I stayed close to the edge of his spacious nest.

"Tired?" he asked. His own voice sounded rough with exhaustion.

Normally, a royal wedding would take days to celebrate. The coronation then would be another great event that would take place days or even weeks after the wedding. But the king didn't have weeks to wait. He might not have many days left, either. Everything needed to be done fast.

I sighed. "It was a crazy busy day."

He exhaled a laugh. "I never thought I'd end up getting married in this lifetime."

I turned on my side to face him. "Do you have any regrets about doing it, after all?"

He lifted a braid from the side of my face and moved it over my shoulder.

"No, my river orchid. No regrets about that. I'd do it all over again if just to see the pissed-off looks on the High Lords' faces as the crown they so desperately wanted got out of their reach." He chuckled.

"They'll fight it."

"Oh, I know they will. But I also have faith that you will hold your own against all of them."

I didn't feel as confident as he sounded, but the stubborn determination to keep the crown I'd been gifted had already taken root in me.

"I will," I said firmly.

He stroked my cheek, his rough skin scratching mine even through the veil.

"I do have some regrets, though," he said somberly. "I keep thinking about some things that happened well before you were born, Amira."

He addressed me, but it sounded like he was talking mostly to himself, not requiring an answer, so I said nothing, letting him speak.

"I regret some things I did when I was younger. I keep thinking about the people I've wronged."

His was a long and turbulent life, and lately, he had plenty of time to analyze it all.

"They say it's never too late to make amends," I suggested softly.

"Oh, it is too late, child. Way, way too late for that. None of those people are here any longer. I've made sure of that," he added with a bitter laugh.

"Well, maybe you'll meet them in the afterlife, then?"

"And hope they don't spit in my face when they see me?" he scoffed.

"Maybe they won't. Maybe they'll give you a chance to atone. Because what's the point of an afterlife if not giving people a chance to right the wrongs they've committed during their lifetime?"

He didn't reply, but his hardened features relaxed somewhat. Sliding his arm under the covers, he found my hand and took it in his.

"You give me comfort, little human, always have," he said, his eyelids drooping as sleep was descending upon him. "I wish I knew you earlier, back when I could still be a proper husband to you."

That could've never happened. Had we met earlier, he would've broken and ruined me the very first night, and I would've hated him for the rest of my days, had I survived.

But I didn't tell him that. Right now, the king believed that at some point in his stormy, violent life he could've been a proper husband to someone like me, and I didn't argue.

I simply held his hand as he drifted to sleep.

Chapter Eighteen

AMIRA

"Your Majesty," Councilor Delahon addressed the king when he and I took our seats at the round table in the council meeting room.

It had been ten days since our wedding. As the queen, I now attended every single one of the king's official meetings and functions. I was no longer sitting on a cushion at the king's feet, either, but had my own chair placed to his right.

"We received a message from Sarnala," the councilor reported. "The werewolves accepted your proposal for the levee."

"They're offering their assistance with design and construction, too," Councilor Zivras added, adjusting the wide sleeves of his purple robe.

I wasn't that surprised at the werewolves accepting our proposal. The prosperity of their border communities largely depended on the trade with gorgonians. Desperation was often the reason behind their raids and attacks when the trade was forced to stop.

"That's great news." I smiled, elated.

Councilor Delahon acknowledged my excitement with a slight bow.

"They're requesting the maps we have of the area and sending gifts for the king to celebrate the start of this collaboration."

"Building the levee is a wise decision." Councilor Zivras nodded. "New for Lorsan, but necessary in this case."

"A clever solution," Councilor Oharen praised.

His words were met with a rumble of approval from around the table.

The king smirked. "Tell them to send the presents fit for the queen."

"The queen?" All twelve councilors turned to me, and I straightened my spine under their attention.

Since I became their queen, the councilors no longer dared dismiss my comments outright, but they rarely voiced their approval, either. Without the king's endorsements, even the crown on my head didn't add much weight to my words yet.

Now, they muttered in confusion, casting questioning glances at me.

"You're fools!" the king barked. "The levee was Queen Amira's idea all along. She was the one who came up with it. She knew better than to present it as hers, though, because you would've had a much harder time accepting it if she did. But she deserves all the credit for it, nevertheless." He moved his heavy stare along the table. "You're idiots if you can't see the value of a thought regardless of whose head it came from."

The councilors shifted in their seats. Some wouldn't look at me, but those who met my gaze had a new respect in their eyes.

I tossed a grateful glance at the king. It'd take time, patience, and many more sound decisions on my part to convince the Council to fully accept me. But this seemed to be a step in the right direction.

When I climbed into the king's nest that night, he found my hand right away. Since our wedding night, he hadn't sent me back to my nest by the window or to the queen's quarters. I'd been sleeping in his nest, holding his hand and listening to the deep rumble of his snoring every night.

"Thank you," I said. "Thank you for speaking for me today."

"Let's hope I'll never have to do it again," he replied. "The councilors are old and set in their ways, but they have to realize you have a mind of your own and opinions that are worth listening to."

The next morning, on the eleventh day of our marriage, I woke up to an unusual quiet. There was only the soothing trickle of water in the waterfalls, the soft rustle of the wind in the branches outside, and the hushed crackling of the wings of the lighting insects.

The snoring was gone.

And I knew. I knew the king was no more.

I sat up in bed. I put his head in my lap, his *senties* stiff and motionless, and I cried.

Things had happened just the way they had between us for a reason. I knew the king would've never taken his time to get to know me or to form any kind of attachment if I met him when he was younger. He would've irreparably hurt me, ruining any chance for us to ever become either true lovers or friends. But I still wished he'd lived longer. As much as I had been preparing to lose him, I didn't feel ready when he passed. I cried bitterly, mourning him.

But I also hoped that the king's turbulent spirit was whisked by the Great Serpent into the afterlife he'd believed in.

King Zeldren might've been a true monster most of his life, but I had been lucky to witness the kinder, gentler side of him. I'd glimpsed his remorse, and I wished he'd find peace and forgiveness in whatever world he had gone to.

That was how Kiris and his helpers found us that morning—the king dead and me crying with his head in my lap.

"Goodbye." I kissed the king's forehead, his skin cold and rough like the bark of an old tree. "Thank you for being my friend when I needed one so badly."

The funeral took place in the afternoon of the same day. They dressed him in a gray-brown robe—the color of decay and mourning in Lorsan—and put a dress of the same color on me.

King Zeldren's body was laid to rest upon the Funeral Mound under the great royal tree—the place where every king before him had lain.

I stayed under the tree long after the official ceremony was finished, all proper seals had been attached to the records, and most people had left.

The sun touched the horizon, its reddish-golden glow highlighting the ripples on the surface of the lake. It got darker under the dome of the tree trunk. Even the people most loyal to the king or most curious to see the human queen up close had left already.

The guards assigned to protect me kept to the edges of this water crypt. They obviously preferred the crimson golden rays of the setting sun to the eerie green semi-darkness under the tree.

It was time for me to go, too, but I lingered.

King Zeldren had never needed anyone. On the contrary, he'd been fiercely protective of his personal space. Yet at the very end of his life, he didn't like being alone. I wondered if that was why he'd kept me to begin with—he'd needed the company of a live person to keep the ghosts of his past at bay.

Not a soul remained near the Funeral Mound now, and I couldn't bring myself to leave him completely alone here.

Sitting on one of the large river rocks surrounding the Funeral Mound, I adjusted the edge of the king's silk robe over his chest.

"How about one last goodnight story, Your Majesty?" I said. "I don't believe I've ever told you about Kyllen's learning how to shoot a bow, have I? It's a funny one."

My eyes still felt sore and swollen from all the crying, but I smiled, remembering the stories we'd shared, the king's dry chuckle, and the way he rubbed his hands in anticipation.

Sorrow gripped my heart. My chest tightened.

King Zeldren had been a friend and a mentor. I'd grown genuinely attached to him. And now...I lost him. Just like I'd lost Radax. And Kyllen... Was it my fate to lose everyone I ever cared about? Was I destined to go through life completely alone? With no friends and no family?

"I'd love to hear a funny story," a male voice said. Its echo bounced off the ceiling, resonating under the dome.

I recognized the voice and the man who stood upright on a paddle board that slowly drifted my way.

"Lord Adriyel." I lifted a hand in greeting. As the queen, I was no longer required to bow to a lord, so I didn't.

His long robe was of the same mourning color as my dress. Only instead of water lilies in silver-thread like on the hem of my gown, his robe was trimmed with ribbons of golden dragonfly wings stitched together.

"Greetings, my queen." He bowed his head with a deference that hadn't been there before I'd acquired the crown. "If you were to tell a funny story, I would listen." A smile played on his pale face.

I discreetly wiped away the tears and managed a smile in return. "I'm so sorry, my lord, but I'm afraid I overestimated my abilities when I made that offer. I don't think I can do funny tonight."

"I understand. It's easy to overestimate one's abilities." He was holding a paddle in his hands. Dipping it in the water, he moved the board closer to me. "Challenges often appear smaller from a distance. Then, when they approach, we realize we could use some help."

Clearly, he was no longer talking about the story.

With another quiet splash of the paddle, he aligned the board with the rock I was sitting on, then got down on one knee, positioning himself at eye level with me.

"It kills me to see you this upset, my queen." He fitted the paddle into the groove carved for it on the side of the board. "Is there anything I could do to ease your mourning?"

"Thank you, Lord Adriyel. Your kindness means a lot," I replied sincerely. Maybe one of the reasons I didn't want to leave here was that with the king gone, I'd be left utterly alone in the royal quarters tonight.

As if sensing my vulnerability, he leaned closer, but stopped short of touching me. Pale green light unexpectedly shimmered around his shoulder closest to me, then spread out in concentric waves through the air between us.

He jerked back.

"What was that?" I stared at the space around him, but the light dissipated quickly.

"Wards." He winced, rubbing his shoulder. "There's enough of them in here to make the ceiling glow." He pointed at the dome above us.

"What are they protecting? The king?" I touched King Zeldren's elbow. The wards hadn't impeded *me* from coming close to him or from sitting here for hours.

"The wards protect the Funeral Mound and anything that's laid upon it. Once placed here, the body belongs to the Lorsan lands. No one can touch, remove, or desecrate it in any way."

"That's good." I stroked the king's hand. His arms were laid straight along his body. His skin now felt not much different from the rock I was sitting on, hard and cold. "But how come I can touch him?"

"The Crown of Lorsan." Lord Adriyel stared longingly at the golden diadem with the delicate turquoise spikes on my head—the king's crown. It had replaced my copy after the king's body was laid on the Mound. "It carries the magic of the Lorsan Wetlands. It makes you a part of it, too."

For once, I truly felt like I was a part of something. I belonged to this place, and I loved the feeling. The land had accepted me.

Lord Adriyel shifted in his position, making his board sway. He steadied himself by placing his hand on a rock he could touch, the one that must be outside of the ward circle.

"I'm here for you, Amira," he said with passion. "I mean it. Anything you need."

A kind word was exactly what I needed right now. I reached across the ward-protected barrier and placed my hand on his.

He flipped his hand quickly to grab mine and squeeze it tightly.

"Ruling a kingdom is not an easy task," he said fervently. "You'll have enemies who will be watching your every move, waiting for you to make a mistake. And when you do make one—not *if*, Amira, *when*—they will strike. Will you be able to thwart the attack? On your own?"

"Oh, I know many perils await me, Lord Adriyel. I don't expect this to be easy, but I'm ready."

He shook his head with a skeptical look in his silver-blue eyes. "It takes years of preparation to wear this crown—centuries. You're a smart woman. You've been learning, I've heard. But you're still so young, so inexperienced, and so very vulnerable." He brought my hand to his lips, placing a gentle kiss on the inside of my palm. His warm breath tickled my skin. "You need a man to help you, someone you could rely on to make hard decisions."

"Not necessarily." I closed my palm. "Women have successfully ruled Lorsan before, with no men by their side."

Gorgonians were a largely patriarchal society. The majority of its rulers had been men. But I'd learned of at least two women who were successful on their own. Their situations were similar to mine. Both had been widowed and inherited the crown from their husbands.

"Queens Exear and Utiya—" I started.

Lord Adriyel didn't let me finish. "Both were gorgonians. Each came from a prominent family that groomed her to become a wife of a noble one day. You didn't have that." He yanked on my arm, making me slide to the very edge of my rock and past the ward barrier. He cupped my face through my veil. "Amira, Lorsan has never had a human queen before."

"Well, there is a first time for everything." I tried to sit back on my rock, but he drew me closer, not letting me move away.

"The people of Lorsan will never accept a human queen," he said firmly. "You're just too different from us."

"Don't gorgonians love the *different?*" I bit back.

"The nobles do. But the regular, common people prefer the stability and the predictability of the tried and familiar. The risk of turmoil is just too high with a human monarch on the throne."

"How so?"

"You have no magic, which makes you weaker than fae. It makes Lorsan a tempting target for other kingdoms to attack. Even as young as you are, you'll live only for a few more decades—not a very long period of stability for our people."

He was right, of course, so very right. But his reasons for saying this were clear—Lord Adriyel saw himself as the next king. The unexpected twist of the crown landing on my head had messed up his plans.

"Thank you for your concerns." I worked my hand out of his grip. "But I'll manage, my lord."

With a deep sigh, he sat back on his board.

"I'm sorry, Amira. I didn't mean to frighten you, or to doubt you. And I most certainly don't wish to underestimate you. You are a strong woman and a proven survivor. It's impossible not to admire you."

"Thank you," I repeated flatly.

"I didn't want to upset you. Especially today." He gave me a polite bow. I couldn't fault him for speaking the truth, though his timing certainly wasn't the best. "Perhaps this would cheer you up?"

He reached inside his robe, then stretched his hand to me. As he unfolded his fingers, a blue-and-green dragonfly barrette lay on his palm. The twinkling of its delicate wings blended with the faint shimmer of his skin and the green glow of the magical light above us.

The sight of it struck me like a lightning bolt.

"How?" I muttered, words lodging painfully in my throat. "Where did you...get this?"

I hovered my fingers over the barrette, afraid that if I touched it, it'd be gone, just like everything else dear to me had disappeared.

"You sent a commission to Ellohi."

"The king did that, as a favor to me." My voice shook.

"They returned this morning."

"And you intercepted them?"

"There was no one else to receive them. The king was gone, and you've been grieving."

He held out the barrette to me. "A palace maid from Ellohi gave them this. She insisted it was yours and that you would want to have it back."

Geltar. She remembered me.

"Yes. It's mine. Thank you." I closed my fingers over the dragonfly. Getting it back felt like a puff of breeze from the past, filled with the memories both painful and comforting at once.

"It was clearly made by a gorgonian, though not by one of our best masters..." Lord Adriyel let the end of the phrase hang in the air, as if inviting me to explain.

Clutching the barrette to my chest, I said nothing.

"It means something to you," he prodded.

It meant so much. To most, it may be just a trinket, too crudely made for a sophisticated eye. But to me, the dragonfly was a rare gift, the only thing I had from my past, and a memory of Kyllen.

As I clipped the barrette to my braid, my fingers trembled. It didn't escape Lord Adriyel's attention.

"Is there someone in Ellohi you care about?" he asked.

I shook my head. "No."

Not anymore.

"The High Lord of Ellohi *sold* you," he reminded me.

I met his stare. "And you *gifted* me. Please explain to me what's the difference?"

He bristled with indignation. "I gave you to the King of Lorsan. And look where it has brought you. *I* made you the queen."

"You..." His audacity rendered me speechless.

"Amira..." He caressed the side of my face. "You're young. So beautiful. You have a whole life ahead of you, but you do need a man by your side. Someone who could protect you." He slid his hand down and under my veil, gliding his fingers along the sensitive skin of my neck. "Someone who could be a true husband to you, in every sense."

His touch sent a ripple along my skin, but it was in alarm, not pleasure. Adrenaline coursed through my veins, sending a shudder across my shoulders.

He misread it.

"Look how your body reacts to me," he murmured, hovering his lips over mine. "You're trembling with need, and I can take care of it for you. I can take care of you, Amira."

I knew Lord Adriyel wanted me from the moment he saw me, but he wanted my crown more. It was the reason he gave me to the king in the first place, to gain favor with him, to come just a step closer to what he truly longed for—the throne.

He gripped my hip through the layers of my skirts.

"Marry me, Amira. Make me your king. And together, we'll be unstoppable."

His other hand slid down my shoulder. He hooked a finger into my neckline, stroking the top of my breast.

I shrank back.

"You didn't make me the queen, my lord. The king did it because he believed in me. I earned his trust. He saw his successor in me. *You* have nothing to do with that. And no, I don't need a man to prove myself worthy of this crown, definitely not a man who sees me as a piece of property to be bought and gifted."

I shoved hard at his chest, needing to get his hands off me. The board lurched. Lord Adriyel lost his balance. He tipped backwards, his arms flailing in the air. Then he fell into the lake with a splash.

I didn't wait to see him climb back up. I guessed he'd have less dignity and far more fury then.

Leaping from rock to rock, I dashed to the other side of the Funeral Mound, then waved to the guards floating on their paddle boards by the tree roots to pick me up.

Loud cursing and spattering came from where I'd made Lord Adriyel take a tumble into the lake, but I didn't look back. One thing was clear, by refusing the lord as my ally, I'd made him an enemy.

Chapter Nineteen

AMIRA

That same night, I met with the king's emissaries who had returned from Ellohi. We talked in the council meeting room, as it was one of the few public rooms in the palace with an actual ceiling, which provided privacy.

It was late. The poor men seemed exhausted by the long journey. I felt tired and drained, too. But I needed to speak with them.

"How did Lord Bherlon die?" I asked.

"Lord Kyllen killed him."

"That makes no sense," I argued. "How could they both have killed each other?"

Another emissary stepped forward. "There was a duel..."

"The argument sparked over the succession to the High Lord's throne," the head of the commission explained. "It grew into a fight. Lord Kyllen was wounded in the back. Before Lord Bherlon delivered the final blow, Lord Kyllen stabbed him through the chest with a poisoned weapon. Lord Bherlon ended up dying the very next day from the effects of the poison."

"A duel?" I scoffed. A duel would've been a much more dignified way to resolve the conflict than what had actually happened. "Who told you that? Udren?"

"Yes."

Of course, the father would want to defend his son's memory, even if that meant distorting the facts in his favor.

"Lord Udren wasn't there when the attack happened," I said.

"His account was supported by many eyewitnesses," the emissary insisted.

I was an eyewitness, too. I had seen Kyllen getting wounded. Was it possible that he managed to stab Bherlon before being killed?

That very well could have happened. Udren had lied about how the attack started, but that didn't mean its outcome wasn't the same.

If so, Kyllen had avenged his death on his own.

I spent that night in a fitful sleep with my fist pressed to my chest. My dreams were short and disturbing—a collection of dark images, backlit by an eerie green light with monsters lurking in the shadows.

Even Kyllen's normally comforting presence couldn't keep them at bay. Instead, it made me restless. I searched for him in the shadows, but he kept evading my touch. So close, yet forever out of reach.

Heavy and fragmented, the sleep kept me in bed well past sunrise. For once, no one burst through the doors with trays and towels that morning. The king was gone. And they had mercifully let me rest.

I sat up in the nest and unclenched my fist. The rumpled wings of the mechanical dragonfly sprang open, trembling in the sunlight. The rays broke in the facets of the beads Kyllen had used to make the barrette, bursting into a myriad of sparkles on my palm.

Crushed and crumpled, it was not broken.

And neither was I.

I drew in a long breath, then clipped the barrette into my hair. Next, I took the crown from where I had left it on the side table last night and put it on, over the veil on my head. Then, I got out of my nest and stood in front of the window.

The queen.

This was *my* kingdom out there. *My* people. I'd pledged my loyalty to them, and I vowed in my heart to earn their love in return. For once, my life had a true purpose, one I felt ready to fulfill or die trying.

It wouldn't be easy. Everything Lord Adriyel had said to me last night was true. I was an outlander, a human—the species considered by many to be inferior to fae.

But dammit if I wasn't going to try my hardest to make it. Where I lacked in strength and magic, I would make up for it in determination.

Not waiting on the maids, I changed from my nightshirt into another gray-brown dress. By tradition, a widow was not required to wear the mourning colors past the day of the funeral, but some did.

In my case, I didn't feel ready for bright colors yet. Or maybe it was the security I felt when wearing the mourning clothes. As the king's widow, I had more rights and power than I'd ever had before.

I opened the doors to the room, letting in the noise of the palace life.

"I'm up," I announced to the sentries on guard in front of the royal bedroom. "Please send a maid up with my breakfast. Just one maid, not all of them. Uzyni," I said the name of the most reserved woman of the bunch. Today, I couldn't handle any idle chatter. "Let Councilor Delahon know the council meetings will proceed as planned. I'll see them all in an hour."

I was the queen. And I had a kingdom to rule.

"It's unheard of for a woman to rule on her own!" Councilor Oharen shouted, his *senties* flaring into a halo of aggravation.

"Actually," I stood my ground. "There is a record of at least two female queens in Lorsan's history."

"Queen Exear and Queen Utiya," Councilor Delahon helpfully supplied.

I sat in the king's seat at the round table with twelve councilors flanking me, six on each side. The table was shaped like a doughnut with a bite taken out of it on the opposite side of me. The person presenting a proposal would usually stand inside the "doughnut" hole in the center, so they could rotate to face any person sitting at the table if they so wished.

The space in the middle was currently vacant. The meeting had gone fairly smoothly, all the items on the agenda discussed and dealt with. The protests started when someone brought up the tournament.

By tradition, if a king died without a successor, the Council held a tournament. The High Lords competed with each other, the crown going to the winner. In theory, anyway, that was how it worked. Historically, however, some tournaments had resulted in full-blown wars.

"We don't need a tournament," I said firmly. "The throne of Lorsan is not vacant, and its crown already belongs to me."

"The kingdom's strength is in its political stability. But you are a woman. A human one, too," Councilor Oharen pointed out.

"Are you saying I can't give stability to my people?" I glared at him.

Councilor Delahon raised his hands in a pacifying gesture. "No one is contesting your right to be the queen, Your Majesty."

"Oh, really?" I bristled. "Because it certainly has been implied I'm not suitable for the role."

A man to my left, Councilor Azorin, shook his head. "Every woman needs a husband."

"And as a human," another one chimed in, "you really don't have that much time to choose one, Your Majesty. Your life is short. The sooner you get married, the better."

"What are you talking about?" I slapped both hands on the table. "My husband just passed away yesterday. His body has not even been absorbed by the land yet, and you're trying to marry me off to someone else, already?"

Councilor Delahon nervously tugged at one of his bright pink *senties* while chewing his lip. "A swift marriage would be to the benefit of the kingdom, Your Majesty."

"You're the queen. King Zeldren made you one, and the queen you shall remain," Councilor Azorin said in a pacifying voice.

"But for the sake of Lorsan!" Oharen roared. "Marry a High Lord and give the kingdom a king."

"A gorgonian man. A true ruler," someone said so softly, I couldn't tell who that was. I shot a glance along the table, but they all avoided my eyes.

Anger boiled in my chest, speeding up my heart rate and heating my face. And maybe it burned so strong because deep inside, I knew they were right. Lord Adriyel had said it all before. And I was sure every other person in the kingdom felt that way.

For them, I was a weak human girl who had somehow tricked their dying king into giving her the crown. In their eyes, I was a huge risk to the kingdom's stability.

I might feel capable, but they wouldn't even give me a chance to prove myself.

Clasping his hands together, Councilor Delahon leaned over the table to me. "It really would be easier, Your Majesty, if you let a High Lord take over as the ruler of Lorsan."

My back stiff, I fisted my hands under the table, bracing against their words.

Oharen slammed his fist on the table. "People of Lorsan are expecting the tournament. The High Lords and their champions have been arriving all night yesterday and all morning today. Let them compete."

Councilor Zivras gripped the armrests of his chair. His terracotta-colored *senties* undulated agitatedly. "Let the Crown of Lorsan and your hand in marriage be the prize for the winner."

"Let the strongest man win. This crown is too heavy for a human woman's head." Councilor Azorin threw his hands in the air in frustration.

"Queen Consort is an honorable position with fewer responsibilities," someone offered.

"Exactly! You're not really giving up anything." Azorin shrugged.

If I let the tournament take place, someone strong and agile would win—a man, a High Lord, from a noble gorgonian bloodline. The marriage to someone like that would pacify the Council. It would nip at the bud any competition or speculation about finding me a suitable husband in the future.

Lorsan would have the king it wanted instead of the queen it got saddled with.

And where would that leave me?

The Queen Consort.

It was a supporting role, which might suit me better than the lead role I'd so boldly taken upon myself. Maybe I wouldn't mind being supportive. I could be a partner in a true partnership, based on mutual respect. But that wasn't how my future husband would see me.

It didn't matter which one of the twenty-four High Lords would end up the winner. As their wife, they all would see me the way Lord Adriyel did—a crown to take, a body to use, a mind to ignore.

"Trust no one."

I'd heard these words often. Wise words. But they weren't entirely true. There was one person I absolutely had to trust. Always. It was me. I had to have faith in *myself*.

Clenching my hands into fists, I slowly rose from my seat.

The councilors stopped their bickering, staring at me. Silence reigned over the table.

"There will be no tournament," I announced, my voice firm, my tone unyielding. "The crown will not be contested. Lorsan already has a ruler. Me." I moved my gaze around the table from one face to another, giving time for my words to sink in. "The kingdom has a queen. There will be no king."

A murmur of protests rolled through the room, but I wasn't finished yet. I raised my hand, calling for silence.

"Instead of the tournament, I want a ceremony where each of the High Lords publicly pledges fealty to me."

Throughout the history of Lorsan, the lords swore their loyalty to their sovereign. I might as well make a celebration out of it.

Councilor Oharen stared at me. "Are you demanding all twenty-four of our High Lords come to Ufaris? Now?"

I tilted my head, folding my arms across my chest. "They are coming already, aren't they? I may as well make their trip worthwhile."

He blinked, saying nothing.

"When would you like to have the ceremony?" Councilor Azorin inquired.

"As soon as possible." I turned on my heel, heading for the door.

This session was over.

"Your Majesty." Councilor Delahon hurried after me. "A jolly celebration after the somber funeral has always been the way to part with the dead and rejoice in life. The crowd expects entertainment. The tournament was supposed to give that..."

I paused at the threshold.

"We'll give them entertainment. Let's celebrate with food and drinks. Let's do games and shows. But there'll be no tournament, no prize, and no winner."

Once back in the king's bedroom, I paced the room restlessly. Putting my foot down today was important, but defending my position would get much harder over time. This was just the beginning. The pressure to marry wasn't going to disappear. With all the High Lords gathering in Ufaris now, it would only mount higher.

The very reason they all flocked to the king's palace was to get a chance at the crown. I had just snatched that chance from them.

They wouldn't give up that easily.

When Uzyni brought my lunch, I went to the king's wardrobe room. It remained unchanged as I hadn't ordered to clear it out yet. It felt too soon. Getting rid of his clothes and other things felt like banishing his spirit from the rooms that had been his for so long.

I took one of the king's formal robes from a trunk.

"Take this to the Wardrobe Master." I handed it to the maid. "Tell him to make me a dress for the ceremony. And tell him it has to be the best he's ever made. Fit for the queen."

King Zeldren had worn this emerald-green robe stitched with black and gold serpents to several formal functions before his death. I could wear it as is, to remind the crowd whose shoes I was filling in. But I wanted it altered.

I wished to send a message with my outfit, to show the High Lords that even though my power had been bestowed on me by their king, I intended to tailor it to fit my style. My governing the kingdom would be entirely my own.

That was a perfect way to shed the widow's clothes and to transition into my new role—not just the king's widow, but the queen in my own right.

Chapter Twenty

AMIRA

The dress turned out exactly how I envisioned it.

A tight, bustier-style bodice fully concealed my breasts, leaving my neck and shoulders exposed. A long train of emerald silk embroidered with gold-and-black serpents went atop a gauzy skirt. But best of all was a tall, stiff collar that opened like a fan over my shoulders. It framed my neck and provided the background for my face with the crown over it.

Gathered around my neck, my veil served as a scarf. But for once, the sensation of it was more restricting than comforting. My veil was a limitation I wished I could get rid of.

Fully dressed, I took in my reflection in the floor-to-ceiling mirror in the king's wardrobe room.

I hardly recognized the woman who was staring back through the veil at me. It was no longer the timid, abused girl from the menagerie. The only thing left from her was the dragonfly barrette I had clipped to one of my braids under the veil.

Compared to the priceless royal jewels adoring my arms, legs, and chest, the dragonfly was rather modest. But it was more precious to me than any treasures of the world.

"It's cute," one of the maids who did my hair said. "But do you think it fits with your outfit today, Your Majesty? It's rather plain."

"If you knew what the man who made it had to work with to create it, you'd know it's a true masterpiece," I replied, keeping the barrette on.

This was all I had left of Kyllen. He might be gone from this world, but he had never left my heart. I felt his support, his affection... No, it was stronger than that. What I felt was his undying love for me. It gave me strength.

I drew in a long breath and squared my shoulders.

The crowned woman in the mirror, dressed in the regal gown, looked every bit the person I wished to be—Amira, the Queen of Lorsan.

"Let's do it," I whispered to the queen in the mirror, and she nodded back at me in support and encouragement.

For this ceremony, I had ordered a floating platform built right on the lake. Surrounded by the seven trees of the royal palace, it was the perfect place for as many of the people of Ufaris to be a part of the ceremony as possible. And so many of them were already there when the boat procession took me from the royal tree to the platform.

Servants, merchants, soldiers, artisans—citizens of Ufaris and visitors from all over Lorsan—all gathered on their paddle boards, vendor rafts, and fishing boats. Hands raised in the air, their *senties* undulating from excitement, they shouted my name and cheered.

Freeing my hands from my long sleeves, I waved at the crowd and grinned.

"To the queen!" someone shouted.

The cheer got caught by the crowd. People raised their glasses and steins filled with drinks paid for by the crown.

This was what I wanted, to be right here, on the same level with everyone else, to be a part of the crowd. The feeling of belonging flooded me.

These were my people.

My home.

The crowd parted, allowing for my boat to pass. It was followed by a flotilla of guards on paddle boards. A string of them carried the long train of my dress over the water.

The crowd of courtiers on the raft-platform greeted me by bowing their heads. I ascended the dais to the royal throne erected for me. Once I sat down, the ladies-in-waiting arranged the train of my dress around the dais. In brilliant green, glistening with the gold-and-black embroidery, the train of the dress looked like the tail of a slithering serpent draped down the stairs and around my throne.

Royal guards enclosed the dais in a circle. But I spotted Councilor Delahon in the group nearby and gestured for him to come closer. I respected this man for the same qualities King Zeldren used to dislike him for—his thorough knowledge of the law and his strict adherence to it.

Councilor Delahon was an adamant stickler to the rules. He also knew a great deal about all the High Lords whom I was supposed to greet and welcome today and whose promises of loyalty I needed to obtain.

"Could you stay here, please?" I asked the councilor, pointing at the spot to the right of my throne. "I may need your help."

He took the place at my side.

"Of course, Your Majesty." The bright magenta glow bled from his *senties* onto the councilor's ink-black cheeks in a blush. He was obviously flattered by my singling him out.

It had taken a few days, but all the High Lords had now come to Ufaris. Maybe they still hoped for a shift in power in their favor, but today was all about them pledging their fealty to me.

Beautiful music floated over the crowd. Live musicians positioned in the nearby trees played instruments enhanced by magic.

Instead of the usual tables, tall stands with food and drinks peppered the platform. People ate while standing, which not only allowed them to mingle more freely, it also saved space on the raft. The floating platform was almost as large as the main terrace up on the royal tree, yet it had to accommodate more people today.

As far as I could see, the surface of the lake was covered with boats, boards, and people. The royal platform was just a part of this endless sea of people.

A stream cut through it. A flotilla of boats and boards was moving toward us. When the first of them reached the platform, the courtier in charge of the ceremony announced loudly, "The High Lord of Osim, the High Lady of Osim, and their heir, Lord Eforn."

I leaned over to Councilor Delahon. "Question. Purely out of curiosity. How would the High Lord of Osim, for example, compete for my hand in a tournament if he's already married?"

"His heir would compete," he replied.

"What if he didn't have a son?"

"Unless they're bonded mates, the law allows a High Lord to set aside his existing spouse for a more advantageous match. The queen would be considered a far more desirable spouse than any other lady in the kingdom."

Set aside his current wife, like a discarded object.

"That's terrible," I whispered, then straightened my back and plastered a smile on my face to greet the High Lord and his family. "Welcome to Ufaris."

The High Lord of Osim was one of those who had requested a meeting with me before the ceremony. I had spent most of yesterday receiving some of the High Lords one on one and answering their questions in an attempt to assuage their doubts about me as their ruler.

Now, I held my breath to see what he would do.

"Greetings, Your Majesty." The High Lord lowered his knee onto a silk cushion placed on the steps of my dais for him.

Bowing his head, he recited the words of the vow of fealty. A gentle sweep of magic rushed over the platform, sealing his promise.

I exhaled in relief.

Many avenues were still available to the High Lord of Osim to betray me if he so wished. For one, his son and heir remained unbound by any vows to me. However, the lord's willingness to come here and publicly declare his loyalty to the human queen was a sign of goodwill already.

After the High Lord of Osim, the other High Lords arrived, one after another. Boats delivered them to the platform. I greeted them and their families. They stared at me in wonder, curiosity, and appraisal, then congratulated me on my coronation, or expressed their condolences on the loss of my royal husband, or both. The High Lords then took a knee to recite the vow before moving on to mingle with the courtiers around the tables laden with food and drinks.

"The High Lord of Ellohi," the next announcement came.

My heart made a loud thud at the name of Kyllen's home.

I suspected Udren might not travel all the way here in his condition. With Bherlon dead, he'd probably just send a courtier in his stead to represent his lands. In which case, the vow of loyalty would have to be obtained later, from whoever would become the High Lord after Udren's death.

My guess proved correct. The man who jumped from the boat onto the platform had the agility Lord Udren had long lost to old age. The delegate looked like he'd just arrived in Ufaris. He still had his travel hood on.

He approached my dais and kneeled. "May the Great Serpent watch over the glorious Queen of Lorsan."

That voice!

With that very familiar teasing note in it.

My heart pumped faster. Blood rushed through my veins, echoing with a swishing sound in my ears. The noise of the crowd fell away. I gripped the armrests of my throne, afraid I would pass out.

He lifted his head and slid the hood off. The bronze and green *senties* spread wide. The face I'd only seen in my dreams for so many nights was right in front of me now.

"As the High Lord of Ellohi, I pledge my loyalty to you for as long as you remain the Queen of Lorsan," he recited the words of the vow. "That is my promise to you, and may I perish in the Garden of the Cursed if I break it."

His golden eyes remained pensive as he studied my face, his expression anxiously expectant.

He flicked his gaze from my eyes, to my mouth, to my hands, down my legs, as if he wanted to take all of me in at once. Then, his searching stare came up again, pausing on his dragonfly barrette in my braid over my shoulder.

His eyes returned to mine, and a wide grin spread on his face, so achingly familiar, with the cheeky bit of a fang sticking out.

I hadn't dared hoping to ever see this smile again.

Everything inside me melted.

"Kyllen..."

Councilor Delahon gripped my hand.

"Your Majesty? Are you well?" he whispered, leaning closer.

With a polite bow, Kyllen had slipped away into the crowd.

But I couldn't let him go.

"Wait..." I rose to my feet.

The music stopped abruptly. The courtier in charge of the ceremony tripped over the name of the next High Lord who was already sauntering my way along the platform. The High Lord frowned. The crowd stared at me in confusion.

I was breaking the protocol, and no one knew why.

"Not all High Lords have been received yet, Your Majesty," the councilor urgently reminded me.

I made a move to go down the stairs. The long, heavy train of my dress, wrapped around the throne dais, held me in place more securely than any restraint.

"Your Majesty?" Panic slipped into the councilor's voice. "Are you all right?"

I hardly heard him, desperately searching the crowd for the head of the green and bronze *senties*. There were some here and there, but they didn't belong to the man I was looking for.

My gaze crossed with that of Lord Adriyel instead. Standing by the railing of the platform, he watched me carefully. As the heir to a High Lord, he was not required to pledge his loyalty to me. Dressed in a celestial blue tunic, he reminded me of a beautiful, deadly viper, looking for a weakness to strike.

The next High Lord approached and kneeled in front of my dais. "Greetings from Dejahr, Queen Amira."

Managing a smile in return, I forced myself down into the throne, then accepted his vow of loyalty.

The ceremony continued, as if Kyllen hadn't just come back from the dead.

Maybe he had not?

This could have been just another vision, more vivid than any before, but still not real.

Was I the only one who'd seen him?

I leaned over to Councilor Delahon. "I want the High Lord of Ellohi to be brought to me at once."

He gestured to one of the guards to come up, then relayed my order to him.

"Is something wrong, my queen?" The councilor looked concerned.

"Did you recognize the High Lord of Ellohi?" I asked.

"That was not Lord Udren." He shook his head. "The old lord must be too fragile for the journey now. This must be his heir, Lord Bherlon."

The councilor clearly hadn't read the report of Bherlon's death yet. Both Kyllen and Bherlon had been reported dead, but what if that had been a deception?

"Was it Bherlon? Are you sure?" I wouldn't mistake Kyllen for anyone else. I would've recognized Bherlon.

The councilor frowned with uncertainty. "Well, I only ever met Lord Bherlon once or twice. Long ago."

Kyllen's sudden appearance seemed impossible. Fantastical. Magical... Too good to be true?

The way he had disappeared just as quickly was even more suspicious.

I'd dreamed about him so often. It wouldn't be the first time when my mind conjured images of him while awake, too.

Or did someone else conjure them for me?

"How common are illusion spells?" I asked.

Bherlon carried a family resemblance to Kyllen. Both had the same coloring, the same height, and a similar build. How hard would it be to magically enhance that resemblance to fool my grieving mind?

I turned Kyllen's ring on my finger.

"It won't protect you from every peril in existence," Lord Adriyel had said.

Councilor Delahon chewed on his lip, looking worried. "Illusion spells aren't easy to create. Only a skilled, powerful hag can do it believably enough. But I suppose it's possible. What is your concern, Your Majesty? Do you suspect someone might be playing tricks on you?"

I shook my head, unsure whether I should voice my suspicions yet.

The guard whom the councilor had sent after Kyllen returned, unable to find him.

"The High Lord of Ellohi must have left the royal platform, my queen." He bowed.

The remaining High Lords continued to arrive. I smiled and accepted their greetings and vows mechanically.

The image of Kyllen's face remained in my mind.

Could that smile and those eyes be fake? Everything in me desperately wished for the miracle to be true, but my hope had been crushed before. When that happened, a part of me died with it.

I was afraid, so afraid to hope again.

Chapter Twenty-One

MONTHS EARLIER

KYLLEN

"Kyllen!" Amira's voice rang high with anguish that cut through his heart like a knife.

His brother's guards dragged her out of the bedroom and away from him. Something in his heart snapped, as if a part of him had been broken off.

"Let her go," he gritted through his teeth.

Four guards held him down on his knees. Each rivaled him in strength. With the wound on his back, he stood no chance against the four.

Bherlon fisted a handful of Kyllen's *senties*, yanking his head back to expose his throat.

"The human is no longer yours to worry about," his nephew hissed. He raised his dagger, aiming it at Kyllen's neck. "Fraud and imposter. You should've stayed in the filthy human world—"

Bherlon suddenly choked with a gurgling sound. The dagger slipped from his fingers, harmlessly bouncing off Kyllen's shoulder and landing on the floor at his thigh.

Kyllen took no time to ponder what had just happened and how.

The hands holding him slackened for a moment, and he lunged sideways. Freeing a hand, he grabbed Bherlon's dagger, then stabbed the closest guard holding him.

The man howled in pain.

Kyllen whipped around to stab the one on the other side, too.

Screams of pain and clashing metal came from another direction. Someone else was fighting the guards with him.

Bherlon wailed, a sword pierced through his chest.

Kyllen shoved a guard away, leaping to his feet. His back burned in agony from the slash wound. The weapon that had inflicted it was made of iron. But it was no ordinary iron. The pain festered and spread, setting his nerves on fire and paralyzing his muscles. If he were to survive the night, he needed to know exactly who his foe and friends were.

"Hapon!"

The man stood in front of him, a bloodied sword raised high in his hands. Leaning back, Hapon jammed the blade into the guard lurching toward them.

Two of the guards separated from the group, sneaking to the door and out. They'd bring more guards, no doubt.

Hapon must have thought so, too.

"My lord." He offered Kyllen his arm. "We need to leave the palace. This way." He yanked him to the window. "Can you climb down?"

The room swayed around him. His wound burned. The weapon that inflicted it must have been laced with poison. It rushed to his head, making him unsteady on his feet.

Hapon dragged him to the window.

"No. I need Amira." Kyllen shook his head, trying to shake off the fuzziness that shrouded his vision and mind.

Someone brandished a sword, and he slashed across the man's throat with his dagger. His aim remained good for now, but the strength was slowly draining from him.

"Here, my lord." Hapon hauled him out of the window. "Climb!"

He clung to the branches framing the window as Hapon shoved his legs over the low sill. Another guard lunged for him, but Hapon stabbed him through the chest before tossing him out of the room. The guard's body flew past him, then splashed into Layahi Bay far below.

He followed it with his gaze, watching the concentric rings of ripples spread on the moonlit surface of the water.

His vision swam again. He found his footing, clinging to the tree. The trick was to lean as close to the trunk as possible, almost becoming one with the tree. Usually, he'd press his belly to the bark, flatten himself against it, using his *senties* to search for any groove or protrusion in the smooth trunk to get hold of.

But the poison stole his coordination. He tried to climb down when his heart urged him to climb up, to search for Amira.

His muscles shook, and his *senties* trembled. His fingers slipped on the smooth bark. His feet lost their purchase...

And he fell.

He plummeted into the dark abyss and didn't remember hitting the water.

Four months later.

It was hot. Hot and muggy, like what the inside of the belly of the Great Serpent must be.

Did he die?

Then why was his entire body in agony? Wasn't the afterlife supposed to be free of pain?

A groan reached him. Then he realized the groan was his. His throat felt dry, as dry as it hadn't been since...well, since he'd been locked in Ghata's crate.

Was he in a crate again?

The thought jolted him with panic. With a gargantuan effort, he peeled his eyes open.

Wooden rafters came into view. He lay under a roof made of woven willow branches. The light filtered through the tiny slits between the weave. This wasn't a crate.

Where was he?

He closed his eyes again tightly, trying to remember.

Memories came in ragged pieces.

He was lying on a moving paddle board, every move of it jarring with excruciating pain in his back...

Hapon's concerned face leaning over him. "Drink this, my lord." A cup pressed to his lips with something terribly bitter in it...

A woman with a face so crisscrossed with lines, her skin looked like the trunk of an old oak tree...

And before that?

His father's palace. Bherlon's betrayal.

Amira...

She had been close. Somewhere...

"Amira," he groaned, calling for her.

But she was no longer here.

He had to go. He needed to find her.

Flexing the muscles in his jaw so tightly his teeth screeched, grinding against each other, he heaved himself up. Pain lanced through his entire body. He doubled over and rolled off the bed.

It wasn't a nest he'd been lying in. Though, it couldn't really be called a bed, either. It looked like a bench—a wooden cot, covered with hand-woven rugs and linen blankets.

He groaned again, curling into himself against the pain.

A dry chuckle sounded nearby.

"Too impatient for your own good, aren't you?" a raspy voice chastised him.

"I need to go..." His throat burned from thirst.

The voice tsked. "Not for another month or two yet, my pretty lord."

He opened his eyes again, squinting against the light of the fire in the metal hearth by the wall. A dark figure sat by the hearth. It was impossible to tell either by their voice or their appearance, whether it was a male, a female, or someone else entirely.

A door opened with a squeak of rusty hinges, and a man walked in.

"Is everything alright, Grandmother?" Kyllen recognized the man as Hapon by his voice. "I heard a noise."

"Your lord is hot in the head." The figure by the fireplace chuckled. "No patience at all." She handed a wide mug with two handles to

Hapon. "Give him this. He needs to drink all of it if he ever wants to stand on his feet again."

"My lord!" Hapon rushed to him, then helped him back onto the cot.

"Tell your grandmother I don't have a month or two to lie around," he rasped. "I need to heal faster."

Hapon blanched. "She's not my grandmother. This is the village hag, skilled in healing. We're in my family's place again, my lord. Please forgive me, but I didn't know where else to go."

Kyllen dismissed his apology with a wave of a hand. The man had nothing to apologize for. The memories of Bherlon's attack had returned, clear in their horror, now.

"You saved my life," he croaked. Speaking hurt.

Hapon crouched at his cot, the mug of the hag's brew in his hands. "My loyalty was tested that night. And I made my choice. I'm on your side, my lord."

Kyllen accepted the mug and took a few large gulps. The liquid was tepid, but it burned his throat without any heat. The witch's magic. It was strong enough to soothe the pain and smooth his throat at once.

Hags possessed the most powerful magic in Nerifir. But they had to trade their good looks and youth for it. The witch in the room could be younger than Kyllen, and she likely would live longer than him, but she looked like she was about to meet the Great Serpent any day. Her dark, patterned hands gripped a walking stick made from gnarly wood. The travel hood—completely unnecessary in the room with only gorgonians present—was drawn low over her face.

"Why did you kill for me, Hapon?" he asked.

"You are your father's son. The throne of Ellohi is rightfully yours. It's my honor to serve you as my father served your father, my lord."

Kyllen glanced inside the mug in his hands. The dark liquid in it shimmered and sparkled like a piece of night sky dusted with stars. "Honor is an inconvenient thing to have. It can get you in trouble."

"It already did." Hapon gave him a humorless smile. "I slew Lord Bherlon. The High Lord's men are scouting all of Ellohi, looking for me."

"How come they're not here? Your family village would be the first place to look."

"It would be." The man smirked. "If Lord Udren ever bothered to ask where I come from."

Kyllen huffed a laugh. It resonated with a wave of pain through his body. He sank back onto the cot. Just a moment's rest, then he had to get up.

"Where is Amira?" She'd been close before. He'd seen her in the darkness of his delirium. He'd spoken to her. Though, he couldn't remember the words.

He *felt* her.

Hapon diverted his eyes and shifted uneasily.

Kyllen lifted himself on an elbow, despite another slash of fiery pain from his back.

"Where is she?"

The hag cackled. "You need to stop jolting your body like that if you ever want to get your lady-friend back."

"She was here," he growled at the woman. "What did you do to her?"

"Me?" The hag shook her head, making her hood sway around her face. "Is that the gratitude I get for saving your hide from *ebon* weed poison?"

He blanched, reining in his impatience. Being deemed ungrateful by the hag might have dire consequences.

"Forgive me. I meant no disrespect. Please, tell me, what have you done to her?" he begged.

"To her? Nothing. I haven't even seen your woman. But you share a thread of connection with her. I used it to let you visit her at the beginning when your spirit was barely attached to your body. You thrashed and screamed for her like a man possessed. So I set your spirit loose to give your body a chance to heal. But you're not out of the woods yet. Keep jumping and jerking like a grasshopper, and you'll split your wounds open again. Then you won't leave this room for many more months to come, if ever. Only a few survive *ebon* weed poison."

The connection.

He felt it, too. An invisible thread that stretched from his heart to hers. He wasn't quite sure when it'd formed. But he knew exactly what it was. Love. He loved his little sweet pea, even if he was too blind to see it sooner.

"Where is she now?" he insisted. "Where is Amira?"

The hag heaved a breath in frustration. "He just doesn't listen, does he?" she muttered under her breath.

Hapon scratched a *sentie* draped over his shoulder. "We don't know where Lady Amira is, my lord."

Worry squeezed around his chest like an iron band.

"How long have I been here?"

"Four months." Hapon sighed, resting a grim gaze on Kyllen. "You were in bad shape, my lord. Still are, to be honest."

"Four months?"

It was an eternity! Meanwhile, Amira was out there... Alone.

He'd sensed her feelings while he fought for his life, unconscious and weak. He knew she'd been scared, lonely, and in pain... so much pain. The echo of her sorrowful screams still resonated through his heart. It could only stop when he held her again.

He had to find her. Comfort her.

"I need to go." He handed the mug back to Hapon and sat up, a little slower this time.

The hag rose to her feet. She slammed the end of her walking stick into the floor with power unexpected from her frail figure.

"You're not going anywhere!" Her raspy voice carried enough strength to boom under the rafters. "The poison is not out of your veins yet. If you keep moving, you'll die. Not that you could get up to your feet yet, anyway." She cackled and plopped back into her chair, looking every bit the frail old woman again. "If you die on your way to your lover, who will help her then? If your dead body is lying on the bottom of a river somewhere, eaten by eels, how would that help your little human?"

As much as he hated her at the moment, the hag was right. He couldn't even get off this cot without tumbling down. How was he supposed to stay on the paddle board long enough to search the wetlands for Amira?

But she was out there somewhere, alone, frightened or...

What if she was no longer alive?

Fear froze his insides. Then, a tiny petal of warmth flickered in his heart—he felt her. The fae mating bond may not be possible with a human, but his connection with Amira was undeniable, whatever it was.

She was alive. He just needed to find her before it was too late. Amira was gentle and fragile, too delicate for this world. So easy to hurt.

"They wouldn't kill her." Hapon must've sensed his fear. "A human woman is too rare and valuable. Wherever she is, she'll be alive."

Amira posed no threat to a gorgonian, including Udren. On the contrary, she was a beautiful, enviable possession that any lord would love to have.

Which could hurt her, nevertheless.

"Could she still be at the palace?" he asked.

Hapon shook his head. "I really don't know, my lord. I've been hiding from everyone. Only my closest family know we're here."

Kyllen couldn't blame Hapon. The man's priorities had been elsewhere. He'd had a lot on his plate with the unconscious Kyllen on his hands while being pursued for murder.

Hapon touched his arm in a comforting gesture. "I'm sure Lady Amira is alive, my lord. We'll find her. But you need to regain your strength first. Then I suggest you claim your title, too, before searching for her."

He stirred impatiently, but Hapon pressed his hand to Kyllen's arm harder, keeping him in place.

"An old, dying man is sitting on the throne of Ellohi," Hapon said. "The lower lords are swarming him, waiting for him to die. Without Bherlon, they see an opening for themselves. If you don't act fast enough, someone will steal your rightful place the moment your brother dies. It'd be that much harder to wrest it from them then."

Everything inside him urged him to dash in search of Amira as soon as he could get off this damned cot. As the High Lord, however, he'd have the resources to find her faster and the power to punish anyone who took her.

Amira had taught him patience. Patience and trust.

He rolled his head on the pillow to face Hapon.

"Pledge your allegiance to me as your lord, and you'll have my loyalty in return. For life."

Trust was hard to come by. His own family had betrayed him. He'd known Bherlon hadn't been happy about his return from the human world. He'd expected his nephew to challenge him. But he did not anticipate Bherlon to ambush him like a coward in the middle of the night. His mistake had been giving Bherlon more faith than he deserved.

Hapon, however, had proven his courage and trustworthiness. He saved Kyllen's life.

"It'll be an honor, my lord." Hapon lowered his head in a bow, reciting the words of the vow of allegiance.

Kyllen sealed their agreement with the promise of loyalty, too. A sweep of magic rushed around them, binding them for life. Instead of the heavy burden of obligation, however, it brought relief. Some promises were worth making after all.

The hag's brew was dragging him under—to rest, to heal. Through the sleepy haze, the urge to act burned and nudged. He wished to rush into action. Take his throne back. Find his woman. Slay everyone who dared stand in his way.

But he could no longer even open his eyes. The healing potion worked its magic, knitting his skin and muscles together and cleansing his veins from the poison.

"Sleep, my pretty lord," the hag chuckled. "Regain your strength."

He needed his full strength back. He had to use his inherent fae affinity to plot and plan meanwhile.

Amira's image floated to the front of his mind. Her dark, inquisitive eyes. The lips he loved to kiss so much. Amira was so trusting and vulnerable. Every minute he stayed away from her, she might be suffering. He needed to save her. He had to...

Heavy darkness swallowed him again.

More weeks of semi-consciousness had passed. Over a month of tossing and turning in sweat and pain on the narrow cot in the hag's care, until she finally deemed him ready for traveling.

The witch refused to accept any goods or jewels in exchange for her services. It didn't surprise him. The hags generally cared little for material things. They craved another kind of recognition.

"I want a room in whatever palace you'll live, my lord," she said. "A chair at whatever table you'll eat, and respect of whatever court you head."

The demand was high but earned. She had brought him back to life, after all. Strength filled his muscles once again. Energy coursed through his limbs.

"You will always have all of that in my father's palace," he promised.

She chuckled, shaking her head.

"No, my pretty, I wasn't talking about *just* your father's palace. You have to word your promise exactly as I did or remain in my debt forever."

After having managed to promise nothing to anyone for almost eight decades, he'd been giving out promises like candies lately. But he owed a huge debt to the hag now, and it was best to settle it now than let it grow.

So he did as she asked.

And now, he had one more thing to settle before he could organize a thorough search for Amira.

He wished he could just march into his father's palace and claim what was rightfully his. But caution dictated it was wiser to sneak in. He and Hapon came at night—two paddle boards sliding noiselessly over the waters of Layahi Bay.

Hapon tilted his head back, assessing the wide smooth expanse of the royal tree trunk of the palace. "This side is impossible to climb, my lord."

Kyllen shrugged. "I've done it as a kid. I sure can do it now."

After paddling for days, his shoulders ached, but his strength and vitality had been steadily returning. He steered the board closer.

"Wait here," he instructed Hapon. "It's probably best if I talk to my brother one on one first."

Scaling the smooth trunk was difficult, but not impossible. The wards placed on the tall windows of the High Lord's chamber didn't stop him, either. The magic of Ellohi recognized him as one of the ruling bloodline.

He leaped over the windowsill and into the room.

The raspy sound of labored breathing came from the large nest with luxurious bedding piled up high.

Kyllen swept the room with his gaze, making sure the High Lord was alone.

"Udren." He approached the nest where his brother was sleeping. Sliding the sword from the sheath on his back, he pressed the tip of the blade to the old man's chest.

The moonlight reflected blue in the metal, but red sparks ran along the blade where the particles of iron had been mixed into the alloy. Iron of Nerifir was the only metal that could kill a fae.

"Wake up." He poked harder. He had no intention of killing a sleeping man in his bed.

Udren's breathing halted, then came a little softer as he slowly dragged his eyelids open.

"Kyllen? Is that you, brother?"

Brother.

The word made him cringe.

"Get up and wake the court," he ordered.

Udren scrambled to sit up. His arms shook, his *senties* tumbled stiffly. There was not a patch on his face not marred by the deeply engraved pattern of mortal drought. He appeared to have aged years in the months since Kyllen saw him last.

"You killed my son," Udren sobbed.

Kyllen moved his sword away. Threatening Udren felt like kicking a sick puppy.

"It wasn't me." He shook his head. "I wasn't given a chance to defend myself. A man loyal to me delivered the blow that killed Bherlon. If he didn't strike when he did, I would've been dead instead."

By the look of Udren, his brother would've far preferred that outcome.

"Did you know Bherlon was planning to attack me that night?" Kyllen asked.

Udren covered his face with his shaking hands. "My son. My beautiful, noble son," he wept.

"Bherlon made his choice, Udren. I would've given him the fair chance that he denied me. A tournament, a duel, a legal battle in the king's court—any honorable way to resolve this. But he chose a cowardly attack at night, ambushing me while I was in my nest with my woman." He gritted his teeth. Forgiving the wrong done to him would be difficult, but he could never forgive the danger brought on Amira.

Udren uncovered his face.

"*Your* woman?" he scoffed, with a cruel spark in his eyes. "Did you really think you could keep the human? You, a vagabond lord with no throne and no means to protect something as precious as her? A rare thing, she was a pet fit for a king."

Anger flared in him. He grabbed a handful of Udren's stiff *senties*, yanking the High Lord to him. "Where is she? What did you do to her?"

Udren laughed in his face, gleeful at having found a place to hit where it hurt.

"Where? In the king's nest, of course. Likely riding his royal cock as we speak."

"You sold her to the king?" Hot rage speared through him, twisting in his chest with the agony of loss.

"I *gifted* her to him," his brother croaked. "To gain his royal favor. So, if you plan to petition the royal court for my title—"

Kyllen yanked the High Lord by his *senties*, getting him up and out of his nest. Udren's long nightshirt fell to below his knees, obscuring from view most of his drought-ridden body.

"There'll be no petitions, Udren. I no longer need the king's help to take what's mine."

Udren stared at him with so much hate it made Kyllen shudder.

"You weren't supposed to come back!" the High Lord spat out. "You were as good as dead. Gone forever."

"That's what you wanted, didn't you? For me to perish in the human world."

Udren shook with hatred. "Why shouldn't I want that? You always were Father's favorite. He let you get away with everything—the eldest son, the future High Lord. And what about me? I was destined to be second in everything. Why shouldn't I have taken the chance to get rid of you when I saw one?"

The words hit Kyllen like a lightning bolt. "What are you talking about? What did you do?"

"I didn't need to do much. I fell behind when we were paddling to the Teal Stream, remember? You didn't wait for me, going ahead—always faster, stronger...*better,*" Udren spat the word out like it was a curse. "Across the bend, I saw the *bracks* setting up the net."

"You did?" He staggered back, letting go of his brother's *senties*.

Udren smirked, clearly enjoying Kyllen's shock. "I wasn't strong enough to push you off the board, but I knew you would jump off yourself if you thought I was in trouble. So, I pretended to get trapped in the net underwater, then threw it over you when you so honorably tried to 'free' me."

Kyllen had thought he knew all about his brother's treacherous nature by now. Apparently, he did not. There was no limit to the depth of betrayal Udren was capable of.

Rage burned higher, bitter and hot. "They took me because of you... I spent months trapped in a crate. I almost died... All because of you!" He grabbed Udren's *senties* again, yanking his head closer. "I should kill you."

"But you won't," his brother taunted. "Because you're too fucking perfect for murder. Even more so, for fratricide."

"Am I?" Kyllen smirked. "Oh, how things have changed, my dear brother. Trust me, I won't bat an eye slitting your throat. But I'll do something worse than that." He sheathed his sword and drew a dagger instead. "I'll let you live long enough to lose our father's throne and watch me take it." Pressing the blade to Udren's neck, he ordered, "You will raise the court right now and declare me the High Lord. I want you to abdicate. In my favor."

At the contact with the dagger, the skin under the dark-green pattern over Udren's face paled. The mocking expression slid off his face, replaced with that of utter terror.

"Why would I do that?" he mumbled.

"Because you know I have every right to kill you. You're a coward, *brother*. Always have been. There's nothing you wouldn't do for just another day to live. Let's go." He yanked Udren toward the door. "If you do as I say, I'll let you live long enough to die in your own nest from the mortal drought. But either way, you won't be the High Lord of Ellohi for much longer."

Chapter Twenty-Two

AMIRA

Returning to my rooms after the ceremony, I couldn't rest.

Uzyni took off my gown and removed a treasure chest worth of jewelry from me. I had a quick bath and changed into my nightshirt, then threw on one of the king's old robes. Once Uzyni had left, I paced the room, waiting for any news from the guards I had sent all over Ufaris to look for the High Lord of Ellohi.

One by one, the guards returned, but no one had found Kyllen. It was as if he'd really been just a vision, dissipating into thin air.

Or an illusion created to fool me?

"Armed men have been spotted just outside of Ufaris, Your Majesty," the last guard reported unexpectedly.

"Whose men are they?"

"Not sure. But there appears to be a large number of them, hiding in the woods around the lake."

Alarm prickled my skin with tiny invisible needles. "How large?"

"Hundreds. Possibly thousands."

Thousands of armed men, sneaking just outside the palace walls, promised nothing good.

"Are they gorgonians?"

"Yes, Your Majesty."

All twenty-four High Lords had now pledged their loyalty to me, yet someone was clearly getting ready to strike.

"Does the High General know?"

"Yes, Your Majesty."

"I need to see him at once."

It was a long night.

During the emergency meeting with the High General, it was decided to send our men to the lakeshore to watch for any sign of an attack. A defense plan was put in place.

"We're ready, Your Majesty," the High General assured me before leaving my rooms well past midnight. "We will protect the palace and keep you safe."

Once everyone had left. I leaned with my back against the closed doors and shut my eyes, waiting for the inner turmoil to subside. It didn't. Thoughts and worries churned in my head like a hurricane.

I expected to defend my crown sooner or later. It appeared that day had come. I went through the plan of defense in my mind, over and over, searching for any gaps or weak spots. The plan seemed solid enough for me to relax and get some rest, who knew what tomorrow would bring. Yet I still couldn't think about sleep.

A restless fire burned inside me, spattering with sparks of anxiety.

The whisper of the leaves outside sounded a bit too loud for this hour.

A twig snapped.

Alarm shot through my weary mind.

I whipped around to face the windows. There was no one outside that I could see from my spot by the door, but the crunch and rustle of the leaves outside didn't sound normal.

Quietly, I circled the room, then took the king's iron sword from its place on the wall over the nest.

The old weapon was incredibly heavy. I could barely lift it with both hands, tucking the end of the long handle under my arm to balance the massive blade. Though rusty and old, the sword was a mighty weapon. Holding it made me feel safer while I stole closer to the tall window that led out to the terrace.

At the first sign of danger, I'd call the guards. But with my nerves strung as high as they were, it'd be easy to overreact. The sounds outside probably just came from the breeze or a bird.

Creeping to the window with the sword held in front of me, I leaned closer to take a better look.

A man climbed onto the terrace.

I squeaked, thrusting the sword in his direction, and opened my mouth, ready to scream for help.

He raised a hand in a calming gesture then promptly slid back his hood, revealing the face I thought I'd never see again other than in a dream.

"Kyllen." My limbs grew weak. The sword slipped from my hands, crashing at my feet.

His golden eyes trapped mine. Walking toward me, he stared at me as if I were the most magical, beautiful thing in the world.

"Amira..." He reached for me.

A green glow rippled across the window the moment his fingers came near. He jerked his hand away.

"Wards." He frowned, glancing at his hand. The wards hadn't held him back before, when he was only a spirit. Was this real? "Please let me in, my love."

"My love."

Alarm spiked in me anew. Kyllen and I never spoke about love, though I now knew I loved him with all of my heart.

I took a step back, grateful for the wards. "Kyllen never called me that."

He dropped his hand.

"I should have. I should've told you I loved you every day. Because I do." He leaned with his shoulder against the window frame, looking exhausted. "I love you, Amira."

I wrapped my fingers around the mechanical dragonfly clipped to my braid. My chest tightened. Oh, how I'd longed to hear these words from him. To see him again.

Only how could this be real?

"Nothing is what it seems..."

"How are you alive?" I managed with a shaky breath.

"Amira, please." He shook his head. "It's me. I survived a wound from a weapon laced with poison. They struck to kill, but I lived thanks to Hapon. It took me a while to recover. But as soon as I was able, I rushed here, to you. I spent days on the board, hardly stopping for rest. I brought an entire army here to fight for you. Great Serpent..." His chest rose heavily. "How much I missed you. Seeing you in my dreams could never be enough."

"Did you dream about me?" No one knew about my visions. I never told anyone. "Do you remember what happened? What we talked about?"

"No." He sighed with regret. "The hag who healed me spoke of letting my spirit visit you, but I don't remember much. Just your pain and your loneliness. I know you screamed for me, and I wanted to come to you. So much. I needed to hold you. I still do."

His last words came with a groan. He lurched my way. The pale green lights flared around his chest where it touched the ward barrier, and he jerked back again.

"Please let me in," he begged. "I fear I'll die if I don't touch you right now, my sweet pea."

A strangled sob tore from my throat at hearing my nickname.

Could any illusion feel so heartbreakingly real?

"Please, let me hold you," he pleaded.

If this was an illusion, then I wished to lose myself in it for as long as it lasted.

I reached out the window. "Come to me."

He grabbed my hand, as if I'd thrown him a lifeline, and I guided him through the ward barrier into the room.

"Amira..." He gathered me into his arms.

Burying his face in the folds of my veil around my neck, he breathed in greedily, as if desperately wishing to fill his lungs with my scent, to soak it up with his entire being.

Right then, I knew he was the man I loved. I had no doubts left. No one had ever held me like Kyllen, as if his life depended on each and every hug he gave me.

I knew, even if I still couldn't believe it.

He slid his hands under the robe I was wearing, and my body lit up with life. My skin glowed wherever his hands touched me.

He kissed my face through my veil—hot, hungry kisses. He'd been starving for my touch as much as I had been for his.

"Kyllen, Kyllen…" I kept repeating his name. This wasn't me screaming into the darkness. He was right here… "Wait." I took his face between my hands. "Let me look at you."

His golden eyes met mine. I stroked along his high cheekbones with my thumbs, taking in his familiar features after so many months. He parted his lips with the glint of his fangs.

"It's me." He grinned. "And it's real."

"It's you…" I breathed out, my body melting into his. He and I—two parts of a whole.

He shoved the robe off me, kissing my bare shoulders, my collarbone, my chest. I arched my spine, staggering backwards under the onslaught of his affection. The back of my legs hit the cushioned edge of the nest, and we fell, sinking into the soft, blush-pink sheets.

Gathering my veil, he lifted it to my eyes. Then he took my mouth with his. His kiss was a drink of cool, clean water, and I was the woman lost in a scorching desert for months. I couldn't let it end. Ever.

I gripped the back of his head. His *senties* spiraled up my fingers and wrists, binding me to him.

Hold me.

Kiss me

Love me.

Don't let go.

With my eyes closed, I couldn't see him. And it terrified me that he might just disappear again.

I wrapped my legs around him, anchoring him to me.

"Stay," I begged when he let me come up for air.

"I'm not going anywhere, Amira. There is no life for me without you, no place I'd rather be but next to you."

He let the veil slide over my face again as he trailed his kisses lower. Desperate in his hunger, he covered my chest with hot, messy kisses. Finding my nipple with his mouth, he sucked at it through the thin fabric of my nightdress, then yanked at the neckline impatiently, ripping the flimsy material to get to my naked body.

Desire zapped hot through me as his lips connected with my bare skin. His *senties* circled my breasts, peppering them with tantalizing nibbles.

I reveled in every sensation. Each touch was physical proof that Kyllen was here with me. He had come back to me. He was alive. He was...

Oh, God. He was kissing lower now. His *senties* snuck in between my legs, gliding, rubbing, exploring.

"Oh, how I missed this," he murmured, kissing below my belly button. "Your scent, your taste. The feel of you..." He kissed the tender spot between my thighs, making me whimper in pleasure and need.

My senses had been lying dormant for so long, only now truly awakening under his touch. I gripped handfuls of his *senties*, lifting my hips to his mouth. I needed his lips, his tongue, his fingers, and *senties*. But I also needed more...

All of him.

"Kyllen..."

"Yes, my treasure?" The low rumble in his voice vibrated against me in a most delicious way.

I gripped his shoulders. "I want you, without these..." I tugged at his clothes.

He shifted up to me, ripping off his tunic over his head.

"Yessss," I hissed.

Pure bliss spread through me like melted butter as I splayed my hands on his bare chest.

"Just like that." I kissed his collarbone, flicking my tongue out to lick his skin through my veil. I missed his taste, too. "Take me, Kyllen," I begged. "I want you as close as a man can be to a woman." I tilted my head back, locking my gaze with his. "I want you inside me."

His eyes opened wider. The focus in them sharpened.

"No one has touched me like this since you." In my life without him, there had been a marriage to another man, but there never was another love.

"I know," he said with his usual confidence. "I know you've never given your heart to another. You couldn't' have, because your heart is mine already, and I'm not giving it back."

"It's yours," I whispered. "It's always been yours."

"As are you." Carefully sliding the veil up, he kissed me again. Moving his hand between us, he unfastened his pants, his hard length pressing against my thigh. "It'll hurt. At first," he warned.

"I know." I hooked my arm around his neck, not letting him pull away from me. "I'm ready." Tingles of anticipation rushed through my lower belly, mixing with trepidation. I'd dreamed about this very moment, but I could never envision anything past this point.

He fitted himself between my thighs. A shudder of pleasure ran through me at the contact.

"I've dreamed about this," I whispered.

He gently slipped the very tip inside me. "Was I there? In all your dreams?"

"You've always been there, Kyllen. Every step of the way."

"I promised I would." He sank a little deeper, stretching me wider.

The discomfort grew painful. I bit my lip and pushed my hands into his chest, closing my eyes.

"Look at me." Bringing his hand between us, he found that one spot that drove me mad with lust when he touched it.

Desire spread low in my belly and down my inner thighs, numbing the pain. I opened my eyes to meet his.

"Stay with me, Amira," he rasped, his muscles straining. He rubbed between my legs. "I want you with me."

He used his *senties* to play with my breasts. A wave of pleasure rolled through my body again, melting the discomfort.

"You and I." He thrust into me. "Together."

Sharp pain cut through my pleasure. I threw back my head, my mouth opened to scream.

"Shhh." His kiss swallowed my cry of pain. He moved both his hips and his finger, rubbing me gently.

The pain dulled, drowned in a swell of sweet sensation. It flooded every vein in my body, making me feel both weak and powerful beyond belief.

Instead of a scream, a moan left my lips.

"Just like that, my sweet pea..." His body undulated over mine. "Stay with me."

His every thrust inside me still stung a little, but something incredible happened. The ache amplified the pleasure he was reaping from me by stroking me with his fingers. The faster he moved his hips, the harder his fingers pressed, making me moan under him.

"Kyllen..." I gripped his shoulders as my climax neared. "Oh God... I can't. I..." Words stuck in my throat as the pleasure erupted.

"Oh yessss," he hissed, letting go of his control, too. As my hips jerked, his lurched into me in response.

I gripped the back of his neck, pressing my temple to the hard ridge of his jawline, as we both fell over the edge. It really felt like a freefall through the clouds of intense pleasure. I no longer knew where it was up or down. There was only Kyllen, and I clung to him with all my might.

He collapsed over me, panting. I tightened my hold on him, afraid again that he'd disappear like a dream. "Don't let go. Don't ever let go of me."

He rolled to the side, taking me with him. "Never."

Chapter Twenty-Three

AMIRA

Kyllen rose on his elbow at my side. "Was this how it happened in your dreams?" He grinned, raising a brow ridge in an elegant arch. "Or was it even better?"

Sunny sparks of humor bounced in his golden eyes. My heart ached at how familiar everything was about him.

"This is better than any dream, Kyllen." I traced the curve of the *sentie* hanging in front of his face, and it nibbled at the tip of my finger when I reached its "head." "This is real."

"It's hard to believe it is." He rolled onto his back, pulling me on top of his chest. "I've come here to rescue you, thinking I'd find you lonely and scared. And here you are...a queen."

"I *was* lonely and scared." I thought back to all the months without him—the months I'd believed would stretch into years and decades of missing him for the rest of my life—and shuddered. "I thought I lost you. I've been told more than once you were dead. I saw Bherlon ready to strike..."

"I'm so sorry." Pulling me closer, he kissed my forehead, my cheek, then my lips. The veil was caught between us, but I didn't care, and neither did he, it seemed. "I was wounded. Poison was in my blood for months, making me delusional. Hapon took me to his home village, on the border with Olathana. Udren's people were searching for us to avenge Bherlon. I heard about King Zeldren's death only when I got here. I came to Ufaris ready to either fight for you or steal you from whoever had you."

He'd mentioned earlier that he'd brought an army with him.

"Wait a minute." I rose over him, spurred by the sudden realization. "Are those *your* men lurking in the woods around my palace?"

He shrugged in that carefree manner of his. "In my defense, I didn't know it was *your* palace now."

"Oh, Kyllen," I groaned, scraping a hand over my face. "I'll have to call off my men, then. So, you came prepared to storm Ufaris?"

He nodded. "To storm, to crash, to burn it to the ground, whatever it took to get you back." He glanced at the Crown of Lorsan in its place on the side table by my nest. "I did not expect to find you wearing *that*."

He looked stunned, and I felt the need to explain again. "I cared about King Zeldren, Kyllen. But it wasn't a marriage for love."

"I know." Cradling my face in his hand, he stared at me, as if learning anew every feature of my face. "I also know that I shouldn't be this shocked at seeing what you've become. I always knew you had the patience and determination to go as far as you wished to go. I just never could imagine you'd go *this* far. This quickly. And...without me." He frowned slightly.

"Is that what bothers you?" I smiled. "Are you upset you've missed the coronation?"

"What bothers me the most is that I wasn't there for you." His disappointment was real.

I sat up. "Kyllen, darling. You *were* here. The memories of you never left me. I felt your support every day. I saw you in the dreams that were more vivid than any dream I've ever had. You talked to me. You kept me alive."

"I did?"

I nodded. "You were as real as you are now. But you said you were in darkness and pain. I thought you were visiting me from the afterlife. But I didn't care, because I just wanted you with me. I needed you."

He played with the edge of my veil, looking lost in thought for a moment or two. "The hag said my spirit roamed freely while my body was healing. Clearly, conscious or not, there is but one way for me to travel—to you."

"You don't remember visiting me? Talking to me?"

"No, my sweet pea. But I remember you being close. When I woke up, it didn't feel like months had passed since I saw you last."

I drew in a long breath, shoving aside the memory of all those months without him.

"Let it be in the past, now. You're here. That's what matters." I splayed my hand on his chest where his heart beat strong and steady. "I love you, Kyllen. I thought I'd never get to say it to you."

A huge grin spread on his face. "I feared you might never say it."

"You did? But why?"

He covered my hand with his. "You tend to keep inside even the strongest of feelings. In fact, the stronger they are, the deeper you try to bury them, like they're treasures to hide and protect."

"My love for you is the biggest treasure." I lifted his hand to my lips, kissing his palm. "But I've found my voice. I've been learning to speak up. I love you, Kyllen. And I'll say it again and again if just to see that smile of yours over and over."

"I love you, too." He sat up, taking me in his arms. I wished we could stay like that forever, but he shifted away from me way too quickly.

"Stay." I gripped his arm.

"I wish I could. But I haven't slept for days. I'm afraid I may fall asleep right here, now."

"Then sleep. There's plenty of space. Rest." I'd just gotten him back. I couldn't let him leave again.

He rubbed his eyes with a hand. "There are guards at my door. They'll expect to see me leaving my room in the morning. I need to be there."

"What guards?" I frowned. "The ones I've sent to look for you have all come back. You've evaded them all."

"I couldn't let them take me to you."

"Why not?"

A spark flashed in his eyes. "Because it already took all I had not to grab you from the throne when I saw you at the ceremony. I was a second away from kissing the life out of you right then and there, in front of everyone."

I bit my lip. "I wouldn't have objected to that."

"But the others would. If the High Lords catch wind of you favoring me in any way, they'll assassinate me without a doubt."

"No," I protested. "I won't let them."

"They'll find a way. Lord Adriyel has already placed his guards at my bedroom door to spy on me. Of course, he claims they're there for my protection."

"How dare he!" Anger boiled hot in me. "I'll get them removed at once."

Kyllen just shrugged. "Don't bother. It would just confirm his suspicion that you favor me."

I seethed. "He's made himself way too comfortable in *my* palace."

Kyllen gazed at me for another moment.

"My queen," he said, as if testing the sound of my new title. "It was the most thrilling experience to see you upon the Throne of Lorsan and then find you here, wielding King Zeldren's sword. You looked magnificent."

Wielding was too strong a word. I barely managed to balance it without dropping it. Still, my cheeks heated at his praise.

"A sword instead of a chair. I've come a long way." I smiled, stroking a *sentie* draped over his shoulder. He promptly wound it around my wrist.

"You really have, my love. I'm amazed, humbled, and proud of what you've accomplished and the person you have become. You've broken out of your shell and emerged as what you truly are..." He sat up and bowed his head. "My queen."

His admiration thrilled me. Warm pleasure glowed inside me at his words.

"Well, as your queen, I order you to stay with me..." I paused before adding, "For the rest of my life."

He took my hand in his. "Will you marry me, Amira?"

"Yes," I said quickly, maybe way too quickly, but I didn't care.

His grin turned rather smug, very much like the Kyllen I knew. Though, he seemed to be lost for words for a minute, just sitting there, grinning happily at me.

I placed a quick kiss on the corner of his smiling mouth. "I'll gather an assembly and make a formal announcement first thing tomorrow morning."

His smile dimmed. "It won't be that easy."

I dreaded to hear these words. Nothing had ever been easy in my life.

"For years," Kyllen explained, "the High Lords have expected their chance to compete for the crown."

"My showing up threw a curveball in their plans," I added with a nod. "They aren't happy, but they've been dealing with it rather well, so far."

"Hm." He looked skeptical. "They're holding on to the hope that not all is lost. One of them can marry you to become the next king. If I sweep in now and take that chance from under their noses, they will not take it well."

"They can't tell me whom to marry," I argued, even though I feared they very well could. A queen's marriage was of state importance. Every High Lord and every councilor would have something to say about that.

"You canceled the tournament," Kyllen said. "That left the lords feeling cheated out of their chance for a crown. Now, if you tell them you're marrying me, without giving any consideration to the rest of them, they'd take that as an insult. The crown is slipping away from them for the second time, through a marriage arranged behind their backs, to someone they consider an outsider. I've been away for too long. I've made no alliances and can't count on any of their support."

"They will assassinate me." His words echoed ominously through my mind.

"If I can't marry you, I'm not going to marry at all," I said firmly.

"Oh, it'll be me. It can't be anyone else." Kyllen leaned toward me, taking my hands in his. "But I need to *earn* the right to marry you."

"How?"

He straightened, squeezing my hands. "Make the tournament happen."

"What? No!"

"Amira, please. Declare your hand in marriage as the prize. And let all of us compete for it."

I kept shaking my head. "No. I'm not playing with your life. I just got you back. I'm not losing you again."

"A win at the tournament, witnessed by thousands, would be the one uncontested way for me to claim you," he insisted. "It's one of the oldest traditions. There was a lower lord once who claimed a princess like that. They weren't bonded mates, but they were in love. I forgot his name."

"Lord Grelen." I remembered reading about that in one of the books on succession laws. "He won the hand of Princess Rhelore, King Anior's daughter, in a tournament and set a precedent that centuries later helped Lord Urick and Lord Oflyn claim their brides from two more prominent families."

He tilted his head, regarding me with new curiosity. "You know Lorsan's history better than I do."

"I've been doing a lot of reading, especially on the Kingdom's laws. I still have a lot to catch up on."

"I never knew of the other two lords," he muttered under his breath.

"Did you skip that lesson, too, as a kid?" I teased.

He shrugged with a guilty expression that made me laugh. He reached for me again, and I gladly crawled into his lap. I hated being apart from him, even if the distance was just a foot or two between us now.

He pressed a kiss on the side of my neck. "Fine, I may not be scholarly, but I'm really good at riding water serpents and winning tournaments. I'm in excellent shape, too, you know. I've traveled by board across the kingdom for days. Don't discount me as the winner yet."

I sighed, snuggling into his arms. His life was at stake. But even if he survived, taking any place other than the first, I'd be obligated to marry a stranger. The chilling dread wouldn't leave me.

"It's too much of a risk. The stakes are too high for me to gamble."

Excitement sparked in his eyes. "But I'm good at gambling, remember?"

"This is not the human world," I argued. "A tournament is not a roulette table. You can't manipulate it in your favor."

"There are always ways to make one's odds higher." He remained undeterred.

"No, Kyllen, please. There has to be another way."

"The other way is this." He tipped his chin at the Crown of Lorsan on the side table. "Leave it here for whoever wants to find it. Come with me to Ellohi. I can't make you a queen, but I'll make you my High Lady. I'll build a fortress around my palace and fight anyone who dares come for you."

Because they would come.

"They will hunt you..." King Zeldren had said.

They would. Now, the prize would be even greater. No longer would I be wanted just as a rare pet. As the former queen, I'd retain some claim to the throne for the rest of my life. It would also mean a death sentence to Kyllen if he stood in the way of any ambitious High Lord who wished to take me from him.

I sighed. "They won't let us live in peace."

"They won't. You see now that the victory in the tournament is the best way for me to claim you? Fair, public, and uncontested. Besides, you'll remain the queen."

I wished I could dismiss that last point. But even if I said I didn't care for the crown, it wouldn't be true.

"You want that, don't you?" he prompted.

I nodded. "I gave Lorsan's people my promise, and despite what gorgonians may think, human promises are important, maybe even more important than fae's, because nothing holds us accountable but our honor. Yes, I want to be the queen worthy of my people's trust. I don't want to give up."

"Then so it should be."

"Kyllen." I shifted to face him fully. "If I have to choose, I'll always choose you over the crown. Without a doubt or a second thought. There is nothing and no one in the world more important to me than you."

"I know. But wanting both doesn't make you a bad person." He smiled. "You can have it all."

I could easily lose it all, too.

The sky had grayed with the first rays of sunrise. The birds in the tree branches outside the windows chirped, greeting it. Still, I clung to Kyllen, the man I had thought I'd lost before and risked losing for good, now.

"I need to go." With a tender hug and a kiss, he freed himself from my arms. "I have to sneak back to my room before the lake gets too crowded. No one can know I've been here or that I love you. No one can know you love me back."

He got out of the nest and searched for his shirt. I watched him getting dressed, wishing I had the power to keep him with me.

"Announce the tournament, my queen, and set the date as soon as possible. There's no need to wait."

"Kyllen." I climbed out of the nest and walked into his arms for one last hug.

He kissed me, holding me close for a little while longer. "I won't be able to see you before the tournament. Not sure how I'll manage that."

"Promise me you'll be careful," I begged. "I want you to win, but I want you alive even more."

He grinned, shaking his head. "I'd rather not make another promise, sweet pea. I've made so many, it's getting harder to keep track of them all. Just trust me on this—I have no problem risking my life, but I can never lose you again."

Chapter Twenty-Four

KYLLEN

He pushed the lightweight board ahead with even strokes of his paddle. The lake was choppy from all the water traffic at this evening hour. He had to spread his feet wide apart and crouch down a bit to keep his balance.

It'd been two days since Queen Amira announced the tournament to the cheer of the people. Excitement had been buzzing in the air ever since. The nobles welcomed the chance to compete for the crown, even if it came with the queen's hand attached to it. And the common folks cherished the prospect of more games and festivities. It wasn't every day that High Lords were willing to die for their entertainment.

The tournament was the day after tomorrow, and he was on his way to secure an ally.

The golden season had started, cooling the air and replacing the green in the tree canopies with yellow.

The sunset was in full bloom, painting the sky and the lake in a vivid palette of gold, orange, and red. Gold-winged dragonflies glided over the water. The tavern where he was heading was already surrounded by swarms of lighting bugs. Clusters of them hung under the lattice that served as an awning over the rafts with tables. The sectional rafts were placed around a thick trunk of a tree on the outskirts of Ufaris.

Several patrons were sitting at the tables. Some were still finishing their dinner. Others had already taken enough of the after-dinner wine to be unsteady on their feet.

A customer stumbled to one of the paddle boards tied to the dock by the entrance.

"Hey, Ezon!" A barmaid carrying six steins of sweet wine, three in each hand, yelled at him. "Are you sure you can get home on your own?"

Ezon waved her off, mumbling something incomprehensible. With a lurch forward, he stumbled onto one of the boards, lost his footing, and plopped into the water, face first.

The patrons at the tables laughed, stomping their feet and slapping their thighs. Setting the wine steins on the table, the barmaid snickered, propping her hands on her ample hips.

Kyllen braced his legs against the wake from Ezon's fall. Once the swell had passed, he maneuvered his board next to the unfortunate fellow.

The man was floating in the lake, his face down, his light brown *senties* spread in a circle around his head, making it look like a twenty-four-legged squid.

Kyllen grabbed the rope from the front of his board and threw it over one of the pegs in the dock. Once on the more stable surface of the tavern raft, he reached for Ezon and grabbed him by the back of his tunic. He hauled the poor fellow onto one of the tied-up boards. The man snorted, shifting into a more comfortable position, but didn't wake up.

"Thanks, my lord." The barmaid sauntered toward Kyllen. "He's a lightweight, that one. A jug of lily ale was all it took. He'll be fine after a nap. Are you here for dinner?"

"I'm meeting someone here."

"Oh, of course." She wiped her hands on her apron. "Well, follow me inside then."

Unlike the much larger outdoor portion of the tavern, the inside of the small building attached to the tree was completely empty save for one customer. Dressed in black, he sat at the table by the window. With his chair placed away from the golden glow of the sunset, he remained shrouded in the shadows.

"Is that the man you are here to see?" the barmaid asked them both.

The other man nodded.

"Yes." Kyllen moved another chair to the table and took a seat.

"Wine?" the barmaid offered.

A blown-glass stein full of golden honey wine stood on the table in front of the other lord.

"Sure." Kyllen nodded, and the barmaid departed.

Lord Adriyel, the heir to the High Lord of Mevon, folded his hands on the table in front of him. His dark-blue *senties* lay motionlessly on his shoulders, demonstrating the enviable control he'd mastered over his emotions. He waited until the barmaid delivered Kyllen's wine.

"I believe I know the reason you requested a meeting with me, my lord," Adriyel said in a calm, even voice when the woman had left.

"Right. The tournament." Kyllen took a swig of wine from his stein. Cool and sweet, it was rather strong. He had to pace himself, drinking that.

"You're looking for an alliance." It wasn't a question. Adriyel didn't seem surprised.

The rules of the tournaments were clear and simple, every contestant performed solo, each competed for himself against the other twenty-three participants.

However, contestants had rarely been punished for bending the rules. In fact, forming alliances had long been regarded as a cunning strategy to improve one's chances of winning. Though in the true fae fashion, backstabbing also happened often.

Adriyel slid the tip of his finger up his stein. "Many others have already asked me."

"But you haven't agreed yet, have you? Otherwise, you wouldn't be here now."

The lord gave only a noncommittal shrug in reply.

A century older than Kyllen, Lord Adriyel was in great physical shape. He also seemed exceptionally motivated, more than any other

High Lord that Kyllen had the pleasure of interacting with in the past two days.

"I've seen you on a board," Adriyel finally said. "Your skills are impressive."

Kyllen smirked. "I've won quite a few tournaments back in my time."

"I've heard." Adriyel wrapped his long fingers around the handle of his stein but didn't take a drink.

There was nothing exceptional about Adriyel's skills on the board, but that wasn't why Kyllen wanted the lord on his side.

"I've heard you're ruthless in battle."

"Mhh," Adriyel conceded with a hum. "I'm unstoppable," he said with obvious pride.

"We'll make a great team, then."

Adriyel cast a glance from under his brow. "Depends on the promises you're willing to make."

A trickle of unease prickled down Kyllen's spine.

Promises severely limited one's freedom. Some of them were short and straightforward. They only lasted until they were fulfilled. Some were conditional—if one party failed to deliver on the condition, the other was automatically relieved from their part of the agreement. Others, like the one he had made to Amira, were a lifetime commitment.

The promise to her didn't burden him. Giving one to Lord Adriyel, however, was a different matter entirely.

Adriyel continued with a slightly bored impression, "So far, I've been tempted with riches, favors, lands, and a couple of rather appealing brides. What do you have to offer me?"

"The Crown of Lorsan."

A ripple ran down Lord Adriyel's *senties*. His eyes flashed with ambition. He quickly schooled his expression into that of calm indifference again. But Kyllen knew his offer got the lord's attention. Adriyel wanted to be the next king. Badly.

With the High Lord of Mevon on his death bed already, Adriyel was the sole uncontested heir to his father's throne. But he obviously aimed higher.

"The crown is not yours to give," Adriyel said skeptically.

"It could be if I won the tournament the day after tomorrow." He leaned forward and lowered his voice. "Help me defeat the others. Then, when it's only the two of us left, the crown is yours. I'll give it up in your favor, even if I win. With me, your chances of getting the crown would be that much higher."

Adriyel stared at him suspiciously, and not a little confused. He then leaned back with a smirk.

"Do you honestly think I believe you? Why would anyone give up the prize they won?" The heir of Mevon certainly wouldn't. Everything in his posture and expression screamed that.

Kyllen laced his fingers on the table in front of him and said as earnestly as he could, "I don't want to be the king."

Adriyel just scoffed at that, making a move to get up.

"Are you familiar with my story?" Kyllen stopped him.

It was safe to assume that Adriyel knew everything there was to know about him. He'd been watching Kyllen like a hawk ever since he'd arrived from Ellohi.

However, it didn't hurt to reiterate it in this case. "I spent many months in the human world, which cost me about five centuries in this one. Meanwhile, Ellohi learned to live without me. I intended to reclaim the title of the High Lord only to be attacked by my own family. One of my men killed my nephew, defending my life. There is still a lot of turbulence in my court. Enough for me to deal with for the rest of my life."

"Becoming a king would give you the power to crush any unrest in Ellohi," Adriyel replied dryly.

"But it'll also bring that many more problems and responsibilities. Not to mention, a human wife." He made a face.

Adriyel squinted at him. "Don't tell me you don't want her in your nest."

Kyllen's cock twitched at the thought of Amira sprawled in his nest for him. But he chased that vision away, for now.

"Sure," he agreed. "I'd take her as a plaything, but I'm not ready for a wife or the king's throne. I'm not even a century old yet. I have far better things to do than sit in meetings or entertain dignitaries. I'm most certainly not interested in leading wars, with their endless marching and sleeping in tents. I spent months in the human world, locked in a wooden crate and wrecked by thirst-induced drought. I want to have some fun now, and I want to do that in comfort."

Adriyel's mouth twitched with disdain. "Why would you even care about making it to the final round, then?"

"Because I want to live, for one. Losers have a much higher chance of dying, as I'm sure you know." Kyllen paused, letting the other lord absorb his words, then added, "And I could certainly use a favor from the new king, too."

Adriyel narrowed his eyes at him in understanding. Finally, Kyllen was speaking his language.

"What kind of favor?"

"As I said. The situation in Ellohi is troubling for me. My brother's wife was from Prusim. Her family is threatening revenge for the murder of her son, my nephew. Sooner or later I'll have to deal with them, and I could use the support of the king."

"Do you want the king to rule in your favor in this succession matter?" Lord Adriyel's expression remained unchanged.

"Well, I want a bit more than that."

Adriyel placed his elbows on the table and steepled his fingers. "More?"

"Yes. If I refuse the crown in your favor, I want you to help me fight the High Lord of Prusim when he attacks Ellohi."

The Court of Stevali might join the Court of Prusim in their aggression against Ellohi. Lady Igaed, Bherlon's widow, had returned to her father's palace in Stevali. The lady might not be as violent in her ambitions as her late husband, but Kyllen didn't entirely discount the possibility of trouble coming from that direction, either. With the death of Kyllen's father, the peace treaty between Stevali and Ellohi was no longer supported by magic. It could be broken at any time.

Fighting both Prusim and Stevali would be difficult for Ellohi without the support of a strong ally.

"Is the attack imminent?" Adriyel inquired.

"Absolutely." The threat was a high possibility.

"And you don't think Ellohi could stop it without royal intervention?"

"Maybe we could." Kyllen moved his stein in a circle, making the wine in it swirl. "But it'd be much easier with the royal army on our side, don't you think?"

"I see." The contempt in Adriyel's voice deepened. "So, you don't want to take on the responsibilities of the king, but you want the royal power to solve your problems."

"Exactly. The best of both worlds." Kyllen grinned.

Adriyel shook his head, picking at invisible lint on the sleeve of his midnight-blue tunic. "Are you sure you even want the title of the High Lord of Ellohi? It comes with certain responsibilities, too, I imagine."

Kyllen stretched out lazily in his chair. "True, but you see, I'm not ready to give up the comfort and privileges the title of High Lord provides. Besides, it's my birthright after all."

"Of course." The disdain in Adriyel's eyes was now replaced by a calculating expression. "What exactly will you be asking from the future king?"

"To fight the High Lord of Prusim on my behalf."

That was worded too broadly for any fae in their own mind to accept, but Kyllen trusted Adriyel to make the necessary corrections. And he did.

"You'll get one battle," Adriyel countered. "If you help me become the next king, I'll send enough soldiers to help you fight off one attack by the High Lord of Prusim."

Kyllen flexed his jaw with a contemplating expression, taking his time to consider the bargain. He waited silently until the tips of Adriyel's *senties* twitched impatiently.

"You will get to choose which attack that may be," Adriyel added. "You'll tell me when, and I'll send in the army immediately."

Kyllen inclined his head as slowly as possible.

"Deal," he finally said.

"I'll need a formal promise," Adriyel urged.

"Right." He cleared his throat. It felt too dry, and he had no choice but to take another gulp of wine before continuing, "I promise to refuse the Crown of Lorsan even if I win the tournament, in exchange for you helping me defeat the other twenty-two contestants in the tournament the day after tomorrow."

Magic buzzed under his skin.

It was a short, simple promise. It had no added clauses, no stipulations, and only one condition. It also held no reference to the favor Kyllen had asked for from the future king. That was the way an inexperienced fae would word it. And it didn't escape Adriyel. Gleeful satisfaction briefly lit up his face.

"Deal," he murmured. "It's a pleasure to do business with you, my friend."

He made a move to get up again.

"Wait." Kyllen stopped him. "I need a promise from you, too."

"Of course." Adriyel settled back into his chair and started slowly, carefully choosing every word, "If you help me become the next King of Lorsan, I promise to send a portion of my army to help you fight one attack of the High Lord of Prusim on Ellohi."

There were quite a few holes in the way that promise was worded. The size of the "portion" of the army had not been specified. And "help you fight" was too vague. It didn't promise a victory.

Overall, Adriyel had left himself plenty of openings to evade the commitment of helping Kyllen in any way. None of that mattered, though.

"Deal." Kyllen stretched his hand across the table.

Adriyel took it. The prickle of magic that had been coursing under Kyllen's skin since the moment he had uttered the words *"I promise..."* surged forward. It blended with the similar current rushing from Adriyel's side, sealing their fates.

Now, they both were bound and in mortal danger if the promises they gave to each other were ever broken as worded.

They let go of each other's hands and sat in silence, absorbing the heavy magic of commitment weighing down on them.

"Well." Adriyel audibly inhaled.

Kyllen heaved a breath, too. "Our biggest worry now is to defeat the other twenty-two men. We only have one day left to get ready."

"Right." Adriyel rubbed his chest. "Do you have a plan?"

Kyllen glanced out of the window. "Is there still a nest of water serpents in the bend of the Olore River?"

"I believe so."

"How about we meet there at sunrise tomorrow?"

Adriyel squinted at him. "You want us to practice riding serpents?"

"I want to figure out a strategy that would combine our strengths and weaknesses in a most effective way. And yes," he grinned, "I want to do that while riding serpents."

Chapter Twenty-Five

AMIRA

Ufaris was ready for the tournament. Both ends of Loop Bend on the Isafaris River had been blocked by grates, allowing the water to flow unimpeded but keeping the twenty-four giant snakes inside the reservoir.

Thick pillars had been hammered into the marsh on both riverbanks inside and outside of the bend, and benches were constructed, with a tall podium for my throne in the middle.

I arrived by boat, escorted by the ever-present ladies-in-waiting, councilors, and courtiers.

By now, the golden season had come full swing. The grass and the leaves on the trees had turned golden-yellow. The temperature and the humidity in the air had lowered slightly, requiring clothing to be worn. The ladies' dresses now provided far more coverage. And the shirtless look for the men had been mostly retired until the warmer days.

My gown of tea-green silk fully covered my chest and back. The long, voluminous sleeves gathered at my wrists, ending in wide embroidered cuffs. My skirts had a few more layers of tulle than before, swaying around my hips and legs like a misty cloud with the freshwater pearls for raindrops. My neck remained exposed, covered only by the folds of the veil gathered around it.

As soon as I took my place on the throne, a gong sounded the signal for the contestants to assemble. My heart sped up as the line of them paddled into the middle of the stream, then moved closer to the river-bank with the sitting area.

Since Kyllen had left my bedroom that night, I'd hardly seen him. He'd shown up to all official gatherings along with the other High Lords but remained distant. He'd been courteous and polite without seeking my company or special attention.

I knew his behavior had nothing to do with the way he felt about me. He'd warned me we needed to pretend we shared nothing special, so I did. I treated him the same way I treated the rest of the High Lords. Or at least I tried very hard to pay him an equal amount of attention as to everyone else.

All I'd gotten from him lately was a cool half-smile or a courteous bow. But I missed him terribly. Whenever I saw his easy-going grin, it was all I could do not to jump on him and kiss him into oblivion in front of the entire court. I felt him in my heart, but my body also craved him. Every time I glanced at his hands or *senties*, I thought about all the places they had touched me.

He was seventh in line of the contestants, and I spotted him long before it was his turn to greet me. Keeping a wide stance on his board for balance, he held the paddle in his left hand.

Despite the cooler temperatures, the contestants wore only calf-length olive-green pants, no shoes, and no shirts. Many had daggers and swords strapped to their bodies. Kyllen had a short sheath with a dagger around his right thigh and a long sword across his back.

He looked relaxed and exuded confidence, which eased the tightness of worry in my chest somewhat.

A smile played in the corners of his mouth. When it was his turn, he brought his board forward with two long strokes of his paddle and stopped it with one dip in the opposite direction, turning to face me.

His smile grew wider.

"Greetings, my queen." He made up for his rather casual tone of voice with a deep bow, somehow managing not to fall off the board in the process.

"May luck be with you, my lord." I said one of the responses I had ready for today.

I wanted so much to say more, to do something to show how much I rooted for him. But that would be like painting a bull's eye on his back and making him a target for every other contestant during the tournament. Instead, I discreetly touched the dragonfly barrette clipped to one of my braids.

A twinkle of recognition flashed in his eyes, then he had to move aside to make room for the next contestant in line.

Only eight of the twenty-four were High Lords. Seven were the heirs, taking the place of their married or aging fathers. The other nine were champions, sent in their lord's stead.

A High Lord could select a lower lord or even a commoner as his champion to represent him at a tournament. If the champion won, the High Lord was declared the winner and reaped all benefits of the victory. If the champion lost, he'd end up either wounded or killed, saving the High Lord's life. Using a champion was considered less honorable than competing themselves, but many obviously preferred safety over honor.

Councilor Delahon walked to the front of the seating area where the sound amplifiers were positioned. He produced a scroll from one of the long, wide sleeves of his robe and unfurled it, then read the rules of the tournament out loud.

There weren't many rules. Each contestant was to select one of the giant water serpents. The yet-undisturbed creatures peacefully glided under the surface, their wide dark backs glistening in the sunlight.

"A contestant loses if he is dead or wounded so gravely he is unable to proceed. The last man standing will be declared the winner." The councilor reached for the large gavel positioned next to a table-sized gong hanging nearby to signal the start of the tournament.

"Wait!" I rose from my throne.

Everyone turned to face me.

"I wish to make a change to the rules," I announced.

"Your Majesty," the councilor mumbled cautiously, shifting my way.

"It's not prudent to alter traditions, especially ones as important as the rules of the Royal Tournament."

He was right. I was pushing it. The spectators on both riverbanks stirred unhappily, a grumbling noise rising from the benches.

I wished I could just stomp my foot and yell, "That is my royal wish!" However, I was so new to the throne, I had to tread carefully. But I'd also just gotten Kyllen back from the dead, and I wouldn't risk losing him again in this stupid contest, just to appease the public.

I walked down the stairs to the voice amplifying devices.

"People of Lorsan," I said loud and clear. "The kingdom has just lost its king. My heart is still filled with sorrow. Let us not add more death and loss so soon. Today, falling off the serpent will be enough to be declared a loser. One does not need to die to exit the competition."

The unhappy noise grew louder. People hurled shouts like stones in my direction.

"That's not how it works! The losers die!"

"We have rules!"

I glanced at the row of contestants. Kyllen frowned, scanning the crowd. He seemed concerned for my safety.

"The rules state 'the last man standing is the winner.'" I raised my voice. Even with the device's help, speaking over the noise of the agitated crowd proved challenging. "I'm not changing it much. The last man standing *on his serpent* will be my husband and your king."

I swept the crowd with my gaze, trying to gauge their mood. The noise had quieted to a rumble.

I continued, "It's a tournament, not a life-or-death battle. Do you want a king who's been fished out of the river? The only one alive and therefore the winner?"

A few shrugs and some muttering came from the crowd in reply. They obviously didn't care about the condition of their future king, as long as they got some good entertainment today.

"Well, I don't feel like searching in the river full of dead High Lords for one alive enough to be my groom." I gave them a smile. "I want my future husband to be well enough to perform his marital duties on our wedding night." I slipped a playful note into my voice. "Is that too much to ask?"

That seemed to work. Some men guffawed, but many women nodded in understanding.

Encouraged, I continued, "Let there be a celebration, not a mourning, today. The contestants will live. The winner will become my husband." I grabbed the gavel and hit the polished disk of the gong. "Let the best one win!"

The high, clear ring of the gong rolled over the river, and the contestants jumped into action.

Each aligned his board with a serpent gliding underwater, matching the speed of the beast. Choosing the right moment, they dropped their paddles. With a harness spread at the ready in their hands, they jumped into the water and onto the serpents' heads.

Lord Adriyel was the first one to catch a giant snake for himself. Kyllen caught one just a moment later. He dropped the wide noose of the harness over the top jaw of the serpent, sliding it past the creature's sharp teeth to the very back of its mouth where it couldn't bite through it.

The second the serpent had been leashed, it lifted its head above water. Pulling on the harness with one hand to steer, Kyllen bent his legs, holding his other arm out for balance.

Councilor Delahon followed my gaze to Kyllen.

"The High Lord of Ellohi is a very capable serpent rider." He nodded approvingly.

The councilor had accepted my assurances that there hadn't been any illusion spells at the pledging of allegiance ceremony. I'd blamed my confusion on being tired, which seemed to have put his concerns to rest.

Kyllen had told me he was good, and now I saw it hadn't been just empty boasting. His bare feet appeared to be glued to the flat spot right behind the serpent's head. His body moved in sync with the creature, as if he'd merged with it and they became one.

"All contestants are good," I said, forcing my attention to another man.

I wasn't supposed to have a favorite. Although my future depended on the outcome of the tournament, I was expected to remain impartial at this stage.

What I said wasn't a lie, though. All contestants showed great expertise in the sport. Every single one had caught a serpent and not only stayed upright but rode the creature with confidence.

Kyllen had formidable competition. I sighed. Worry vibrated through me stronger.

Lord Adriyel yanked on the harness of his serpent, making the giant snake slide left sharply. Drawing the sword from the sheath on his back, he stabbed through the neck of a competitor.

I gasped, pressing my hands to my chest. Shock speared through me. The murdered man dropped into the water, a red ribbon of blood flowing in the stream.

"Why?" I demanded from Councilor Delahon. "Lord Adriyel didn't need to do that! I changed the rules. He could've just knocked him off the serpent."

The crowd cheered. Bloodthirsty gorgonians.

The councilor shrugged. "Murder is expected at the Royal Tournament. Some see it as an added benefit—an opportunity for revenge against the lords who've crossed them before. By changing the rules, you didn't forbid killing a contestant, Your Majesty. You just added falling off the serpent as another way to lose."

True. All I did was give them a chance to spare a life, assuming they would take it. Obviously, that wasn't the case.

"I changed nothing." I clasped my hands in anguish. The body of the murdered contestant floated down the stream where the attendants in palace uniforms waited to fish it out.

The councilor patted my arm. "Don't be sad, Your Majesty. Your new rule does give the contestants a chance to survive. Some may still use it."

I hoped so. Though all of them already had their swords out. Zipping through the water on their serpents, they brandished their weapons. The rules forbade attacking the snakes, but the men had no reservations when it came to cutting and slicing each other.

The calm waters of the Isafaris River churned and roiled, agitated by the giant bodies of the serpents.

A contestant steered his snake toward Lord Adriyel, aiming his sword at his back. Lord Adriyel was caught in a battle with someone else. He seemed oblivious to the threat, barreling toward him at full speed from behind.

The crowd gasped as one entity.

I held my breath, too, bracing for yet another unnecessary death.

Kyllen yanked at his reins, turning his serpent sharply. Crouching low, he slammed his elbow under the knee of Lord Adriyel's attacker.

The contestant's leg buckled from under him. He lost his balance and plummeted into the churning white water.

The crowd cheered.

Kyllen flashed a grin toward the benches. Cocky as ever.

I released a breath, unsure whether helping Lord Adriyel was a wise move on Kyllen's part. The lord had proven himself a formidable opponent. He was steady on the serpent and confident with the sword. The crowd seemed to prefer him over anyone else. His spending so much time at the royal palace must have something to do with that. People could easily imagine him as the next king.

On the other hand, Kyllen's assistance to Lord Adriyel put him in favor with the crowd, too. They seemed pleased, cheering and shouting encouragements to the High Lord of Ellohi.

Lord Adriyel sent his direct opponent into the turbulent waters of the Loop Bend. He then swung around in search of the next. Bypassing Kyllen, he went for another contestant right behind him.

He either didn't wish to engage in a fight with someone as capable as Kyllen. Or...they had made some kind of agreement.

Judging by the pattern of the fight unfolding, I guessed, quite a few of the contestants had colluded with each other, at least for some part of the competition.

Worry gnawed at me, at the thought of Kyllen trusting Lord Adriyel enough to form an alliance. I wouldn't want to rely on a partner like him.

For now, however, the advantage of the alliance was apparent. Both men were capable on their own, but together, Kyllen and Lord Adriyel seemed invincible.

Their serpents glided through the chaos of the battle with ease, taking down more and more contestants. When faced with the menace, some of them used the way out I'd given them by changing the rules. At least one of the contestants, a champion of a High Lord, jumped off his serpent to avoid being impaled by Lord Adriyel's sword. He forfeited his chance at winning but stayed alive.

All the other champions fought with ferocity, though. Whatever their High Lords had promised them for the victory must be worth risking their lives.

The fewer contestants that remained, the more viciously they fought. Those were the most determined to snatch the prize.

I shifted forward on my throne, clutching my hands together so tightly my fingernails nearly pierced my skin. Only one contestant had my entire attention now. I no longer cared what the court thought about my favoring him. I watched Kyllen as if my life depended on his every move, because it did.

He was my life.

Soon, it was just the two of them left, Kyllen and Lord Adriyel. After fighting side by side for close to two hours, they turned against each other.

It happened instantaneously. The only other contestant slipped from his serpent, pushed off by Kyllen, and Lord Adriyel swerved in the current, directing his sword at Kyllen.

"Oh no..." I groaned.

The two had advanced so far by fighting together and watching each other's backs. With only two of them left now, they had no one else to fight but each other.

Kyllen parried Lord Adriyel's attack. But the moment the lord's serpent slinked by him, it lashed its tail unexpectedly, knocking the sword out of Kyllen's hand.

To my knowledge, a rider had little control over his serpent's tail. Yet I couldn't shake the feeling that Lord Adriyel had influenced the move somehow.

Swerving around, he steered the giant snake back, barreling at the disarmed Kyllen.

Kyllen's sword sank to the bottom of the river quickly. To retrieve it, he'd have to dive for it. If he jumped off his serpent, he'd lose.

He remained on the snake. Holding the reins tightly, his feet spread wide for balance, he waited for Lord Adriyel to come closer.

The lord's sword against Kyllen's bare hands. He didn't even grab the knife he had strapped to his thigh.

"Kyllen... Please." I rocked on my throne, silently pleading for his life with all gods of both Earth and Nerifir.

Adriyel brought his serpent flush with Kyllen's, thrusting forward with his sword.

Evading the weapon, Kyllen let go of his reins and jumped. Grabbing the harness from Adriyel, he shoved his shoulder into the lord's chest, knocking him off his own serpent.

Lord Adriyel splashed into the river, still wielding his sword.

The impact cost Kyllen his balance, too. He landed on the serpent with both feet, but then staggered and plopped backwards on his butt, his legs draped on either side of the serpent's neck.

Councilor Delahon chuckled. "Well, that'd be 'the last man *sitting*.'"

A few snickers and giggles came from the crowd, too.

The next moment, Kyllen leaped to his feet. He steadied himself in the upright position before triumphantly raising his free arm in the air.

A winner!

The crowd erupted with cheers. They might not have known him well before, but Kyllen had earned their admiration during the tournament. His bold move of taking over Lord Adriyel's serpent seemed to especially endear him to them. They laughed at Lord Adriyel spluttering in the water and cheered for Kyllen, who waved and grinned, energy and excitement beaming from him.

He swept the crowd with his gaze, stopping it on me.

I jumped off my throne. Happiness bounced inside me, warm and thrilling. Lifting my skirts so as not to trip, I dashed down the stairs to the deck over the water.

Councilor Delahon hurried alongside me. "Your Majesty!" He fought with the billowing layers of my skirts as they floated all around me, getting in his way. "The winner is supposed to ascend to the queen, not the other way around."

"Oh, but I don't care!" I laughed.

Kyllen's smile drew me in like a beacon. He steered the serpent closer to the wide dock constructed along the riverbank, then hopped off the beast, dropping the harness. Set free, the fantastic creature submerged its head back into the river and the harness slipped off.

One of the attendants on a paddle board had fished Lord Adriyel out from the stream. The lord reached the dock the moment Kyllen set his foot on it.

Councilor Delahon rushed by me, inserting himself into my path to Kyllen.

"My queen." He panted, out of breath. "You haven't pronounced the winner yet. The tournament couldn't possibly conclude without the announcement."

I leaned sideways, catching the glimpse of Kyllen over the councilor's shoulder. My man's smile was all I wanted to see right now. I wished to leap on him, to wrap my arms and legs around him, to cover him with kisses head to toe...

But the crown on my head came with certain expectations.

I drew in a breath to proceed with the formal announcement.

"The High Lord of Ellohi, I declare you the winner—"

"Not so fast, my dear queen." Lord Adriyel shoved the councilor aside, taking his place in front of me. "Some promises need to be honored first. Isn't that so, my lord?" he tossed the question to Kyllen over his shoulder.

"Promises?" I moved my gaze from one man to the other. "What are you talking about?"

Soaking wet, Lord Adriyel had every reason to feel ashamed. However, instead of slinking away, like all the other surviving losers of the tournament had done, he displayed the confidence of a winner. His shoulders rolled back, the sword still clutched tightly in his hand. He stared at me possessively. His glare pressed heavily on my shoulders.

"Lord Kyllen has some obligations to honor." He shrugged, looking dangerously self-assured. "The Crown of Lorsan is mine." Greed flashed cold in his eyes when he flicked his gaze to the crown on my head.

"How?" I glanced at Kyllen for an explanation.

He took a wide stance, crossing his arms over his bare chest.

"Not true." His smile didn't waver, which allowed me to breathe a little easier.

"We made a deal!" Lord Adriyel bellowed. "You know what happens to promise breakers."

Kyllen shrugged.

"Oh, I fully intend to keep my promise, which was to refuse the Crown of Lorsan if I won the tournament. I didn't lie. I don't want the crown."

Roars of disbelief rolled from the audience.

Lord Adriyel smirked triumphantly, sending a chill of trepidation down my back.

Kyllen looked at me, and his expression melted with so much love and affection, it floored me.

"Lorsan already has a sovereign," he said. "A much better one than I could ever be. Queen Amira is the rightful owner of the Crown of Lorsan." He lowered his head in a deferential bow to me. "And the crown she shall keep."

Fury distorted Lord Adriyel's normally calm expression.

"The crown is mine! You promised to forfeit it."

"But the crown has never been the prize of the tournament," I corrected. "It was my hand in marriage, nothing less, nothing more."

"You see, my lord..." Kyllen rested his hands on his hips. "When we made the deal, you were so blinded by your greed and so eager to take advantage of me that you didn't pay enough attention to my wording. I promised to give up the crown, not the queen." He tilted his head, arching a brow ridge. "There is a huge difference between you and me, Adriyel. You fought for the throne, but all I've ever wanted was the woman who sits on it. The queen will keep the crown. But I'm keeping the queen. She is my prize. And I'm claiming her as my own."

"You!" Lord Adriyel raised his sword, aiming it at Kyllen.

The merry expression flew off Kyllen's face. His eyes narrowed with murder as he yanked the dagger from the sheath on his thigh.

Adriyel pivoted to me.

I was the one standing in his way to the throne. The crown was on *my* head. And at me he directed his rage.

"No!" Kyllen leaped at Adriyel's back.

But the lord's sword had already descended.

I shrank back, but not fast enough. The sharp blade pierced the veil in front of my face.

Adriyel staggered back, Kyllen's dagger sticking out of his neck, buried in his flesh almost up to its handle. Crimson blood pulsed out around the blade. The metal glinted red with the deadly Nerifir iron.

Lord Adriyel sank to his knees, then dropped to his side onto the deck. His sword sliced through my veil all the way down. A breeze from the river caught the air-light material, blowing it open.

"Close your eyes, Amira!" Kyllen yelled, his voice filled with horror.

But it was too late.

Frozen in shock, I stared into the silver-blue eyes of Lord Adriyel at my feet, without the milky haze of the veil between me and the gorgonian's eyes.

He smirked. Life steadily trickled out of him in the pulsing ribbon of blood from his neck. But he knew he got his revenge.

"No, Amira. Please!" Kyllen leaped over the dying lord to me. "Close your eyes, my love." He cupped my face.

I could see it on his face. He knew it was too late, way too late. My insides chilled. My heart dropped, crushed by the agony of parting from him. I froze, rooted in place.

"Oh, Amira..." He held my face in his hands. "You can't leave me. You can't leave me, my sweet pea."

Sorrow rose in a swell of darkness inside me. It lodged in my throat, suffocating me. Tears burned my eyes, blurring my vision. They rolled down my face. Hot tears against the chilled skin on my cheeks.

I felt them.

I felt Kyllen's warm palms cupping my face.

I felt the whispering caress of my gauzy skirts moving in the breeze against my legs.

I smelled the fragrant, moisture-rich air of Lorsan. And I heard its people murmur in wonder around us.

Tears gathered in my eyes, obscuring Kyllen's beloved face. I blinked them away to see him better.

I blinked.

I drew in a breath. My chest expanded. I could breathe.

Hope flickered in Kyllen's golden eyes. "Amira?" My name fluttered from his lips like a dragonfly, subtle and fragile.

Slowly, I lifted my hands to his.

I could move.

I was staring straight into his eyes, but I did not turn to stone.

"How?"

He exhaled sharply. "You're alive." Moving his hands down my body, he squeezed my shoulders, my arms, my sides. "You're alive," he kept saying, as if needing to hear the confirmation again and again.

"But how?" I repeated, shaking my head.

"I don't care." His chest rose and fell with shallow, ragged breaths. His eyes glistened with unshed tears. "I don't fucking care *how*. Just please, please stay alive."

He crushed me to him. I hugged him back tight, so tight that if I turned to stone now, he'd be trapped.

Still, I remained flesh and bone. Feeling, breathing.

Living.

"I love you," Kyllen groaned, kissing me.

The breeze moved the veil against our faces. Kyllen grabbed the useless piece of fabric and ripped it off, tossing it aside.

He leaned back. "You're glowing."

"What?"

"When I touch you, your skin glows."

I lifted my hand to stroke his face. When my fingers connected with his skin, a golden glow shimmered up my hand. I thought I'd seen this before, the night he had climbed through my window. Only it had been so subtle then, I hadn't paid much attention to it, overwhelmed by his miraculous return.

The glow was beautiful. And it felt...right, making me light at heart.

"What does it mean?" I smiled.

A sound of someone clearing their throat came from the side. Only now did I remember about Councilor Delahon still standing next to us on the dock.

The world came back, rushing in. The river. The tournament attendants around us. The rows upon rows of benches full of spectators. They all were watching us.

The councilor cleared his throat again, inching a bit closer. "There are some myths... Stories about human love that's capable of transcending magic."

"Humans have magic?" Kyllen didn't sound very surprised or concerned. He just sounded happy, staring at me as if I were better than any magic in the world to him. And maybe I was?

The councilor rubbed his chin in thought. "Do you feel any different, Your Majesty?"

I felt love. But it wasn't anything new. I'd loved Kyllen for some time now.

"I *feel* her," Kyllen replied for me. "I know when she is sad, worried, concerned...happy. I felt her alive. Here." He pressed his hand to his chest. "Even as I knew in my mind that without the veil, she should've been dead."

I knew instantly what he was talking about. I'd carried his presence in my heart for months, and it'd been growing. In the days since his return, I sensed his hopes, his love, and his confidence. They gave me strength.

I placed my hand over my heart. "You've always been here, Kyllen."

"Interesting," the councilor muttered under his breath. He then spoke loud enough for the people around us to hear, "The legend says human love—if it's strong enough—can link with fae magic to create a bond, a mating bond. As bonded mates, things that can't harm Lord Kyllen won't harm the queen, either. She will share his longer lifespan, too. The queen will live as long as her mate."

I no longer needed the veil.

"How did no one say anything about that before?" Kyllen groaned.

The councilor shrugged.

"It's an obscure, ancient legend. I thought it was just an old story when I read it long ago to pass the time. Honestly, I never thought there might be any truth to it as it contains a lot of obvious lies. It says, for example, that humans trade in pieces of cut-up paper with numbers printed on them. Surely, no one is that stupid to trade their goods or services for a stack of papers. Or that they can fly above the clouds with no magic whatsoever." He scoffed, shaking his head. "I thought the entire story was just hearsay."

Kyllen laughed, placing a quick kiss on my lips. "I really need to read more."

I gave him an apologetic smile, too. "I've read so much since I came to Ufaris, but I still haven't made it to the myth section of the Archives. I've been mostly catching up on Lorsan's history, which is quite long, as you know."

He stroked my hair, gazing at me in wonder. "A mating bond. The one thing I doubted would ever happen to me."

"And with a human..." the councilor echoed.

"My very own human." Kyllen leaned his forehead to mine. "I'm going to marry you, my little sweet pea."

"You'd better." I couldn't stop smiling.

Councilor Delahon perked up. "Oh! That needs to be announced." He hurried back to one of the voice-amplifying devices.

"People of Lorsan!" His voice boomed over the crowd, undoubtedly reaching the opposite bank of the river. "Queen Amira is announcing her impending marriage to Lord Kyllen, the High Lord of Ellohi and the winner of today's tournament! Lorsan will have a king again. The King Consort."

The crowd cheered. They had gotten to know Kyllen a little during the tournament, and they seemed to like him. They also must cherish the fact that their fate was no longer just in the hands of a lone human woman. They surely were looking forward to the royal wedding celebration with lots of parties to come, too.

"Who knew the day would come when you'd make me a king?" Kyllen laughed, the merry, carefree sound I loved so much. Grabbing me, he spun me around, sending my skirts in a twirl around us.

I wrapped my arms around his neck. Happiness floated inside me, comforting and invigorating at once.

"I love you, my very own king."

Chapter Twenty-Six

KYLLEN

He stretched on a long, padded bench as two men and two women massaged and kneaded the muscles in his arms and legs.

A group of six servants had already bathed him, then four of them rubbed fragrant oils all over his freshly scrubbed body. He'd never had so many people trying to please him at once, but he could certainly get used to being pampered.

Such was the life of a king.

The best part about it, of course, was that Queen Amira was waiting for him in her bedroom for their wedding night. All this scrubbing and rubbing by an entire army of servants was happening because the court etiquette demanded he please his wife tonight. And for once, he wished to comply with the court etiquette fully and completely, with no reservations.

Kiris, the commander of this "army of pleasure," touched his shoulder. "You can turn on your back, now, Your Majesty."

He did as he was told, lying on his back and folding his arms under his head.

One of the female attendants diverted her eyes from his now completely exposed body. But he caught her furtive glance at his crotch.

He smiled to himself. He wasn't nearly as shy as Amira about nudity. And frankly, he had nothing to be ashamed of. His body was a pleasure to behold. His cock would look even more magnificent had it been up. But for now, it rested flaccid against his thigh.

The female masseuse was pretty. With a light, skillful touch, she worked on his left leg. But he felt no attraction to her or anyone else besides his wife.

Amira had stolen all his affection. She had ruled his mind and body long before they had known anything about their bond. And now that she was his wife, his queen, and his bonded mate, there could never be anyone else. The thought of spending the rest of his life with his little human made him so happy he felt giddy like a little girl.

Amira was just behind the wall that separated her royal chamber from his. As King Consort, he got the rooms reserved for royal spouses. This bedroom had been predominantly occupied by queens throughout Lorsan's history, which didn't matter to him in the slightest.

He hadn't exactly lied to Lord Adriyel when he'd said he didn't care about being the king. Born and raised to govern, he knew all about the responsibilities that came with such a high position. The mere idea of sitting in daily council meetings, discussing levee construction plans or reviewing thousands of complaints from cranky High Lords and peasants alike, made him want to cry from boredom.

Amira was so much better at that than he could ever force himself to be. She had the patience he never had. He'd watched her during the weeks of preparations for their wedding. He'd seen how cleverly she solved issues or how tactfully she handled the pushy councilors and the capricious courtiers. He had no doubts she was well suited for the crown on her head.

He couldn't wait to watch her grow into the best ruler Lorsan had ever had. He didn't doubt she'd do much better than the past king, that vicious brute who Prince Zeldren had grown to be.

Kyllen knew Amira was fond of her predecessor. She had somehow tamed the bastard and made him fond of her in return, so fond that he even passed his crown on to her.

It amazed Kyllen, but it didn't surprise him. There clearly was no limit to what his woman could accomplish without any tricks or brutality, but simply with kindness, patience, and perseverance.

He was fully prepared to be by her side every step of the way. He'd be her partner and adviser whenever she needed to run her decisions by someone. He'd be her ear on the ground, listening for any trouble among the lords and commoners alike. As King Consort, he could keep a lower profile than the ruling queen, which provided more opportunities to hear and see things that might escape her.

And if all her negotiations failed, he'd lead her armies in battle for her. He'd defend his queen to his last breath, both in peace and war.

As his bonded mate, Amira had centuries to live now, too. And he was looking forward to each and every day spent with her.

"Let's get you up, Your Majesty." Kiris offered him an arm for support as Kyllen climbed off the bench in all his well-oiled, naked glory.

The attendants wound a golden, bejeweled snake-clip around each of his *senties*. His forearms were circled with iridescent spirals, carved from the giant rainbow snail shells.

They then dressed him in a long robe made from a transparent material, light and flowing like feather clouds during the green season.

Kiris gave him a critical once-over and nodded, obviously satisfied with the results of his team's work.

"Her Majesty awaits," Kiris declared.

Two of the attendants dramatically flung the doors open between his and his wife's bedrooms.

Amira rose from the edge of her nest. She closed her long silk robe in grass-green, concealing the thin white nightgown she was wearing underneath.

Her unbound, dark hair streamed in thick waves down her shoulders. Without the veil over her face, he could see every single one of her beloved features. He wished to kiss each of them, too.

With a brief nod to Kiris, he crossed the threshold into her bedroom and shut the doors behind him. "I'll take it from here."

His wife gave him a long look, then slowly slid it down his body.

"You look...nice." A soft, tantalizing blush colored her cheeks. She wetted her lips with her pink, delicate tongue as if about to take a bite of a dessert. If the dessert was him, he was all for being eaten.

He chuckled at her loss of words. Clearly, the sight of him was breathtaking.

"Just *nice?*" He raised a brow ridge. "I believe Kiris and his people were going for 'alluring and enchanting' for my look tonight. They aimed to make me as enticing to you as possible."

She took a step toward him, then another. Slowly. He knew her hesitation didn't come from fear. She was taking her time, savoring every moment of this night. He knew it, because he felt the same way, too.

"Well." She came closer. "They succeeded. I am *enticed*."

"Is it the robe?" He tilted his head. Mischief bubbled in his chest, adding to his excitement. "It displays my best features ever so splendidly, doesn't it?" He adjusted the see-through material on his hips, turning to show her his backside then his front again. "Or is it the oils they've bathed me in?" He waved his hands in front of his chest. "They've used at least twelve kinds, I think. There's no way to tell what flavors they all are now."

She giggled at his antics. Reaching out with a finger, she stroked his nipple through the thin robe. His cock jerked to attention, as if connected by a string to the tip of her little finger.

"No nipple clips, I see?" She pouted with a teasing glint in her dark eyes. "I was kind of hoping they'd put them on you."

"Nipple clamps? You want those?" He blinked in surprise. His little sweet pea never ceased to amaze him. "I'll wear them if you will," he quipped.

She bit her lip, the expression in her eyes heating.

"I've been curious how they work. And with you, I wouldn't mind trying." She kept circling his nipple through his robe. The light caress ignited sparks of pleasure throughout his body. His cock swelled rock-hard—one touch was all it took with her.

He slid his gaze down to her chest where her hard nipples pushed against the silk of her robe. Imagining them decorated with clamps sent another rush of heat to his groin.

"There are many toys and trimmings..." He licked his lips. "And with the right person, all of them can be fun."

His hands fisted at his sides. He struggled to remain in control of his own body when hers was so close. A *sentie* slipped her way, as if on its own. Its mouth open, it clamped on to the tip of her breast.

She gasped softly. Her eyes opened wider, her breathing speeding up as she swayed his way.

The most beautiful woman he had ever met.

Emotions overtook him. She was his love, his wife, and his entire life.

"Come here, my queen." He grabbed her, making her squeak as he carried her to the royal nest.

He lowered her into the soft bedding but didn't let go. His arms wrapped around her, he lay next to her and placed his head on her chest. His face cushioned by her breasts, her warm scent enveloped him.

Love and comfort.

Peace.

All the wonderful things he'd only felt so deeply when in Amira's arms.

He closed his eyes, breathing her in. Oh, he would make tender love to her tonight. Then he'd fuck her hard, too. He'd make her scream his name quite a few times before the night was over. But right now, he wanted to enjoy the moment of simply being close to her.

She sensed his mood. Of course she did. She was a part of him. Gently running her fingers between his *senties*, she stroked his head, his neck, then his back. Her touch sent ripples of pleasure along his skin.

"Will you stay the night, Kyllen?" she asked, her voice like the sweetest music floating over him.

He lifted his head.

"I will. Tonight and every night."

He'd always enjoyed sleeping next to her, and he knew she loved that too. Why would they ever be apart? Just because they now had more rooms than they knew what to do with?

"You can use the other bedroom as an extra closet or something," he suggested.

"A nursery?" she blurted out, then shut her mouth quickly.

He chuckled. Children hadn't really entered his mind yet. But now that she'd mentioned it, he found he wasn't opposed to the idea of having them sooner rather than later. Children were rare and always wished for by fae. His chances of fathering one with a human wife were higher, according to what he'd heard.

"Well. Shall we start working on producing the residents for the nursery, then?" He slid her robe aside then lowered the neckline of her nightgown to expose her left breast. The sight of her hard, perky nipple made his mouth water and his cock twitch.

He dragged his tongue over the tip of her breast, savoring the taste of her skin, then rolled the hard bud between his teeth. His fang tugged at her tender flesh. Her moan broke with a gasp in response.

She gripped the back of his head, arching her spine to keep him at her breast.

Humming a groan, he wrapped some of his *senties* around her wrist. With one *sentie*, he reached under her nightshirt, searching for her other nipple. Finding it, he clamped the mouth of the *sentie* to it.

The taste of her intensified. Her scent teased his senses. She whimpered, writhing under him. The spice of her arousal flavored both her scent and her taste, heady and intoxicating.

Hooking her leg over his side, she rocked her hips into him. Her hot, slick core pressed against the ridge of his erection as she rubbed herself against him.

Oh, she was ready, so ready for him.

"Kyllen... Oh, God," she moaned. "More."

He smiled, lifting his head.

"More?" He gripped her hip, keeping her in place.

"Don't you tease me, Kyllen. I'm your queen. I can order you, you know." She was so deliciously adorable in her frustration.

"Oh, is that how it's going to be, *Your Majesty?*" He sat back on his haunches.

She propped herself on her arms, glaring at him in challenge.

Thrill rushed through his chest and straight down to his groin. His little wife proved delightfully exciting.

He met her stare. "Well, my sweet pea. Tonight, I feel like giving orders to *you*. So, lift your nightshirt and spread your legs. Instead of a throne, you'll be sitting on my face for the next little while."

He freed her from her robe, then hiked up the skirt of her nightdress.

"Oh," she exhaled as he yanked her knees open and dove between her legs.

Desire raged through him, hot and desperate. He dipped his tongue inside her, then lapped greedily, unable to get enough of her taste.

She moaned, riding his tongue.

Grabbing her hips, he flipped them over, rolling to his back and dragging her over his face.

She gasped, her knees shaking as he wound his *senties* around her thighs, slid them along her tender flesh, tasting her with their tongues and his own. Opening the mouth of one, he clamped it around the sensitive bud at the apex of her thighs, nibbling on it.

"So good..." she exhaled with a whimper. "Kyllen, my darling... I love you so—"

He knew she loved him. He felt every emotion raging through her body. Her lust rolled over him in swells, radiating through him. He was so hard, he could probably hammer nails with his erection. But he was determined to bring her to a climax first.

Her voice cut off. Her breathing halted. She bucked her hips against his mouth. Her orgasm crested, and she fell over the edge.

It was delightful.

He felt every spasm of her pleasure as it echoed through him. And he needed more. Grabbing her hips tighter, he slid her down along his body, then impaled her on his cock in one smooth movement. He fit in snugly, but she was so hot and slick inside, he moved easily.

She clawed at his shoulders, whimpering in pleasure. The last tremors of her orgasm still rocked through her when his climax already teased him. He thrust harder, chasing it.

The orgasm erupted through him. For one blinding moment, the world fell away. Only one thin, shimmering thread tethered him to life —his bond with Amira. He growled, pumping his release into her, then dropped to his side next to her. Spent.

She threw her arms around his neck, panting. "I've no idea how I survive this with you... Every time. Is sex always like this? Mind-blowing, body-shattering, heart... Oh, I have no words to describe it."

He smiled in satisfaction. She had described it well enough. His muscles still shook as he rose on an elbow at her side.

"No, not always. Sex has never been like this for me before you." He kissed her shoulder, then her neck, moving up to her mouth. "It never could be like this with anyone else, my love. Because we are two parts of a whole, coming together. You and I."

Epilogue

ELEVEN YEARS LATER

AMIRA

"Look, Mama!" Radax, my little boy, lunged forward. Slicing through the air with his wooden sword, he nicked the skin on his father's wrist.

"Aw!" Kyllen lurched back with a severely exaggerated howl of pain. "You got me! The Great Serpent released my spirit. And…" He tossed aside his own wooden weapon and chased his son. "My spirit is going to get you now!"

Dropping his sword, Radax dashed across the clearing inside the Loop Bend of the Isafaris River. Narrow side streams crisscrossed the ground. But our son leaped over them, evading his father's hands that grabbed for him. Kyllen's shouts of fake disappointment at failing to catch his son and Radax's happy giggles filled the warm air of this peaceful afternoon.

I laughed, watching them from my chair on the dry patch of the riverbank.

Lily, our five-month-old baby girl, calmly sucked at my breast. Her little eyelids, delicate like lily petals, fluttered closed as she let go of my nipple, falling asleep. I gently placed her in the rocking crib at my side, then laced up the front of my dress.

It was a balmy afternoon at the very end of the golden season. The yellow leaves on the trees had been slowly regaining their fresh green color. Another week, and the entire Kingdom of Lorsan would be dressed in the vibrant green of summer again.

I touched Lily's crib. The gorgonian magic coursed through my fingers, setting the mechanism of the crib into motion. A thin but sturdy canopy rose over my baby, shielding her from the breeze.

Ancient legends called love "the human magic," and it certainly held power. I wasn't born as Kyllen's bonded mate, but through my love for him, I had become one. Through our bond, I could also use his magic whenever I wished.

Making sure Lily was warm and comfortable, I drew my shawl around my shoulders. The breeze from the river was still brisk at times. Though Kyllen had already shed his shirt. He must be warm enough from chasing our little Radax.

A child of a fae and a human was always a fae. Radax was every bit like his dad. He had the same bronze-and-green *senties*. They flared in a wild, tangled halo around his head as he ran, laughing. Leaping over yet another narrow creek, he tore off his lime-green tunic over his head.

"Radax!" I took a step away from the crib. "It's still too cold to run around naked."

"But Father is doing it." The little rascal pointed at his dad. "And we aren't naked. We have our pants on."

"Thank God for *that*," I muttered, shaking my head.

Kyllen just laughed. Sneaking behind his son, he grabbed the kicking, giggling boy and spun him around. "Got you!"

From the corner of my eye, I caught a boat approaching the Bend from down the stream. It appeared to be heading in the direction of the royal palace just up the river.

Iven, one of my guards, gestured to Hapon, one of Kyllen's men. Together they jogged down the riverbank to the water to meet the boat.

Carrying Radax over his shoulder, Kyllen glanced at the approaching boat, too—always alert.

As King Consort, he'd been deeply involved in all state matters. As my husband, he had been my rock to lean on, my support, my shoulder to cry on whenever I felt overwhelmed or frustrated. Shrewd, clever, and outgoing, Kyllen had proven incredibly resourceful at getting any information I ever needed. I couldn't have done it without my king.

Being a ruler was not about brawn or even magic. It was about taking care of my people. It required a lot of knowledge, honed diplomacy skills, and an infinite amount of patience. Some of that I already had. The rest, I was determined to obtain and improve. Learning was a long process—a lifelong one.

King Zeldren had loved a good game, and I often wondered if by giving me his crown, he had tossed another game piece onto the board, to watch me either sink or swim for his amusement from the afterlife. Wherever he was now, though, I hoped he wasn't disappointed. For the eleven years that I'd been the queen, the Kingdom of Lorsan had been thriving.

The boat turned toward the riverbank, with the clear intention to land in the clearing.

Kyllen gently set Radax back on the ground and stepped in front of the boy.

I turned to the royal hag, who was picking flower buds from a bush nearby. "Grandmother? Would you keep an eye on the princess, please?"

The hag nodded, the dark hood over her face swayed. Looking frail and weak, the woman was more powerful than any man.

Kyllen had brought her from a small village on the Olathana border the year he and I got married. He said she'd saved his life once. Ever since, the hag had been living in the palace with us. She tended to injuries, brewed potions, cast wards when needed, asking for nothing but lodging and respect in return.

I trusted her to keep Lily safe while I turned my attention to the boat. Hapon appeared to speak to one of the gorgonian crew on it. He then headed up the slope toward me.

"Your Majesty, the boat is from the village of Egrus. It's on the border with Sarnala."

Lorsan had been enjoying a long period of peace with the kingdom of werewolves. Together, we had constructed enough levees to ensure passable trading routes through many parts of Lorsan, and the trade between our two kingdoms had flourished ever since.

The negotiations with other kingdoms had gone smoother, since the fae of every kind could look the ruler of Lorsan in the eye. Despite being able to use gorgonian magic and gaining an expanded lifespan, I remained a human. I had no *senties* and couldn't kill with a look.

Kyllen jogged to my side. "What do they want?"

"They caught a werewolf," Hapon said.

I frowned. That could cause complications to my peace treaty with Sarnala. "Tell them to release him."

"He ran away."

Kyllen huffed a laugh. "So. Why is it important, then?"

"The werewolf was in his beast form." Iven climbed up the bank to us. "Unchanged for days."

One of the villagers from the boat accompanied Iven. He carried a bundle wrapped in a homespun piece of cloth.

"Greetings to the glorious Queen of Lorsan." The villager, a handsome man with dark senties and serene gray eyes, bowed to me.

"Greetings." I inclined my head. "Tell me, how is it possible for a werewolf to retain his beast form past the night of a full moon?"

Even Madame—the goddess that she was—couldn't make Lero shift completely. All she had managed was to keep him in mid-shift for some time.

The man shook his head.

"Normally, it's not possible, Your Majesty. The Moon guides werewolves, changing them to beasts for one night a month only. But there have been a few of those abominations lately, stuck in their beast form. They can't speak. However, some have been able to communicate through other means. They conveyed that they had come from the human world."

My old world.

It had become as distant as a long-forgotten dream to me. Just a random tendril of nostalgia would drift into my heart every now and then. Or a few shadowy shreds of a nightmare would remain with me in the morning. But the memories of the man who'd raised me never left. I promised Radax to always remember him. And I always would.

"We sent inquiries to Sarnala towns across the border, Your Majesty," the villager continued. "But they are just as confused about these beasts as we are."

Why would a group of werewolves arrive from the human world?

The only werewolf I knew in my old world was Lero.

"You said you've been able to communicate with some of the beasts who don't shift. Did you learn their names?" I asked.

"We've learned only one name so far. Nerkan."

Breath caught in my throat. Nerkan was one of Madame's *bracks*, not a werewolf. I turned to Kyllen, then back to the villager.

"It couldn't be..."

As hard as I'd tried to escape my past, it caught up with me in one sweeping wave of darkness.

There had always been reports of *bracks* sightings here and there. Since timelines crossed and looped when moving from one world to the other, the *bracks* had come to Nerifir for supplies for Madame's menagerie at all times throughout the history of Nerifir. The one thing they had been sourcing in Lorsan the most had been our lily honey that Madame liked in her tea.

"Are you sure Nerkan was a werewolf, not a *brack?*" I asked the villager.

"Yes, Your Majesty. He had fur and a tail. He looked nothing like a *brack*."

Weird. Of course, there could be more than one Nerkan between the two worlds, but the coincidence was just too unsettling.

"Where is he now? Do you know?"

The man twisted the bundle in his hands. "We don't know, Your Majesty. He ran away toward Sarnala, and we haven't heard from him since."

I hoped it was a good thing.

"What are your concerns?" Kyllen stepped in. "Are you worried the beast will attack your village?"

"He might, though that's not why I'm here." The man hurriedly unwrapped the bundle in his hands, then thrust a silver-colored plaque my way. "I should've mentioned this first."

Kyllen quickly stretched his arm in a protective gesture between the man and me.

The villager turned the plaque in his hands, visibly hesitating. "It has your name on it, Queen Amira, but no one can read the rest."

Kyllen took the silver object from the villager and inspected it closely. Satisfied it carried no harm, he passed it to me.

"Is it in English?" he asked.

Once we'd crossed back to Nerifir, Kyllen had lost his ability to read or speak English. I, however, had gained the ability to speak the fae language in addition to English, just like he used to be able to speak both, back in my world.

I took the plaque from him.

"Amira" was engraved in large letters at the top, just over the picture of a cupcake. All horizontal lines of the letters were straight, typical for writing in Sarnala. In Lorsan, most of them would've been wavy. Both styles, however, were similar enough for the people of both kingdoms to read.

The rest of the writing was in the language that did not come from Nerifir.

"You're right, my love. It's English..." I skimmed the text all the way to the signature below.

"Radax."

My knees gave in, and I stumbled back to my chair. Emotion gripped my throat as I re-read the writing, taking in every word. I couldn't say a thing, reading silently.

"What does it say, sweet pea?" Kyllen crouched at my side, holding onto the armrest of my chair.

I swallowed the lump in my throat before drawing a long breath in.

"It's from Radax."

"From me?" My son poked his head from around his dad's arm.

"No, my sweet boy," I smiled through the shimmering film of tears obscuring my vision. "It's from the man whose name you have. The one who saved my life and raised me. Who had been my only family growing up. And whom I left behind..."

The man I had shot, leaving him bleeding on the floor of the truck trailer. Not knowing anything about his fate had been like a needle buried in my chest all this time.

Kyllen took my free hand and squeezed it gently. "What did he write?"

I took a few more deep breaths before feeling strong enough to continue.

"Ghata is gone. Her *bracks* are free, including Radax." I turned to meet his eyes. "She is dead, Kyllen. She won't torture anyone ever again."

His chest rose with a heavy breath. His shoulders straightened as if a weight had dropped from them. I felt so much lighter at heart, too.

I placed the plaque into my lap and traced the outline of the cupcake engraved on it.

"He sends me a picture of the cupcake for all the birthdays of mine he has missed and for all those he will be missing." I swallowed hard again. Somewhere out there in another world, in the timeline that twisted, curved, and looped compared to ours, Radax was living a happy life, the life he had earned. "He is free. At last. And he met someone, a human woman. They're in love."

Tears overflowed, rolling down my cheeks.

Kyllen took my face in his hands, wiping my tears with his thumbs. "Looks like he got his Happily Ever After."

"He did." I sniffled. "And he so, so deserved it." I wiped my eyes with the end of my shawl. "These are happy tears, my darling. Very happy tears."

He kissed my face, and I buried it in his chest. His warm, familiar scent felt more comforting than ever.

"Do you want to write him back? To let him know you have your own Happily Ever After, too." He arched a brow ridge dramatically. "You do have it, don't you?"

"Yes, I do," I smiled through tears. "You are my Prince Charming."

"King," he corrected, lifting a finger for emphasis. "Not just a prince, sweetheart. Though, admittedly, I am a charming one."

And just like that, my tears dried up. I laughed, shaking my head. He grinned, happy that he'd managed to cheer me up.

"How would I write to Radax, though?" I asked. A regular correspondence wasn't possible between the worlds.

Kyllen rubbed the back of his neck. "Ghata may be gone at some point and time. But the *bracks* who have been crossing over would continue to do so for a while. They would just be coming from the earlier times, from when Ghata was still well and alive, running her menagerie and obtaining the supplies for it."

He was right. The *bracks* could still be coming from a more distant past into our future. And when they left here, Ghata would pull them to her across dimensions, back into the time of the menagerie.

"I will need to catch a *brack* and make him deliver a message..." I thought out loud. "No, it has to be something that doesn't look like it contains a message but appears to have some value. So Ghata would keep it to display it in her menagerie until Radax can open and read it."

Kyllen stirred enthusiastically. "I'll help you make it. It could be a communication box, with the message recorded in your voice for Radax to recognize you. We can commission Wuveus, the master who created the grand clock in the main hall of the palace, to help with the design."

"A communication box?" The words triggered my memory.

In her menagerie, Ghata had displayed something she called "a communication device from the Wetlands of Lorsan." And now I wondered if it had been my message box all along.

"I think I know how I want it to look," I said. "And I'll ask you to lock it so that no one but Radax could ever open it. Will that be possible?" I held out the tablet with Radax's engraving. "Can you do that by using this?"

My husband gave me one of his cocky grins that always made me weak in my knees.

"Can I?" He wiggled his shapely eyebrow ridges. "By now you should know, my queen, that when it comes to fulfilling your desires, nothing is impossible for me."

I leaned over to kiss the tip of his nose. "Well, you go ahead then, my magnificent. Make it happen. Meanwhile." I rose to my feet and waved to one of the guards nearby to come closer. "Go find Councilor Delahon, please. I need to make a kingdom-wide announcement when we return to the palace."

The guard left with my order, and I turned back to Kyllen again.

"I want the next *brack* who crosses into Lorsan captured and brought to the palace. I'll tell him I have a gift for his goddess and as much lily honey as he can carry for her."

Wrapping his arms around me, Kyllen drew me to him. "If they deliver the box in the time while you're still at the menagerie, would you like me to make the lock so you could open it too, not just Radax? Would you like to have known your fate, back before you met me?"

I took a moment to think about that.

"No." I shook my head. "I don't want to change anything in the past because I can't risk inadvertently changing our future." Now that I knew Radax was happy and free, I didn't dare spoil it for him, either. "We all suffered for our happiness, my love. We earned it. Now, I wouldn't change a thing."

He searched my eyes. "Are you happy, my sweet pea?"

Our son ran to us, slamming against us and hugging our legs.

I laughed, placing one hand on his slim shoulder while keeping the other arm wrapped around my husband's neck.

"I'm happy, Kyllen. Happier than I've ever thought I could be."

Thank You for Reading

If you're not ready to say goodbye to Kyllen and Amira, I have a short story sequel, Serpent's Promise.
It's available on my Patreon on all tiers:

https://www.patreon.com/posts/sequel-to-touch-80389319?utm_medium=clipboard_copy&utm_source=copyLink&utm_campaign=postshare_creator&utm_content=join_link

If you enjoyed the Serpent's Touch duet, you may also like Madame Tan's Freakshow trilogy which is set in the same world, with stories of Radax, Lero, and Zeph.

Or flip the page to read the excerpt of Fire in Stone, the next duet from this world. It's the story of Elex, the gargoyle, who is currently frozen as a dragon-man statue in Madame's menagerie.

Fire in Stone

CHAPTER 1

"Sorry, Amber. You know I would let you stay. At least for another month, maybe. But Jonah..." Michelle scrunched her lovely face into a pained expression. "You know he's all about business."

"I know." I nodded, wrapping my cardigan tightly around myself.

The Georgia air felt fresh this March morning. Today, however, the chill running through my body had little to do with the weather. I was being evicted from the place I'd called home for almost a year now.

Michelle and I had been getting along great since the day I'd moved into their basement apartment a year ago. Technically, however, the house belonged to Jonah, her fiancé. And he was "all about business." His business as a landlord was to collect rent. As his tenant, I hadn't paid rent for a second month in a row. I had nothing but change in my pocket, a fat, round zero in my bank account, and no means to replenish that any time soon.

Less than an hour ago, I'd found out I no longer had a job. The real estate office where I'd worked for a few months now closed unexpectedly. I got no notice, other than two of my paychecks had been delayed.

One was cut short. And now, it looked like the last one wouldn't be paid at all. Which sucked. A lot.

I was told I should file a claim. When my employer's assets were liquidated, I might get some of my unpaid wages back. Maybe. Eventually. Except that the rent was due right now. I'd lived paycheck to paycheck. Missing one literally put me on the street.

I wished I could just turn around and leave. But where would I go? I had no one.

"Michelle, can I at least talk to Jonah? Please. I'll start looking for another job, right away—"

She pressed her lips together, tenting her eyebrows with pity.

"Well... He's not around at the moment."

His truck stood in the driveway next to my beat-up car. The light was still on in their second-floor bedroom, despite it being midmorning.

I ran a trembling hand through the stubble of my undershave on the left side of my head. "He just wants me out. He's not interested in talking, is he?"

Michelle heaved a sigh, folding her arms over her ample bosom. "Well, Jonah is a businessman..."

"He has another tenant for the basement, doesn't he?" I took a guess.

She shifted uncomfortably, avoiding my eyes.

"A buddy of his is moving to town," she finally confessed.

Coming to the town of Creek Bent had meant a new start for me. And for several months, it'd felt like I was going to make it. For once in my twenty-five years, I had an honest job and a place to live that I paid for, all on my own. I'd even started taking college classes after work at night. I'd thought I had finally done it—I'd built a life for myself. I'd gotten the taste of some stability and safety. And it truly sucked to give it all up again.

Michelle shifted her weight to another foot. Her leather sandals displayed her sparkly toenails, painted with the same pearly pink polish as mine. We'd painted them together, right here on Jonah's porch, last week. Back when I still believed I had a job, a place to live, and a friend.

She shrugged uncomfortably. "Amber, you know Creek Bent is small. Things have been hard around here, with the economy being the way it is and stuff. But you'll find something somewhere. Maybe in Atlanta? Things always seem to be better in a city."

"Right." The hollowness in my stomach wasn't just from the missed breakfast. Dread pressed heavily on my chest.

"I'll help you pack," Michelle offered, her voice lifting.

Packing didn't take me long. The basement came fully furnished. All my belongings easily fit in two suitcases and a couple of boxes, all of which I shoved into the back of my car.

After driving just around the corner from my old place, I pulled into the parking lot of the only grocery store in town and turned the engine off. There was no need to burn gas if I had no plan.

Dropping my forehead on my forearms folded over the steering wheel, I blew out a breath.

Now what?

I was behind on my car payments. My cell phone bill was due any day now. All of that was supposed to be taken care of by the money I'd thought I'd be getting any minute. Instead, I lost my job. And now, there was no money coming from anywhere.

Michelle was right about one thing, there was nothing waiting for me in Creek Bent. I had to try my luck elsewhere. Only with a tank just half-full of gas, that "elsewhere" couldn't be very far away.

I needed a plan, a destination. I had to find a new place to live, and even more urgently—something to eat. Soon. My stomach rumbled. I usually had toast and coffee at the office in the morning. Today, I had no chance to have anything at all.

Thoughts were spinning in my head like a twister. Most were filled with panic.

How long before I lose my car?

My phone?

Before I have to return to the streets again?

Before hunger will force me to beg and steal?

Again...

I drew in a long breath and tried to focus on one thought at a time.

The situation was bad. But I'd been through worse. I just really didn't want to go back to that *worse* again...

I never met my father and didn't remember my mother. She'd left me with my grandma when I was a baby and never came back. Grandma was the one who raised me. Thanks to her, I had a good childhood with school, friends, Sunday dinners, birthday celebrations, and other nice things that children get when they have adults who love them.

Grandma passed away when I'd just turned sixteen. With no other living or known relatives, I ended up with one foster family, then another, then another one, in less than six months. None of them were like my grandma. Not even close. The last couple were especially nasty, and the two teenage boys in their care seemed outright dangerous. That was when I ran. I'd figured I'd be better off on my own.

Except that at sixteen, I was too naïve to realize how much nastier the outside world could be to a young girl living on the streets. It hadn't been pretty. And the man who had finally saved me from that life was no knight in shiny armor.

Chris was older than me by over a decade. He had a shady reputation and quickly drew me into his life of crime. When I'd finally realized that was not the future I wished for myself, it had taken everything I had to break free.

I rubbed my nose, fingering the hoop piercing in my left nostril—the only piercing I'd kept besides the earrings, after switching to a "cleaner," more professional look for the job as a receptionist at the real estate office last year.

I'd worked hard to earn an honest living. I'd done it for almost a year. And I could do it again, dammit. I still had my phone and enough gas to drive for a few hours. My car needed some work, but hopefully, it would last long enough for me to find a new place to settle down.

I took my phone out. The screen flicked to life. The service was good here—all bars.

Little blessings.

If I found a few suitable job postings in the area, I could arrange for some interviews as soon as possible. Except that it took me less than a few minutes of searching to realize how horribly right Michelle had been about the poor state of the economy. Wanted ads were few and far between. And judging by the wages advertised, I'd need at least three of these jobs to make ends meet, which also meant there would be no college classes for me any time soon.

The red circle with number one was glowing over my text messaging icon. I'd been ignoring it for a day now, since it was from Chris.

He and I were done. I'd told him that the last time I saw him back in January when he took me for a "romantic" country drive on his fancy motorbike. He'd said he wanted me back, promising that things would be different between us—better. But there was nothing he could do or say that would make me change my mind.

Why did I not delete his message, then? I had no idea.

I clicked on it now, fully intending to get rid of it. The number with way too many zeros to ignore jumped at me from the screen.

"$200,000..."

Chris clearly knew how to get people's attention. My thumb hovering over the screen, I read the rest of the message.

"Long time no see, baby girl. I've got a job for you. Quick and easy. Pays $200,000 cash."

The zeros danced in front of my eyes. I shouldn't be thinking about what that money could mean for me, but I did think. It meant food in my stomach, a roof over my head, a finished college degree, a better job...

A new life.

All I had to do was to take a step back for this one last job, to dive into the muddy swamp of my past once again, before I could leave it all behind for good and move forward even faster than before.

He didn't put in the message what the job entailed. But knowing Chris, it was definitely something illegal. I'd worked for him for years and had done many things I wasn't proud of. I'd sworn I was done with all of that.

But maybe, at the very least, I could find out what he wanted. I could always say no, couldn't I?

I quickly typed, *"What job?"* and hit *"send"* before giving myself a chance to overthink it.

The reply came almost immediately.

"I'll see you at the Chicken Wing in twenty. My treat."

Chicken Wing was a diner in the town thirty minutes from here. I had enough gas to get there and would at least get a breakfast out of this. But a heavy feeling pressed down on my chest when I started the car and pulled out of the parking lot.

"Hello, beautiful." A crooked smirk stretched across Chris's face in the way I used to find irresistibly attractive.

At first glance, he didn't appear to have changed at all. He wore one of his usual band t-shirts, a trendy leather jacket, and a pair of designer sunglasses. Only when I took the seat across the table from him, and he removed his sunglasses could I see more lines around his eyes. Even in the couple of months since I last saw him, the bags under his eyes had grown heavier and the shadows deeper.

Chris was eleven years older than me, and time, aided by his many bad habits, were slowly destroying the good looks he was born with.

When I first met him, I was seventeen. It happened in a very similar diner. A teenage runaway, I hadn't eaten for days and had snuck in, lured by the smell of fried food.

At that time, I'd survived mostly on what I could shoplift. Chris had bought me lunch. By the time I'd finished wolfing it down, he'd completely stolen my heart. For the seventeen-year-old me, he seemed so mature, confident, and in control.

I hated how similar my current circumstances were to those that had brought us together eight years ago. I hated that I still hoped Chris would feed me.

"Hi, Chris." I leaned back in the fake leather seat of the booth, hoping my empty stomach wouldn't make any loud noises in this place filled with delicious breakfast smells.

He passed me the menu, and I had no willpower to refuse it.

"It's real nice to see you, baby girl." He kept his pale blue eyes on me. Years ago, I'd found the contrast between his light eye color and his dark stubble alluring.

As a teenager, I'd seen Chris as my savior. By the time I'd met him, I'd been on the streets for months, fighting hunger, homelessness, and a lot of assholes who were always ready to take advantage of a lonely girl who had nothing and no one.

Chris had fed me and—at the beginning, at least—hadn't asked for anything in return. He'd waited for three whole weeks before making any sexual advances on me. Then one day, he'd pumped me with some cheap wine, and I'd practically climbed into his lap myself, begging him to make love to me.

I was seventeen. He was twenty-eight. Back then, I thought we were in love. Now I knew better. That night, I was underage, drunk, and desperate for affection, and he was a groomer, taking advantage of my naïveté and situation.

Deep inside, however, some long-torn string still tugged at my heart when he covered my hand with his and said in that husky voice of his, "You ain't looking too good, baby girl. Things must've been hard."

"I'll manage." I jerked my hand away.

"I know you will. You're a smart cookie. Always were." He tilted his head, watching me as the waitress brought our food.

I tried to hold back, faking not being hungry, pretending I didn't need his charity. As if I was doing him a favor by joining him for a meal, not the other way around. Gingerly, I picked up a strip of bacon off my plate and...finished it in three huge, hungry bites.

Dammit, it tasted so good! I grabbed another one right away, forgetting all about playing it cool.

Chris watched me with a knowing smile.

"I wish you'd let me take care of you, Amber, like in the good ol' days," he drawled.

The food stuck in my throat at the memories of those "good old days."

It hadn't been all bad. I'd been fed. At some point, I'd even thought I was loved. But I hadn't been free. For years, I'd belonged to Chris—body and soul. He had to approve everything from the clothes I'd worn, to the friends I'd had. We had sex whenever *he* wanted and only the way *he* wanted it. I had no say in what I ate or what I did. Until recently, I'd had only a vague idea about what kind of person I even was.

Leaving him was the hardest thing I'd done, but there was no coming back.

"I no longer need to be taken care of, Chris," I said around a mouthful of egg, toast, and bacon.

With that ever-present smirk of his, he ripped open a packet of sugar, dumped its contents into my cup of coffee, then added some cream, just the way I used to drink it. I'd switched to milk instead of cream recently, but Chris wouldn't know that, of course.

"Rumor has it that realtor's business you worked for went belly up." He slowly stirred the coffee for me.

The rumor couldn't be more than a few hours old, yet somehow it had reached Chris already. I said nothing, keeping my eyes on my plate while eating.

"It's a good thing, you know. You don't need that shitty office job, anyway." He slid the coffee mug my way.

Clearly, he was steering the conversation to whatever it was he wished me to do for him in exchange for two hundred thousand dollars.

I took a long drink of coffee, my first one that day. It tasted divine, even with cream. I closed my eyes, savoring every drop.

"It was just a job," I said, putting the mug down. "I'll get another one."

He lifted an eyebrow in a skeptical expression.

"Might not be that easy. There isn't that much work nowadays."

He was right, which made irritation flare in me. Even the warm weight of the food in my belly didn't soothe it.

"What do you know about the job market?" I snapped. "You never worked a day in your life."

"I'm a businessman," he said, as smoothly as ever. "I need to know things like that, even if I don't work for others."

Fighting the irritation, I silently finished my breakfast. The fuller my belly got, the more I wondered why I'd ever agreed to meet with this man. Nothing good had ever come from my being with him. Chris's way of life had always been crime and violence, and he'd dragged me into it headfirst.

"I shouldn't have come." I put my fork onto the now empty plate. "Thanks for breakfast, though. I really appreciate it."

He quickly placed his hand on top of mine again. "Aw, don't leave yet. I've missed you—"

"Don't." I jerked my head with a huff, having no patience for the softness in his voice or the playful squeeze of his hand.

Only he wouldn't listen. He never did. His fingers tightened around my hand.

"You know I never wanted it to end between us, Amber. I'd take you back in a heartbeat. To me, you'll always be my baby girl."

The sound of his old nickname for me was grinding on my nerves.

"Stop it. Chris. We're done. I'm not coming back, and you know it."

He let go of my hand and leaned back against the squeaky pleather of the booth seat. The look in his pale eyes hardened.

"Fine. Keep playing your emancipation game for a bit longer if you wish," he said, as if indulging a child in their tantrum.

An unpleasant feeling scraped inside me. I thought I'd been strong by leaving Chris, but he obviously believed he had *allowed* me to stray for a while. He sounded confident he could stop my "game" at any time.

"All I need from you right now is to do this one job for me," he said.

I shook my head, running my hand through the shoulder-length hair on my right.

"I—"

He raised a finger, not letting me finish.

"It's easy money, Amber. The job is perfect for you." He took my hand from the table again, playing with my fingers. "There is magic in these little hands of yours. It's a shame to have a talent like that go to waste."

Flattery would get him nowhere. But curiosity got the best of me. I wasn't interested in the job, but there was no harm in asking about it, was there?

"What do you need to have done?" I kept my tone of voice neutral.

His features relaxed, as if I'd agreed already.

"I want you to get something for me. In and out. Like I said. Easy-peasy."

I took my hand from him. "And what do you want me to steal?"

"*To take,*" he corrected. "Clean and quiet. Like I know you can do."

"What do you want me *to take?*"

"A statue," he said, casually flicking his wrist.

"Is it like a piece of art or something?" I didn't peg Chris as a lover of fine art. However, if the piece had a market value, he'd certainly appreciate it.

"Something like that. The statue is with the traveling menagerie, the one I took you to see in January, remember?"

Memories of the country fair sideshow rushed over me. The striped canvas tents had been filled with fantastic animals that didn't exist in our world yet looked so real. I'd never seen anything like that either before or after that visit to the fair.

I'd had a few days off at work that week. In a moment of weakness, I'd agreed to let Chris take me to the fair happening nearby. Visiting it had been fun. Having Chris as my travel companion had been more intense than ever. It had reminded me how trapped he'd made me feel.

On the way out of town in a parking lot of a grocery store, I'd spotted the girl who sold tickets for the menagerie. She seemed shy, even skittish when I tried to speak with her. But I imagined she must lead the most exciting life—traveling with the menagerie, never belonging to any place or any man. Free. Just how I longed to be.

I sighed through the echo of all those emotions resonating through my chest. "Yes. I remember."

Chris shifted closer in his seat.

"So." Eagerness slipped into his voice. "The menagerie is in Europe now. In Germany. They're leaving Munich soon. All their stuff will be shipped out in a few days. The statue will be in transit, with minimal security. That's when it'll be the best time to get it."

I shook my head. "I told you, I'm not doing this shit again."

He took both my hands in his. "Look. It's just taking a piece of useless rock from one rich asshole and selling it to another. Your moral sensitivities don't have to be offended here. It's not like you're stealing from a museum or some starving orphans."

"Well, thanks for that." I rolled my eyes.

"I'm telling you, some rich guy wants this stupid statue that someone else has, and he's willing to pay good cash for it. It'd be dumb to miss out on a chance like this."

It was a lot of money. And that would be just my share. Chris must be in to pocket at least as much, maybe more. He wouldn't tell me the actual number if I asked, but I knew he always looked after his interests first.

"What is so special about this statue? Why does the buyer want it?"

"Fuck if I know. Maybe it's an ego thing? He wants what he doesn't have. I don't care, and you shouldn't either. As long as he pays when we get him what he wants."

"*We?*" I clarified.

Chris faltered, glancing aside.

"Well, *you*. It's a one-man job." He gave me a teasing smile. "A one-*woman* job, I should say."

"So, you wouldn't be there?"

I hadn't done anything like that on my own before. My role in Chris's "business" had been largely a supporting one. I'd mostly helped with the planning of his heists and then with the disposing of whatever he and his thugs had stolen. I was good with forgery and with some aspects of money laundering. I could pick locks like no one's business. And I'd been a getaway driver on a few occasions. But I'd always worked as part of a team before, never on my own.

"So, where would *you* be while I'd be doing your dirty work for you?"

"The job is overseas," he said. "And I... Well, I can't board a plane for the time being."

I squinted at him, tilting my head in question.

Wincing under my stare, he rubbed the back of his neck, then scratched the dark stubble on his chin. "It's a long story. Let's just say I've had some trouble with the police that resulted in out-of-country travel restrictions. *Temporarily.*"

"I see."

"I'll take care of it. I always do. But the timing isn't the best. But hey..." He perked up. "You'll do fine on your own, Amber. You're a pro."

"Pro at stealing," I scoffed. "What an accomplishment."

He rolled back his shoulders. "Of course it is. There's some good money in what we do, baby girl. Much better than what that realtor dude was paying you. Cheap bastard."

So much was true. I would've had to work close to a decade in that realtor's office to earn the same amount Chris was offering me for a few days of my time.

"Two hundred thousand dollars," I said softly.

"That's right." He looked at me like a cat at a mouse clasped in his paws. "Plus, all expenses paid." Reaching inside his leather jacket, he produced a thick envelope and placed it on the table between us. "Three thousand euros, baby doll. To get you to Germany. A nice European vacation that pays for itself and then some."

I stared at the envelope stuffed with cash and tried not to think what it meant in terms of meals, warmth, and comfort.

"You deserve a break. That realtor asshole overworked and underpaid you," Chris scoffed.

Maybe. But with no education, no references, and with my sketchy past, I considered myself lucky to have that job. I'd felt so elated when I got the call that the position was mine. It'd been as if the door had finally opened to a life I'd only ever glimpsed from the outside—the normal, honest life I'd had no access to since my grandma's death.

For almost a year, I didn't have to invent lies when people asked me what I did for a living. I'd had a future ahead of me. I'd proudly told anyone who cared to listen about my work and my college plans. It'd felt like my past was firmly behind me.

Now, my past was sitting across the table from me again, with the familiar all-knowing smirk.

"No, Chris." I shoved the envelope back to him. The spark of excitement at the sensation of the thick stack of money under my palm flashed and went. "I'm done with this. Thanks for breakfast."

I got up from the table.

His eyes followed me with the dangerous glimmer of temper, the temper I knew way too well. But he remained in his seat.

"Suit yourself, baby girl." He leaned back, casually draping an arm over the back of the bench seat. "You know where to find me if you need me."

I prayed I never *needed* anything from this man, ever again. Leaving the diner, I closed its door firmly behind me.

With every step I took along the parking lot on my way to my car, however, the worry pressed harder and harder on my chest. All the panicky questions of earlier had returned. The one pulsing most anxiously in my brain was, *"Now what?"*

I was back at square one. Jobless and penniless. The only difference was the feeling of fullness in my stomach. But I knew it'd be empty and gnawing with hunger again way too soon.

The door of the diner opened and closed behind me. I forced my head not to turn in that direction, but I felt Chris's stare on my back.

He watched me. Waiting.

Putting as much confidence in my step as I could muster, I approached my car, opened the door, and slid into the driver's seat.

"I can figure it out," I kept saying again and again in my head, turning the key in the ignition. *"I don't need Chris or his money."*

The dead silence of the engine chilled me with dread. The damn car made no sound, no matter how many times I turned the key. I stopped trying, dropping my hands into my lap.

Fear—cold, paralyzing terror—spread through my limbs. Without the car, I truly had nothing. I couldn't even get to an interview, provided I somehow managed to get one.

Taking small, shallow breaths, I lifted my gaze. Through the windshield, I saw Chris. Leaning against his large, black motorbike, he was turned to me, his arms crossed over his chest. With his face hidden behind the glass of his helmet, I couldn't see his eyes, but he appeared to be waiting. My fire-red helmet conveniently lay on the seat next to him, as an invitation for me to join him.

Knowing Chris, he might have something to do with my engine not starting at this very moment. Though, my car was old enough to fail on its own, too.

At the end of the day, did it really matter how it happened? One thing was clear, it didn't take much to crush my life completely and turn my situation from bad to desperate.

I was tired. So tired of fighting every little thing that always went wrong while waiting for the other shoe to drop. Tired of constantly strategizing which of the bills piling up to pay first. Tired of not having a reliable roof over my head. And I was scared because I knew things would get worse, much, much worse now that I had no job *and* no car.

Chris might take a lion's share of the proceeds, but he always paid his people what he promised. At this point, two hundred thousand dollars was life-changing for me.

Maybe I needed to take that one step back to be able to move forward? One brief trip to the past to ensure my future?

I blew out a breath, taking a moment to gather my resolve.

I couldn't see his face, but I *felt* Chris smiling when I got out of the car and headed his way.

Available Now

More in the River of Mists

Joyless Kingdom

Somber Prince, book 1

Wingless Crow

Crownless King

Fire in Stone

Hearts on Fire

Serpent's Touch

Serpent's Claim

Madame Tan's Freakshow Trilogy

Call of Water

Madness of the Moon

Power of Rage

More by Marina Simcoe

SCIENCE-FICTION ROMANCE

My Holiday Tails

Married to Krampus

My Tiny Giant

My Birthday Getaway

New Year, New Planet

Mail Order Mom

My Pumpkin

What Makes an Alien a Dad?

Dark Anomaly Trilogy

Gravity

Power

Explosion

Stand Alone Novels

Experiment

Enduring (Valos Of Sonhadra)

About the Author

Marina Simcoe likes to write love stories with human heroines and non-human heroes who just can't live without them. She firmly believes that our contemporary world could always use a little bit of the extraordinary.

She has lots of fun exploring how her out-of-this-world characters with their own beliefs, values, and aspirations fit into our every-day life.

She lives in Canada with her very own extraordinary hero, their three little offspring, and a cat who is definitely out of this world.

facebook.com/MarinaSimcoeAuthor
twitter.com/MarinaSimcoe
instagram.com/marinasimcoeauthor
amazon.com/author/marinasimcoe
tiktok.com/@marina.simcoe
goodreads.com/MarinaSimcoe
bookbub.com/profile/marina-simcoe

www.ingramcontent.com/pod-product-compliance
Lightning Source LLC
Chambersburg PA
CBHW030349310726
48979CB00001B/236

* 9 7 8 1 9 8 9 9 6 7 2 6 3 *